EDEN'S ENDGAME

An Eden Paradox Novel

The Eden Paradox
Eden's Trial
Eden's Revenge
Eden's Endgame

Front Cover Art by John Harris

B A R R Y　　K I R W A N

Copyright © 2014 Barry Kirwan
All rights reserved.

ISBN: 1503228711
ISBN 13: 9781503228719

CONTENTS

Galactic Timeline ix

Prologue xiii

PART ONE - KALARAN 1
Vortex 3 – War Council 10 – Awakening 29
Failsafe 43 – Recode 52 – Savange 64
Insurance 75 – Machines 82 – Spies 90
Tunnels 100 – Prisoner 105
Releasing Angels 112 - Titans 123

PART TWO – BLAKE 135
Experiment 137 – Plan F 147
Siege 160 – Sentinels 168
Preparations 182 – Resurrection 190
Massacre 197 – Breach 209 – Star Storm 218 – Antigen 229

PART THREE – MICAH 241
Goliaths 243 – Gabriel 251 – Missions 264 –
Upgrade 276 – Ghost in the Machine 286
Lair 296 – Hell's End 313 – Diaspora 335

Epilogue 339

Glossary 341

For Chris and Dimitri

ACKNOWLEDGMENTS

Many thanks to my writing colleagues in Paris (MWP): Dimitri Keramitas, Chris Vanier, Mary Ellen Gallagher, Marie Houzelle and Gwyneth Hughes. Thanks also to my pre-readers, reviewers and proofers: Andy Kilner, Lydia Manx, Mike Formicelli, Jacob Bergsteiger, Gideon Roberton, Ruth Sims and Joanne Crawford, and to artist John Harris for the truly inspiring front cover artwork. Last but not least, thanks to all those readers who kept demanding this fourth and final book in the series.

ABBREVIATED GALACTIC HISTORICAL TIMELINE

2 billion years ago
War between Kalarash and Qorall in Jannahi Galaxy. Qorall believed dead. Galaxy destroyed. Seven Kalarash escape to Silverback Galaxy (human name: "Milky Way").

The Dark Age
Various civilisations rise and fall. Five Kalarash leave Galaxy. Only Kalaran and Hellera remain.

10 million years ago
Grid Society founded under Kalarash guidance. Grid is a transport hub traversing a third of the galaxy. Grid Society strongly hierarchical based on Levels of intelligence. Kalarash are Level 19 [Humanity is later graded Level 3].

2 million years ago
Kalarash disappear. Level 17 Tla Beth (energy beings) left in charge, supported by Level 15 Rangers (reptilian).

50000 years ago
Anxorian (Level Sixteen) Rebellion threatens Grid. Tla Beth genetically alter Grid species 195 [Q'Roth] to become galactic foot-soldiers. Rebellion quashed. Anxorian species extinguished.

40000 years ago
Ossyrian (Level 8) race patronised by Tla Beth, become Medical race for the galaxy.

Every 1000 years
Due to their genetic alteration, Q'Roth new-borns must feed on life energy of unsponsored species Level 3 or below, occasionally (where sanctioned by the Tla Beth) Level 4. Such species are becoming rarer.

1000 years ago
Q'Roth harvest pacifist spider race on Ourshiwann (renamed Esperia), but fail to discover hidden egg nests.

1000 years ago
Q'Roth scouts land on Earth and broker a deal with the future Alician sect. In exchange for upgrading Alicians to Level 5 and promised sponsorship by Q'Roth, Alicians must keep humanity from advancement and from maintaining weapons harmful to Q'Roth (nuclear/nanotech)

900 years ago
Ranger Shattrall crash-lands on Earth. Realises humanity targeted for culling, despite early signs of Level 4 evolution. Warns local Tibetan tribe who become Sentinels. Sentinels engage in silent war with Alicians.

500 years ago
Q'Roth terraform Eden, plant egg nests, then enter hibernation period.

40 years ago
Alicians secretly release nanoplague on Earth. 50 million people die. Nannite technology banned.

30 years ago
Third World War on Earth. Environment sent into irrecoverable global warming. Nuclear weapon stockpiles dismantled. Alicians gain widespread power via the religious sect known as Fundies.

20 years ago
Eden discovered. Blake and crew arrive and find Q'Roth eggs hatching, and Hohash artefact, whereby they discover Q'Roth intent. Micah uncovers Alician plot on Earth. Battle ensues. Earth decimated, refugees flee to Esperia. Alicians escape.

19 years ago
Alician known as Louise hunts down and destroys one refugee ship, killing 2000. Attacks Esperia. Humanity prevails.

19 years ago
Qorall and his forces attack, break through the galactic barrier, and bring dark worms inside the galaxy.

18 years ago
Micah and crew enter the Grid. After the self-defence killing of a Q'Roth ambassador, humanity is put on trial by the Tla Beth. Humanity acquitted but placed in protective Quarantine for one generation. All children to be genetically upgraded by Ossyrians.

18 years ago
Kalarash presence detected on Esperia along with spider egg nests. Kalarash ship disappears with three humans on-board. Believed to have left galaxy, reason unknown.

Past year
The Tla Beth, aided by the Q'Roth and other races, have lost half the galaxy to Qorall's armies. The eldest human 'genned' child is now eighteen. The Spider eggs have long-since hatched and live in Shimsha, near Esperantia.

Two months ago
As Quarantine fell, the Alicians led by Sister Esma attacked Esperia. Humanity prevailed but with significant losses, and sixty captives were taken back to the Alician homeworld, Savange. Kalaran has returned to wage war against Qorall, who has unleashed a new weapon.

PROLOGUE

Bangkok, 2252, Eve of WWIII

Thirteen years before the Fall of Earth

Louise fidgeted in the long silk dress with the red dragon pattern; give her combat fatigues any day. But Nick had never seen her in a dress – naked, sure – and they were being called up tonight, so it was now or never. She shifted her weight in the bamboo chair, sipping her second Lao Pane, a kiwi whiskey shake, and mopped her brow with a paper serviette; it was forty-five in the shade, and the café aircon was bust again. Nick was already an hour late, but she'd wait. It was the fourth day in the past month they'd been put on high alert, the difference this time being that the tactical nukes had been armed, their mid-range delivery missiles prepped.

Through the dusty window she watched people in bright colours and straw hats scurry past. Bangkok always bustled, but there were fewer smiles and animated interchanges than usual. Everyone knew a third world war was just around the corner. According to the indie sav-minds, half the population would perish. Many still didn't accept it, but she did. Man had always waged war, on increasingly large scales. All you needed to make it go truly global was to interconnect everyone and everything. Nowhere left to hide or run to, nowhere neutral. The screen behind the counter blared out the latest last-ditch peace talks, another excuse for a barrage of rhetoric whipping up normally sane people into a frenzy. One trigger-happy finger, one inflammatory event, and the world would ignite.

Louise leant forward, caught her reflection in the glass table-top, saw the hardness behind her features. Her state of mind wasn't the best brochure for humanity. Twenty-two years of life had been pretty shit so far, more than her fair share of uninvited adult attention as a teenager, and once she could fight back, she'd tried and failed to reinvent herself as a teacher. Instead she'd ended up a marine after one of her few real friends pointed out she had a killer instinct, having witnessed her break a guy's jaw in a nightclub punch-up on her eighteenth birthday.

Her sex-life had been a disaster zone until a few weeks ago. Nick, a Canadian commando monitoring the US war games in Thailand. Love at first fuck. And now gung-ho politicians and insanely radicalised religious leaders were going to blow it for them, and for everyone else. She could forgive them all if she and Nick could have one last afternoon of passion. Staring over people's heads outside, she searched for his six-six frame. Come on, Nick, don't keep a girl waiting.

She took another sip as she watched a woman in a burka enter the café – must be baking alive inside – and take a seat opposite a man with slick black hair, shiny business attire and mirror sunglasses, none of which suited him. He looked like one of the Green-Shirt politicians who'd been warmongering over the Thai vid channels. The two of them made an odd couple, especially as she seemed to be the one running the meeting. The woman's eyes suddenly locked onto Louise, so she turned back to gazing out the window.

Across the busy street she spied Nick, taller than the locals, sailing towards her like a yacht cruising into harbour. She stood up to show him the dress. His shades were down but when he saw her he stopped dead and lifted them and mouthed "Wow." He walked faster, waving his hands in the air, pretending to be exasperated by the constant flood of people and biofuel tuk-tuks in between him and the café; it made her smile. Wait till he saw what was underneath her dress.

Another man crossed her gaze as he glided towards the café entrance ahead of Nick: athletic frame, bald, no hat, no sunglasses, and grey one-piece jumpsuit despite the heat. Her instincts kicked in as he cut effortlessly through the crowded street, his features concentrated and alert; he was on a mission. She noticed a tattoo on the side of his neck, like a cross but with an oval at the top; the ankh symbol, she recalled. Then she remembered a briefing three days ago: a US politician had been killed in broad daylight right outside the Senate; there had been a photo of the assassin's body, riddled with bullets, the same tattoo on his neck… She glanced down at the bag at her feet. No pistol, just her knife.

The door tinkled as the man stepped inside, his eyes an intense emerald green. He took one brief look around, reached into his pocket, then sprang towards the woman in the burka, brandishing a metal rod. The woman, without even turning around, flung herself flat, as a thin blue blade whipped above her, finding instead the neck of the politician who was rising to his feet, a gun in his hand. The politician dropped his weapon and clutched at his throat, unable to speak or scream, only gurgle as blood gushed through his fingers. He crumpled to the floor.

Louise stumbled backwards as the speed of events caught up with her; she couldn't move properly in that damned long dress. Cursing, she fell to the floor, amidst the scraping sounds of furniture being kicked aside, swishes of the assassin's ultra-thin sword, and high-pitched screams and shouts of the clientele as they clambered for the exit. Louise glanced up while her left hand dived into her bag and unsheathed her stiletto. Nick burst through the door, almost taking the frame with him, and thank god had his pistol drawn. Louise found the knife, grasped its smooth handle, and got to her feet.

Nick was right behind the assassin, who seemed oblivious as he hacked his way through tables and chairs towards the woman in the burka, who was far more agile than she looked. Nick shouted at the guy to stop, or he would fire. The assassin didn't turn around, just flicked his blade backwards, its blue edge slicing first through Nick's pistol arm before it carved a line through his chest; Nick went down. The woman in the burka had her back against the wall.

Louise darted forward and flung the knife at the killer just as he raised his sword. The stiletto plunged into the side of his neck, severing his carotid artery, a curtain of blood spraying over the wall. The woman in the burka dived to the floor. The assassin staggered backwards a pace, glared at Louise once, then tapped the sword hilt with his other hand as if entering a code, ignoring the blood spurting from his neck, and collapsed.

Louise didn't see him hit the ground.

Everything turned blinding white, and she heard a deafening crack as a wave of searing heat scorched her entire body, lifted her off her feet and threw her to the other end of the café. She landed in a puddle of melting plastic furniture and burning bamboo. Her left eye still worked, the right was fused shut. She looked down her body: the dress was largely burnt off, her skin a hideous landscape of red and black, the flesh on her right arm barbecued to a crisp. Flames licked her legs, the only saving grace being that she couldn't feel them. She was glad she couldn't see her face. Acrid fumes made her cough and her eye water. Getting up wasn't an option. Through the smoke and fire she tried to make out Nick's remains.

A tall figure walked over: the woman in the burka. Steam poured off the black material that now looked more like very fine chain mail. It flickered silver and white as if there was some kind of tech underneath. The woman was unharmed. She removed her hood and facemask, and bent forward, her eyes the blackest Louise had ever seen. Two sets of footsteps rushed in, speaking urgently in foreign accents, not Thai.

"Your Eminence, are you alright? Thank Alessia! We must leave straightaway, the police will arrive quickly; you cannot be found here!"

The woman did not answer them. She spoke instead to Louise.

"You saved my life. But you have fourth-degree burns over most of your body."

Louise coughed, tried to speak, couldn't, her throat and tongue dried leather, tasting of charcoal. That extent of burns meant only one thing. Louise closed her eye as the pain asserted itself with a vengeance, as if she was being boiled alive. Her body began to shudder. A single whimper of agony escaped through clenched teeth.

The woman continued, amidst shouts and wails outside, and the crashing of the burning roof caving in all around them.

"The assassin who did this to you – and murdered your friend – is called a Sentinel. There are fifty of them roaming this doomed world. You have a choice: I can put you out of your misery here and now, or I can save you – if you agree to join me and help kill the rest of the Sentinels. The choice is yours. If you wish to die, keep your eye closed. You have ten seconds."

Louise thought of Nick; he deserved to be avenged. But what if this woman was evil, and the assassin had been trying to kill her for a good reason? No way to know. And right now, the world could go to hell as far as Louise was concerned. Besides, if she was dead, there was nothing after, of that she was convinced.

She opened her eye.

The woman touched Louise's neck with something metallic that made a short hiss, and her body numbed as if she was wrapped in a cool cloud.

"Bring her," the woman said.

Rough hands grabbed Louise's listless body, lifted her from the sticky floor. The sirens grew louder.

"What about the Minister, Your Eminence?"

"Leak a report that the Fundies assassinated him. It is the spark we have been waiting for. The war starts tonight."

Louise's head tilted back as she was bundled out of the café into a hover car. Behind her, in amongst the smoking carnage, she glimpsed Nick's cremated corpse. In that moment, she hated the world and everyone in it, and was prepared to watch it all burn, until there was nothing left but ash.

THIRTY YEARS LATER

PART ONE
KALARAN

Chapter 1
VORTEX

Louise could hold her breath a long time. Thirty seconds earlier she'd been standing on the bridge of a Q'Roth Battlestar with three of her Alicians and ten Q'Roth warriors, including the captain. They'd begun a routine Transpace jump, the last on her journey to the Alician homeworld Savange, taking back their precious cargo of sixty human captives. Three seconds later the front part of the ship had been breached by a vortex of unknown origin. Now she clawed her way toward an auto-sealing hatch as air roared past her, dodging equipment and anything else not lashed down as it flashed past. She snatched a breath then held it again. The doorway to the next section of the ship, where sanctuary lay, was closing. In fifteen seconds she'd be locked into a vacuum.

Louise's face stung with the cold. She slit her eyes almost closed to stop them freezing, and pounded her Q'Roth claw into the metal floor to prevent herself sliding into oblivion. A sharp-edged metal object hurtled towards her, ricocheted off the corridor wall and narrowly missed her face. It caught her second-in-command, Arteus, who screamed as he tumbled into the vortex devouring the ship. Louise hauled herself forward, her eyes set on the closing hatch.

The Q'Roth captain overtook her, his six powerful legs and sharp claws finding better purchase. The exit was almost sealed, but they both kept going, moving faster as the airstream diminished. The captain punched a claw into the last sliver between the closing hatch and its frame, and roared as he brought all his strength to bear against the motors trying to protect the rest of the vessel. He forced open a narrow gap, his upper legs shaking violently with the effort. Louise scrambled over his blue-black trapezoidal head and squeezed through, landing hard on the deck.

She made a quick assessment: the captain was wedged in the crack, unable to get through, while air continued to bleed out of the ship. Grabbing a handhold with her Q'Roth claw, she drew her pistol with her human hand, and fired repeatedly at him until he began to lose his grip. Louise let go and slid towards him. She braced herself, one foot on the hatch, the other on the frame, and fired point blank at the two remaining claws keeping the hatch open till they glowed red. Her pistol's charge ran out. The captain still clung on.

She yelled through the wind, feeling the tug on her lungs. "You're already dead, don't take the ship with you."

The captain's six vermillion eyes flared once, then settled to a deeper red.

"It's yours, for what little time you have left."

He let go.

Through the sealing hatch, she watched him topple backwards, then regain his footing and rise almost casually, then stride towards the vortex that had already swallowed his entire bridge crew and three of her Alicians. Its swirling blue and white surface crackled with sapphire arcs of electricity that lashed out at the captain, flash-frying him before it sucked him into its depths. He did not cry out.

She wondered if the vortex was some new weapon. There were no stars behind it, which meant the Battlestar was outside normal space. She had a hunch what was causing it. Just before the hatch sealed, she calculated how quickly it was eating the kilometre-long ship, how much time she had before the next breach, and the one after that, which would wreck the Battlestar and empty all its occupants into the vortex. Twenty minutes, call it eighteen to be on the safe side. She began a background mental count, a trick she'd learned from her Alician mentor, Sister Esma, a lifetime ago.

At last the hatch clunked into place. She sat with her back against it, her chest heaving, and checked herself over: ears ringing from the decompression, all exposed flesh seared with frostbite, lungs raw. Good enough. The air was thin and cold, so she took a few long breaths, then got to her feet. She stared down at her new Q'Roth claw; it had been meant as a temporary replacement, though it had probably just saved her life.

She ran along the corridor, but as she reached the next hatch two Q'Roth warriors emerged and barred her way, towering a metre above her.

"You killed our captain. We watched you on the monitors."

She stood her ground. "He put me in charge, you heard that, too."

Their eye-slits pulsed a brighter shade of red. "We heard, though we do not know why."

She took a deep breath. "We're foundering in Quickspace. The ship will be catastrophically breached in sixteen minutes. I know what is attacking us and how to stop it."

They said nothing, but she knew Q'Roth psychology: she had to give them more or they'd kill her, and one of them would become captain, though not for long.

"All remaining crew must assemble in the battle bridge in the aft section," she said.

Still they barred her way. "And where are you going?"

"To my two ships, in your hold. That's where the problem is. If I don't join you in fourteen minutes, void them into space and fire on them. Destroy them and everyone on board."

They let her through. Louise sprinted down the corridor leading to her two Raptors, knowing that the Q'Roth wouldn't wait fourteen minutes.

Louise stopped at the first Raptor holding thirty human captives from the raid on Esperia, all perfectly still, frozen in stasis. She'd been away from her fellow Alicians for so long, and had known nothing of the Plight: genetically-upgraded Alicians had barely been able to breed since Earth's demise, and needed a steady influx of DNA from their human predecessors. The irony of the situation wasn't lost on Louise. Alicians had twice tried to wipe out their genetically outdated cousins, only to discover that without them they would perish within a generation.

The unmoving humans were huddled together like a pack of frightened goats. Like Sister Esma before her, she'd prefer to be rid of them. Humanity had squandered its chances, and as far as she and other Alicians were concerned, had long ago forfeited the right to exist. But for now – and the next fifty years – a few would be kept alive in order to replenish Alician society. Qorall's armada sweeping across the galaxy would eliminate the rest of humanity back on Esperia.

Her gaze settled on two of the women at the front: Antonia and Sandy. She reckoned their leader, Micah – responsible for Sister Esma's death and her own missing arm – still cared about these two. Good; he'd come to Savange on a fool's errand to rescue them, and she would finally be able to kill him. She hated long goodbyes.

Could these humans have stopped a Q'Roth Battlestar dead in Transpace? No. She exited the first Raptor and walked quickly to the identical short-haul transporter next door.

Twelve minutes.

Inside the second storage cell a single large black Spider hung upside down, its four legs clamped to the ceiling. Wires and tubes smeared with blue blood hung in loops from the Spider's flattened cylinder body, and fed into a console. One of the two remaining Alicians, a tall male of fair complexion – Jura, she recalled – manned the console and pored over the latest readouts. Jura didn't know what was happening to the rest of the ship, and Louise wasn't about to distract him from his task.

"No change," he said. "We still can't scan it. It disrupts any form of electromagnetic wave. We can only see where we penetrate its flesh, and then not much that makes any sense."

His baritone voice soothed her. She'd missed Alician contact. Eighteen years away from her people, most of it spent with alien species who bore no resemblance to her own kind; aliens often stank, were visually repulsive or else grated on her ears.

A human corpse was strapped to a nearby chair, the deceased woman's face streaked with sweat and tears.

"What did you get from the human?"

Jura turned from his displays to Louise, his eyes steady. "Not much. The current batch of Spiders hatched on Esperia sixteen years ago, but they have lived apart from the humans. What the human subject knew was mainly myth and supposition."

"Indulge me."

He cleared his throat. "The human subject – we picked her at random and pulled her out of stasis – believed the Spiders were originally raised by the Level Nineteen Kalarash being known as Kalaran, though she didn't know why. Apparently no one does."

Louise thought while Jura talked. Qorall wanted one of these Spiders at all costs. He, like his Kalarash enemies, was from another galaxy. Qorall was currently winning the war, but what if the Spiders were also from another galaxy, a secret weapon brought here by the Kalarash aeons ago? Evidently these Spiders could influence space and Transpace without technological aid. That was unique as far as she knew. But she wanted to know more before she handed over this prize to Qorall.

"… the Spiders communicate via the coloured band around their bodies. Otherwise, they appear to be deaf and mute. They are also non-violent. They've never been known to kill anything, even when provoked. I'm afraid we've learned as much as we are likely to." He glanced at the corpse. "She died under the interrogation. Their hearts are so fragile."

Louise ignored the dead woman and stared at the Spider. The Q'Roth believed they had eradicated the Spiders centuries ago, yet now they flourished again on Esperia, sharing that dustbowl planet with humanity. They looked docile, but no one except the Kalarash knew their purpose and their capability, and now one of them had stranded a Q'Roth Battlestar in Transpace. The most important currency in the galaxy had always been information. But she was running out of time.

Eight minutes.

"Send in borers," she said.

Jura's brow creased. "It will die."

Louise said nothing. It had to die anyway, she was convinced of it, to free the Battlestar. But this was her last chance to understand this species, and a dead but intact Spider would still be of considerable value to Qorall. Jura nodded, and went to fetch the burrowing micro-cameras.

Kaarin, a female Alician who had been quietly listening, spoke up, her eyes sharp. "If it dies while we are in Transpace, what will happen to us? And why are we conscious in Transpace anyway? We always believed Transpatial travel was instantaneous. What did you see on the Bridge?"

"I saw nothing," Louise lied. "This is an anomaly, nothing more. When it ends we will wake up on arrival at Savange." She spoke with complete conviction; Alician leadership required overt self-assurance. Yet Kaarin was right; all species experienced Transpatial travel as instantaneous. That didn't mean it was. The Spider didn't want to be taken to Qorall, and had somehow snagged them in mid-flight – there were no stars outside – and had opened up a vortex that would kill them all. They would disappear without any trace.

Seven minutes. At four she'd have to kill it.

Jura returned and injected the Spider with six borers at equidistant locations around its body: they would navigate their way through it, chart the Spider's anatomy and neural activity, and then invade its brain. The Spider's legs tensed, then began to shiver. Blue blood spattered onto the metal floor, like the first heavy drops of rain in a brewing storm.

Jura returned to his console. Louise joined him, looking over his shoulder, his face reflected in the screen where numbers and curves scrolled past. Suddenly his eyes went wide.

"Well I'll be dam –"

Louise felt the familiar chill – like a sudden ice breeze – of entering Transpace. Every surface, every line on Jura's face, every hair, turned silver and froze, as did everything else Louise could see, including her own hand resting on his shoulder. She could no longer move. This was all expected when travelling through Transpace, except she should have been unconscious. She guessed the Spider was dying, but not yet dead. She wondered if Jura and Kaarin were conscious too, but she had no way of knowing.

She heard a thud as the Spider dropped to the floor amidst the sounds of wires and tubes ripping from its flesh. It hobbled over and stood next to her, its soft fur brushing against her thigh. Its communication band, dark until now, lit up, and a focused beam of amber light swept over the console. When the beam shut off, all the complex analyses and data had disappeared from the screen.

The Spider leant against Louise, then tilted its body, and one of its legs kicked with ferocious speed at Jura's head. Louise heard his neck snap. She would have gasped if she'd been able. From all she knew, what she'd just witnessed was unheard of. The Spiders had always been peaceful, not even defending themselves when the Q'Roth had culled them. Had the Spiders recently changed in some fundamental way? She doubted it; species rarely changed that much, even over millennia. No, they had been waiting, biding their time, until Qorall arrived. Somehow they were a real threat to him. Louise was glad she hadn't seen what Jura had gleaned from the data: the price of such information was clearly too high. But the intel that the Spiders could manipulate Transpace, and were capable of extreme violence, would be highly valuable to Qorall.

The Spider sagged next to her, heavier than she'd imagined. Something pricked her calf, cold seeping into her veins. The display screen was now silver like everything else, and Louise watched as the Spider staggered away a couple of paces before its legs buckled and it collapsed, its body twitching on the floor in a spreading pool of blood. Good, it was dying, which meant the ship and all aboard would be saved. But what had it injected her with? Even as she thought about what she had just witnessed, and the need to tell Qorall as soon as they arrived at Savange, her mind began to fog. She struggled to hold onto the past few minutes' events, but they slipped from her memory's grasp. Louise heard a gurgling sound she presumed to be the Spider's death rattle, and slipped into unconsciousness.

Chapter 2
WAR COUNCIL

Blake had never trusted aliens. It wasn't that he didn't like them. It was just that when it came down to it, there weren't that many habitable worlds in the galaxy. Viable planets in the so-called Goldilocks Zones were few and far between. Pierre had said one in a thousand worlds was capable of evolving and sustaining intelligent life. Given the size of the galaxy, the statistics should have made it easy pickings once Transpace travel had been discovered. But there were plenty of races out there. Once you subtracted all the planets destroyed in countless wars over the aeons, even if you added in those rare terraforming successes, prime real estate was still a rarity. Each race looked out for its own; altruism wasn't a winning trait when it came to galactic survival. But there was one species he trusted, who his wife had given her life for, and he would too: the Spiders.

Blake stood on Hazzards Ridge with two of them. They each had four sturdy legs and a fat round body that also served as a head. When they'd first hatched, growing to full size within a year, the tops of their furry bodies barely reached Blake's elbow. He'd joked to Glenda that they looked like walking charcoaled hamburgers, which wasn't such a smart idea around a hungry human population. She'd scolded him, rightly so. Now, laying a hand on the top of the one he considered his best friend, he stroked the soft velvety fur. The Spiders didn't speak or utter any sound, they communicated with colours via a jagged three-sixty band around their bodies, and right now his friend – he'd never named any of them, out of respect for their own way of life – emanated a waxy, shimmering purple. It signified concern. Blake wondered how the Spiders could read him better than his own kind.

He and Glenda had raised the Spiders on Esperia as soon as the eggs, stored in deep caves, had hatched, bringing them back to the small town where their ancestors had been slaughtered by the Q'Roth a millennium ago. The two of them built pens so the puppy-sized fur-balls didn't go wandering off into the desert, or come into contact with humans, most of whom couldn't handle cohabitation with an alien species. He and his wife led the young to the underground feeding stations, where the infant Spiders waited patiently in silent queues for hours till all of them had fed. Together with the rapidly-maturing and fast-growing Spiders, Blake and Glenda tried to work out how the homes and other buildings in Shimsha, the Spiders' ancestral home, functioned.

The task had brought him and his wife closer. After they'd lost their son in WWIII three decades earlier, their love had turned platonic. Blake had accepted it, and never once looked elsewhere, even though Glenda had even pushed him towards the idea once or twice. But the energy of the Spiders, their exuberance when at play, had rekindled fires in both of them.

The Spiders became family. He smiled, recalling happier times with Glenda when they'd got it all wrong, the most embarrassing case when they watched what they thought was some kind of athletic display, only to realise it was an annual group mating. But what had amazed him was how fast the Spiders learned; he only had to show a single Spider anything once, and it would transmit to the others, until the whole society knew it as if they'd been shown first-hand. Glenda taught them to lip-read human speech – something he'd never told Micah, and in return they had taught Blake and Glenda how to read their colour language. He and Glenda could have left at any time and gone back to the nearby town of Esperantia to re-integrate into human society, but they didn't. Instead they watched the Spider society grow and flourish.

In the mornings the Spiders farmed the land, producing a single crop, a bitter sorghum that could be pulped into an oily yellow residue, bland but nutritious. In the afternoons most Spiders met in groups of nine – never less or more – for several hours, usually out in the open in the ubiquitous broad plazas. Blake had tried to attend such meetings, but the way they flashed colours to each other was too fast and complex; they were Level Four, after all, more advanced than most humans, him included. Once or twice he had been gently ushered out of such discussions. At first he'd thought nothing of it, assuming it was maybe something more personal to them, but as Qorall's armies neared Esperia, the frequency of such events increased, and since Kalaran had come back, many more secret meetings occurred all over town, less in the plazas and more behind closed doors. Good for you, he thought. He knew they were fundamentally pacifist, but he hoped the Spiders might put up some kind of fight when the time came.

At night they painted the sky with fluorescent displays, sometimes abstract, other times evoking battle scenes from forgotten wars. He had no idea how they knew anything about history, but occasionally a few Ossyrians had come to watch, and they would tell Blake and Glenda about wars in distant times. When he'd asked them how the Spiders knew, the Ossyrians didn't answer. Recently, the Spiders had constructed six towers around Shimsha's perimeter to create new night-time displays; one of the few remaining things he'd been looking forward to.

After Glenda passed away, he stayed in Shimsha; they'd shared too many memories for him to ever leave this place. Besides, the Spiders were so at ease with each other, and with him. Whenever he visited his own kind, he quickly tired of the complex social interactions, tensions, and egos. Humanity was fatally self-obsessed.

Blake had been feeling increasingly burned out – not in a bad way, he'd just had a very full life. He missed Glenda every day; the passing of time made no difference. And the Spiders; well, he had the feeling their time was coming, and they didn't need him anymore. They would look after him in his old age, if it came to that. But he'd never wanted to be a burden. And in his heart, despite all this time in a pacifist society, he was still a soldier. Blake wanted to die on his feet.

Emerging out of his reverie, he noticed his friend's jagged band was now a warm green. But the other Spider shimmered red, reminding Blake it was almost time. He gazed upwards.

The noon sky above Esperia was criss-crossed with a chaotic web of milky lines. Filaments left by the Shrell stretched all the way out to the edge of Esperia's system, preventing any normal ships – and Qorall's dark worms – from entering. Looking up, Blake saw a single ship, ten kilometres long and shaped like an elongated crossbow, with an arrowhead for the cockpit. Its hull rippled scarlet and emerald, shapes emerging then disappearing into the general flow of colour. It suddenly struck him that it wasn't for decoration – it was talking, perhaps to the Spiders, perhaps to someone or something else.

The ship hung silently in low orbit above the two towns of humanity's refuge planet: Esperantia, the human one whose roofs glittered in the sunlight – zinc being the one metal found in thick, accessible veins inside caves nestling in the Acarian Mountains – and alabaster Shimsha, or as Micah had once dubbed it, Spider Central. The ship belonged to Kalaran. Blake didn't trust him, even though the legendary Level Nineteen being had protected the Spiders for half a million years, and now preserved humanity. Blake reckoned Kalaran had his reasons, was playing the long game, and that in his case altruism was a 'nice-to-have' characteristic that could easily be sacrificed if needed.

Blake's friend nudged him, as if sensing his slipping back into a sombre mood. Blake patted it, then used the light glove on his left hand to flicker a message to both of them: "Okay, I'll make an effort."

No sooner had he said it than his skin prickled and his vision turned first grainy, then black, as if he'd blinked, and he found himself on the ship he'd been looking at. He felt dizzy for a moment, as if the outside world was whirling around him, and then it felt more as if he was spinning on the inside, behind his eyes, the merry-go-round sensation accompanied by a rushing noise, the sound of his own blood coursing through his veins. He blinked hard and the visual and auditory after-effects vanished. Blake felt a shiver as the tingling dissipated, and shook himself. *Whisking.* He'd heard that very few ships could teleport, none below Level Fifteen, and that it used up a tremendous amount of energy, and even then only worked at short range and in line-of-sight. He wondered why Kalaran had expended such resources on him.

He was inside a vast pearl bay where forty or so shuttles of varying sizes and description stood, many floating a half metre above the hangar deck.

Some appeared outlandish, others sleek, and several looked downright hostile and tooled-up with gun ports to prove it. Most had large semi-transparent tubes – some empty, others filled with viscous liquids or opaque gases – snaking into the walls of the hangar.

A diminutive figure approached, and as she got closer Blake recognised Petra, Esperia's President, in matching beige pants and jacket, very smart and formal, though she didn't look altogether comfortable. She had the same short-cropped, unruly salt and pepper hair, the same crooked smile across her lips, and the same slate-grey eyes as her mother, Kat, far away on another of the galaxy's outer spirals with Micah and the others. They'd gone to retrieve the sixty human captives, and to kill Louise. The thought flashed through Blake's mind that he should have gone with them, then he dismissed it; he'd made his decision, and had never been one for second-guessing himself.

"Still in one piece, Commander?" She grinned, then threw her arms around him, her head against his chest. He stiffened at first, unaccustomed to human contact, then relaxed, and hugged her back.

"The others are already here," she said. "We had to come the conventional way, by shuttle. Only you got the luxury treatment." She folded her arms.

"Good to see you, Petra. How are you enjoying being President?" Blake hated small talk.

Her face grew serious. She hooked her arm in his, and started walking towards the opposite end of the hangar. "After only a month of this job I can see why both you and Micah resigned. Come on, the others are waiting. Oh, and…" she paused, turned to him again, mock-conspiratorially. "Some of them smell a bit weird; try not to let it show."

He knew what she was doing, trying to put him at ease. Blake reminded himself she was a Genner, genetically advanced by the Ossyrians to Level Four, approaching Level Five, more intelligent than he was. Petra also had more emotional intelligence than most Genners. He wondered if she sensed the dark thoughts in his head. The Spiders certainly did; the past few weeks they never left him on his own, one of them even sleeping at the foot of his bed. He patted her arm, the same way he'd patted the spider; Petra was special, one of the few humans he still really cared about. She let go and separated from him, walking towards a doorway which he was sure hadn't been there earlier.

"Follow me, and don't look down."

He should have taken her advice. As soon as he passed through the opening into the ship's dazzling interior daylight, he had to cross a long and narrow glass bridge. Inevitably his gaze dropped to what was below, and vertigo swept through him. There was no frame of reference but he was sure it was kilometres straight down towards a bubbling mercury lake. Pierre had warned him how vast the ship was, but still…

"Keep your eyes on my shoulders, and you won't fall."

She said it like an order, and it worked; he was a soldier, after all. He lifted his gaze and tried to keep in line with her, like he'd learned a lifetime ago in boot camp back in Montana. The bridge twisted slowly in the air. Unfortunately his peripheral vision worked just fine, and he could see that they were slowly rotating, defying gravity. After a hundred metres, he reckoned they were upside down from where they had started.

"Don't look up, either."

He did, of course, and sure enough the boiling lake was there, confirming his suspicion about their orientation. Looking 'down', he saw a dozen spheres floating or hanging, all different colours, like giant marbles drifting in a pale azure sky. Daring a glance sideways, he couldn't see the walls of Kalaran's ship, only a hazy blue with no horizon. He tried to make his jaw relax, and focused on her shoulders as instructed.

He and Petra were half-way to a rust-coloured sphere. From this angle he could see tubes that wound their way vine-like from the hangar behind him, reaching across the ship's internal sky until they pierced the sphere's outer shell. Curiosity trumped his nagging nausea, and he sped up, almost treading on Petra's heels. She didn't slow down as they neared its metallic surface, and passed straight through it. He hesitated a second, then followed her.

It felt like a veil over his eyes, a small jet of cool air blowing on his skin, and then he was on the inside. He stopped dead. An assortment of creatures were sprawled around the inner surface of the sphere. A few species he recognised, most he did not. But his eyes were drawn to the centre of the sphere. He tried to process the creature he was seeing. Its body reminded him of a sea anemone, fleshy tentacles waving lazily in every direction from a central mass lost in a brown fog. At the end of each undulating tentacle was a mouth that, when opened, revealed a glinting ruby eye. One of those eyes was staring directly at him.

Take your seat.

Petra grabbed his arm, tugged at him.

Blake didn't move; he needed confirmation. "What did you just say, Petra?"

She flicked her eyes to the anemone. "*I* didn't say anything."

Blake let her lead him along the inner curve of the sphere. They weaved between several alien species he didn't recognise, each on a clam-shaped recliner, facing the anemone. Blake was looking up and nearly tripped over a brown scaly tail. Ukrull, he thought, the Ranger.

"Manota," the Ranger said, correcting him, and sure enough he realised it was not Ukrull; the tone of voice was lighter.

"Female," she confirmed, flicking a manicured claw in the direction of the anemone. "Translator for Kalaran. War Council meeting started. You late."

He stared at her awhile. The rumour of Rangers being telepathic appeared to be true. When he looked away, Blake was relieved to spy his former mentor, Kilaney, who looked remarkably feisty despite his seventy-two years, a full head of white hair and bushy eyebrows atop smouldering brown eyes. Blake reminded himself that trying to apply age comparisons made little sense anymore. Kilaney was technically seventy-two, but had been killed, then his memories and DNA had been downloaded into a Q'Roth warrior, and only recently had he been restored as 'mostly human'. Underneath his human skin were a number of Q'Roth organs. Kilaney was allegedly as strong as an ox, and very fast. Added to that, everyone aged more slowly on Esperia, something to do with its weaker sun and more oxygenated atmosphere and benevolent if dry climate. A number of people in their eighties and even nineties still worked Esperantia's outlying farms every day.

A shimmering, platinum avatar of Pierre was present, too, Blake's former science officer aboard the original Eden Mission, now half-human, half…

well, no one really knew, since Pierre's nannites had been constantly rearranging his body chemistry for two decades. Yet despite his enhanced Level Ten intelligence, Pierre still had that look of scientific wonder on his face. At least his eyes had become a decent human blue again, and his hair was only partly silver, the original jet black colour reasserting itself. Pierre looked enthralled by the alien menagerie all around him.

Pierre addressed him. "Take a seat, Commander, so far it's only been introductions."

"An hour of them," Kilaney added.

Blake's former mentor was trying to sit up straight in the clam, but it was clearly meant for a reclining position. Petra nodded to an empty one and Blake climbed in. It had a spongy feel and moulded to his body. Despite lying down, he felt clear-headed. He heard Kilaney grunt and guessed he'd finally settled in. Petra also took her place in an adjacent clam.

"So, how exactly does this work?" Blake asked.

No sooner had he spoken than he found himself sitting in a dark, lozenge-shaped room around a white table with Petra, Kilaney, and Pierre. The walls were opaque and soundproof. Pierre looked more human, more normal, though Blake reminded himself Pierre wasn't really there.

"This is a construct," Pierre said. "The actual meeting place is disorienting, and most of it is going to be impossible for you to follow, a lot of it is too much for me, to be honest."

Petra took control, her prerogative as President.

"But you're Level Ten, Pierre."

Pierre's face had a residual tinge of platinum – he was still undergoing his transformation back to being human – and when he smiled at his daughter, Petra, whom he had only met a month before, cobwebs of tiny silver lines etched around his mouth and eyes.

"Ten is the *average* level back there. Thankfully, Ukrull is on the Ice Pick and is listening in. He's translating most of it, though the speed of communication is giving me a headache."

Blake didn't want to interrupt. He knew Pierre and Ukrull were off on a secret mission for Kalaran in the Ice Pick, heading towards the outer edge of the galaxy, along with Jen and Dimitri. Pierre momentarily seemed elsewhere, as if someone was talking to him, no doubt Ukrull. Kilaney broke the silence.

"So why the hell are we here, Petra? What possible use can we be in a War Council with aliens far more intelligent than we are? I don't recall inviting ants into my strategy meetings back on Earth during our little war."

Blake smiled. Although their 'little war' had been horrendous and had almost destroyed Earth, back then he'd always known who he was, what to do, and who the enemy was. His smile faded. Now he and the rest of humanity were caught up in something far beyond their comprehension; legions of aliens warring on behalf of two titanic races, Kalaran on one side, Qorall on the other. Kilaney was right. Blake felt like an ant on the Somme battlefield. He realised Petra was staring at him, about to speak.

"Kalaran said we have a role to play. Us and the Spiders." She touched Blake's hand.

Pierre 'returned'. He looked agitated. "Okay, a lot has just been discussed. Qorall's new weapon is being used all along the front. They're discussing combative measures to –"

Blake found he was no longer in the lozenge, but back in the clam on the inner surface of the sphere. He sat up. The others were all still immersed. One of the anemone's eyes watched him, but he ignored it. On impulse he stood up, and began walking around the inner surface of the sphere. None of the other aliens paid him much attention, except the Ranger Manota, whose yellow eyes flickered once in his direction.

He passed a pack of Ossyrians, mankind's guardians on Esperia these past eighteen years. The collie-like aliens, in full ceremonial headdress of horizontal bars of gold, garnet and lapis lazuli, were huddled together in a single clam, snouts upright, quicksilver eyes flashing shapes at almost subliminal speed. One of them turned its head towards him. Its eyes stilled. Blake walked on.

Next he came upon a Finchikta; a birdlike upper half atop a forest of centipede-like legs. The third eye on the top of its head opened, a sad pale blue, and watched him independently while the bird's beak emitted squawks and shrieks.

He stopped dead two metres from a Q'Roth Queen, her swollen, armoured blue-black belly resting on the floor, curling upwards to end in a square head with six blood-red slits serving as eyes, her gash of a mouth open, hissing in the direction of the anemone. A Q'Roth warrior appeared in front of him, barring the way. Blake's hand automatically slipped to his holster only to find it empty; his pistol hadn't whisked with him. That figured. The warrior wasn't armed either, not that it needed to be with those mandible-like upper claws and six-inch thorns along its middle and lower pairs of legs. Blake took another path.

After passing a dozen other alien species too weird even for drug-induced nightmares, his eye snagged on something on the opposite side of the sphere, almost back where he had started. Blake didn't know if it was one alien or many. A set of pale globes the size of soccer balls were joined together by arm-width purple blood vessels, and each globe had fronds sticking out of it, waving in the air, puffing out short jets of green gas. Blake moved closer. It reminded him of an ancient Greek fable about a woman with a head full of snakes; Medusa. The creature shied away from him, then advanced. Blake didn't move. There was something unsettling about it…

A flicker of movement in the corner of his eye made him turn. One of the Spiders was walking on a parallel path. Blake recognised him, the friend who had been down with him on the surface. The Spider scuttled along in his usual stop-start manner, which should have attracted attention from the other aliens, but it didn't. *They can't see him.* The Spider passed Manota, but even the Level Fifteen female Ranger seemed oblivious. The Spider's communication band was a dull brown, when suddenly it flashed a message to Blake. It took Blake a half-second to translate, then he dived to the ground as several of the Medusa's fronds lashed out, spear-like, to where his head had just been. Blake looked up to see the Q'Roth Queen looming over him, all six eyes blazing. The Medusa withdrew.

"Not safe here, human." The Q'Roth Queen's voice was like the rustling of dry leaves; Blake didn't speak Q'Roth, and assumed the anemone was translating, which should be a two-way process. Good, he'd always wanted to address one.

Blake rose to his feet fast, fire in his veins, confronted by the leader of the race who had culled both humanity and the Spiders. He thought about punching her jaw, knowing he would break his hand in the process. The fact that she might have just saved his life didn't stop him calling her to account.

"You destroyed my world. Seven billion dead."

She reared back on her hind legs, her mouth opening slowly like a razor cut.

"One more, then," she hissed.

One of the central tentacles swung down between them, its eye facing first the Queen, then him. Blake got the message. He looked for his Spider friend but he was gone. On his way back to his clam, Blake pondered what the Spiders' role in all of this was, and why the other aliens had not seen the one walking in their midst, but no sooner had he laid down than he was back in the lozenge.

He expected them to ask him where he'd been, but they carried on as if he'd never left. Pierre had just finished speaking. He gave Blake a sidelong look. "What do you think, Commander?"

With a shock, Blake realised he knew everything they'd been discussing, though he hadn't been there. Obviously Kalaran didn't want them to know he'd been absent. Blake decided to play along. "Sounds good to me, Pierre."

Petra narrowed her eyes. "You're sure?"

Kilaney folded his arms, grinning. "Well, why don't you run it past us again?"

Much to Blake's surprise and relief, the words poured out of him.

"We'll take two ships to sector 143-511-873 first thing in the morning. Kilaney will command a Q'Roth Battleship with a complement of Genner Youngbloods. I'll take a Scintarelli Dart. We'll join the local forces and try to fend off the Orb en-route for the planet, or failing that, gather as much intel as possible and return here inside the Shrell-wires."

"Good enough for me," Kilaney said. His avatar vanished.

"So," Blake said, "an hour for introductions and five minutes for the main agenda?"

Petra's brow furrowed. "What do you mean five minutes?"

Blake cleared his throat, guessing more time had passed than he'd thought. "Never mind, an old Earth joke." But even as he smiled and waved a hand dismissively, he wondered if he'd been somewhere else as well as back in the chamber with the other aliens; had Kalaran done something with him, or to him?

Pierre spoke. "The others are leaving. Kalaran suggests we leave last. Quite a few of the alien species registered formal protest at having such low-breds – that is, humans – present. Kilaney is ex-Q'Roth and wanted to have a word with the Queen out there, presumably about borrowing a ship. I have to go in any case, the Ice Pick is almost out of range." He faced his daughter Petra, and Blake turned aside, trying not to listen to the words spoken in hushed, urgent tones.

When it became quiet, and Pierre's avatar had left, Blake turned back to Petra. "What really happened here today?"

She inspected her fingernails. "Newly forged allegiances, alliances that will dissolve as soon as the war is over, promises of Upgrade as well as territories if and when we win and get to pick up the pieces." She faced him. "Mostly they were here to meet with Kalaran, to know he's really here and means business, because if he and his Kalarash mate Hellera leave, then most other races won't even attempt to stand up to Qorall – they'll pledge allegiance to him."

"But that's –"

"Survival." Her face became stern. "Once you cut through the politics, rivalries and envy, they're all scared, Blake. We were in quarantine for eighteen years. They've watched Qorall's progress unchecked for that same amount of time, and he already controls half the galaxy. And now there are these damned Orbs…" She folded her arms, and sat back. "They're also here to see which races might defect; there was an awful lot of posturing out there before you arrived. But the news that Qorall is going to attack the Tla Beth homeworld stunned all of them." She got up and paced. "Think about it; for two million years the Tla Beth have ruled Grid Society with no serious challenge." She sat down again, looking older than her years.

"Leadership can do that to you," he said.

"Do what?"

"You carry too much responsibility, so when you think you're going to lose, you feel guilty. Doesn't make any sense, and stops you from being the leader people need."

Petra leaned back, a thin smile across her lips. "Getting philosophical in your autumn years, Blake?"

He parried the remark, focusing on her again. "How are *you* doing?"

She laughed. "Try 'what am I doing?' I seem to be making this all up as I go along. Want your old job back?"

Blake shook his head. "I meant how are you doing with Pierre gone God knows where, and your mother gone to Savange to rescue Antonia and the others?"

Petra grew serious again, her voice colder. "I keep myself busy, Blake." She fixed her eyes on him, and then banged her fist down on the table. "I won't allow us to be snuffed out or turned into Qorall's slaves."

Blake nodded. He made to stand up, but she leaned forward and placed a firm hand on his arm.

"We still need you, Commander. War is almost here, on our doorstep."

He didn't reply and tried to stand up again but her arm pressed down harder.

"I'm not reaching you, am I? Then let me try another tack: the Spiders need you. Especially when Qorall's troops arrive here, which we all know is going to happen eventually, despite the Shrell wires."

He laid his hand on top of hers. "I know my duty, Petra."

She let go. "You could take my place as President in the wink of an eye; but I could never take yours." She stood, glanced aside as if deciding whether to say something, then spat it out. "One of the Spiders came to see me."

Blake found he was standing, too. "But you can't understand them!"

"We're Genners, remember? We worked out their colour speech years ago, and Virginia made a translation device."

Blake's heart pounded. "What did it say?"

"They're worried about you." She swallowed. "But they respect you, and your wishes. You're like a father to them, and they want what's best for you. The way they expressed it, your mind's made up, even if you think it isn't.

They have a concept somewhere between mathematical psychology and karma; quite interesting, actually." Her voice quavered, and she cleared her throat. "They said you were near cusp time, a cliff edge on your karmic trajectory. All the probabilities of a terminal conclusion converge."

He stared down at the table. Hearing it second hand, even if couched in psychobabble, made it ring true. He'd been denying it, but even the Spiders had confirmed it. "And what do you think, Petra?"

"You're tired of it all, you've given way too much already, and you want out, to be with Glenda, or simply not to be without her anymore." She softened a little. "I don't blame you, Blake. As for me, I don't want to lose you. None of us do. You mean too much to us."

Blake knew it was a lifeline being thrown in his direction. But he didn't take it. He pursed his lips. "And what does the President think?"

She let out a hollow laugh, then pressed her fist down onto the wooden table as she looked him in the eye. "The President expects you to make it count, Commander."

Blake smiled, then stood to attention, something he thought he'd given up a long time ago, and saluted.

"Then we'll both play our parts, Madam President."

"See you back on the surface, then," she said. Her avatar vanished.

Blake waited. Nothing happened. He got up, walked around, and still nothing. For a while he wondered if he'd somehow been forgotten. Then someone appeared, and Blake fell back into his chair with a gasp.

A large, bald black man stood before him in a cobalt Eden Mission uniform, grinning.

"Zack," Blake whispered, then caught himself. "Kalaran," he corrected, and folded his arms.

"Sorry, Boss, he made me do it." Zack belly-laughed.

Blake knew he was being manipulated, that this was Kalaran, not Zack, but dammit to hell, it was good to see his best friend in the flesh after all these years. He resisted the urge to return Zack's beaming smile. It wasn't easy. To compensate, and to register protest, he spoke with a tone just short of contempt.

"What do you want, Kalaran?"

Zack nodded. "You giving up, Boss?"

Blake felt anger welling up inside him: the recent battle, the last vestige of Zack finally gone, Marcus, Virginia and Gabriel all dead, along with most of the Ossyrians. He'd thought they'd have some peace on Esperia. Why couldn't the galaxy just leave them the hell alone? He closed his eyes. At least Kalaran wasn't using Glenda.

Zack's voice softened. "I wouldn't do that to you, Boss."

Micah had told him Kalaran did this; picked an avatar that was so close to you it made it difficult to retain emotional control.

"What do you care about me, about any of us? Why are you taking an interest exactly? Us fighting Qorall? It's a sick joke, might as well use bows and arrows against a nuke. What's the point?"

Zack frowned. "You're a soldier. You want to fight, but you feel impotent, is that it, Boss?"

Blake stood, thumped both fists on the table. "Stop calling me that. You don't deserve to be Zack. Stop this charade, show yourself to me right now or send me back to Shimsha!"

Zack disappeared, the lozenge too, and Blake stood on a small jade sphere, still inside the ship, but much lower down, near the boiling mercury lake. Something was rising out of it, something huge.

It was hard to fathom. A sphere, definitely, but the outer surface was like a layer of cigar-shaped clouds, the layer underneath an electric green mesh of shifting shapes – squares, diamonds, triangles, and other more complex polygons; and beneath that, swirling red blobs against a black brick-like mosaic… Blake felt he was falling inside it, the effect was so hypnotic. He tried to count the layers, but there were too many. He stopped trying, as two words bubbled to the surface of his mind: kaleidoscope and Babel.

You are on the right path – a long way to go, of course. Your species has no adequate conceptual metaphor. Not yet.

However, Blake intuited that he was looking at the equivalent of the brain, the central core, whatever it was, of Kalaran. But there was no body. He remembered something Micah had said, and decided to verify it.

"You merged with the ship, didn't you? So, you control it with your mind, and it does everything you want? The ship, those other spheres, everything else, it's you, isn't it?" Which meant that if the ship was destroyed, Kalaran died along with it.

Correct. We have not had independent bodies for aeons. All Kalarash elect this path.

There was no voice, the thought came straight into Blake's head. It felt strong, not just communication, but the direct imparting of knowledge. Blake almost felt violated, as if someone was trespassing in his mind, someone who could rearrange things in his head, even re-write his mental software.

Do you want Zack's avatar instead?

"No," Blake said. "Just me and you."

The brain rose level with him, rivulets of mercury – or whatever it was – cascading down its sides, falling and splashing into the lake below, sending puffs of silver steam into the air. Something gelatinous oozed out of the pores every few seconds, pulsing.

In front of Blake, between him and Kalaran's brain, an image arose of the War Council. Various aliens flashed past in the moving vista, until it paused on the one Blake had settled on, the Medusa creature consisting of white globes.

Level Sixteen. Nchkani. Why did you stare at them?

Blake's anger at Kalaran ebbed. At the end of the day they were on the same side. But those Medusas unnerved him… "I don't trust them," he said.

Instinct?

Blake thought about it. It must be true, he had nothing else to go on. But any field commander knew that gut feelings could be just as important as more objective intel.

A grating voice came from behind Blake. "Concur."

Blake whirled around to see the reptilian Ranger, Manota, on all fours. A pink forked tongue whipped out between hook-like incisors, wiping over her yellow eyes.

"Treachery planned. Next in line if Tla Beth fall." Manota took two diagonal steps towards Blake, ending up with her snout inches from his face. He resisted the joint urges to retreat out of reach of those teeth and flinch at the smell of rotting food.

"Ukrull told other Rangers about humans. I studied files. War with Qorall like your chess, far more complex. But also like poker. You wild card. Keep you in deck. Play you when need."

Blake should have been outraged: he was being used. But instead he smiled. Soldiers are pawns on a chessboard, there to be played. Besides, a pawn can take down a queen, sometimes even a king.

Manota. Go to the Tla Beth homeworld. Hellera will join you when the time comes.

Manota vanished.

The heaviness that had been dogging Blake for weeks lifted. He watched the brain descend back into the lake. Now that Manota was gone, he felt he could ask the question that had been dogging him.

"The Spiders; what is their role, Kalaran?"

It must be a surprise to Qorall.

Blake shook his head, feeling as if he were a kid again in a school playground.

"Suppose I promise not to tell?"

Kalaran's voice took on an edge. *Time will prove otherwise.*

Blake bristled, and raised his voice. "Then how come I could see the Spider in the chamber when no one else could, not even Manota, who is Level Fifteen?"

You have some of their DNA in you. I implanted it before sending you back to the chamber. You will understand soon.

Blake's temporary indignation dissipated. Kalaran was going to use him, just as Manota had said, as the wild card in the deck. So be it. He was a soldier, this wasn't the first time he was being sent on a mission without full disclosure.

Are you in the game again, Blake?

Blake knew he was. "Yes, Kalaran, I'm in –"

Petra and Kilaney were staring at him, outside the Dome in Esperantia. One of the Youngbloods had joined them, a tall hulk of a teenager. Blake tried to recall his name; he'd given a eulogy at the mass funeral for the fallen Genners: *Brandt*.

"Where've you been, Commander?" Petra asked.

He shook his head, then spoke to the Genner warrior. "Brandt, assemble six of your men and women who are ready to fight and die if necessary. You will lead them and report to Kilaney." He turned to Kilaney. "Did the Q'Roth Queen grant you a battleship?"

Kilaney nodded. "Destroyer, waiting just outside the system."

"Good enough. Get them ready. We leave in four hours."

Kilaney and Brandt exchanged glances then headed off.

Petra was smiling. "Kalaran. You met him, didn't you?"

"We have work to do, Petra."

She shrugged. "Don't I know it. Nice to have you back, Commander."

A though struck him. "Promise me you'll look after the Spiders, Petra." He paused a little too long, then added, "While I'm gone."

Her smile faded. She was a Genner after all, and no doubt guessed the implication. "What happened up there?"

He told her about Kalaran infusing him with some Spider DNA.

"Interesting. But – as usual with Kalaran – not the whole story."

Blake gave her a level stare. "Meaning?"

She leant against a balustrade. "A Spider came to see me half an hour ago. Caused quite a stir, as you can imagine, walking down Main Street right up to my office. There was quite a crowd."

Blake's mind whirled. A Spider had never entered Esperantia, not since they'd hatched. He waited.

"It said that Kalaran put some of your DNA into the Spider you saw on Kalaran's ship."

"Why?"

She shrugged. "Part of the plan, I guess."

"I have to go and talk with them."

"You can't."

"Excuse me? I know you're President, Petra, but –"

"It told me to tell you that you would meet one more time before the end."

Blake felt blood rush to his head. "Well, Madam President, I think I'd like to hear it from them. I have many friends there, I need to say my goodbyes."

Petra remained cool. "That's what it said you would say. But when I said you can't, I meant it's not possible." She handed him a pad. It showed Shimsha underneath a glistening dome.

"Vasquez has been trying to break through for the last half hour. It's impervious."

Blake didn't understand. "But they don't have any tech…" He recalled the new towers going up around the perimeter, the ones he'd assumed were for the night-time displays. The Spiders had erected a shield.

Sixteen years raising them, living with them; he'd thought he'd known them, been part of their family. But they were alien. Blake suddenly felt empty, and very alone. "Is this Kalaran's doing?"

"Maybe. But I can't ask him either." She flicked her eyes upwards.

Blake followed her gaze. Kalaran's ship was gone.

"Hellera's ship is on the outskirts of our system, still keeping the dark worms at bay, though I don't know for how long. We're on our own, Commander. The Shrell-field surrounding our system will keep out most aliens, but not Qorall if he pays a visit."

"Why should Qorall come here?" Blake asked, then glanced back at the pad. The Spiders. Qorall would come for them.

"Precisely," Petra said.

Chapter 3
AWAKENING

Jen and Dimitri shot towards the planet, helmeted heads first, like two silver bullets. The timer in the corner of Jen's visor indicated ten minutes since they'd torpedoed out of the Ice Pick parked safely above them in orbit, another ten till touchdown. Ukrull had refused to land, and as usual declined to explain why. The planet had no atmosphere, so there was no need to worry about burning up. But the silence was eerie: no rushing wind, only her own measured breathing and Dimitri's ragged gasps.

They were on the galactic rim. To one side there were no stars, on the other a disc-like swathe of light. It gave Jen vertigo whenever she glanced towards the inter-galactic void, so she focused instead on their destination below. The planet was dark, even though this was the side facing the system's red dwarf. As she tried to make out details, her helmet visor sensed her eye muscles' effort and zoomed in. But there were no distinguishing marks, only a frozen ocean of metallic dust, all that was left of the Xera, the hyper-intelligent machine race that had almost taken over the galaxy two million years earlier. The other galactic species had barely survived, but had finally conquered the Xera, leaving nothing but this tomb planet, ten kilometres deep with metal ash. It was a memento, and above all a warning. And now she and Dimitri were there to find a machine race remnant if one still existed, and bring it back to Esperia for examination, without waking it up.

The planet grew large beneath her, the terrain stretching far and flat in all directions, and she took one last look towards inter-galactic space. She and Dimitri knew pretty much nothing about the Xera; apparently such intel was only fit for Level Fifteen and above. When they'd arrived, however, she'd asked how the Machine race had started at the galactic rim; it seemed unlikely. Ukrull had replied, "Before Machines, galaxy bigger." She guessed the Xera had somehow chewed up entire star systems for resources. Either that or the purge of the Machines at the end of the war had necessitated a clean-up operation on an unimaginable scale. She felt a chill, and adjusted a control to put a little more heat inside her suit.

Jen glanced across to Dimitri, his bulkier space suit looking awkward, his arms waving in jagged movements as if to stabilize himself, when there was as yet no appreciable gravity, his gloved fingers splayed as if for protection against an imminent fall. Dimitri's helmet visor, like hers, only showed half his face, from nose to eyebrows, but she could see his eyes were wide.

"Are you okay?" she asked.

"Yes."

She knew him better. While she was enjoying the thrill of the ride, he was clearly terrified. This was taking too long. "Pierre, how close are we? I can't see the entrance." She waited, wondering if Pierre and Ukrull, sitting in the Ice Pick, were paying attention, or were involved in deep discussion about tactics in case Qorall had tracked them.

"Twenty klicks to the right, Jen." Pierre's voice still sounded synthetic, although he had most of his humanity back. "I'm adjusting your suits' course direction. When we blasted the drop-shaft there was some blowback debris. It should be safe now."

"Should?" She knew Dimitri could hear Pierre, too.

Ukrull's gruff voice boomed inside her helmet. "Safe."

The altitude readout said one hundred twenty klicks to go. Abruptly her suit-thrusters kicked in, and her head and internal organs squeezed to the left as she and her lover tacked to the right. Within thirty seconds she saw the gaping hole in the dust sea, blacker than its surroundings.

After several minutes she felt the top of her head press against the helmet as they began to decelerate. "Lights, Pierre," she said.

The drones sent down earlier activated, and the ten-kilometre chasm beneath them lit up like a glistening, bottomless shaft, its smooth lipless mouth rising slowly toward them.

"Piece of cake, Dimitri," she said.

Dimitri, normally loquacious, grunted something. Jen had thought the light might help, but it only emphasized how fast and deep they had to go. The decel continued as they plunged into the borehole lasered by the Ice Pick, thirty metres across, its cauterised wall a polished coal mirror reflecting two blurred shapes tearing downwards. She tried to breathe normally. Dimitri's arms started to flail.

"Pierre, can you slow us down?"

"We're on a tight schedule, Jen. You know as well as I –"

"Pierre, just do it."

She thought she heard Ukrull's grunting laugh, but there was no other response. They began to brake hard. Firing her micro-thrusters, she drifted towards Dimitri, within arm's length. The halo of small helmet lights around his face accentuated his dark bushy eyebrows and wide, eager eyes, but covered his dark moustache and goatee. He looked tense. She selected private comms so Pierre and Ukrull would not hear.

"Take my hand, please," she said.

He stared straight down, his eye-brows connected. "I am fine, my love, it is just –"

"I'm not. Please. Take my hand."

Without facing her he reached across and clutched her hand. She didn't flinch, though it hurt at first. She saw him blink hard.

"I must seem a big fool to you," he said.

She said nothing, the best way to get him to talk.

"I'm afraid of heights, my one weakness. That is, I'm afraid of falling."

She laughed, not unkindly. "But you lived on Santorini, high above the Mediterranean waves. And for the record, you have plenty of other weaknesses."

He let out one short staccato laugh. "I left that isle as soon as I could."

"We're nearly there," she said.

"It's okay, I'm feeling better, we can go a little faster. Pierre is right, we're on a tight schedule."

"Just because Pierre is never wrong, doesn't mean he's always right." She flicked a comms switch at her waist. "Pierre, half-speed, please."

Jen gazed downwards into the blackness. She tried to suppress a gnawing intuition that this was going to be a one-way trip, and squeezed Dimitri's hand, glad he was with her.

Suddenly two steady blobs of light appeared on the floor below; their reflections.

"Pierre?"

Decel was severe this time. Her head rammed into the top of her helmet. At first she flailed her arms as Dimitri had done earlier, then she punched the thruster controls on her heels, flicking herself upright. With relief she saw Dimitri execute the same manoeuvre, but they continued to drop too fast, their reflections still a blur on the sides of the shaft. Pierre should have been precision-controlling their descent from the Ice Pick to minimize drop-time, but this was cutting it too fine.

"*Pierre!* Slow us the fuck down!" She felt Dimitri's arm tug around her waist, pulling her against his larger frame, trying to protect her. Abruptly their suit thrusters fired a plume of blue flame, and Jen felt herself slide down inside her suit, compressing towards her heels. Dimitri let go; just as well if they were to avoid an uncontrolled tumble.

Three seconds later she hit the ground. She attempted to roll but instead sprawled, her visor whacking against the smooth metal floor, banging her forehead hard against the padded helmet interior. She ended up on her back, panting. At least the visor hadn't cracked. Her partner loomed over her, holding out his hand. *You're tougher than you let on, Dimitri.* Accepting his help, she got to her feet and checked herself. Nothing broken or sprained. Dimitri was smiling; now that they'd landed and he could go play the explorer.

Jen wasn't smiling.

"Fucking hell, Pierre, you almost –"

"Jen, are you both alright? There was an energy surge down there, off the scale, blocked us for fifteen seconds."

The concern in his normally unemotional voice stalled her anger. "So, something is still down here," she said. The weight of what they had been sent to do finally hit her. She'd thought it was most likely a dead end, it seemed so fantastical, that part of the Xera – the galactic equivalent of an urban myth – could still be alive. How could the other species have been so reckless? How could they have left the job unfinished two million years ago?

She nodded to Dimitri. "Okay, Pierre, we're going in."

"This way," Dimitri said, his voice regaining some of its customary exuberance. He pointed, and she saw the circular tunnel off to the left. Ukrull's precision impressed her: thirty thousand kilometres up, he'd sunk a hole to exactly where he'd detected an underground maze and a single, very faint, heat signature. Inside she felt a shiver again; the Machines had been supposed long dead. There should have been no tunnels, no heat signatures, and no power surges. Jen wished she'd brought along a tactical nuke.

"Let's go, my sweet!" Dimitri said, and bounded towards the tunnel's mouth.

She smiled, happy with his return to form as an eager explorer, but then pursed her lips; she knew how often his enthusiasm got them into trouble. "Wait for me, Dimitri." Jen ran after him, the low grav allowing her to take long leaps as he disappeared from view. She flicked on the finder to locate the heat signature, but it registered nothing. Not good. Staring down the tunnel's entrance she saw that it divided in two, but couldn't see any light; Jen didn't know which way he'd gone.

"Hey, Dimitri, I said wait up!"

Pierre didn't need to look at a clock to know they were on borrowed time. This was the vulnerable phase, with Jen and Dimitri deep inside the ten-kilometre maze of tunnels they'd detected eight hours earlier. If trouble arrived, there was no fast way to get them out. And if they found a live Machine, they'd probably both be killed anyway, and he and Ukrull might have to go to Plan B and attempt to destroy the planet, though they wouldn't have been the first to try. But Kalaran had been specific, as always. Retrieve a dormant Machine relic. Don't activate it, just retrieve it. Pierre assumed Kalaran could control it, dissect it, and get what he wanted from it, without unleashing the plague of Machines again. But then he didn't entirely trust Kalaran, even less his mate, Hellera.

He glanced across at Ukrull, his two and a half-metre-long lizard-like travelling companion, who was chewing on something unsavoury, some kind of meaty bone that didn't smell too good.

"You miss daughter," Ukrull said, in his rock-grinding bass voice.

Pierre had hoped to have more time with Petra before leaving again, having only just rediscovered her after all these years. But the war was headed their way, its front nearing Esperia where Petra and the rest of humanity lived.

Pierre stared at his hands, nearly back to normal, fleshy on the outside, some hairs even starting to grow. Hellera's gift, or punishment; it wasn't clear which way she'd intended it; a retrovirus that was making him human again, though so far his intelligence clung to Level Ten. He suspected that would change as his physiology reverted. But for now his palms were still platinum flow-metal, as was half his nervous system. He had more in common with the dead civilization beneath him than most. He wondered; if Hellera hadn't intervened in his ongoing metamorphosis, would he have become like the Machine race? But then he'd never had any desire to rule the galaxy or purge it of 'organic impurity' – something of a hypocrisy given that the Machines apparently relied on a tiny amount of organic metal for their higher conscious processes. Nor had he arrived at the conclusion that order and logic were better than the semi-chaos of most living species. But perhaps Hellera had done it because he reminded her of the Xera, and though the probability of his evolution into pure machine intelligence was small, the consequential risk was too great.

"Do you remember them, Ukrull?"

Ukrull crunched through the bone, shattering it, a brown jelly-like substance oozing around his yellow incisors. "Not that old." He munched noisily.

"But you have ancestral memories, don't you?" Pierre knew it was true; all species above Level Twelve had such memories to avoid repeating former mistakes. One of Kalaran's gifts to the advanced species in the galaxy.

Ukrull put down the bone, flicked his rust-coloured tongue over his lips and eyes, and settled back, his three-digit fore-claws resting on his tan underbelly. His crescent-shaped pupils narrowed till his eyes were almost pure yellow. "Bad time. Almost lost all. Machines relentless. Cell and DNA principle. Each Machine made of smaller ones: nano-size to Titan, inter-stellar city-ships. Machines originally hard-coded to defend galaxy at any cost." Ukrull looked distant for a moment. "Lost perspective. Spread fast. Mined gas giants for Trancium, hyper-conductive flow-metal, very tough, memory structure in-built at atomic level. Organic species got in way."

Ukrull had never talked about it before. Pierre guessed he did so now due to the proximity to the planet where the final battle had taken place. "What happened then, between the Tla Beth and the Kalarash?" This was what both Kalaran and Hellera had refused to tell him. The Kalarash, Level Nineteen, had been the progenitors of the galaxy, seeding and nurturing life for eight million years, and had just handed over power to the Level Seventeen Tla Beth, when the Machine race emerged, Level Eighteen. Either the Kalarash or the Tla Beth must have created them, or at least fostered their development. Pierre had his suspicions as to who had unleashed them.

"Mistake," Ukrull said. "Misjudgment." He shifted position, his equivalent of sitting up, leaning forward. He fixed Pierre with snake-like eyes. "The Tla Beth –"

A klaxon sounded and their heads both snapped towards a holo-display that popped up in the front of the cramped cabin, showing seven bright red dots at the outer limits of their sensor capability. Pierre and Ukrull both uttered the same word.

"Incoming."

Jen was growing impatient, but at least she'd found Dimitri. Together they walked along black empty tunnel after black empty tunnel, the path always twisting and turning, their lights shining twenty metres ahead before a curve cut them off. "How long has it been, Dimitri? Any sign of those two drones?"

They'd dispatched six fist-sized drones to explore the network, and one had gone missing. They re-directed another to take its place and… ditto, which was why they were walking in the direction both drones had taken. It didn't seem a super-intelligent plan to her, but they had none better. The other four drones were painstakingly mapping out the catacombs, as she thought of them, far more extensive than she'd first estimated.

"Switch off your lights," Dimitri said.

"Getting romantic all of a sudden? There's a time and a place, you know, not to mention a near vacuum down here." She smirked beneath her visor, but she complied and turned off the helmet torch beams. At first she saw nothing, but then she detected a faint turquoise glow up ahead. They both stood, watching. The pale light strobed, very fast, almost imperceptibly. It struck her as odd, because she wasn't sure the Machines would need light. Was something else down here, also come to find a relic? But it didn't add up. The tunnels had been here a long time. If the Machines were active again they'd have replicated and the tunnels would be brimming with them. They weren't. And then it struck her: what if, after the Machine-Organic war, something had been left here to guard the planet and its secrets? It would have to be something very old, a long-lived species. She had a hunch which one.

"Whatever it is probably already knows we're here," she said. Flicking a switch, she directed comms back along the tunnel pathway to the bottom of the shaft, where she'd left a relay to the Ice Pick. The channel was dead. *Now there's a surprise.*

"Looks like it's just you and me, Dimitri."

"I'll go first," he said.

She sighed. "Dimitri, you're the brains, I'm the merciless killer, remember?"

He laughed, but moved aside to let her pass as they both re-activated their helmet lights. She took the nanosword from her belt and held it ready in her right hand. As they rounded a second bend the light grew stronger, flooding from the entrance to a larger chamber. On the ground were two silver smudges. *So much for the drones.* Jen stood behind them, realised what was inside the chamber, then stepped across the threshold, Dimitri a pace behind her. Before them was a Tla Beth.

Jen had heard about these Level Seventeen creatures, erstwhile rulers of the galaxy after the Kalarash had largely disappeared two million years ago, right after the battle that had ended where she and Dimitri now stood. She'd seen fuzzy images of the Tla Beth, but had never met one before. It floated a couple of metres above a raised dais. The Tla Beth at first sight was spherical, with vertical metallic strips rotating around its core, some clockwise, some anti-clockwise. The bands looked sharp, giving her the idea that if she tried to reach inside, her arm would be sliced off. The bands also shifted colour and brightness, creating the strobe effect, so that she had to concentrate to see the Tla Beth's 'body'. It looked like a rounded hourglass, the top half almost pure white, the lower half almost pure black, tiny motes of black and white drifting in the respective halves.

She knew Dimitri would be thrilled, and sure enough he strode past her to get a closer look. She put her nanosword away; it would be of no use against a Level Seventeen being. But a cacophony erupted inside her head, making her reel backwards, eyes squeezed shut with pain, as if a shard of ice had just splintered through her skull. It shut off, and she found herself in Dimitri's arms – he'd caught her, his dark brows meshed, his face a picture of worry.

"It accessed your node?" he asked. "It tried to communicate with you, didn't it?"

Jen watched excitement break through his concern. She didn't mind; besides, talking to a Level Seventeen being was pretty cool. Letting Dimitri help her back to her feet, she nodded gently, the pain melting from her forehead. Then the Tla Beth tried again, slower, less compressed.

<Drones tech, cannot let them near husk. Why are you here? Who sent you?>

Husk? She stared at the dais, and noticed something on it, a flat oblong shape, the size of an old-style briefcase. *Christ, they let one survive!* Her instinct was to slice through it with her nanosword. But she understood what the Tla Beth had transmitted. No tech must be allowed to touch the remnant, as it could be used by the dormant Machine as an energy source – no wonder Ukrull had refused to land his ship. On reflection, tech probably included her nanosword. Better to bury the damn thing then.

But the Tla Beth had asked her a question, and their imminent survival might depend on her answer. Focusing, with eyes closed, she thought a reply: <Kalaran>, imaging his ship in her mind – since she had never actually seen the Level Nineteen being in the flesh.

A shot of black ink spurted into the upper half of the Tla Beth, and the creature descended towards them. Jen's head spun, then the Tla Beth calibrated properly for her brain.

<Is it time?>

"It's asking me if it's time," she said to Dimitri, who was excluded from the conversation. "Oh, and we have to keep any tech away from that." She pointed, and watched Dimitri's eyes sparkle. He took a step toward it but hit a force field and bounced back off. She wasn't surprised: Pierre had told her the Tla Beth used force fields all the time, even for fine manipulation tasks. This one could kill her and Dimitri in an instant, if it so chose.

"How long has it been here? And what are the tunnels for?" Dimitri asked, massaging the spacesuit material around his right knee.

She concentrated on Dimitri's questions, so the Tla Beth could perceive them. But it wasn't easy; Jen wasn't a natural at nodal communication.

"Same response," she said. "It asked if it is time." Jen didn't add that it was probing her memory, images from recent and past events flashing past in the background of her mind. It had also asked her about the other ships, but she didn't know what it was referring to.

Dimitri's gloved hand went to the lower edge of his helmet – she knew he wanted to stroke his goatee, as he often did when deep in thought.

"We need to give an answer, Jen. It could mean time to destroy the machine, time to activate it, or time to transport it somewhere else."

A tremor beneath her feet rocked her, so she had to steady herself. "Did you...?" But she could see from Dimitri's expression that he'd felt it too.

Before she had time to ask what was going on, the Tla Beth supplied the answer. A holo appeared. The Ice Pick and the planet were both under attack from seven large ships whose design she didn't recognize.

<Confirm which ones are friends> the Tla Beth transmitted to her.

She whipped out the sword and flicked the electric blue nano-blade to point at Ukrull's craft, which was jumping around like a mosquito, avoiding heavy weapons fire. <Friend> she transmitted.

A tactile alarm on her belt told her the other four drones had just stopped transmitting. Within seconds, the holo showed silver ellipsoids spiriting upwards from the planet's surface, from the borehole, homing in on the seven ships. Each of the enemy vessels was quickly engulfed by a blue cloud that crystallized around its host. She'd originally trained as a biologist, and it reminded her of an antibody attacking an uninvited pathogen. The firing stopped, the encrusted ships drifting in space, dead or dying. She blew out a long breath. Now she knew what the tunnels had been for – they hid defences, ones she and Dimitri had not been allowed to see.

She transmitted again to the Tla Beth: <Can I talk with our ship?> Then added. <There is also a Ranger aboard called Ukrull.>

After a few seconds Pierre came online. "Jen, Dimitri, are you okay? Ukrull says you're with a Tla Beth. Is it true?"

Jen looked at the creature, its black and white halves stabilized again, its bands rotating calmly. "It's a Tla Beth alright. Has some cool toys. Think it wants to share?" She noticed Dimitri circling the dais, his hand by his hip, testing the force field with an outstretched forefinger. She tried to ignore what he was doing.

"What species just attacked us?" she asked.

"We didn't recognize the ships at first, but the Tla Beth confirmed they were Level Sixteen, Nchkani, more powerful than the Ice Pick, but no match for Tla Beth weaponry."

Jen mentally filed away the intel of a Level Sixteen race joining Qorall's side; bad news indeed. "Pierre, it keeps asking if it's time. Does Ukrull know what it means?" Jen waited. She guessed the Tla Beth and Ukrull would be communicating at a far greater speed than humans could tolerate.

"Jen, Dimitri," Pierre said. "You need to run back to the shaft. Go now."

Pierre's voice sounded shaky. Jen swallowed.

"What's happened, Pierre? Why –"

"Just run! Holy –"

The channel went dead.

Jen whirled around to see Dimitri staring at the Tla Beth. Its bands had stopped moving, and the air around it shimmered. Abruptly there was a screeching, banshee-like noise in her head. Her hands went uselessly to the sides of her helmet. Her legs buckled and she dropped to her knees. Tilting her face upwards she saw a micro-storm of jagged jade lightning surrounding the Tla Beth. Its hourglass body swirled black and white, and then Jen felt like she'd been stabbed in the stomach as a deep scarlet cloud mushroomed inside both halves of the Tla Beth's body, swirling like blood in water. The Tla Beth screamed through her node, sending her head crashing backward onto the floor. Jen's instincts told her it was fighting for its life. She shook violently as if her entire nervous system was in spasm. She bit down on an urge to vomit; throwing up inside a space suit would hardly help matters.

An arm scooped around her waist and picked her up as if she was a rag doll. The ground skated along underneath her to the rhythm of Dimitri's powerful stride, making easy progress in the low gravity. She felt something warm and sticky trickle from her nose and her ears. But tears also came; the connection with the Tla Beth was still there. It was in terrible pain, shocked at what was happening, and the realization that the external attack on the Ice Pick had merely been a lure to find and kill it. A cascade of images, some making no sense to Jen whatsoever, flickered in her mind's eye. The Tla Beth had lived for aeons, and yet she sensed that same dread of any being about to die, who still had so much to do. This Tla Beth had been a star engineer, painstakingly creating new systems where life might take root and flourish. She saw nebulae condense into star fields, planets sculpted into habitable worlds, oceanic habitats precipitate in open space, held together by force-fields while they were ferried to barren waterless star systems, Dyson spheres the size of Earth's solar system, and even a ring-world slowly turning around an ice blue star; wonders she had never imagined. But there was something else.

For the last period of its life – the time-frame impossible to gauge accurately but possibly tens of thousands of years – it had been the guardian of this tomb planet, and its secret. And then its mind remembered she was there, and Jen had the feeling that a god-like creature was staring at her, seeing everything she was, her life, her thoughts, her very being, and through her the species she represented, all in an instant, judging her and humanity. It transmitted a fast thought-stream through her node:

<You must survive. Will protect you as long as able, will mask your life signs. Planet ninety-eight per cent Trancium, very tough, hard to destroy, even for Qorall. You must hide. Message dispatched to Kalaran>.

She felt its life-force sputter, then it seemed to rally one last time. It said two more words to her, then with a feeling she equated with compassion, it cut her mind loose. Jen's body stilled, sadness welling up at the loss of such a super-being.

Dimitri was almost knocked off his feet by a massive quake. A curtain of blue flame rushed over them, burning itself out in a second, never really hot, she gathered, instead pure energy on some wavelength she'd probably never comprehend. A whirlwind of black and white confetti flushed through the tunnel as if expelled by one last gasp of life. Myriad tiny motes settled on her and Dimitri before melting like snowflakes, until the space around them was clear again, and Jen knew simultaneously that the Tla Beth was dead, and that they were hidden from Qorall's sensors.

They reached the drop shaft, and Dimitri set her on the ground. Nothing happened for a while. If Pierre and Ukrull were still in control, they'd have lifted them out of the hole using the Ice Pick's gravitic scoop. She gazed upwards and thought there must be some visual after-effect from the nodal transmission. The entrance, ten kilometres above them, was green. Space itself was green, if it was still normal space. She'd heard about Qorall's fondness for 'liquid space'.

"He's changing the rules of the game," she said, still feeling weak.

Dimitri knelt next to her. "I fear Qorall himself is here. Only he and his ship could do this."

Then we're screwed. That was when she noticed what Dimitri was carrying in his other hand: the husk, a dull, harmless-looking slab of grey metal, the last remnant of the Level Eighteen Machine race, the Xera.

"We can change the rules of the game, too, if we so desire," he said.

She thought about it, as another impact rocked the planet. "Qorall's trying to destroy it, along with us in the process." She took a breath, staring at the remnant. *Kalaran, I hope this is the right thing to do.*

She got to her feet, remembering the last words the Tla Beth had transmitted. And deep down she felt it *was* right, even if there would be hell to pay later. Probably sooner.

"It's time," she said.

Dimitri nodded, his eyes flattening, so she knew he was smiling. "You know me, my love. I've always wanted to open Pandora's Box."

She handed him the nanosword. Re-activating the blade, he gingerly touched the black, flat object with the tip of the nanosword. Nothing happened for a few seconds, then the blade blazed purple and was gone. Dimitri studied the hilt, but Jen already guessed it was drained. She watched the box, waiting. A single point of light shone faintly, dead centre on the top side, then began to stretch into a line, reaching towards the edges of the box. She knew what it meant. It was going to open.

"Dimitri, time to go."

They set off, jogging back into the tunnels, following the last map the drones had provided, heading down to the deepest level. As she began to sweat with the effort of running, she thought of Pierre and Ukrull, and prayed they'd escaped. But her mind kept swinging back to the Machine husk. Although there was no sound or light behind them, and she was sure nothing was following them, at least not yet, the back of her neck prickled, and she had trouble controlling her breathing. She lengthened her stride.

"Faster, Dimitri. We need to run faster."

Chapter 4
FAILSAFE

Sandy wondered if the concept of a cell was universal, or at least galactic. She and Antonia occupied a drab room just large enough to pace in: low ceiling, no windows, a wall-length glass front, and no apparent door. An uncomfortably narrow marble-hard bench, impossible to fall asleep on, tempted Sandy to sit but then made her want to stand. A seated contraption in one corner, with various controls neither Sandy nor Antonia had any idea about, had an obvious function which they'd both avoided so far; the fact that they'd had no food or drink for some time helped in that respect. The overall package put her on edge, and she guessed the set-up was aimed at priming them for interrogation.

They had both awakened there, a few blurry days after the long trip to Savange. Neither of them had spoken much; they'd never been friends, exactly. Yet Sandy knew they had to work together, even though they were almost certainly being watched. She decided to test how well they were being monitored, by saying some things openly, and others more secretly. She made eye contact with Antonia, who still looked immaculate – tall yet slight build, two-tone hair, perfect skin, classic almond eyes and high cheekbones – aside from a faint puffiness around the eyes. Sandy hated to think how she herself looked, and was grateful the thin glass wall didn't offer her reflection.

She could see why Micah liked Antonia. She stopped herself, and switched tracks to her husband Ramires, who loved her unconditionally, never looked at another woman, let alone… She closed it all off. Micah was ancient history.

Ramires was the perfect husband. She'd made the right choice. He would come to rescue them for sure. Sandy paced.

"They'll come for us," she said, unsure if it was a good or bad thing, since if they did, they might be captured or killed. But it was as good a place to start a conversation as any.

Antonia's eyes stared back a moment at Sandy, unblinking. The look conveyed openness and honesty, but to Sandy it was a mask dating back to Antonia's aristocratic upbringing; she had no idea what Antonia was thinking. Nonetheless, it looked as if her porcelain façade might finally crack.

"You mean Micah?" Antonia said, then her face flushed a little, and she said in a quieter tone, "and Ramires of course, and your son, Gabriel."

"Kat, too," Sandy added. She tried not to say the next thing on her mind, but it slipped out on account of her trademark 'mouth', as her long-dead brother used to call it.

"If any of them are still alive." Sandy knew she was inflicting as much pain on herself as on Antonia. Immediately Sandy thought of her son; the last time she'd seen him, Gabriel had gone with Petra and Micah to defend Esperia against the Alician attack force. Somehow she knew he hadn't made it. She'd dreamt of him, and in her case that only meant one thing.

Antonia looked aside. "They'll come." Her eyes pressed closed, lips squeezed tight, and her face closed like an antique China doll.

Sandy had a fleeting urge to sit next to Antonia and put an arm around her. But that would break the habit of a lifetime.

"Do you buy that bitch's story, about why we're here?" Sandy knew saying such things openly might get her into trouble, but she didn't care. Besides, that should get some kind of response from whoever was watching them.

Antonia opened moist eyes, drew her knees up to her chest. "The need for genetic material? Well, we're alive, and Alicians don't normally take prisoners."

Sandy thought about it. Her right fingers were twitchy. She really needed a stimlette; the withdrawal was making her antsy. At least Ramires wasn't there to tell her off about her minor addiction. But images of Gabriel growing up on Esperia flooded unbidden into her mind: as a young boy running around the farm chasing pigs, then as a young man doing martial arts with Ramires, and being heroic in the last sim-battle with Micah. She was convinced he was dead, such intuition a mother's curse. Turning away from Antonia, she walked up to the glass, took a deep breath then hammered her fist into the barrier. The glass wobbled slightly, a dull boom quickly fading, her two front knuckles stinging where they had just connected, leaving a bloody smear on the glass.

"That's normally a guy thing," Antonia said.

Sandy gave a short, humourless laugh. "Try living with a Sentinel for eighteen years."

"We need a plan, Sandy."

Sandy turned around. She sucked noisily on her knuckles to stem the flow of blood, then swallowed. "We also need to be realistic. This is the Alician homeworld. Their chances of getting us out of here alive are remote."

Antonia folded her arms. "So what's your plan?"

Sandy sat next to Antonia, cupped her hands around Antonia's ear, and whispered very softly. "Deprive them of the genetic material. Then they'll die out."

Antonia cupped her hand around Sandy's ear and whispered back. "You mean we kill ourselves?" She drew away, her brow furrowing before it smoothed. It was her turn to utter a mirthless laugh. "God, Sandy, that's what Zack used to call Plan F."

"Exactly, when there are no better plans."

Antonia took her turn to stand up and pace, and shook her head. "You really have been living with Ramires too long."

Sandy approached her, made Antonia stop and face her. Again she whispered, close. Antonia was clearly uncomfortable with Sandy's proximity; too bad. "But this way we're not victims, we're actually a weapon."

Antonia grimaced. "Listen to yourself." She placed a hand on her shoulder. Sandy flinched, so Antonia withdrew it.

"The answer is –" Antonia enunciated each word slow and clear – "no – fucking – way. There's always hope. The others are coming to get us, and they won't give up. We owe it to them –"

Sandy grasped Antonia's shoulders, holding her there. "They'll die if they come here. We could save them."

Antonia stood there, then spoke in a quiet voice, her eyes narrowing. "No. That's a word you should understand, Sandy, you've used it often enough in the past."

Sandy let go. "What's that supposed to mean?"

Antonia shook her head again, and returned to the bench. "Forget it. Forget I said it. But the answer will remain 'no', and in any case you'd never convince the others to go along with such a plan. At the first whiff of trouble the Alicians will put us back in stasis and harvest us when they need to."

That was the problem. Sandy knew her plan was shit. But sometimes better ideas grew out of bad ones. Shit makes good fertilizer, her Gramps used to say, and a wrong track can lead to a new perspective, and a better path. She just hadn't gotten there yet. Besides, she was worried her intuition about Gabriel was right, and wanted anything to take her mind off it. She decided to try to salvage something out of this exchange. Maybe Antonia could help her think around the problem.

"That's what I don't get; why they allow us to be awake."

Antonia looked up. "You think they need us awake?"

"Maybe they're not sure. It all sounds precarious, this genetic extraction process. And they've only got one shot, sixty of us. They botch it, they die out: no kids." Which was why her idea of revenge tasted sweet.

Antonia nodded. She did the whispering thing in Sandy's ear.

"We need to try to find out where all the other captives are. If the Alicians split us up around the planet, rescue will be next to impossible."

Sandy had thought about it. She whispered to Antonia, this time without Antonia shying away. "We're lab rats. They'll be analysing everything, comparing, looking for the most successful genes. We'll be kept close together, at least to begin with, in the same complex."

"Then we need to find a way of communicating with the others, when we find them, so that we can all react when rescue comes, so –"

Sandy shushed her by drawing a line across her throat with her fingers, and nodding to the other side of the glass. Someone was coming. The two women moved apart on the bench.

Louise came into view from around a bend, blond ponytail swinging from side to side as she strode purposefully towards them. Sandy raised an eyebrow when she saw that Louise had a Q'Roth left arm, black with a dark blue sheen, ending in a crab-like claw.

"Hello girls, bonding nicely?" Louise walked straight into and through the glass shield, slowing slightly as it traced the outline of her body then sealed again behind her. "It's coded for my DNA," she added.

"Latest Alician fashion?" Sandy said, staring at the Q'Roth arm.

Louise lifted it to shoulder height, opening and closing the claw, making a sharp clicking noise. She was clearly proud of it.

"Sister Esma had one. When I lost my own arm, I decided to be symbolic, given that I was taking over from her as leader. By the way, you should be proud, Sandy; your son Gabriel killed Sister Esma, sacrificing himself in the process." She shrugged. "Got me promoted."

Sandy's breath went into overdrive, her fists closing tight. She focused on Louise's pretty face, wanting with all her might to smash it into bloody pulp, to turn it inside out, to let her brains see daylight. Suddenly Antonia locked her arms around Sandy, part consolatory hug, but Sandy knew it was primarily a restraint.

Louise smiled. "I see you two are getting on. That's good; you're going to be together a long time."

Sandy remembered Ramires' training. Calming her breathing, she gathered saliva in her mouth by swirling her tongue around, and swallowed, repeating the process three times. Her arms relaxed a little, and Antonia let go. Sandy didn't take her eyes off Louise. She felt her son's presence next to her, telling her to wait, reminding her that a wise warrior never lets the enemy dictate the moment to strike.

Antonia broke the silence and stood up. "Where are the others? Why have we been separated? And what do you want from us besides genetic material?"

Sandy only half-listened. She was thinking tactics. When Louise departed, she would turn and slow as she passed through the glass; one lunge and a precision tiger punch to the vertebrae sticking out at the base of her scrawny neck. If she was quick enough, she could kill Louise.

"You two have been separated from the others because I want you to lead them, to do what's best for them, to keep them in line."

Antonia snorted. "And why would we do that?"

Sandy studied Louise; the bitch had an ace up her sleeve.

"Because then I will allow you to raise your child."

Antonia folded her arms. "Child? Are you deranged, Louise, I –"

"You are pregnant, Antonia. Guess who the father is?"

Sandy watched Antonia's face blanch, saw her stagger back a pace, the backs of her knees meeting the edge of the bench, making her sit, her mouth open, her eyes wild, as if searching. Sandy's rational mind wondered for two seconds who the father could be, but she already knew in her heart whose baby it was. Damn Micah again. He hadn't changed.

"What about me, Louise," Sandy said, "why should I cooperate?"

Louise walked up close, far less than spitting distance. "Don't you still care for Micah, Sandy? He escaped, you know. I'm hoping he comes here to rescue both of you. We have unfinished business."

Sandy willed herself not to react. "My question still stands, Louise."

"Alright, then. I want the Sentinel Ramires alive. On Esperia he beat two Q'Roth warriors in close quarters combat, something no Alician can do, despite genetic upgrading. I have a vid of him fighting; impressive, even by my standards. If you cooperate, I'll spare him when he comes for you. He can train my people."

Sandy laughed. "He'll never –"

"But he will. If he was Alician, he would not, because we rise above what you call love. Honestly, you humans are so sad, so easy to manipulate. You'll cooperate to keep him alive, and he'll do the same."

Sandy tried to keep the words in, but they edged out. "And Micah?"

Louise walked away. "You prove my point." She turned back around, and waved her hand in Antonia's direction. "But as your new best friend recently said, 'no – fucking – way'. If he shows up, he dies on sight. You'll have to settle for Ramires; which is what I hear you've been doing these past eighteen years."

Sandy lunged forward straight for Louise's throat, but instead something that felt like a sledgehammer – Louise's claw – smashed into her right cheek, knocking her clean off her feet. She hit the stone floor, her right shoulder thwacking the edge of the bench. She gasped for breath, unable to see clearly, dizzy from the blow.

"One more thing," Louise said. "While you were all in stasis, we implanted a failsafe device in your heads, a neurotoxin. It induces frontal brain death in three seconds, while leaving the core and brain stem working. We prefer to have you alive and functioning, but you might call it our 'Plan F'. Every fifteen minutes a signal is sent out that prevents the toxin from being released. If you *were* to escape, you'd have that long to enjoy your freedom. And by the way, if I am killed, the signal will stop."

She crouched down towards Sandy's face. "Your suicide plan won't work. You're right, we don't know all the variables, but we'll have enough genetic material from your limp flesh for it to begin to work. We live long lives, so even with a small number of fertile men and women we can replenish our society."

Louise stood up. "Think about what I said. You can live relatively content lives here, or I can put you all back in stasis and you'll never wake up, never see Ramires, or watch Micah's son – it's going to be a boy, by the way – grow up." She paused, as if deciding whether to say something or not, then she stared at them both, her remaining human hand on her hip.

"How long do you honestly think Esperia will survive? It won't see out the next month. Qorall has already dispatched resources to take it down. The only relics of humanity will be here on Savange. I've studied galactic history and trust me, every single time a race evolves its predecessor disappears. It's the natural order of things. Do you give a shit what happened to the generations that preceded Homo sapiens? Didn't think so. The other Grid races, all they'll see is that humanity shifted from Level Three to Level Five, which is no mean feat. And you two – you three – will be part of that evolutionary process."

Sandy tried to get up but it wasn't happening. She said nothing. At least her breathing had recovered. Antonia also kept quiet.

Louise turned and passed through the glass.

Sandy struggled to her knees, and managed to lever herself up onto the bench. She checked her cheek and shoulder; no breaks, but she was going to be bruised for a while. Antonia had her head down on folded arms atop her knees. Sandy could think of nothing to say. She shuffled along the bench until she was next to Antonia's trembling frame. Sandy decided it was time to break a lifelong habit, and put her arm around Antonia.

She wondered if Ramires and Micah were already on their way. For the first time she truly hoped they were not. All would be killed except Ramires, the last living Sentinel, and he would be trapped into aiding his sworn enemy. But memories of Gabriel flooded into her mind, his entire life from an infant to a child to an adolescent to a man. Such promise, erased out of life so early. She realised he'd died at the same age as her brother. A single tear spilled. Then another. She couldn't stop them. Antonia clasped her hand, and Sandy clung to it, squeezing hard. The full sting of Gabriel's death – that he was really gone – washed over her. Antonia manoeuvred herself so that she held Sandy, uttering soothing noises. Sandy's rage fell away, a gaping hollowness replacing it, a vacuum inside her belly, as if her womb remembered what it had given up to the world for safe keeping, and was now forever lost.

"Is she right about us, Antonia? Love makes us pathetic, weak?"

"No, she's all wrong. And I know you, Sandy, you're hurting now, but you are the strongest woman I've ever met, besides Kat. I know that right now you want to kill Louise despite everything."

Sandy sat up, wiping her sleeve across her eyes and face. "If I do, we'll all end up vegetables, barely-alive cadavers in an Alician lab."

Antonia leaned close, whispering into Sandy's ear. "At least I won't have to go back to my previous job."

Sandy frowned. Antonia had been a Council member on Esperia. What did that have to do with anything? But then she remembered: before that, back on Earth, Antonia had been a comms expert for the Eden Mission, working with carrier waves slip-streaming from Blake's ship, the Ulysses, all the way back to Earth. She thought about it. The signal preventing the neurotoxin being released would be a carrier wave. It was a long shot, but if Antonia could gain access, maybe she could disrupt it…

And there it was, the alternative path born from a dead-end. Sandy sniffed once, wiped her face again, and sat up as straight as she could.

The two women sat side by side on the uncomfortable, too-narrow bench, backs against an unyielding wall. Neither of them spoke. The only connection between them was Sandy's left hand, pressed onto the cool marble of the bench, and Antonia's right hand, covering Sandy's.

Chapter 5
RECODE

Seven minutes to intercept.

Cocooned in the cockpit of a Scintarelli Dart, Blake acknowledged the automated message, and watched the asteroid-sized ochre sphere enter the local solar system at a leisurely pace. It was the first time he'd seen one of Qorall's Orbs. It didn't look like a horseman of the apocalypse, but for the inhabitants on the planet he and twenty-seven other captains were trying to protect, Armageddon had arrived.

The Zlarasi were Level Six: their role in Grid Society was that of aqua-farmers, providing a vast range of seafood, essential oils and underwater tech prized throughout the galaxy. Their world, Alagara, was nine-tenths water, with most of its civilization covered by oceans, the three bare land-based continents reserved for air-breathing traders. Blake had seen a Zlarasi via holo-conference – the creature resembled one of Earth's defunct sea-based dinosaurs, the plesiosaur. At one point during talks over defense strategies they all knew to be futile, the Zlarasi had fixed Blake with stark, unblinking purple eyes. These locals understood perfectly well that their forty-thousand years of peaceful existence was at an end. Blake found he had to turn away. When he looked back, the delegate no longer met his gaze. For the first time in many years Blake experienced a sense of shame.

Six minutes to intercept.

He focused back on the current task. Zooming in via the Dart's visuals, he noticed the Orb's surface ripple. Lines like writing floated to its surface, only to submerge moments later. No one knew what it meant, except perhaps the Kalarash, and they wouldn't say. If it was language, it was presumably in Qorall's tongue. Perhaps it was better not to know.

They'd been losing the war against Qorall ever since he'd unleashed these genetic Recoders, asteroid-sized balls that entered a system, spilling golden rain onto the planets they targeted, rewriting organic 'software' at the chromosome level, turning every sentient being into Qorall's minions. The defensive armada's mission parameters were to defend the planet and evacuate as many as possible before the Orb unleashed its contents onto the doomed world. They would of course attempt to destroy the Orb, but similar engagements were ongoing at fifty locations across the front line, with aliens far more advanced than humanity in charge, and so far all attacks on the Orbs had failed, with heavy casualties.

Blake had received special instructions from Kalaran: to capture some part of an Orb so they could study it and develop counter-measures. He hadn't told Kilaney about this, for two reasons. First, Kalaran had imparted it to him and him alone, and that had to be for a reason. Second, Kilaney would intervene if he knew, and broaden the strategy, pouring more resources into it, which would make it more visible to Qorall. Blake understood Kalaran's tactic, he'd used it himself on more than one occasion during the Third World War: sometimes you send one man alone behind enemy lines to get a particular task done – like the assassination of a local enemy leader – while the battle raged on all around.

Kilaney would recognize the strategy, too. When Blake and Kilaney had worked together back on Earth they'd nicknamed it 'one-shot'. However, Blake had no idea how to achieve this particular mission. Any sentient being touched by Qorall's liquid virus was turned within seconds. The few robot ships and drones that had managed to scoop up some of the golden rain and escape with it, found that the substance degraded into raw elements moments after seizure.

Five minutes to intercept.

Blake checked the other screens, and frowned. Few worlds could evacuate fast enough. Blake tuned in to the elevated chatter from the planet, translated automatically for him by the Dart, but he hardly needed to understand the words: the general cacophony screaming through surface comms told him it was panic beneath the smooth ocean waves. If he'd been down there, he'd be sitting with a pulse pistol in one hand, a whiskey in the other, ready to make sure Qorall didn't add him to his army.

Staring at the pristine Zlarasi world, its turquoise oceans shimmering in the sunlight, knowing it would soon be gone, his mind drifted back to Earth's own demise. He'd managed to help twelve thousand souls escape, but seven billion had been slaughtered. Kilaney had kept the Q'Roth occupied long enough for the transports to escape, only to be captured and turned into a Q'Roth warrior. Luckily, though it had taken many years, they'd gotten Kilaney back. With his Q'Roth battle experience, Kilaney was now more valuable than ever.

Something snagged in Blake's head. What if…?

Four minutes to intercept.

The fledgling idea dangled on the edge of his mind. Rather than chase it, which in his experience only pushed it away, he concentrated on something else. Whenever Qorall took over a race, the virus brewing inside the Orb adapted to the intelligence level of the indigenous species. When the Orbs had first appeared a month earlier, they targeted any species in their path, no matter what level. Now Qorall was being more strategic, sending them to worlds inhabited by higher-level races, such as the Level Six world below. Blake also knew that was why he and Kilaney's small human contingent had been sent here; higher-level allies had been sent to attack the Orbs bearing down on Level Nine, Ten and Eleven worlds.

Apparently a Level Twelve fleet had managed to stop an Orb, by working with the Shrell to cause it to founder in Transpace, costing the lives of a thousand Shrell in the process. But the Orb had exploded, emitting a burst of epsilon radiation over a twenty light year radius, annihilating three species inhabiting unshielded planets, including those on transports fleeing the system.

He imagined the near future as the inhabitants below were killed or turned. All the indigenous species' ships, and the planet itself, had self-destruct systems; no one wanted to be corrupted. Of course, it didn't matter to Qorall. Blake had always loathed terrorists, whom he unequivocally branded cowards, as they targeted civilians. But Qorall had taken it one step further, turning those civilians into his army. Blake squeezed his fist hard inside his palm, then changed hands, repeating the move. Soldiers like him were supposed to be able to protect civilian populations. He took three deep breaths to calm himself down. It didn't work.

Three minutes to intercept.

Movement on the central display came as a welcome distraction. At least the local inhabitants had impressive ships – half of them upgraded with Level Nine tech – skeletal green diamond shapes with a burning white anti-matter core at their centre, held in check by a magnetic brace. Ten of the ships engaged the Orb at the outer edge of the system. Their particle beams and missiles had no effect. Atomics were used next, then anti-matter cluster-bombs. The view screen on Blake's Dart automatically dampened visuals so the blast flashes didn't blind him. He tapped a pad on the console to contact Kilaney, once again his Commander-in-Chief, housed in the Q'Roth Destroyer hanging above the planet.

"The Orb's trajectory hasn't been deflected or even slowed down. How is that possible?" Blake asked.

Kilaney's voice was gravelly, serious in a pissed-off way. "We think they use some kind of contained micro-black hole to power the shields and resist gravimetric attacks."

Blake watched as new Zlarasi ships – massive affairs shaped like conch sea-shells – spewed megatons of rock at the Orb. Mass drivers were crude, but it made sense to try, since shields were usually designed to resist high-energy beam attacks rather than those from kinetic energy. But again, there was no deflection of the Orb's trajectory. Instead the avalanche of rock was parried around the Orb and then compacted, making it glow under heat stress. It briefly gave the Orb a comet-like tail.

Two minutes to intercept.

"They should retreat," Blake said, knowing they wouldn't. He wouldn't if he were there. "Maybe they can salvage more people from below."

"We need to fall back, Blake. I don't see what else we can do here."

Blake made a steeple with his fingers and stared at the ochre sphere. The diamond ships were still firing, when an alarm signified an intense gravimetric shock wave. All of the Zlarasi vessels were sucked violently towards the Orb's surface. Their commanders' shouts and screams tore at him, but he didn't shut them off; that was part of his code, to stay with soldiers when they died. He watched as the ships were engulfed, disappearing without a trace. *Sonofabitch*. He'd commanded troops plenty of times before, but never seen such wasteful deaths.

Kilaney came online again, his voice scratchy. "We have to leave now while we still can, take the intel we've gathered back to base."

"How many, Bill?"

There was a pause before Kilaney answered. "I don't count them anymore, Blake, not since –"

"How many?"

"Dammit Blake… fourteen hundred and fifty-seven souls. But that's a piss in the ocean compared to the billions still on the planet."

Blake closed his eyes as if in silent prayer, then opened them again. "But they were soldiers. Their death has to mean something." *As does mine.* The idea crystallized in his mind, and as soon as it had formed, it made obvious sense. His mind made up, his anger congealed into purpose. "We're not leaving empty-handed, Bill. This can't all be for nothing." He touched a panel, and his ship pitched forward, then accelerated towards the Orb.

One minute to intercept.

"Blake, what the hell are you doing? That Dart won't even get its attention!"

Blake had wondered why Kalaran had suggested he take a Scintarelli Dart, while Kilaney commanded a Destroyer. Now he understood. Probably Kalaran had planted the idea in his head. It didn't matter. Time to play the wild card.

"We need a sample to study, Bill. A live one. In ten seconds I'm passing command override to you. The Dart has antigrav, remember? If the Scintarelli are as good as their word, this little ship can slipstream out of a black hole's event horizon, so it should be able to escape the Orb's local gravity."

There was a pause. "Wait a goddammed minute, Blake. Are you suggesting what I think you are? Hell, you're asking me to watch my best friend get turned into one of Qorall's soldiers. I won't do it, Blake. There has to be another way. We could come back later and capture one of the others who've been turned."

"Later isn't now. So far none of those turned have been captured alive, and the code unravels after death. Bill, in war, intelligence is paramount."

"Blake, dammit, I –"

"One shot, Bill. I can do this. We can do this. That's why Kalaran sent us. That's why he sent you and me."

Kilaney remained silent. Blake continued, committing his friend to the plan.

"Once I've been infected, take me back to Esperia, to Kalaran, or to the Spiders if he's not there."

Kilaney's voice lost its edge. "You think they'll be able to fix you?"

The Orb occupied a third of Blake's view screen. The writing began to look tantalizingly familiar, but he still couldn't make sense of it. Blake wanted to spit, but his mouth was dry. Could he be turned back later, become himself again? He pushed the idea away; he'd never indulged in wanton optimism.

"Both Kalaran and the Spiders have scanned me physiologically and cognitively; they know me well. They can work out how the pathogen functions, maybe derive a defence." He doubted there would be an antidote, not for him at any rate.

Blake's aft screens told him the last transports of local inhabitants had jumped out of the system. They carried only fifteen per cent of the population, but it was better than nothing. They were headed to a water-based planet at the edge of the galaxy, where they would try to start afresh. He programmed a fly-by loop towards the Orb, then sat back.

Ten seconds till intercept.

"Bill, get out of here, recover me from long range. Don't let me die for nothing. No words, either, we've said them all before."

Kilaney stayed silent. Blake was relieved to see the General's ship wink out and then reappear at the far edge of the system, outside the known range of the Orb.

Finish this one without me, Bill.

The Orb filled his screen. Blake watched the writing appear and disappear, wondering again what it meant, and who would read it. Eventually he was so close its surface appeared flat. A fissure opened up beneath his Dart, a golden flare lashing out at his ship.

"Now, Bill!"

The normally-silent Dart engines whined, then roared. Deafening klaxons barked in the cockpit as the pathogen breached the hull, the air around him taking on a golden hue. The ship shook violently as it strained to pull away, and Blake had to clamp his jaw to protect his teeth. The engine pitch rose to a screech, then descended as the Dart catapulted away from the Orb. Blake raised his hand to salute his commander, but halfway his hand stopped. It was golden.

He turned it around to see his palm, the cracks and lines appearing in sharper relief against its golden sheen. It spread beyond his wrist, crawled up his forearm, icy veins sketching a web at first, the area between the veins quickly filling in. It was almost beautiful, save for the ice-burn sensation that had now reached his throat. He thought of Glenda, while he still could. *Pray for my soul, my love.*

His vision blurred as the freezing wave reached his scalp and lanced behind his eyes, which he squeezed shut. Nausea gripped him and he dry-retched, then it passed. His mind felt like it was being squeezed through a sieve. He found it difficult to focus, impossible to think in anything except loose fragments. Through an effort of will, he remembered Glenda, long gone, their wedding, a younger Bill Kilaney with a full head of jet black hair congratulating him, but then the image lost cohesion. Bill who? He struggled to recall the name, knowing it was important, something was really important, he mustn't let it go. But what was it? His whole body, from skin to core, felt like it was made of ice. Yet it no longer felt cold, it felt... pure. It had been so dirty before, so confused, all that detritus in his head, floating like scum on

EDEN'S ENDGAME

the surface of his mind. Impure thoughts drained out of him until his mind was clear as water.

Suddenly he felt powerful, incredibly strong. Opening his eyes, everything was in sepia. It didn't matter, colour was a distraction. For a few seconds he had no idea who he was, where he was, and why he was. Looking at the view screen, he saw and read the writing on the Holy Messenger. It sang to his soul. Qorall's sacred scripture, the call to war. He knew immediately what he must do. Hands dancing over the controls, he tried to disable the command override. He shut off the noise from the planet full of infidels about to be saved, deliverance upon them from all their woes. Why did they always protest?

A voice intruded. "Goodnight, Blake."

Whose voice was that? A face appeared in his mind, someone he once knew, back then a comrade, now an enemy. He shook his head to clear the image; all the past heresy of the biological receptacle he now inhabited must be purged. But none of the ship controls responded. The mother ship was far away, and he suddenly recalled the barbarian Kilaney's plan, to capture a holy soldier in order to develop a counter-weapon. It could not be allowed. Death rather than capture; the writing was very clear on that. He pulled out his pulse pistol, but his arm grew sluggish. Struggling, he raised the barrel to his temple. His index finger slid into place in front of the trigger. One death to protect the cause, preserving the integrity of Qorall's swelling army of trillions. An easy choice. But his vision glazed, and he could no longer feel his arm, or move. His last conscious thought was the realization of what this heathen Kilaney had done to him.

Kilaney closed his eyes and uttered a silent prayer of thanks; he'd activated the stasis field in Blake's ship just in time, paralyzing him in a temporary state of hibernation, slowing his bodily functions down a hundred-fold. The Dart gathered speed, shot past the planet, and headed to join his Destroyer and the rest of the Zlarasi refugee fleet. As he waited, he watched the planet on the screen. The Orb was almost in orbit, from where it would disintegrate and rain over the doomed world. He was patched through to the planetary commanders.

"It is your decision, but if you want to act, you must do so now."

A holo appeared of the Zlarasi military commander, her smooth grey-green body with its long neck and small head undulating slowly in a vast ship-based water container, her four paddle-like fins wafting gracefully. A reply came through the onboard Q'Roth translator system.

"None of us can bring ourselves to do it. It is against our… religion. We ask your assistance."

Kilaney winced as the command codes flashed up in front of him. His bridge crew all turned towards him. It felt like genocide, wiping out a whole planet. Hell, it practically was genocide. Glancing at the other screen, he noted Blake's Dart land in his holding bay, where it was locked down. "I'm not sure I –"

"End this. We would do the same for you. We will do the same for you when it is your time. Can you not hear them?"

Kilaney touched a control, and for a moment the auto-translation switched off. Keening cries echoed around the bridge, like a choir of tormented whale song; it was the saddest noise he'd ever heard. The Genner Youngblood leader, Brandt, rose from his chair, but Kilaney shook his head. Kilaney began entering the code.

A hissing sound interrupted him, and his finger poised as the noise morphed into words.

"Return the Holy Soldier you have stolen, and we will leave this world untouched."

Brandt turned around. "It's coming from the Orb, Sir, though I'm not sure how it's interfacing with our comms system."

Kilaney played the words over again in his head, then stared at the screen. The Orb hung silently, motionless above the planet. It should have begun its attack by now.

As Kilaney expected, the Zlarasi came through on comms a second later.

"Commander, this is an unprecedented chance. Return the one they want."

Kilaney barely breathed. He glanced at Brandt, and said quietly, off-comms, "Raise our shields."

Brandt frowned but entered the command.

The hissing voice came through again. Kilaney had no doubt the entire fleet and planet could hear it.

"One man in exchange for billions. This is not a ruse. We will leave this system and proceed to the next engagement. This world will be declared neutral territory for the duration of the war."

Still Kilaney said nothing. He stared down at the flashing panel beneath his hand that awaited the final three digits to destroy the planet.

The Zlarasi communicated again. "Commander Kilaney, you must hand him back. The potential benefits far outweigh the risks. If this was your world you would not hesitate."

Blake's words drifted back to Kilaney: *This was why Kalaran sent us, Bill, you and me.*

Brandt stood up. "Two Zlarasi ships are now on an attack vector towards us, Sir."

Kilaney nodded. He glanced at the screen showing Blake's Dart in the hangar.

Brandt posed the question that Kilaney guessed the entire crew was pondering. "Can we trust Qorall? It sounds insane, but there are billions of lives at stake, Sir. Tactically speaking –"

"I'm a General. I don't do tactics, I do strategies. You're a Genner. Do the math. Why would Qorall make such an offer, even assuming it is legitimate?"

The Zlarasi commander came online again, her voice elevated. "Commander, we order you to –"

Brandt cut them off, staring at his Commander, standing to attention. "Your call, Sir."

A boom signalled the first Zlarasi shot impacting the Destroyer's shields, shortly followed by another.

"I assume we don't return fire, Sir?" Brandt said.

Kilaney gazed at the hulk-like Genner. This was the young man's first time in a military engagement, and yet he already made a good first officer. "Correct."

Kilaney knew there wasn't much time. His humanity made him hesitate, no matter the brutal logic behind his actions, but he had been Q'Roth for a long time, used to decisions that could mean you never slept soundly for the rest of your life. He entered the final code for planetary self-destruct.

The hissing came through again, despite blocked comms. "You have made a mistake. Your world will pay soon."

The Zlarasi ships stopped firing, as the Orb lost cohesion, shedding a golden aura of death around the planet.

Ugly scarlet gashes opened up on the planet's continents as Devourer Class bombs – used for demolition of unstable planets – ignited under its crust. The two small poles blazed white, as the vast oceans first turned from blue to a sickly green, then began to boil. It was fast, but then it had to be. Inwardly, he saluted a race who could make such bold preparations for the greater good, and wondered how mankind would fare when it was their turn.

All his Genner crew stood, transfixed by the image on the screen, except Brandt, who had his head in his hands. Kilaney made himself watch. The planet seemed to swell, as if trying to hold something in, then its entire surface turned lava red, and the world burst apart. He'd seen planets explode before, but never a heavily-inhabited one. For a moment he felt vertigo from what he'd just done, and gripped the armrests of his command chair.

"Open comms to the Zlarasi Commander," he said, and cleared his throat.

"Commander, I fear I have made an enemy this day, but you must understand my decision."

"We are Level Six. We understand. One man for billions, one planet for the galaxy. But you must understand that you have lost an ally today. Leave now, take your prize back to Kalaran, and pray your plan works."

Four Wagramanian vessels appeared, scorching towards Kilaney's Destroyer from the opposite end of the sector. Kilaney recalled that this Level Seven warrior race had recently been turned by Qorall. It was definitely time to leave.

The Zlarasi Commander continued. "When Qorall's forces come for your world, we will be there to ensure your integrity."

That sounded ominous. But in a flash the Zlarasi fleet was gone. Kilaney didn't bother engaging the Level Seven Wagramanians – he was no match for one of their ships, let alone four.

He leant back into his command chair as the Destroyer prepared for a long range transit. The awful truth of what he had just done settled on him like a crushing weight; billions had just ceased to exist. Despite the strategic advantage, it felt like he had just committed a war crime of unimaginable proportions. His gaze fell again upon the image of Blake's Dart in the bay. Kilaney knew what it was like to be transformed into the enemy. But this was different; Blake was no more, what was left was a fervent Qorall follower. Whereas Kilaney had wanted to exact revenge for years on his Q'Roth captors, Blake would now willingly die for – and kill for – Qorall. Kilaney had earlier considered going down to the bay and putting a pulse bullet in Blake's brain, so he could bury the man while his memory of him remained untarnished. But after what he himself had just done, that was no longer an option. He would see Blake's idea through to the end, including terminating what was left of Blake if – when – necessary.

War was always like this in his experience; terrible deeds, tragedies, injustices, and crimes. Only in peacetime did any kind of justice and morality reassert itself. Those who called for war never understood until it was too late. And now he had committed one of those terrible deeds, and even if it was for the greater good, Kilaney knew there had to be a personal price to pay. The only course of action left to him personally, the only path to any kind of redemption, was to die in battle.

Brandt attracted his attention. The Wagramanians were almost in firing range.

Though Kilaney was sure he'd had worse days, none came to mind.

"Brandt, get us out of here, quickest route home."

Kilaney sank back in his command chair, wishing he could crawl out of his skin. But he would see this through. *Kalaran, time for you to show us what a Level Nineteen being can do.*

Chapter 6
SAVANGE

Micah couldn't deny the space station was impressive. Staring through a view screen the width of Shiva's command bridge, he studied the Alician stronghold floating in space three kilometres away, tethered to the planet Savange, and was thankful for the null field hiding Shiva from any external sensors. The slowly rotating disc-like station was studded with metal spires and flying buttresses, and peppered with particle beam turrets. A surrounding oval bubble glistened in the distant sun's orange rays; the Alicians' orbital spaceport was well-shielded. A taut silver thread attached the station to the planet's equatorial region; this tether was the most obvious target. Two Q'Roth warships patrolled the region, completely black except for Spartan green lights that slowly pulsed. The ships would no doubt react to any incursion with extreme force. Micah hadn't yet tested Shiva's capabilities, but a fire-fight at this stage would jeopardise the mission. For now, silence and invisibility were the best strategies.

His eyes traced the tether downwards to the Alician home world Savange, to the purple and green continent edging its way out of darkness, a smudge of yellow light marking the city where the human captives were most probably held. He walked over to the view screen, felt its cool surface first with his fingertips, then his forehead. "Hold on; we're coming," he said, his breath momentarily misting the screen. In his mind's eye two faces arose, tugging him towards the planet's surface. Micah would have come halfway across the galaxy if there had only been these two women – or even just one of them – amongst the sixty stolen by the Alicians. No matter that neither of them was his. He had to assume they were unharmed, or else he couldn't function, and would endanger the mission. Do your job, he told himself; stay focused.

Pushing off from the view screen, he returned to his command chair set apart from the other seats and consoles, all currently vacant, arranged in an arc behind him. The lights were always low on Shiva, and the ridged, mottled brown ceiling made him feel he was inside a powerful whale. It suited his mood.

Ash entered through the arch at the rear of the bridge. The ship's innards were a maze of corridors connecting larger enclosures, no doors anywhere. None of them were used to it yet. Ash walked barefoot, as usual, hands clasped behind his back. Ash reminded Micah of a priest; no, not a priest, a holy man. Micah had asked him why he'd changed his name from Rashid to Ash. He'd replied it was a diminutive form, but Micah didn't buy it. There was something else. Ash had seen marvels on his inter-galactic 'sabbatical' before returning to this galaxy, and clearly they had left their mark on him, so much so he'd altered his persona, and his name. Yet Micah was accustomed to it now, and felt it suited him better.

Ash's head jiggled when he spoke, an Indistani habit. He flicked a hand toward the view screen. "They do not know we are here?"

Micah shook his head. "They'd attack if they did. We'd look small and relatively defenceless." He glanced at the command holosphere hovering to his left, each convex square on its gridded surface showing a key parameter, one of them the field around Shiva keeping the ship invisible to sight and scans. It indicated a stable shade of green. He frowned. "However, sending a Rapier down to the planet's surface might be problematic."

Ash's voice was unperturbed. "Ramires is working on it. He will find a way."

Micah's gaze returned to the space station. Although Alicians were just two genetic steps ahead of humanity, and only one ahead of Genners, their tech level was far more advanced. Back on Earth scientists had long dreamed of – but never been able to construct – a 'skyhook', an orbital platform tethered to the planet by a single thread of super-strong alloy. Like an upside-down plumb line, the planet's rotation kept everything in place. The tether also served as an elevator, able to transport people or goods up to the station and down to the surface. Micah decided it might prove useful later as an escape route, so it was best left intact.

The stark beauty of the space station irked him. The Alicians had achieved so much in the past eighteen years since they quit Earth's charred corpse, whereas mankind's remnants barely survived above subsistence level, having returned almost to an agrarian status. The adage 'it's not what you know but who you know' evidently applied at the galactic level; the Alicians had powerful allies, willing to share advanced technology. At least the Kalarash being named Hellera had provided Micah with Shiva, a ship way beyond Alician and even Q'Roth technology. Still, it was all so damned unfair, not that fairness had any currency when it came to galactic survival.

Ash cleared his throat. "Perhaps Ramires was right about the Nova bomb."

"No," Micah said. He'd been very clear on that issue.

Ash's head stilled, bowing a fraction. He turned to leave.

"I'm sending you both down to the surface."

Ash's head turned back towards the purple and green ball hanging in star-speckled darkness on the view screen.

"I want you to try the cloak, Ash. See if it works." Micah smiled. "We have no privacy aboard this ship anyway."

Ash nodded and walked to the arch. Micah called after him, still staring at the station, wondering how many Alicians were aboard.

"Ash, you must have seen so many strange things on your travels: wonders, horrors. You never talk about it." He broke away from the screen to face Ash's skinny frame, and stared straight into his all-black eyes; Mannekhi eyes given to Ash by Kalaran, the reason only recently made apparent.

"What most affected you?" Micah asked.

An air of sadness imbued Ash's words. "The rarity of compassion."

Micah didn't buy it, guessing that Ash's response was intended as a message. *I'm not the one you need to convince.* He watched him leave, then reached out for the holo-cube, twisted it, and tapped one square. It expanded into a single table-top sized square of information: weapons status. The Nova bomb was still there, locked down in the weapons bay. It wasn't that he didn't trust Ramires…

He decided to check in with him, Shiva instantaneously opening up a one-to-one channel between him and Ramires, so that no one else heard. Micah presumed this was based on the use of Ramires' name, as well as context and the tone of the speaker's voice.

"Ramires, any prog–"

"I've found a weakness in their detection grid. We can get a Rapier down there, next window eight hours."

Ramires' voice was cutting and urgent; fair enough, given that his son had been killed only a month ago and his wife was one of the captives down on Savange. Micah took a breath, and broadened the communication parameters. "Listen up everyone, briefing in six hours. Until then get some rest."

There were no replies; he didn't expect any. Like him, everyone wanted to act, not hang around in orbit. Although he'd told the others to get some rest, he pulled out a small rectangular patch from his chest pocket and pressed it to the side of his neck. A cold flush bristled across his face and neck, then trickled down his spine. He shivered once, discarded the patch, then began planning strategies and tactics, back-up plans, and back-ups to the back-ups, using the resident in his brain to help him store and compare the scenarios. In his training back on Earth as an Optron analyst he'd learned that chess masters thought five moves ahead; less and they got beaten, more and it made no difference due to the unreliability of predicting that many steps ahead. But he was dealing with Alicians, so he pushed out the boundaries to seven. His resident informed him there were in excess of two hundred and fifty credible scenarios of varying likelihood. "Thanks," he said, to the echo-less walls.

Involuntarily the faces of Antonia and Sandy crystallised again in his mind, making him pause. Shiva, constantly scanning Micah's resident, interrupted him.

<Inquiry: the first one was briefly your lover, and is the wife of Kat; the second is the spouse of Ramires. Yet both women trigger a significant increase

in emotional resonance when you think of them. Which of these two women is more important to you?>

Micah clamped his lips shut, tried not to get angry, the soft option given the broiling cocktail of emotions lurking just beneath his skin. His close connection with the ship mind left him even less privacy than the rest of the crew. Before leaving Esperia, he'd been told that Shiva was designed to anticipate its captain's wishes. He figured Shiva wanted to know his priorities, especially in case not all of the captives could be rescued, and a choice had to be made. But Micah didn't want to answer, and wasn't sure he knew anyway.

"It's a dynamic variable, Shiva. If that decision comes up, I will decide at the time."

<Understood.>

Micah almost laughed. *I doubt it.* He nudged the images of the two women out of his mind and got down to work.

Ash stood in his quarters, holding the cloaking device in his hand, a small yellow rod the size of a cigar. He had asked Shiva how it worked, its scientific principles, but the ship's mind had replied by asking how good his hyper-math was, at which point Ash had shrugged. It had practically no weight. Attaching it to his belt, he activated it and felt absolutely nothing, no change, no tingling on his body. Walking up to the mirror he used each day for shaving and brushing his teeth, he saw, instead of his face, the opposite wall and the archway to his room. After moving left and right to check that he was definitely in front of the mirror, he laughed aloud. He tweaked the control to attenuate any further sounds he might make: his breathing, footsteps, even disturbance of the air around him. Then, with an almost mischievous grin, he set off.

The first cabin he came to was occupied by Vashta, the Level Eight Ossyrian doctor, sitting on her hind legs at a small console, mercurial eyes in her dog-like face dancing over an alien script Ash didn't recognise. He'd only met Vashta a week ago, but had been impressed by her complete and selfless concentration on whatever task she was set. She had a mane of jet-black fur. Her Pharaoh-like headdress made up of horizontal bars of gold, red and blue, was propped up on a chair next to her cot; he'd not seen her without it before. Her pointed ears remained back, not detecting him, not even his scent. With a shock Ash realised she was naked; never mind that she was an entirely different species and covered head-to-paw with fur. Feeling his face flush, he backed out of the room. At least the cloak-field worked. But he needed to test it on more subjects.

Next he headed to the cabin of the brunette Aramisk, the stocky, not unattractive but somewhat abrasive female Mannekhi, the only other humanoid race any of them had encountered. He shared one thing in common with her and all other Mannekhi: all-black eyes, including the irises. But he was surprised to find Kat in the room, and intrigued to find the two of them standing very close, Aramisk's hands on Kat's slender waist.

"Aramisk," Kat was saying, "I told you before. It was just once. You know I'm here to rescue Antonia, to bring her back so we can be together again."

Aramisk's firm hands glided up Kat's thin, almost boyish torso, then one hand reached up and stroked her face and black, short-cropped hair. Kat didn't pull away.

"And I will help you find her. But we Mannekhi work differently, we separate the present from the future. Here, let me show you." Aramisk pulled Kat towards her and kissed her full on the mouth. Kat resisted at first, but Ash could see it was only half-hearted, and soon Kat had her hands locked around Aramisk's neck, kissing her back.

Ash found himself outside the cabin, his head reeling. He recalled that two days earlier Vashta had made a seemingly innocuous remark over crew dinner, that Mannekhi pheromones were far stronger than humans were used to. Now he understood, though he had no idea how Vashta had put it together so quickly. He wondered if he should tell Micah; it could affect the mission. But he knew he wouldn't.

Composing himself, he found his way to Ramires' cabin, where the last-surviving, grey-moustached Sentinel was dressed only in shorts, performing a martial arts kata with a metal staff, a thin sheen of sweat over his muscled torso. Abruptly, eight metallic holo-spheres appeared, surrounding Ramires, each with a single blue meridian running around them. They flew towards the warrior. Ash was mesmerised. Ramires dodged and struck them exactly on their equatorial lines, with two ice blue, ultra-thin foot-long blades that flashed out from each end of his staff. Ramires' feet left the ground, and he twisted through the air. The only sounds were sharp, ringing clangs as he guillotined the spheres one by one. Ramires landed in a semi-kneeling position, head down, one arm stretched outwards, the other gripping the staff, its nano-blades retracted. The last of the hemispheres rolled to a stop on the floor and vanished. Ash, trained in martial arts himself, but nowhere near Ramires' level, resisted a strong urge to applaud. Then he reminded himself that on Savange, if it came to hand-to-hand combat, Ramires would be surrounded by an entire population of Alicians, all faster and tougher than humans; he wondered how many Ramires could fight off it if came to it. An image formed in his head of a battle scene with a lone Sentinel defending himself against appalling odds. Ash shook himself; it felt too much like a premonition.

Ramires hadn't moved, and his breathing didn't seem laboured. The only sign of effort during the exercise had been his greying ponytail flinging out behind him as he'd spun through the air. But Ramires' head jerked upwards suddenly, and he glared toward the archway where Ash stood. Without warning, he flung the staff at the doorway. Ash ducked, the bar brushing the hair on the top of his head before clanking against the corridor wall. Ramires' eyes glared at the entrance, as Ash slowly moved to one side. Then Ramires seemed to relax. "I must be getting twitchy in my old age," he said. He walked over to retrieve the staff. Ash decided not to push his luck, and departed.

His last port of call was back at the bridge, where he found Micah poring over a luminous console, an array of images of all sixty captives decorating its surface. Ash's brow creased, and he felt the heaviness in his shoulders that he supposed Micah carried all the time. Added into the mix was the risk factor: they might simply fail in their mission, or lose some of the people in the extraction. But at least the captives were alive for now. Micah's fingers touched one of the images softly, a woman's face; Ash was surprised to see who it was. Then the images vanished and Micah spun around.

"It works, then," he said, looking straight into Ash's eyes.

Ash was nonplussed. He disabled the field, then he got it. "Shiva, yes?"

Micah tapped his temple. "When you entered the bridge she patched your image through to my resident. Now go get some rest, Ash, and keep it turned it off. Shiva says if you use it for more than a couple of hours you'll begin to fade."

Ash nodded; he disliked subterfuge. "That must be a joke, yes?"

Micah shrugged. "You think Shiva, Level Fifteen sentient tech, has a sense of humour?" He shook his head. "Something to do with cellular fatigue."

Ash jiggled his head, and decided a few hours' sleep might be a good thing.

"Oh, and Ash… The image I was looking at, just now. Don't tell Ramires. He's got enough on his mind already, and –"

Ash held up a hand, and smiled. "What image?"

Micah nodded. "Right. See you soon."

Micah turned around again, summoning tactical holo-displays and maps of Savange's only city, where they believed the captives were being held. As Micah was engulfed by translucent displays, Ash took one last look, remembering what an uncle had once told him, that if you wall off your heart and deny its feelings, it turns in on itself, and eventually seeks its own destruction. The Buddhist solution was to let go, but few could, and he doubted Micah knew how. Ash left the bridge.

Back in his room, he recalled some of the things he'd seen on his travels with Jen, Dimitri and Kalaran: the birth of a new star, the rainbow planets of the Hasrian galaxy, and the heart-wrenching death-song of the Daphnaea males, to name but a few. He'd witnessed horrors, too, and now they had one in their own galaxy: Qorall. Ash wished this business on Savange could be over soon; there were larger stakes to consider. He hadn't been entirely truthful when Micah had asked him what had affected him the most. It had been something that had left an indelible imprint on his mind, one that would be with him until his end.

Kalaran had taken them to the Jannahi galaxy, the place where the Kalarash had evolved two billion years earlier, where Qorall had last waged war. Ash had witnessed the utter desolation of a dead galaxy. There had been no light, all the galaxy's suns long since extinguished in the death-throes of the war. Kalaran's ship had lit up space around it like a lonely flare as they coursed through fields of asteroid-sized debris that stretched across thousands of light years, occasionally finding blackened chunks of unknowable technology drifting amongst the space-dust. They'd spent two weeks there, during which time Kalaran refused any contact. Jen had become distraught, worried about Kalaran, but Ash had understood: it had been a lesson, a vision of what could happen if they lost the current fray with Qorall.

After they left, he asked the others to call him Ash from then on. Asha, meaning 'hope', had been his middle name, he told them, and they bought it. The truth was different, however; he never wanted to forget what could happen if they failed, that an entire galaxy could be reduced to ash.

Kat interrupted his thoughts, knocking on the entrance to his quarters, looking a little sheepish. As usual she tried to brazen it out.

"Hi Ash. Can't sleep either?"

He ignored her dishevelled and wary look, and beamed at her. "I was just about to make some herb tea, would you like some?"

She nodded, wandered over to a large orange cushion and plonked herself down on it.

"Ah, not there," he said, "I was about to meditate. Take the bed."

Kat didn't hesitate, and flopped onto it, the way a child might: face down, arms spread wide. By the time he'd brewed the tea she was fast asleep. He sat in a lotus position on the cushion, setting the cracked china cup on the floor before him, staring into the steam, inhaling the smell of cinnamon and cloves, letting it cleanse his mind.

What had also affected him on his travels was the sheer, incomprehensible vastness of the universe. People, and most aliens too, rushed around as if anything they did really mattered in the larger – or longer – scheme of things. But Qorall had to be stopped, and it seemed humanity had a role to play. His gaze drifted to Kat's inert form. She had met Qorall, after a fashion, though she would give few details. Only one other human – that is, he corrected himself,

Alician – had had that dubious privilege: Louise, the new Alician leader, just returned to Savange.

He picked up his cup, closed his eyes and inhaled the aroma, then sipped the spiced tea, letting the cup's heat warm his hands, and considered their situation. Qorall knew about humanity now, they had moved out of obscurity into the foreground, either because they were the guardians of the Spider-race on Esperia, or due to their association with Kalaran; probably both. He sipped some more tea, then set down the cup. He thought of his long dead wife and two daughters, the love they had all shared, and the more recent affair with Zack's wife – now widow – Sonja. The hollowness he'd been running away from for the past year took root once more. This time he held back from closing it off, didn't deny it; he refrained from walling off his own heart. *How easily we see our own faults in others.* Ash had had little to live for in recent years, but plenty of others did. He let his grief and anger wash through him, he let them have their voice. His lip trembled, but he maintained his upright posture. After a while his inner storm abated, but it left behind a residue of conviction. He chastised himself for having been aloof and self-centred; it honoured neither his family nor his ancestors. Quietly he rose from the cushion and stole from his room.

He met Aramisk in the corridor coming out of her quarters, the unruly state of her hair and half-fastened clothing suggesting she had just woken. He barred her way.

She looked a little flustered. "Have you seen Kat, she's not in her –"

"Kat is asleep in my room. If you truly care for her, leave her wits in one piece before we engage the Alicians."

Aramisk's mouth fell open, but Ash walked on before she could reply. He heard her retreat back towards her quarters.

At least Ramires and Vashta were asleep in their chambers.

He entered the bridge and walked straight through the holograms swamping the command chair and its lone occupant.

Micah looked up, surprised. "Ash, I thought I told you to get some rest?"

"When I am dead, I will rest. Now, show me your plans, Micah, all of them, including those for the Spider Louise captured, whom I assume you intend to destroy rather than rescue."

Micah folded his arms, and cast Ash a quizzical look. "First, a question." Micah paused. "I know you used to be a commando back in the war on Earth, but, well… Look, there's no easy way to say it. While you and Jen and Dimitri were travelling outside the galaxy with Kalaran, for you a year passed, for us it was eighteen. But you seem to have changed more than us, you seem more, I don't know… philosophical?" Micah pushed himself up straighter in his chair. "Ash, it comes down to this. Are you willing to kill if necessary? Because if not, I'll send someone –"

"I will kill if required, Micah. Now, please, the plans."

Micah nodded, and began rearranging holos so Ash could see them in the right sequence.

As Ash studied them, he realised close-quarters combat was almost inevitable, and he knew the Alicians would fight to the death to retain the captives, as their very existence depended upon it. Now that he saw the scenarios right in front of him, including some where they might have to kill guards in cold blood, he wondered if he had just lied to Micah.

Chapter 7
INSURANCE

Louise didn't like surprises; life already had enough of them. She entered the glass booth replete with monitors on each side of a bay window looking over a darkened arena.

"Why am I here exactly?"

Lexa, one of her new Achillia, the six-strong elite personal guard inherited from Sister Esma, gave a faint smile. "Sister Esma kept this secret from almost everyone, Your Eminence –"

"Don't call me that. Louise will do fine."

Lexa nodded slowly, then continued. "Sister Esma called this her insurance policy, in case she didn't make it back." She cleared her throat. "You will see." She touched a pad and the lights in the booth dimmed, while those in the arena came on, lighting it up as if it was in daylight.

They both stared through the glass to the sim-floor below, a reconstruction of a section of the human's sprawling city, Esperantia. Single storey buildings with white walls and zinc roofs lined a dusty unpaved street beneath a hazy orange sky. Louise was a little surprised at the basic amenities, compared to the beauty and technological complexity of the Alician metropolis on Savange; she'd assumed humanity would have done better. *You've disappointed me again, Micah.*

Human figures stood motionless, lifelike automatons she presumed had been fabricated from a Q'Roth training ship: expensive to fashion, easily damaged and usually non-repairable. Whatever this insurance was, it wasn't cheap.

Lexa activated a holo-field and donned a black sense-glove. She clicked her finger and thumb, and as one the people began to move. The noises of day-to-day humdrum lives flooded Louise's ears through the monitors. She watched them; none of the automatons were alive in any real sense. But Louise recognised a few faces, and guessed the function of the simulation. She held up a hand, and Lexa paused the simulation.

"Show me the principal targets."

Lexa's fingers danced and twisted in the holo-field. The sky dimmed. Five stalactites of light shone down on four men and one woman in different locations in the town. Louise glanced from one to the other as Lexa used focusers to zoom in: Blake, Vasquez, Ramires, Jennifer, and Micah. Louise understood. The first and last were the leaders, the priority targets. Vasquez and Ramires were military, the first a colonel, the second a Sentinel, the last left alive. There was a readout next to each figure, and this particular automaton, Ramires, had been programmed with a very high level of fighting skills, as much as human muscles, tendons and skeletal structure could handle – which was less than an Alician. Louise didn't know why the woman Jennifer was there.

Lexa took a breath. "A man is about to enter. He is a clone who has been kept in stasis for some time, and doesn't know this is a simulation. Once he enters, I cannot pause the simulation. You will see why."

Louise eyed Lexa, who busied herself with her monitors. "Continue," she said.

The five lights shut off and the scene resumed. A man with goat-black hair and a taut body walked onto the scene. Louise stood up, and uttered his name. "Gabriel!"

Lexa spoke. "Sister Esma said you met him once, back on Earth. As I said, he is a clone, not the original. Before Sister Esma had the real Gabriel killed, she cut off one of his fingers so as to have enough DNA, and downloaded his memories using a Q'Roth extractor. But he has been grown here, and is Alician in his mind, though he has the reflexes, knowledge and partial memory patterns of the original. The danger, however, is that his memories overwhelm his Alician conditioning, hence the simulation. But if he succeeds –"

"We send him to Esperia. He would be the perfect assassin." Louise knew about this process, being herself a clone. If you tried to partition the memories, the process usually failed, and you ended up with a walking vegetable. But the risk was that he reverted to the original Gabriel's morals and loyalties. Then he would be very dangerous to Alicians, especially Louise.

"Yes, but to be clear, he is not an automaton, he is real flesh and blood. The simulation below is real, and they can kill him."

Louise smiled. Insurance policy indeed, Sister Esma had considered all the risks, all the outcomes, as ever. She regained her seat, then leaned forward as Lexa zoomed in to the action.

Blake and Vasquez were discussing something as the clone – Louise decided to think of him as Gabriel for now – approached them.

Blake faced him. "Can I help you? You look lost. I don't recall seeing you before."

Vasquez moved to one side, his right fingertips making contact with the hilt on his pulse pistol.

"You're Blake, aren't you?" Gabriel said.

"You have the advantage, son. What's your name?"

Gabriel didn't squint or shade his eyes, despite the simulated late afternoon sun shining on his face. "Gabriel."

Vasquez spoke while his fingers slipped around the pistol's hilt. "Nobody of that name lives here. Gabriel was a hero, revered by us all, his acts in the last days of Earth –"

"That was me." He inspected the ground for a moment, then looked back up at Blake. "I am Gabriel."

As he finished the sentence his left foot whipped out and snapped Vasquez' wrist, his fist ramming at the same time into Blake's solar plexus. As Blake doubled over, trying to grab his own weapon, Gabriel snatched it and fired at Vasquez without looking at him, catching the white-haired Colonel with a blast to the face that punched him off his feet, dead before he hit the floor.

Gabriel's right arm wrapped around Blake's throat, then he dropped to his knees, snapping Blake's neck with a sickening crunch.

Louise watched. This was basic, not yet a real test. Any Alician warrior would have gotten this far.

Gabriel crouched behind Blake's crumpled corpse and fired six times at the militia men and women running towards the scene. For a moment everything stilled as their bodies skidded into the dust. Then Gabriel walked calmly to the nearest house, where a family stood watching, too bewildered to run inside. Knocking the father down, Gabriel dragged the woman and daughter into the house, slamming the door shut behind him. A monitor to Louise's left lit up, showing the view inside the room. She watched as he signalled to the woman and girl to stay quiet, placing a forefinger across his lips.

The door burst open, a tattooed warrior stripped to the waist framed in the smashed doorway, holding a thin metal rod in his hand.

Louise stood; this would be a good test. She wondered if the nanosword was real, then decided it couldn't be, it must be a simulation – no Alician, not even Sister Esma, had managed to capture one.

Gabriel touched the girl's forehead with the barrel of the pistol and nodded his head toward the nanosword.

Ramires frowned, and tossed the sword to the floor. "Gabriel, if that's really you... what the hell are you doing? You fought to save these people. We're on the same side. You and I had the same Master, Cheveyo. You're a Sentinel!"

Gabriel tossed the pistol towards the nanosword. He approached Ramires, stood in a loose boxing stance, and held up his right fist.

Ramires shook his head, but followed suit. Their wrists touched lightly.

"This is madness, Gabriel. What have they done to you?"

Louise stilled her breathing, and didn't blink.

For several seconds neither man moved, then Ramires' fist blurred forward like a piston, but Gabriel deflected it and his left fist pummelled into Ramires' stretched ribs. A monitor to Louise's left showed that Gabriel had just driven two of Ramires' ribs into his lung. Ramires tried to counter with a savage back-hand strike to Gabriel's temple, but Gabriel ducked low, as he spun around, sweeping his leg into Ramires' ankles, sending him crashing onto the floor. Gabriel's open hand axed into Ramires' windpipe, crushing his Adam's apple. He then pinned Ramires to the floor while Ramires simultaneously choked to death and drowned as his lungs filled with blood.

"They showed me the truth," Gabriel answered.

Louise doubted it would be so easy to kill the real Ramires; she'd seen a vid of him dispatching two Q'Roth warriors back on Esperia. Still, the clone was good.

The woman and girl ran shouting and screaming outside, and were joined by many voices, including one Gabriel should have recognised from his childhood.

Louise sat back down again. Now she understood why Jennifer was there. "If he fails to kill his sister?"

Lexa didn't take her eyes off the scene. "Then the conditioning has failed, and we will terminate him."

Louise watched.

"Gabe," Jennifer shouted, "they're going to kill you. There's no way out. For God's sake come out and surrender. Gabe, let me see you at least. They told me you were dead. Whatever has happened –"

Lexa touched a pad and studied a Q'Roth display, speaking softly. "We implanted a reader in him, to know what he's thinking more or less – he doesn't know it's there, by the way. It wouldn't work on a normal subject, Alician or human, but we built the infrastructure into his brain while he was being grown."

Louise smiled. Just like Sister Esma: insurance on the insurance.

Lexa continued. "Right now he's remembering playing with Jen when they were children. But he judges that she picked the wrong side, killed thousands of the Chosen Ones. He does care for her, but considers it's better to end her confusion before she can do more damage. She's been seduced by Micah and the others." Lexa frowned.

"What?"

"He's struggling with the decision. This is Jen, his sister, his one true soul-mate." Lexa sighed.

"He's not the first clone, is he?"

Lexa shook her head. "The first four failed here or earlier. He is the last, there's not enough original DNA left to fashion another clone." She brightened. "His confusion has passed. There!" Lexa pointed at a display of his physiology – his breathing deepened. Louise recognised it: Sentinel breath, long, deep and slender. He waited behind the door. A crowd had gathered outside.

"Is Micah there?" he said, not bothering to shout.

"I'm here Gabriel." There was a pause. "It's been a long time."

Lexa nodded to Louise and pointed to a line on the thought monitor, confirming that Gabriel remembered their brief encounter back on Earth.

He picked up the nanosword, activated a control to make the hilt more pliable, anchored it inside his left sleeve against his bicep, where it stuck and moulded to his flesh.

"I'm coming out, Micah."

Louise stood up.

Lexa joined her this time. "He's almost there," she said, not concealing her excitement.

As soon as he was though the door, heavy arms took hold of him, bent him to the floor, cuffed his hands behind his back, and clamped his feet together. He was dragged in front of Micah. Jennifer was there as well, a picture of anguish. She started to say something to Micah, pleading for her brother's life.

Lexa zoomed in on Gabriel. He flexed his bicep and straightened his left arm a little, and the hilt of the nanosword detached and slid down into his left palm. The cuffs looked tight, but he activated the nanoblade, and with a flick of his wrist he sliced through the wire chaining his hands and feet, then whipped around and flashed the blade in front of Micah, who stared a moment, trying to work out what had just happened, before his head and body separated, both toppling to the ground. Jennifer's eyes went wide as Gabriel sunk the blade into her heart, then rushed forward to catch her collapsing body.

"Lexa," Louise said.

A dozen pulse barrels pressed against Gabriel's head, their tell-tale whines rising as they charged...

"LEXA!"

The scene froze, all except for Gabriel, who let go of his sister and stood up, searching. Lexa touched another control and Gabriel staggered a few steps before falling to the floor, unconscious.

"Apologies, I was caught up –"

"Never mind. You've done well. Debrief him. Tell him everything, then bring him to me." After a moment she called after Lexa. "I can't call him Gabriel. Does he have another name, or do you have one for him?"

"You honour me… Louise. We could call him Toran," Lexa said. "My father's name. He was killed during the Liberation."

Louise had almost forgotten the Alician name given to the sacking of Earth, since for them it had meant the freeing of Alicians after centuries of living in the shadows, hunted down by Sentinels.

"So be it. Tell Toran his new name. And you are no longer part of my Achillia."

Lexa bowed her head. "I have disappointed you."

"Not at all. I need someone as a personal aide. I've been away too long. You see, I don't even know what title you should have."

Lexa bowed deeper, then stood straight. "I will be your Hara."

Louise watched Lexa depart, then leant forwards, her fingertips on the glass as she gazed down at the frozen scene, focusing on the corpses. Micah would come to Savange, probably Ramires, too. After they'd been dealt with, she would send Toran to Esperia. Insurance was a waste of money unless one day you cashed it in.

Chapter 8
MACHINES

Jen felt a trickle of sweat run down her spine inside her spacesuit. She panted, her re-circulated air hot from all the running. She leaned against the smooth wall for a moment's respite and glanced at Dimitri. He was bent double, large hands planted on his knees, chest and shoulders heaving; he wasn't cut out for this. But the husk was closing on them. She checked the pad again: two choices as always, now that they were in the bottom layer of the maze of tunnels left by the Tla Beth caretaker: left or right. It had been thirty-five minutes since they'd woken the Machine remnant, and now it was hunting them down.

Left or right? She had to decide quickly, the maze wasn't infinite, and they mustn't get caught in a dead end. But it could move faster than them – it didn't have to choose at each juncture, merely follow their path. Luckily, two of Jen's drones were still working, and were tracking it from a safe distance. She didn't know what it looked like now, but from the blip on the pad she could see that it had grown in size, larger than her and Dimitri put together.

She checked the map on the pad, planning the next five turns ahead. It was tricky, because according to the drones, the husk was leaving some kind of residue behind it, and she didn't want to risk entering any tunnels it had already been down. She could almost laugh; it was as if they were stuck in a child's cheap holo-game, trying to stay ahead of a monster eating the path as it chased them. And now they were on the last, deepest layer in the game, and she couldn't see a way out, except to keep running.

Without warning, the ground shook, knocking her to the floor, Dimitri just managing to stay on his feet. She assumed it was another hit from Qorall; the strikes were arriving more frequently. Ukrull had said the planet had unusual properties, making it hard to destroy using 'conventional' weapons, whatever that meant in Level Fifteen parlance. But Qorall was Level Nineteen; so it was only a matter of time. She hoped Ukrull and Pierre had made it out of the system.

She got to her feet. "Left," she said, and they sprinted down the tunnel. They came to an open chamber, and she slid to a halt. Before them was an array of upright, shiny cigar-shaped objects, each one about six metres in length. She recognised them as the weapons the Tla Beth had used against the Level Sixteen attackers. There was no obvious means of propulsion, nor any device to launch them, nor hatches leading to the planet's surface. Level Seventeen, she reminded herself; why should she understand how they worked? And in any case it wasn't her priority.

"Do you think it might prefer these to us?" She doubted it; in her experience good fortune usually slid downhill out of her grasp.

"No, if… I am right… it is… hunting organic material," Dimitri said, between pained gasps, as he blinked hard and tried to catch his breath.

He didn't complain, nor did he look at her. Yet she knew him well. He would be feeling ashamed he had never kept fit, that he was endangering her. She kept expecting him to tell her to go on without him, which was exactly when she would tell him to go to hell and keep moving. But he said nothing.

"Let's go," she said, and set off at a slightly slower trot.

She knew he was right about the husk. It wanted them: the only organic material on this dead planet. They'd passed other stashes of Tla Beth equipment earlier and it hadn't even slowed down to take a look. Pierre had briefed them before their descent that it would need an energy source to re-awaken, and Jen's nanosword had provided that. But the power of the Machine race was in their ability to replicate, and the planet was ten kilometres deep with inert metal residue. So, given that the planet was under attack from Qorall, she'd assumed the husk would simply replicate and engage in battle. Wrong. And now she and her lover were running out of both time and tunnels.

Next junction. She glanced at the pad. The husk had just entered the section behind them. "Right!" she shouted, and dashed down the tunnel. Dimitri's wheezing rattled over the intercom. Just keep running, Dimitri, *please*.

Jen tried to reason it out for herself; she was sure Dimitri already knew, but he needed all his oxygen for his muscles, not speech. The Machines were based on organic metal; she didn't really know what that was, presuming it was a metal that was literally alive and grew. But what if it needed a small amount of living organic material, either as a base or as a catalyst in order to replicate? If it took one strand of DNA per replication, then she and Dimitri would offer the husk the chance to replicate billions of times.

Her helmet torch-beams lit up a cathedral-like chamber ahead. But she skidded to a stop as the floor disappeared. Cave-in. *Shit*. She glanced at the pad; the husk was in the tunnel behind. Dimitri bumped into her, almost sending her over the edge, and peered over her shoulder. The floor had collapsed, no doubt due to Qorall's bombing, and she couldn't see the bottom. Her mind raced.

"Thrusters, Dimitri. We have to go down now. Are you ready?"

"Always, my love."

She should have heard it in his voice – the way he said it like an epitaph – before she leapt downwards. But no sooner had she started falling, her thrusters almost depleted from the initial descent to the planet, than she knew Dimitri was not following.

Panic seized her. She flipped around and stared upwards. "Dimitri, don't you fucking dare! Come on, we can still escape!"

She saw his helmet peering over the ledge as she tried to flare her thrusters to ascend again, but it was no use.

He gasped a few more urgent words. "Tla Beth… must… have…"

No. Not like this. No, no, NO! She tapped her visor to zoom in as she fell, not caring where the floor was, her thrusters sputtering. Something was behind him. His body stilled. Shadows of black dust grew up his legs, over his torso, creeping towards his helmet. On maximum zoom she could just make out his large eyes, baleful, remaining open until dust encrusted his helmet and took on a shinier, metallic form. Through the intercom, she heard his last breath being sucked out of him, and she knew the Machine had taken him.

Jen screamed, an anguished, deafening cry inside her helmet. She couldn't believe it; the one thing about Dimitri was that he was always so full of life. A flood of memories of their life together skated across her mind: seeing him for the first time lecturing in Athens University when he captured her heart; seducing him a week later in his office; cramped together in a submersible in the depths of the Mariana Trench where they located the first Q'Roth ship; finding Dimitri looking so ragged and alone in the caves on Esperia after she'd sent him away; and in Kalaran's vast ship where they'd spent the past year, a year she'd never wanted to end. The galaxy had just stupidly thrown away a brilliant, vibrant mind. It didn't make sense.

She called out to him again, somehow hoping he would reply, knowing it was futile. Jen found it hard to breathe. She wanted more than anything to get out of her damned suit.

And then she decided.

Still falling, barely able to see Dimitri up on the ledge, Jen's hands moved to her helmet seals. She'd never been religious, but she'd always believed that if your lover died, there was a short moment when maybe, just maybe, you could go with him, be with him forever. The time with Dimitri eclipsed everything else. Besides, the husk would get her soon. Better to go this way. She knew he'd stayed above to give her a chance, but it was her life, hers to do with as she pleased. She hooked her index fingers under the release catches and took a breath, just as the ground slammed into her, knocking her out cold.

When Jen roused, she lay there, not moving, as if dead on the rocks. For a moment she forgot what had happened, and turned left and right searching for her lover. Then she remembered, waking fully into her nightmare. Her breathing became ragged, and a wave of pure grief rose through her chest and up into her head. She squeezed her eyes shut, as her gloved fingers clawed at the ground, her body trembling.

She didn't know how long she stayed there. Eventually three thoughts seeped into her mind; first, that the window of opportunity to join Dimitri had closed. He would be glad of that, and would have chided her for even considering suicide. Second, the husk had not come to harvest her as it had her lover. Third, Qorall's shelling of the planet had stopped. She reckoned the last two were linked; the husk had enough genetic material – for now – to begin its defence against Qorall. But if the legends of the Machine race were true, its appetite for replication was insatiable, so it would return for her.

Jen got up slowly, and checked herself over: bruised, but nothing broken. She'd been lucky. But her one remaining torch beam faltered. A passageway far across the field of rubble beckoned. Memorising the rock pattern between her and the opening, she turned off her torch to conserve power and began making her way across the boulders. She had no plan, but Dimitri had sacrificed himself so she could live a little longer. After several slips, trips and falls, she reached the mouth of the tunnel, and glanced back upwards to the cliff edge. All was dark.

Her drones hadn't entered this hidden fifth level, so she had no map, and her pad was smashed from the fall so there was no way to call them. She paused, recalling Dimitri's last words. He'd been trying to tell her something, something about the Tla Beth. It had built these tunnels. Why had this level been sealed off from the others? What was down here? She played back Dimitri's words in her head. *The Tla Beth must have…* And then it came to her: a ship.

Thank you, Dimitri.

The LED on her wrist flashed a dim red; her oxygen supply would fail soon. She ignored it. With one hand stretched out in front of her, the other touching the wall, she walked forward in darkness, in search of the Tla Beth ship. Jen didn't know if she would be able to access it or use it, assuming she even reached it before her air ran out, but as Dimitri used to say to his students, one leap at a time.

Pierre had never seen Ukrull so concentrated. His tail was perfectly still, his muscular shoulders hunched over the controls, eyes closed as he mind-plexed a distress call via the Hohash. Pierre held onto his seat, the Ice Pick shaking violently as they tried to outrun Qorall's black hole. The grinding noise from the engines told him they weren't going to make it.

Pierre glanced at the display, the dark, insatiable mouth of the vortex, the deadliest natural phenomenon in the galaxy, continuously sucking them towards it, as if it only ever breathed in. As an astrophysicist back on Earth he'd studied black holes, and had always found their awesome power fascinating. But soon it would crush them, absorbing them into its singularity. No being, no matter what Level, had ever come back from one.

This black hole sat amidst a translucent dark green swathe of space, like a negative image of a moon reflecting in a lake. This was Qorall's liquid space – not truly a liquid, but not empty space either – a feature imported from his own distant galaxy, which even the Kalarash hadn't yet fathomed. Every few minutes gravitic shock waves emanated from the black hole, colliding both with the Ice Pick and the planet, before they swept back towards the singularity. Each wave buffeted them, then yanked them backwards.

Whatever Qorall had done to normal space, it prevented the opening of Transpatial conduits, so the Ice Pick could not simply jump out of the system. Pierre nudged a control and switched displays to see the planet. It was cracking up, fissures opening on the dead Machine world's formerly smooth surface. The planet no longer had a molten core, so at least there were no volcanic eruptions. Pierre presumed Qorall didn't want to get too close to it, knowing what was there, not wanting to awaken it. Staring at the slowly lengthening trenches, Pierre wondered if Jen and Dimitri were still alive on this tomb planet. He juggled the probabilities and uncertainties in his head. Whichever way he analysed the available data, their prospects didn't look good.

But there was one curious thing: towering dust tornadoes were flashing up from the planet's surface, rising kilometres above the surface. He had no idea why this should be happening, since there was no atmosphere. It could be due to the black hole, but he didn't think so; they looked too uniformly spaced. But a sound like metal tearing apart reminded him of other priorities.

"No use," Ukrull grunted. "Abandon ship."

At first Pierre thought he must have misheard, then he remembered the Ice Pick could teleport the two of them across a short range; in all their travels they'd never once used it, as it required so much of the ship's energy, but that hardly mattered now. Ukrull stood up on his hind legs, his bony head brushing the ceiling, and began donning a self-sealing suit. Pierre stepped onto the suit-forming platform, the black gel crawling over his feet and up his legs, like cool wet leather, until it reached his neck. Ukrull tossed him a helmet and back-pack. While his helmet auto-sealed, Pierre watched Ukrull interfacing with the Hohash, gripping its rail-like outer edges with both fore-claws. Ukrull slipped on his own helmet, with an elongated visor to accommodate his snout, and turned to Pierre.

"Ready?"

Pierre didn't know exactly what to expect, but he nodded. Besides, the noise from the ship suggested strips of the hull were shearing off; it was time to leave.

The ship around Pierre appeared to dissolve, and for a moment his mind seemed to catch, as if someone had pressed 'pause' in his head. For a tantalising fraction of time everything was a uniform grey, featureless and silent, and he wondered where he was. Then he found himself standing on the planet's surface, next to Ukrull, watching a tiny dot streak across the dark green sky towards the black hole. Pierre's helmet visor magnified, tracking the Ice Pick's trail. For the first time he saw something else, a black disc on the edge of the event horizon – Qorall's ship. The image continued to magnify and Pierre became aware of the spherical shape of the ship, the size of a large asteroid.

"Watch," Ukrull said.

Pierre didn't know how this level of magnification was possible, unless... ah, the Hohash – it was in space, transmitting to their visors. He followed the Ice Pick as it attempted to ram Qorall's ship. Suddenly the closest wave to the black hole grew in size, a ghostly green tsunami. It closed around the Ice Pick like a vice, then crushed it until the ancient craft was nothing but debris.

Ukrull let out a long hiss, his booted foot stomping against the ground.

Pierre didn't know what to say; Ukrull had forged a deep attachment to his ship over thousands of years; it had been a gift from someone special, though Ukrull had never said who.

"What about the Hohash?" Pierre asked.

"Is okay. Not affected by gravity."

That was something Ukrull consistently refused to explain, but Pierre decided now was not the time. Besides, they had new priorities. Perhaps this was all simply a stay of execution. The planet did not have long before it would be torn apart, them along with it. Or else the Machines might find them in order to replicate – Ukrull had explained about the organic catalyst requirement only after Jen and Dimitri had gone down to the planet's surface.

Pierre scanned the broken horizon for dust tornadoes, but saw none. But as he looked upwards again, he was sure he could see less stars than should be visible. Stars were winking out, Qorall's green, liquid space being slowly occluded by a spreading black curtain. Within a few minutes there were no stars, although a dull grey light emanated from somewhere. The Machine must have awakened, and erected a shield. No sooner had Pierre thought it, than a section overhead glowed green briefly, then returned to black. Other green splodges peppered the shield, but none of Qorall's attacks broke through.

"Not shield," Ukrull said. "Shell. Protect new-borns."

Pierre realised that they were both safe and trapped at the same time.

"What do we do now?" he asked.

Ukrull snorted. "Run from those," he said, flicking a gloved fore-claw to Pierre's left.

Pierre stared into the darkness and detected giant beetle-like objects scurrying towards them, fast. He turned back to Ukrull, who was already bounding away in the opposite direction.

Pierre didn't need to be told twice.

Chapter 9
SPIES

It felt odd to walk unseen amongst others, especially to Ash. He had been blind for a whole year before Kalaran had given him his Mannekhi all-black eyes. Ash recalled how it had felt knowing others could see him while he saw nothing. Initially, before learning to use his other senses, the over-riding feeling had been one of helplessness, of utter dependence. Now he felt the reverse, the raw power of the disguised assassin, the camouflaged predator surrounded by prey. It was narcotic. Ash forced himself to concentrate on his mission: to find the entrance to the shaft leading to the sixty human captives held underground.

Trained long ago to move without making a sound, Ash slipped between Alicians as they went about their business. Even in the noon sunlight the citizens of Savange were oblivious to him. He was cloaked so effectively that there was neither shadow nor shimmer of air as he made his way through twisting streets that wound up a gentle slope towards a cluster of gleaming glass and metal towers, and Savange's central spire.

Alician men and women – he'd seen no children – strode through sun-drenched streets, the ground a pale terracotta muffling their brisk pace. He was surprised to see a wide range of skin colours and features; North and South American, European, African, Chinese, and even one wizened, Indistani-looking man. That stopped him; so few of his own nation had survived the Alician-Q'Roth purge that had left Earth a barren, airless lump of rock. His breathing grew heavy. They had tried to exterminate humanity, yet here in this citadel they had preserved a wider gene pool than the human refugees Ash had left behind on Esperia.

Yet this appeared to be a truly merged society; he could see it in their posture. All held themselves upright, confident to the point of arrogance. And they were agile: he paused to watch a group of twenty or so performing some form of slow martial art in a gravel courtyard; long, slow, sweeping movements and deep crouching postures, all of the Alicians, young and old, in perfect synchrony. Their tan clothing – no skirts, all men and women sporting skin-tight pants – did not hide these genetically-advanced humans' powerful yet graceful gait, as if they were all gymnasts.

Ash noticed something else: few of them spoke as they passed one another, looking each other in the eye for a split second before walking on with firm purpose. Yet there was no tension in the air. They appeared to trust each other, with no need or desire to indulge in idle banter. Alicians weren't conflicted – as humanity was and probably always would be – they embodied unified purpose, and so would be harder to take down. Ash shivered; the air was cooler and damper than on dry, semi-desert Esperia, and the field keeping him cloaked chilled him, something he'd been warned about. He remembered his mission and walked on.

Suddenly there was a commotion off to his right. A couple with a child were mobbed in a friendly manner by other Alicians whose demeanour shifted gear, becoming softer, almost sentimental, especially the women, as they crowded around this utter rarity, an Alician infant. Ash knew this was the reason the sixty humans had been captured, to serve as a genetic catalyst to fix the faulty Alician genome, so they could reproduce again. He listened to the soothing, cooing noises, and for a moment there seemed to be a bond between this species and Ash's own. Then he remembered his two daughters and wife lost in the Q'Roth invasion of Earth, perpetrated by these same Alicians who had lain low, plotting humanity's demise for centuries. He turned his back on the near-human scene and continued onwards.

As he made his way up curved streets towards the centre, the style of buildings around him altered. He left behind the functional two-storey terraced houses, and strode between tall towers, many with high, open terraces without railings, speaking simultaneously of a gentle climate and a people who did not age appreciably, and knew neither infirmity nor suicidal tendencies. He wondered what went on in those buildings, what industry they housed, but he had no time. Gazing upwards through a gap in the maze of increasingly tall buildings, he spied the distant orbital tether, at least twenty kilometres away, its sleek outline hazy as it stretched up into the sky like a silver arrow, glinting in the afternoon sun. He knew that Micah had Shiva's weapons locked onto its base, in case a distraction was needed.

Seeing Alician society up close, rather than simply considering them as a distant enemy, made him wonder about his mission. He'd seen many species on his travels, almost none of them humanoid. Qorall's army and fleets were overcoming entire species on a weekly basis as they raked across the galaxy, and it seemed hopelessly tribal for two so closely-linked species – human and Alician – to be warring at such a time. He wished there were an alternative; but he knew that Ramires, for one, would love to Nova-bomb the entire planet once the captives were recovered. Even if Micah had ruled it out, that decision was borne mainly from a moral code than any compassion for the Alicians. Ash stopped walking. He had never thought of it before, but now he wondered if humans and Alicians could fight alongside each other, against Qorall, if it became necessary. It seemed a ridiculous idea, yet the question held him; something Kalaran had said once, long ago. Not for the first time Ash felt that humans and Alicians, and a number of other species, were all pieces on Kalaran's chessboard, and that Kalaran would use them as he wished.

He heard something: the sound of someone stopping suddenly, sandals braking to a stop on the pavement. Ash began paying more attention to his surroundings. At that very moment, despite being effectively invisible, Ash's instincts told him he was being followed. He didn't see how it was possible, since the cloak was Level Nine tech and Alicians only had access to Level Six, but the prickling hairs on the back of his neck insisted. Without turning around or altering his speed, he set off again and branched down a shaded alley in between two squat blocks, and sure enough quickened footsteps followed. At least it was only one. The scene around him looked normal, relaxed even, as people went about their business. But he suspected that if he were unmasked, they would tear him apart and ask questions later via brain autopsy.

Rounding a corner, Ash froze as he saw a three-metre-tall Q'Roth warrior barring his way, blue-black serrated thorns decorating its three pairs of legs. The footsteps behind sped up, but Ash stayed where he was. The Q'Roth did not seem to be aware of him, but Ash couldn't be sure. Its waxy eye slits gave no indication of what it was looking at, and it was so still it could almost have been a statue. Ash didn't feel like squeezing past the warrior, who could kill him with a single slash of its claws. But the footsteps were just around the corner.

Ash made up his mind, and quickly stepped through an archway into a passage barely wider than a man's breadth, and a good thirty metres to the other end. He glanced at the ceiling; about a foot below, on either side was a small ledge that could serve as a handhold. It had been a long time since he had wall-climbed, but he had been training intensely with Ramires throughout the voyage from Esperia; he was fitter now than he had been for years. Added to that, Vashta had injected him with an energetic booster based on an ancient Ossyrian soldier recipe – adapted to humans – that temporarily augmented his physical prowess and healing faculties, and dulled his pain receptors. It was time to put it to the test.

He took a breath and pushed against both walls with his palms and soles, and scaled his way upwards, manoeuvring his back flush against the ceiling, feet and hands balanced precariously on the narrow ledges. He was face-down, his arm and leg muscles straining to keep him from falling. Breathing out slowly, he took a deep breath, and held it.

An urgent voice on the street spoke Q'Roth. Then a fair-haired Alician male walked into the passage a metre beneath Ash, squinting in the dim light, a pistol drawn. He shouted "Stand clear!", then fired, its laser pulse crackling the air, a faint metallic burning smell from the gun's barrel reaching Ash's nostrils. Nothing happened. The man walked a few paces forward and stopped.

Ash's muscles held, but tremors began in his biceps and thighs, and the strain to keep them firm made him clench his jaw. The urge to suck in a breath clawed at his lungs. Ash suppressed it, remembered his apnoea training, and let a small amount of air expire silently from his nose. The Q'Roth warrior joined the man, with a clumping sound of its hoof-like feet, right underneath Ash, the top of its head a mere hand's breadth under Ash's chin. A bead of sweat ran from Ash's right temple to the centre of his forehead. He resisted the urge to swallow.

The Alician walked a few paces further, turned and said something to the warrior, then sprinted to the far end, disappearing out into the next street. The Q'Roth warrior didn't budge. Shaking began in Ash's biceps, and the bead of sweat threatened to fall, so he lifted his head slightly, whereupon the drop slid to the bridge of his nose. The warrior shifted, turned around, and made to leave, just as the drop left Ash's nose and fell towards the floor. As it did so, Ash recalled three things: first, what it was like to be blind; he would have heard such a drop hit the tiled floor. Second, that a Q'Roth warrior's hearing was superior to that of a human; and third, that the warrior's reactions would be quicker than his own. Ash simultaneously let go with his hands and kicked off hard with his legs, frog-like, away from the warrior. He felt wind on his feet as the warrior spun back around and slashed upwards into the ceiling, making the brickwork explode as if hit by a shell. Ash rolled as he hit the floor then sprang up and sprinted away from the warrior, gasping in air. The warrior didn't give chase, and for a moment Ash thought he would escape, until the light at the end of the passage was cut off by another Q'Roth warrior barring the way. Ash slid to a halt, panting.

The warrior in front began walking towards him on its lowest pair of legs, the other two pairs slashing up and down, chopping through the air from floor to ceiling. There was no way past. It came as no surprise when he heard an identical air-whipping, thrashing noise behind him. *Think*, Ash said to himself. *Think fast!*

Ramires joined the small group of Alicians near the passage. He'd been watching from afar, ready to intervene, but the Alician male had made his move on Ash too quickly. If he'd had his staff with its nano-blades he could have taken down the Q'Roth, but then he'd be discovered, and the mission would be finished.

Though he had been walking amongst the Alicians, and even acting like them, his insides were aflame. His adopted son Gabriel and so many others had been killed by Sister Esma's third attempt to wipe out humanity, and now his wife Sandy was amongst the sixty captives somewhere beneath his feet. He'd been proud when he'd heard how she'd volunteered to go with the Alicians to save more fragile people from being taken. Their marriage hadn't always been smooth, and he knew he loved her more than she loved him, but she'd been loyal all these years, and the perfect mother to Gabriel. It was her safety, and hers alone, that kept him focused.

He didn't expect the others to understand, not even Micah who had lost so much since Earth's fall – including losing Sandy to him. For the others, the Alicians had appeared twenty years ago. But Ramires was the last of the Sentinels, whose war against this genetic abomination had endured nine centuries. Micah had said their mission parameters were to take the captives and leave. Ramires had done something rare, something he was ashamed of; he had lied, agreeing with Micah. Once the captives were safe, Ramires would target this planet with the Nova bomb on board Shiva – he already had the access codes.

Right now he had to rescue Ash; he'd seen too many comrades fall in battle. Calming his breathing, he tried to think like an Alician, and sauntered up to the fair-haired man at the alleyway entrance.

"Louise may want to question whoever is in there."

The man turned around, his eyes a startling blue, offsetting a chiselled Nordic face. "I don't know you." The man's right arm, holding a weapon, tensed.

Ramires held his gaze. "Rodriguez, Keftan Sector." He nodded to the alleyway, the noise of threshing claws scraping the walls getting louder. "A spy always has a watcher," he said, citing an old Alician proverb.

The man relaxed a little. "You call them off, Rodriguez. Let's see how good your Q'Roth is."

Ramires did not smile or show any indignation; such traits were human, and might give him away. Instead he bellowed a Q'Roth command, adding a colloquial swearword for added effect. The whipping noise ceased amidst a guttural response from the nearest warrior, which included its own far more severe curse.

Ramires moved to the entrance, and shouted in clear English. "You have five seconds to make yourself visible, after which time they will recommence until blood bursts from your shredded corpse."

The fair-headed man and a few others craned their necks to see beyond the Q'Roth warrior. Ramires didn't bother. Micah's plan had five back-ups, though Ramires judged they were already on Plan C. He counted the Alicians around him: fifteen, too many to skip to Plan F, which was barely a plan in any case.

Ash was man-handled out by the Q'Roth warriors, lacerating his forearms in the process. One of the warriors swiped at the back of his legs whilst pressing down on his shoulders, dropping Ash to his knees.

"Mannekhi," Ramires said, with disdain, pointing to the all-black eyes. "I'd hoped for a human."

The lead Alician drew his right arm back, then punched the side of Ash's face with full force, knocking him to the ground. "That's for my brother, pathetic Mannekhi Q'Tach! One of your Spikers took out his ship while he was on a med-evac run!"

Ramires turned to the rest of the crowd. "Anyone else? He needs to be able to talk, otherwise, feel free."

Ash lifted his head from the ground. Blood mixed with saliva spooled from his mouth into a small puddle on the terracotta ground.

A slightly older woman moved to the front. "My husband," she said, her voice shaky, "his name was Anton."

Without hesitation she kicked at Ash's ribs with surprising power. Ramires held his face poker-neutral, as Ash rolled over, clutching his sides, his face contorted in pain. Ramires hoped Vashta's elixir lived up to its reputation. He squatted, held out his hand.

"The field emitter."

Ash struggled onto his hands and knees, then snapped a button off his belt, and handed it to Ramires without looking at him. Ramires stood, and passed it to the Alician male. He took a gamble.

"Lucky the new detector worked."

The man studied Ramires. "How do you know about it?"

Ramires kept his face serene, but he was making it all up as he went along. In his Sentinel training in the Himalayas – a lifetime ago – he would often be put in situations like this, having to talk his way out of situations, like a lobster bartering its way out of a pot of boiling water. He knew he had to gain this man's trust, get away from the crowd, and lose the two Q'Roth warriors. He banked on an old piece of Sentinel intel, that Alician leaders were notoriously secretive about their plans, even to other Alicians. Information was power, and was often on a 'you don't need to know' basis.

Ramires puffed out his chest a little. "I was a member of Louise's Achillia."

The man drew back, even as some of the others moved closer around Ramires.

"We were told Louise acted alone," the man said, eyes narrowing.

Ramires nodded, then turned to face the crowd, catching their eager eyes. "That is what Louise wanted people to believe. How else could she gain the trust of Qorall?" He turned back to the Alician male to clinch it. "It was, of course, Sister Esma's idea all along."

The man's brow furrowed, then smoothed, against a background of chatter from the others; the lie resonated with their adulation for their recently deceased leader.

"Her Eminence always played the deep, long strategy." He gazed at the floor.

Ramires continued, sealing it. "Such a loss. But Louise – whilst not Sister Esma – is her rightful heir."

"Yes," the man said, the others murmuring agreement. Then, as if suddenly remembering something, he said, "My name is Torkell. It is an honour to meet you, Rodriguez. Do you wish to take the prisoner to Louise yourself?"

It was tempting, but it would cut across their traditions. "No, Torkell. The capture," he flicked a hand towards Ash, still on the floor, "and the kill, are yours. But, with your consent, I will accompany you."

Torkell nodded, almost graciously.

Two Alicians hauled Ash to his feet, and the Q'Roth moved in to follow. Ramires stood in their way, then spoke Q'Roth. "The tether. He or his accomplices have probably rigged explosives to it, to serve as a distraction. You will be fastest to secure it."

Torkell nodded, adding his own supporting instruction. They galloped away on all six legs, Alicians scattering in front of them as they sped around a corner. Ramires had forgotten how fast they ran.

Torkell and four others, weapons drawn, escorted Ash to the central spire, amidst a growing crowd of Alician onlookers pointing to Ramires as much as Ash. Ramires knew his lie had worked too well, and that gossip had spread like wildfire. He could have made some excuse and departed, but then he would probably never see Ash alive again.

He and Ash were now on Plan F, as Zack used to call it. He had a nano-sword in an inside pocket, and a small triggering device for the explosives on the base of the tether. Ash looked beaten up, but was tougher than he seemed, and Ramires trusted Vashta's skill. However, once he and Ash met with Louise, they would be quickly undone.

The central, gleaming spire, two hundred metres tall, almost all metal with narrow slits instead of windows, loomed up ahead, and Ramires knew he was out of options. *Micah, whatever you're planning, now would be good.* But they kept walking, and nothing happened. They crossed the threshold guarded by six Q'Roth warriors and entered the building that housed Louise and her true Achillia, the elite personal guard inherited from Sister Esma, and Ramires knew that he and Ash were on their own. *Sandy, I fear I've screwed up; forgive me.* He and Ash had run out of options; it would be up to Micah now.

A small group walked briskly toward them, led by a woman with a blonde ponytail and pretty but hardened features. Louise. It felt to Ramires as if all the deceased Sentinel masters suddenly sat up out of their graves, and watched intently. As if guided by their chilled, ghostly fingers, Ramires' left hand slid into his pocket, the one holding the nanosword. He strode forward, past Torkell, as if to greet an old friend.

Chapter 10
TUNNELS

Jen drifted along yet another dark tunnel, having managed to cross-connect power to get one of the helmet torch beams working again, at least for the moment. According to her wrist monitor she had thirty minutes of recyclable air remaining – it was already hot and stuffy inside her helmet, and there was only so much the oxygen recycler could do. She'd been walking in a daze for nearly an hour, and a stubby rock protruded from the normally smooth floor, the first she'd seen since leaving the chamber where Dimitri had… Anyway, it was too inviting a chance to miss. She sat down, and acknowledged that she might never get up again.

Jen was tired. No, she decided, she was weary. She knew enough psycho-physiology to understand that grief was depleting her resources, her motivation, and her will to live. Added to that was a sense of futility. She'd given up on her idea that a ship was down here, having wandered endlessly through the subterranean maze using a grid-based search pattern that should have found something by now. Pile on top of that the bleak darkness and slow but inevitable loss of oxygen, and, well… She didn't need to finish that thought process.

Jen figured there were two alternatives. The first was to take off her helmet. It would be painful for a couple of minutes, then she'd be gone, it would be over. Sooner or later it was going to happen in any case. The advantage of sooner was that she was fully conscious now, but as the oxygen molecules disappeared from her micro-environment, she'd enter a semi-conscious fugue; it might be better to die fully awake.

The second alternative was to go to sleep. It should work. She could activate a delta wave inducer in her helmet. It was there to induce a pseudo-coma and save oxygen in case a rescue mission was on the way, which wasn't the case. Going to sleep sounded pretty appealing. She could lay down, think of Dimitri, and slide into the arms of Morpheus.

<Not yet.>

She sat up. At first Jen thought she was hallucinating. But it had the feel of nodal communication, a light pressure like a breeze on the left side of her brain where the speech centre housed her node. She closed her eyes and concentrated on nodal communication, which was a different process for each individual. For Jen, it was like imagining a slow-moving but wide river, and she had to keep it flowing without letting it speed up or stop. Given that she was deep underground, Jen guessed at the only person it could be

<Kalaran? Where are you?>

Six sentences came in 'choired', all hitting her node at the same time, like sudden turbulence in the river:

<Not far from your sector. I am unlikely to arrive before your air runs out. I'm calling via Ukrull's Hohash, though there is interference from the Machines. Thanks for waking them, saved me the task. Sorry about Dimitri, I liked him. You can't die yet, Jen, I have plans for you.>

That's what it was like with Kalaran, multiplexed communication all the time. Jen knew he was having to slow things down dramatically for her, and even then the thought stream was intense, but she'd gotten used to it during her one year sabbatical with him. Kalaran always jumped ahead, covering a lot of ground in a short space of time, leaving her to play catch-up. He didn't do small talk, and conversations with him were usually short and sticky, leaving her to ponder about them for hours afterwards. So she always kept her side pointed as well.

<Qorall is here.>

<Which is why I'm coming. He wants to destroy the Machine race, the Xera, which must not happen. The Xera are essentially inorganic, they can

fight Qorall's Orbs; their matrix won't be susceptible, and they are powerful enough at Level Eighteen to inflict some damage, if they get the chance to reach maturity. But Qorall's vortex is very strong. There isn't much time until planetary shield breach. I need you to find the Tla Beth ship. It's hiding from you.>

Normally, Jen would try and infer what Kalaran meant; it had become an educational game during her stay on his ship. But she was very tired. <What?>

<The ship is there. You have passed it twice. It is in stealth mode. I need to alter your brain chemistry. I'm sending harmonics through your node. You must keep the nodal channel open until I speak again. This will hurt a little. Actually, a lot. I'll slow it down so you don't go into neural shock. >

<Thanks, I think.>

Jen waited, idly wondering what she saw in Kalaran. At the end of the day, he was a taker, using her for his own ends. But he was also the smartest being in the galaxy, so she cut him some slack.

The first wave hit, literally like a surge of flood water flowing down her river. Not so bad. Then she felt the next one building, a tidal wave that made her want to shut off nodal comms and hide behind the boulder.

Jen found herself on the floor, face down, her helmet lights showing the dusty ground centimetres from her eyes. There was a terrible smell.

<Jen, I'm not finished. Don't move. You've vomited, and if you roll onto your back you will choke. The microbes in your suit are cleaning you up. Take a breath.>

She no longer had control of the node, otherwise she would have cut it off as a freezing ocean fell on top of her. She began to convulse, as if being electrocuted, and all she could think of was getting her tongue out of the way so she didn't bite it off.

After a while, the pain abated, and she imagined herself on the riverside, the waters calming down.

<It's over, Jen, you're fine. But Qorall's nearly ready to destroy the planet, and the Xera's shield is faltering; I don't know how much longer communications will last. I need you to get up, and to go and find the ship. Now. >

<Fuck you, Kalaran.>

It was the first time she didn't get an immediate response from Kalaran. When she did, it wasn't what she was expecting.

<I'm not a taker.>

<Prove it.>

Again, there was a delay. She'd meant it as a rhetorical question. What the hell could he do for her that would matter?

<I have done something for you. You will see. But only if you live.>

<Bastard.>

Again no response.

<What have you done for me? What could you possibly do that could persuade me to get up after I've lost everything that matters to me?> It was difficult to rant in nodal comms, or imbue the words with anger, but Jen made a good effort.

<Your nephew.>

Gabriel? Sandy's son? But he was dead. She'd never met him; while she'd spent a year with Kalaran outside the galaxy, eighteen years had slipped by on Esperia, so he'd grown into a full adult and been killed before she could even meet him. She'd only had a short chance to talk to him right before he'd died, and she'd seen him once via the Hohash. He had looked so much like his father, her brother of the same name. And the way he had died… He deserved that name, his father would have been proud if he'd still been alive.

Jen got onto all fours, then stood up. For the first time she could feel the interference on nodal comms, as if the water level in the river was dropping rapidly. Not now, dammit! Time was running out, and for the first time ever, Jen 'choired' a message back to Qorall.

<What about him? He's dead. You tried to download his personality string and memories but the Hohash link was destroyed when he killed Sister Esma. Are you saying you can bring him back?>

<Hellera got some of it. It can only be a partial reconstruction. It will take some time. He may not remember you, or much at all. He will be an approximation.>

Jen's eyes misted. The riverbed was almost dry, just a trickle now. <Doesn't matter, do it.>

<Hellera will do it. She is better at this than me. Goodbye Jen. I'll miss you.>

She didn't understand. <Kalaran?> She paced in a circle, wondering at those last three words. She tried one more time, using all her mental effort. <KALARAN!>

She waited, but there was no reply. She closed her eyes a moment, recalling the good times with Kalaran, Dimitri and Ash on the ship, exploring other galaxies. Who could have asked for more? *Thank you.*

Jen took three deep breaths, despite the stink from her vomit. She began walking. After ten minutes her torch sputtered and failed. She stopped, tried to get it working again, but it was no use. Then she realised she didn't need it; she could see in the dark.

Nice one, Kal.

Chapter 11
PRISONER

Blake walked towards the wall of fog, his bare feet sinking into the soft sand, then stopped. He looked back. The mist completely encircled his private beach – for want of a better word – which was the size of an old football field. Hazy light filtered through to where he stood, while the slowly swirling fog wall was impenetrable. He reached its edge. It was as if there was a barrier keeping it out, or keeping him in. He raised a hand and let his fingers sink into the mist. Cold, damp. Like fog. Not a barrier then. He looked back one last time at the beach. Nothing there. "So be it," he said, about to take a step.

"I wouldn't do that, Boss."

Blake spun around. Zack. But Zack was dead. Kalaran?

"No, Boss, just me this time, sort of. Kalaran put me here, in your head, to stop you going in there." Zack waved a finger at the fog. "Walk away from it, over here, that stuff gives me the creeps."

Blake took a few steps towards Zack. It looked like him: a burly six foot guy, black, bald, with an infectious grin and a voice to match. Blake hadn't said what he'd needed to say to Zack last time, because then it had really been Kalaran. He knew it still wasn't the real Zack, but better than nothing.

"Where are we, Zack?"

"Like I said, Boss, in your head. Qorall's Orb attacked you, it's trying to re-write you. Kalaran created this hiding place in your mind, though it won't last long."

It didn't make much sense to Blake, so he focused on what did, on some unfinished business with his best friend.

"Zack, I'm sorry about what happened to you back on Esperia, when Louise attacked. I should have seen it coming, should have read the signs. I already suspected Louise had put the implant in your head."

Zack stood just out of arm's reach, and squatted down. "Ancient history, Boss. I almost killed you, then went travelling with Micah to see the galaxy." He dug his fingers into the sand, pulled them out, and watched the sand fall back through them. "Point is, Qorall's Orb has done something similar to you."

"Where am I, Zack?"

"A bubble in your mind. Kalaran put it there. Well, actually the Spider did."

Blake sat down, crossed his legs. "You'd better start at the beginning. We have time, don't we?"

"Some, anyways." Zack looked up, grinned, stretched his legs out in front of him, and leant back on his elbows. "Once upon a time…" He belly-laughed, then shook his head. "Okay. Seriously, because this is serious. We need you to fight what Qorall's done to you."

"How, exactly?"

"There's the problem, Boss. You're not in conscious control, so how do you fight something you're not aware of?"

Blake stared at Zack and waited, then realised that what his former friend had said wasn't meant to be rhetorical. "I don't know."

"No. So, this is how we have to do it. I need to plant something in your head that will help you fight back emotionally, when the time comes."

"This isn't making much sense, Zack. You're beginning to sound like Kalaran."

Zack got to his feet. "Better move, Boss."

Blake felt a chill down his neck. Stepping forward, he turned to see why. The fog was right behind him. "It's expanding."

Zack sighed. "Actually, the bubble's shrinking. Come on. It's exponential, I'm afraid, we'll have more time in the centre."

Blake followed Zack further into the middle of the beach. The beach had lost around thirty metres in diameter.

Zack talked while they strolled. "Emotional trauma can cross the boundary between conscious and unconscious."

Blake looked over his shoulder. The fog was following. "If you say so." A thought struck him. "Are we in Transpace?"

"Bingo! Well, kind of. Kilaney's ship is travelling in Transpace with you locked down in stasis in the hold, and the Spiders can access you, 'cause you have some of their DNA. Qorall can't touch you here, but as soon as you exit Transpace, this bubble will close."

"And you'll be gone."

"Along with your consciousness, Boss, which will dwell in that fog until you die, so back to the reason I'm here." Zack surveyed all around them. "This'll do."

Blake reckoned they were dead centre.

Zack squatted again. "You're going to kill a Spider."

"What do you mean?"

"One of your friends. Your best friend. You're going to kill him. You know, the one you and Glenda secretly called Robert, after your son."

Blake stepped backwards. "Jesus Christ, Zack. I will not! What the hell are you saying?"

Zack remained unperturbed. "You're going to claw Robert apart with your bare hands, and rip him to pieces."

Blake felt his heart race, his skin grow clammy. "Zack. I would never... I'd rather die, you know that!"

Zack stood up, came closer to Blake. "You'll sink your teeth into his flesh like he was a hamburger, then spit it out."

"For God's sake, Zack, stop this!" Blake tried to back away, but Zack grabbed his shoulders, pinning him there.

"But you will do it, Blake. Or something like it. Hell, we don't really know. But that's what being taken over by Qorall means. Like when I attacked you because of that implant. I'm sorry, Boss, really."

The fog accelerated. With a rising hiss it swept towards them over the sand.

"What can I do?"

Zack shrugged. "It's already done. Most – well all of Qorall's minions – don't know what they're doing when they do it. Now you do, or you will. You'll understand at the end."

"Will I? How will I see in the fog?"

"Just don't move from that spot. Try to hold on, Blake. And think of Robert."

The fog enveloped Blake, a frigid embrace. It chilled his lungs. He couldn't see his friend anywhere. "Zack?"

But Zack was gone, and the fog became denser. He couldn't see anything, or even feel his body, and then he couldn't think.

Petra tapped the black oval object on her antique wooden desk.

"General?"

Kilaney answered, and began his report. She didn't interrupt, as this wasn't instant Hohash communication; Kilaney was just outside the Esperian system, and while the ten minute lightspeed delay had been compressed, the lengthy pause and echo were both noticeable. His report didn't improve her mood. She'd asked Blake to act, but she hadn't anticipated this.

"How are his life signs? His EEG?"

Again, a short delay. "He's strong as an ox right now. Thank God he's in stasis, I don't think restraints would hold him. His metabolism has sped up three hundred per cent, heart rate one-ninety even in the stasis tube. We've suspected for a while that the turning does this to those it infects. Makes them exceptional warriors, and they don't sleep. It must shorten the host's lifespan, though, there has to be a cost." He paused, but Petra kept quiet.

"As for his EEG, that's the strange part. All the normal waves – alpha through delta – are gone, replaced by a square wave, very strong. For a short time there was a sinusoidal wave, but it diminished, then flat-lined about half an hour ago. We have no idea what it all means."

"Bring him here, General, a contingent of Ossyrians and an Ngank surgeon are setting up a lab."

There was a longer pause, so she broke it. "General… Bill. Is there something else?"

"Yes, Madam President. It's Hellera. Her ship is gone."

Petra stood up. "The dark worms! Are they still –"

"… worms are gone, so… Sorry, you are speaking, please continue."

Petra deliberately slowed her breathing. "No, General. Please continue, I need to know everything, including your suppositions." She sat back down again.

"Her ship is gone, but so are the worms. According to the intel from the satellites we placed around the system perimeter, the worms left first, then Hellera's ship followed them."

Petra scratched at a knot in the desk wood grain. Why did the Kalarash never tell her what was going on? "So, we're defenceless."

"No, Madam President. The Shrell field will keep out invaders. No one knows how to get in except…"

Petra waited. Then waited some more.

"Sorry," Kilaney said, "I was just checking the hourly data-stream I saw earlier, something snagged my memory."

She heard him sigh.

"The Mannekhi, their twelve worlds were hit by a dozen Orbs in a coordinated attack five days ago. That's not all. The Mannekhi worlds weren't at the war front. Their planets shouldn't have been attacked for another month. I saw the spike in Qorall's front line but neither I nor the other commanders knew what to make of it."

Petra didn't need Kilaney to join the dots. The Mannekhi knew how to navigate through Shrell wires, since the Shrell had poisoned their space many times in the past.

She leant closer to the oval transmitter. "Bring Blake here, General, as soon as you can without slicing your ship in two on a Shrell filament."

Kilaney acknowledged, then broke the connection.

Petra needed to think. It would take Kilaney a couple of hours to arrive. She knew where she had to go.

On Silent Hill, Petra stood over the graves of Gabriel and Virginia. She wanted to cast off the mantle of President, if only for a short while. She missed her friends. Rather, she missed Gabriel.

"Gabriel, you'd know what to do. They're coming again." She sat on the rough grass, drew her arms around her knees. "They're never going to leave us in peace, are they?" She stared up at the cracked sky. At night the stars were no longer visible. Somewhere up there were her mother, Kat, and in a completely different direction, her father, Pierre, whom she'd only just begun to get to know.

"Petra, are you okay?"

She got up quickly. Brandt, the leader of the Youngbloods following Gabriel's death. Her cheeks flushed at the interruption. "Are you following me? And it's Madam President to you." She knew she was over-reacting, displacing her anger.

Brandt approached until he also stood over the two graves, towering above her.

"I miss them, too, you know, especially Gabriel. I can never replace him."

"You're right about that." She almost spat it out, then berated herself. "I'm sorry, Brandt. That was uncalled for." She folded her arms. "Things are closing in on us again, and it sits heavy on my shoulders."

"You're not alone, you know. You only…" He stopped under her glare.

"But I want to be alone, Brandt. That was the point of coming here. Why did you follow me?"

Brandt shifted from one foot to the other. He cleared his throat. "Petra, all those years you… I knew how you felt about Gabriel. You hid it well, but I knew, Virginia too. You see, I knew because –"

"Stop! Don't say it, especially not here."

"Why? There are no lies here, Petra. You can't lie to dead people. Here we have to speak the truth."

"Look, Brandt, I can't deal with this right now. Maybe later."

Brandt gazed up to the sky. "There probably won't be a later, we both know that."

Petra turned away from him. "I'm sorry, Brandt."

She heard his feet turn to go, then he paused. "If I could swap places with him, Petra, I'd do it in a second. You'd be happy, and we'd all be better off."

He left. She waited a long time before she turned around to see him descending back to Esperantia, then spoke to one of the graves.

"I know what you would say, Gabriel. But it wouldn't work. Maybe if there was more time." She took another look. Brandt was almost at the Dome. "Anyway, I should leave you two alone, you've both earned some peace."

She began her trek down the escarpment. Despite the undesired encounter, or because of it – she didn't know which – she felt lighter, and began planning defensive strategies. They included the Youngbloods, so she'd be dealing with Brandt again, but she could handle it, and so could he. She called Vasquez. "Commander, we need to meet. My office in fifteen, please."

Chapter 12
RELEASING ANGELS

The doors to the atrium closed, sealing Ramires and Ash inside the Alician headquarters. Ash had his hands bound and was surrounded by six guards, so Ramires couldn't count on any help from him. He walked calmly towards Louise, his left hand on the hilt of the nanosword inside his jacket pocket, his right hand concealing a skin-coloured wafer. Louise stood at the head of six armed Achillia, her personal guard. Ramires estimated that with the advantage of surprise he could take her down and maybe three of the others, though he and Ash would not survive. A fair trade.

Time slowed for Ramires as he neared his target; he and countless others wanted Louise dead on account of her crimes during and after the fall of Earth. Her succession of Sister Esma only served to underline that objective. His son Gabriel had killed Sister Esma, now he would be the one to execute Louise.

Diagonal shafts of sunlight from high windows bathed the Alician leader and her entourage in an orange glow. She looked younger than he'd expected, but then Alicians barely aged once re-sequenced by the Q'Roth. Her eyes, though, reminded him of some of his fellow trainees back in Tibet who had gotten a taste for casual killing. His Master, Cheveyo, called them 'shark-eyed', because they had lost perspective, and were highly dangerous. Ramires noticed the claw where her left arm should be; no matter, the nanosword would slice through it, he'd tested it on enough Q'Roth.

Louise's eyes narrowed, as if she recognised him, though they'd never met. Two more steps and he'd be close enough. He froze; she'd drawn a pistol unbelievably fast – one moment it wasn't there, the next it was – her arm steady, the weapon aimed at his face; quicker than a normal Alician, quicker than a Q'Roth.

"Ramires, isn't it? I've heard so much about you."

Guns ripped out of the guards' holsters, and pointed at his head. The moment had passed. He let the nanosword slip back into his pocket and stood, feet splayed, ready to spring in any direction. Ramires folded his arms, one palm concealing the wafer. He recalled a Sentinel maxim: never converse with the devil.

Louise spoke again. "I watched the vid of you fighting two Q'Roth warriors back on Esperia. Impressive. The last Sentinel." She put away her pistol. "Well, not quite the last."

Ramires kept his poker-face, but wondered what she meant. All the other Sentinels *were* dead.

Her demeanour changed, a little more tension around the eyes and lips. "Where is Micah?" she said in a flat, controlled tone. "We have some unfinished business."

He stayed silent.

"We could torture you, but I've studied the history of our so-called Silent War. Sentinels are notoriously resistant, almost as if you relish pain."

There were twelve Alicians around him and Ash, all armed. Too many.

"Or we could torture this one," she said, nodding towards Ash. "Looks like someone already started."

Ramires wondered if Ash would hold up under torture. Perhaps he should kill him now with the sword. But Ash was four paces behind, Ramires wouldn't get close enough in time.

"Or your wife, Sandy."

Ramires outwardly showed no reaction. Inside, his heart slowed, and his muscles loosened. In nine hundred years of unseen war between Sentinels and Alicians, there was one maxim both sides shared: better to die than be captured, because the latter path never ended well. So be it. He was less sure he could kill Louise, but he could take out several of the guards. Better to die on his feet than chained to an interrogation rack.

Without moving his eyes, he pictured where each man stood, and their most likely pistol aim trajectories, given that the wafer would catch them off-guard. He envisioned the layers of pulse-fire. In the initial confusion, blinded by the flash as soon as the wafer ignited, they would fire towards his trunk or head; he would have to duck low. A second later he would need to be above three intersecting layers of pulse fire. He estimated that there was a sweet-spot where the guards' lines of sight would be conflicted: they would hesitate, in order to avoid killing each other in the crossfire. It would require a high leap but he could do it. Next he calculated the place where he would be least easy to target, but from where he could still shoot Louise. After that it didn't matter.

The assessment had taken two seconds. He'd trained blindfolded hundreds of times back on Earth, and had continued to practice with Gabriel and the other Youngbloods on Esperia. His right hand gently squeezed the wafer inside his fist so that it split open. Now it just needed a little air.

Louise studied him, then the corners of her mouth lifted a fraction. "Let's see how good you are, Sentinel." She took a step backwards then spoke to her personal guard. "Take him."

Ramires took in a sliver of air, and then held his fists out in front as if to be cuffed, but as two of the Louise's personal guards seized his wrists, he blinked hard and dropped the wafer. It burst into a curtain of blinding light that smarted his retinas even through closed eyelids. He locked the wrists of the two stunned guards, then drove them into each other. Ramires ducked amidst a sizzling eruption of pulse-fire that fried the two guards. *Two down.* He leapt up high and spun mid-air, flailing the nanosword around him, decapitating two more guards and slashing the arm off a third, releasing a pistol that he snatched before it reached the ground. He breathed in more air. *Five down.* He landed behind one of the collapsing bodies, and used it as a shield while he fired at the two guards on either side of Ash, striking them in the middle of the neck, sending them tumbling to the floor. *Seven.* A pulse strike speared through his pistol arm, rendering it useless. He took another sliver of air as he dropped the sword and grabbed the pistol with his left hand and fired at Louise, who had vanished. The pulse round found another of her guards; they moved in a zigzag pattern aimed to defend and distract. *Four left.* They shot Ramires' corpse-shield again and again, blowing off its head and limbs, leaving Ramires with only the torso as a barrier, the tang of ozone and charcoaled flesh sharp in his nostrils.

Two more of Louise's guards toppled backwards; Ash, hands still bound, had fired two weapons from a prone position. *Two left.*

Ramires' legs exploded with pain, making him gasp in air. With a grunt, he flung the charred torso away from him and rolled to the right, firing two quick shots, dropping the last two guards.

Louise was nowhere to be seen. He reached for the nanosword, but it was gone. There was a 'pfft' sound, and Ash slumped forward, a feathered dart sticking out of his neck. Ramires fired towards the likely point of origin, but only hit shadows.

"Here," Louise whispered, behind him.

Ramires made to turn, but felt ice on his neck, and found he couldn't move. His chest muscles locked, and he rocked forward, his forehead striking the floor with a thunk, his eyesight growing blotchy.

She whispered two more words to him. "Not yet." With her boot, she flipped him over onto his back.

Ramires struggled to remain conscious; whatever Louise had used on him was powerful. He let his face muscles, closed eyelids and neck go slack. He heard soft footsteps, like those of a cat, approach Louise.

"I didn't need you to fire the dart, Toran," Louise said, "everything was under control."

"This one is good, very good. I admit I could learn from him. I have the knowledge, the latent memories. Sparring with this one would activate them, translate them into real skills and reflexes. Your next set of guards could do with more training, though. They were complacent, unattuned to the shock of a sudden, violent attack. They have grown soft."

Ramires listened to Toran's voice. He didn't recognise it.

Louise nudged Ramires with her boot. "That's why he isn't dead," she said.

"I doubt he'll help you, Louise, even if you use Sandy as leverage. He'll just as likely kill her quickly. It's what I'd do. It's what we were trained to do if the situation ever arose with a partner or children. We call it 'releasing angels'."

Ramires' mind sprinted. Louise had implied there was another Sentinel. And this man knew one of the most guarded secrets. Ramires thought about opening his eyes. But Toran started to walk away.

"Where do you think you're going?" Louise said.

"He's still awake. Some of the training school memories from my original host are still intact. I heard rumours about this particular Sentinel. We never knew each other's names, but during early training nicknames were common. His was 'possum'."

Ramires opened his eyes in time to see Louise crouch over him, and he felt the ice cold touch of something on his neck again. This time there was no resisting it. But as he slid towards unconsciousness, he quickly put the pieces together. Toran must have been cloned from a Sentinel, probably with Alician enhancements to make him even tougher. An abomination, yes, but that was irrelevant now. He could only exist for one reason: to infiltrate Esperia. Infiltrate and assassinate. Yet Toran was not ready; borrowed memories are not the same as honed skills. If Ramires could kill him, then the problem was solved. But if they fought and Toran survived, that could catalyse Toran into the strongest Sentinel ever.

Ramires' mind clouded, and he gave up on thinking about the never-ending war between Alicians and humans that had already consumed so much of his life, and thought instead about the one woman he cared for, the only person who had ever given him some respite, and happiness. He prayed he would see Sandy before the end.

Kat stared down at the Q'Roth carcass at her feet. "Vashta's rifle works."

Aramisk finished inspecting the second bubbling corpse and joined Kat. "Of course it works. You have to stop thinking Level Three. The higher intelligent races – and Vashta is Ossyrian, Level Eight – don't brag or exaggerate."

Kat hated lectures. "Whatever."

Aramisk held a hand under Kat's chin, the Mannekhi way of saying 'listen to me'. It was aggressive, but Kat liked it, because with Aramisk it was often followed by a kiss, sometimes more.

But this time Aramisk's demeanour was serious.

"Not 'whatever', Kat. It is never 'whatever'. You humans must look deeper, seek understanding, or else you will remain at the bottom of the galactic heap." She sighed and removed her hand.

"We Mannekhi are precise because we deal with higher Grid species." She glanced down at the fizzing Q'Roth mass as the nannites turned its body into mush. "When higher races visit your world for the first time, they assess you quickly; culling and enslavement are never far off their agenda." She met Kat's eyes. "First impressions count in the galaxy; you have no idea."

Kat knew of the Mannekhi's 'patronage' by their Masters – not far short of enslavement – for tens of thousands of years. She lay a hand on Aramisk's shoulder. "I'll try."

Kat touched her wristcom. "Micah, there's been a development. She angled her wrist downwards, showing the two dead Q'Roth.

"So I see," he said. "I'm checking sensors. No one else is around you, but they'll be missed for sure. I want you to enter the city, Kat."

"Aramisk can't, her Mannekhi eyes –"

"Aramisk needs to stay with the Rapier, keep a target lock on the base of the tether."

Kat turned to look at it, a hundred metres away, a cylinder of glistening metal as wide as a house sunk kilometres into the ground, rising impossibly straight, disappearing into the haze of blue sky above.

"Ramires and Ash?" she asked.

Micah's voice sounded taut. "Captured. That's why I'm sending you in. Plan D: recon only, Kat, nothing more, understood?"

"Sure," she replied, a crooked smile playing across her lips as she caught Aramisk's eye. Aramisk shook her head.

"I want open comms, Kat, and continuous cam-feed. And don't forget the Spider, we need to locate it as well as the captives."

"Okay, I just need a minute." She broke the connection. Aramisk had her back to her. "Are you okay?" Kat asked.

Aramisk spoke but didn't turn around. "Ash told me to leave you alone."

Kat flared "He had no right –"

"But he is right, Katrina. Go find your wife and the others. Concentrate or you will perish here, dragging the rest of us down with you."

Kat suddenly felt foolish; she'd been behaving like a teenager; it was her way of dealing with intense situations, always had been. Aramisk and Ash were right. Still, she'd developed feelings for Aramisk these past few weeks. Kat lowered her voice. "Let me see your eyes one more time, please."

"When you return." She walked away and left the clearing.

Kat watched her go, then walked to the camouflaged Rapier's airlock, and stepped inside, putting down Vashta's Q'Roth-killer rifle – she couldn't very well walk into the city toting it. She picked up a set of stiletto blades and a single barrel device which she stuck in her pocket, and switched on the cam bracelet, as well as the mike, lodging the micro-earpiece in her left ear.

"Okay, Micah, I'm heading in." Kat walked back out, half-expecting to see Aramisk there to wave her off, but she'd disappeared into the bushes.

"Fucking Level Six," she muttered.

"What?" Micah said.

Kat broke into a trot. "Nothing," she replied.

Threading a pathway through the foliage towards the city's outskirts, she began thinking about Antonia, who she'd not seen for two years. Images of happier times coursed through her head. Though her body had occasionally begged to differ in the past, Kat knew in her heart that she could only love one person at a time. Reaching the top of a hill, she glimpsed the central tower where Ramires and Ash had last been seen. She took one last look behind, toward the Rapier, the tether, and wherever her alien lover was hiding. *Thanks for saving my sanity.*

Kat launched herself down the other side, gathering speed with each long pace.

Ramires awoke with his head in Sandy's lap. She stroked his hair.

"You didn't kill the bitch then?" she said.

With an effort, grimacing from residual pains in his legs and right arm, he sat up. They were in some kind of glass-fronted cell. Antonia sat at the far end of the same narrow marble bench, watching him.

"How do you know?" he asked. His head cleared. "And how long have I been here?"

"Six guards brought you about an hour ago." She gave him a smile. "An impressive escort given that you were lashed to a stretcher and unconscious." Then her smile faded, and she filled him in on the failsafe chemical device implanted in all the captives, and the fifteen minute fuse if they left the compound or Louise died.

"That complicates matters," Ramires said.

"Or simplifies them," Sandy replied.

Ramires drew back. "I didn't come all this way –"

"You're a Sentinel. That's why I fell in love with you."

Ramires considered their options. The failsafe was unanticipated. None of their plans took it into account. And he and Ash – where was Ash? Being interrogated probably, or more likely mind-scanned, so they'd find out about Micah and Shiva soon enough. Louise had too much leverage now. The time-proven Sentinel solution to such a scenario was clear. Sandy was right.

"Why did she keep me alive?" he asked.

Sandy spoke to the floor. "She wants you to train the Alicians to be better fighters, so that they are ready when the war reaches Savange."

He got to his feet. "Train the enemy? A Sentinel training Alicians? She… Louise is deranged! We're not just blood enemies, our war goes back almost a thousand years."

Sandy stood up. "And I don't want her to have any hold over you. I know your DNA is practically hardwired to fight Alicians, and Louise is the sickest –" Sandy cut herself off, and turned away.

Ramires studied her a moment. Most people hated Louise because she'd sent one of the refugee ships into the heart of a sun, two thousand souls vaporised in an instant. But for Sandy, Louise had taken her prior lover, Vince. It was personal. One of Sandy's traits was that she never forgave; it meant she had fewer friends than most, but from his point of view it made her the perfect partner for a Sentinel.

She turned back, laid her hands on his shoulders, and cleared her throat. "She can't... mustn't have a hold on you. It would destroy you, and me." She bit her lip. "Do you... do you remember what you told me once, about... releasing angels? We have to show her we can't be controlled like... like goats, being nourished until the day they slit our throats."

His mouth opened, but no words came out. Though he'd considered it earlier, now, with her right in front of him... Ramires swallowed, then clasped her shoulders, pulling her close to him.

"Do it now," she said. "I don't want that bitch to control you, not for one second. Just make it quick."

He inhaled the scent of her hair, felt the soft warm flesh of her cheek against his. He kissed her neck, felt the pulse in her carotid.

"Now," she whispered.

His left hand moved to her neck, her body trembling against his. He closed his eyes and imagined that his master Cheveyo was standing there. 'Release this angel', he'd say. Ramires took a deep breath, brought his other hand up to the back of her head. His hands shook. They'd never shaken before, not once in all those kills. He began to apply pressure, Sandy not resisting in the slightest.

Antonia collided with him, her elbow jabbing into his ribs with more power than he'd have given her credit for. Pushed aside, he let go of Sandy.

Antonia stood, red-faced, and howled at him. "What the *fuck* do you think you're doing?" She turned on Sandy, who stood like a statue. "Both of you. Stop this crap right now!"

Ramires took a step towards Antonia, raising his palms. In all the time he'd known her he'd never once heard her swear. Before he could speak, she shouted again, clenched fists shaking by her sides.

"I don't want to hear it, Ramires, whatever you're going to say." She pointed to the glass wall. "They must be… pissing themselves laughing at us." Her voice quavered. "We're giving them quite a show, don't you think?"

Sandy reached out for one of Antonia's wrists. Antonia slapped her hand away.

"Antonia," Ramires said, "You don't understand –"

"And I don't ever want to. You're a warrior, the last and best one alive so I've heard. Well, prove it to me. Damned well fight them. Find another way."

Ramires glanced from Antonia to the glass wall, then back to Sandy, who stood bolt upright, but was trembling. He gently put his arms around her.

Antonia moved back to where she'd been sitting earlier, drew her knees up to her chest, and locked her arms around them, eyes glaring at the glass wall.

Ramires brushed a lock of Sandy's blonde fringe out of her eyes, and spoke softly, nodding his head towards Antonia. "Is she normally like this?"

Sandy tried to laugh, but it caught in her throat. She buried her head in his shoulder.

A while later Ramires walked across to Antonia.

Without looking up, she addressed him, anger in her voice. "We're being monitored, you know."

"Then sing," he said, "sing loudly."

She glared at him once, then complied, something in Russian, from what he could tell. He bent forward and whispered into her ear that Kat had come for her. Antonia's voice cracked and descended into a cough.

He wondered if he could find another way, wondering if Micah had moved to Plan F yet, in which case it would all be over soon.

Ramires heard heavy, booted footsteps. Ten armed guards arrived. They fired at him point blank through the glass wall and he buckled onto the ground, fizzing blue arcs of electricity dancing over his body. Amidst shouts of abuse and hammering fists from both women, the guards disengaged the glass door and took him from the cell, binding his hands and feet with mag-cuffs. As he was dragged away, he saw Antonia on the ground, her lip split. She met his eyes, defiant, and he recalled her words.

Half an hour later, Ramires was shoved through a doorway into a circular pit with high walls. He landed roughly on a sandstone floor, tasting dust, and was nearly deafened by angry jeers from spectators above. The cuffs around his wrists and ankles opened and fell to the floor. He brushed himself off as he got up, and kicked them aside. He stared upwards at the faces peering down at him over metal railings.

The door opened again and three young men sauntered in, muscular, tattooed, brimming with bravado, each brandishing two curved knives. They were greeted by cheers. The door closed.

Eight seconds later they were on the floor, one dead, the other two wracked by spasms as blood spurted from slashed throats. The crowd hushed.

"Lesson number one," Ramires shouted to the audience above. "If you want them to survive long enough to learn anything, don't give them weapons."

Scanning a sea of hostile faces, he found the one he was searching for: Louise. It wasn't too hard. She was the only one smiling. And then he saw someone sitting next to her. Their eyes locked in recognition, one Sentinel to another.

Chapter 13
TITANS

In Kalaran's judgment there was no such thing as a good day to die. And yet here he was, about to challenge Qorall, one-on-one. As a Kalarash, he felt responsible; when they'd first come across Qorall, he had been an outsider from a backwater sector of the universe, Level Eighteen, an incredible find, a prodigy. They'd taken him in, and Kalaran and the others had helped him advance. Only Hellera had urged caution, but she'd been over-ruled. That had already cost them their home galaxy, and although there were plenty of galaxies around, Kalaran wasn't going to let it happen again. Even so, it wasn't easy after two billion years of sentience to contemplate one's own demise. It wasn't simply about ego, either; how do you sacrifice for the higher good when you are the higher good?

His plan had been running in the background for millennia. He had been the only one of the seven remaining Kalarash that had developed a contingency plan in case Qorall had survived the last war, the others believing him dead. Unfortunately, Qorall's onslaught had been far more vicious than anticipated, with many new weapons, and a base that seemed impregnable. High stakes required bold moves, and Kalaran accepted that at the end of the day, the Kalarash weren't Gods, weren't permanent fixtures in the universe, they were just players in the game who had a limited time like everyone else, just longer than most. Still, it was difficult to make his final move knowing he wouldn't be there to see how the game ended.

His ship held the full spectrum of weapons, from molecular scramblers and subspace mines to dark-energy disruptors and star-imploders, but when fighting an equal, the small stuff didn't count. Both his and Qorall's ships had vastly resilient immune systems capable of identifying and rejecting invasive organics. It came down to who hit the hardest and the smartest. And in Kalaran's case, just how much he was willing to sacrifice.

His ship punched into the system where the Xera homeworld was in the process of resurrection. Qorall had flooded the sector with liquid space rendering it a ghostly green. Four of Kalaran's allies – Ukrull, Pierre, Jen and Dimitri – remained in play. He vowed to get them out before the battle got too hot. He trimmed his ship's shields and drives to adapt to the liquid space properties that would otherwise leach power from his weapons.

Six Level Sixteen Nchkani vessels took up position at the outer edge of the system. Kalaran held a tinge of admiration for their design, there was a certain panache about them – obsidian ovoids festooned with feather-like spines, each holding a dizzying arsenal. But the Nchkani were only Level Sixteen, and did not yet possess the ability to manipulate gravity, unlike the Tla Beth, whom they aimed to replace if Qorall won.

It was never easy to kill a species he'd helped evolve over millions of years, but the Kalarash always squashed rebellions, one of their few rules. He dispatched a gravity weapon Qorall knew well enough but was unheard of in this galaxy, a Hell-Class weapon he'd not used for aeons, and had once argued should be banned. But the rules of war were bound only by three factors: the laws of physics, ingenuity and sheer force of will. He had to send a message. Besides, the weapon had a side-effect that fitted his plan. Kalaran watched, knowing any Nchkani caught by it were already dead, their short ten thousand year lifespans about to be snuffed out.

The net, a purple veil, fluoresced through space as it sped toward the ships. Three of the captains had the sense to jump their ships out of the system. The other three separated but were sucked back together. As the net closed around them, first their spines crumbled, melting like wax, then the hulls cracked apart, spilling their occupants into a gravity gradient that pulverised them. A torrent of explosions erupted in a spasmodic and futile fit of rage, then all three ships melded into a ball, becoming smaller, harder, silent; a uniform brown speck that flashed crimson, a stunning bloom of what humans called Hawking radiation, before collapsing into a pin-prick black micro-singularity.

A communiqué arrived from Qorall. That was unexpected. It said <Leave>, meaning quit the galaxy. Qorall wanted Hellera, in order to build the foundation, his progeny.

Not going to happen.

He considered the field laid out between him and Qorall: the gaping black hole; Qorall's asteroid ship hovering just above its event horizon; the Machine planet; and the red dwarf sun, all set in a jade haze. Nothing else around, the nearest star system well out of harm's way in one direction, and in the other, the shimmering galactic barrier. Ukrull's ship, the Ice Pick, was missing. Kalaran extended his senses and found the subspatial trace signature that told him the ship was no more. He tried to see beneath the planetary shield the resurrected Xera had erected, but could not penetrate it. Interesting. A solitary Hohash drifted nearby. Kalaran pinged it with an info-burst, and it shot towards the shielded planet. As it reached the barrier, it morphed into subspace to slip through, but was blocked. That was also unexpected, definitely on the wrong side of 'interesting'. He signalled it to wait there.

Hellera contacted him from the other side of the galaxy, her ship inside the nebula sheltering the Tla Beth homeworld. Accessing her sensors he saw dark worms and Nchkani ships swarm.

"I should be there, with you, Kalaran. Together we stand a better chance."

"If the Tla Beth fall, other species will surrender to Qorall. And if you come here and we lose, Qorall will be unstoppable. Once he conquers this galaxy, he'll go after the rest of the Kalarash."

Several nano-seconds slipped past, a long pause for Hellera. "These humans. You still believe they are important."

"A catalyst for the Spiders."

"I've been in their heads; chaos and conflict."

"Sometimes they're happy for a fleeting moment."

"An illusory and pathetic state we abandoned a billion years ago, with good reason."

"Do you remember, though? You and I were happy once."

Again, several nanoseconds pause.

"I remember."

"I have to go now, Hellera. Are the Hohash in place?"

"Of course. Are you sure about this, Kalaran?"

"Never surer, Hellera."

"Then do it." She broke the connection.

Two billion years alive. As Jen would say, he'd had a good run for his money. Kalaran readied his ship. Its ten kilometre-long outer hull shifted from its usual scarlet and green hues to a deep blue, except for a single ivory ankh, the sign of the Kalarash. His ship sprang towards Qorall's, and opened fire.

Jen staggered along a passageway of gnarled rocks and boulders seen in ghoulish shades of grey in the utter darkness, courtesy of her new visual capability, Kalaran's parting gift. She sucked in the last morsels of oxygen from her suit, holding each skinny breath for as long as she could before gasping another. It was tempting to lie down, to accept that life had finally kicked her ass, to give up. But she kept going, for Kalaran. Dammit, she was worried about him.

A faint glow rippled ahead, like a light underwater, so dim she thought at first that it must be an illusion, her new vision playing tricks on her. But no, it was there. She breathed out, and breathed in, having to suck hard, and realised this was her last breath from the suit. If nothing else, she wanted to see the ship before she died. The glow led her around a corner, and there it was.

A gyroscope was the first image that sprang to her mind as she gazed at the ship hovering just above the floor, the size of a three storey house, emanating blue light that pulsed like a heartbeat. Similar to the Tla Beth themselves, it had four vertical rings of shifting rainbow hues, turning slowly, two in one direction, two in the other. The inner part was diamond-shaped, its swirling surface masking any doors or windows that might offer her a sliver of hope.

The aching in her lungs grew to breaking point, and she exhaled a little, glancing at the red dial on her wrist indicating zero oxygen. Jen wanted to touch the ship, to try and make contact, and staggered a few paces forward. She exhaled some more as the onset of dizziness began. The thirst for air yanked at her lungs, and waves of nausea swept over her. One of the rings collided with her, knocked her off her feet, and spilled the last air out of her chest.

Jen tried to breathe, but there was nothing. Her mouth gawped uselessly, like a fish tossed onto dry land. She knew the pattern: muscles would fail from the extremities inwards, her brain being the last organ to shut down after the others stopped. Her body started to convulse, but even through the tremors she saw something silver above her, snaking its way towards her. It touched her helmet. She tried to sweep it away but her limbs refused to comply, and she watched a mouth open on the outside of her visor, reminding her of a lamprey, an Earth-based sea creature that latched onto fish and ate their intestines. She tried to push her head back inside her helmet, but her muscles ignored her.

Without warning, it pierced her visor, writhed into her mouth, and slithered down her throat. She wanted to scream, to fight this last violation, grab the worm and smash its head against the floor. But she was practically catatonic; even her gag reflex was inactive due to the oxygen depletion in her cells. Her body stilled, and Jen waited to die, thinking about Dimitri. She guessed she had a little time before complete brain death; maybe thirty seconds.

Jen felt a sharp jab inside her head, and found herself thinking about the Tla Beth, though she didn't want to. She relived those last moments before it was destroyed by Qorall, images playing back in her mind of its accomplishments. She could still see its ship above her – but that wasn't right – her vision should have faded by now. In fact, coherent thought should have ceased altogether. And then she breathed in the sweet taste of pure oxygen, just once, her chest suddenly rising, her back arching off the floor before collapsing again.

A surge of information screamed into her mind, she presumed via her node.

<Where?>

It wanted to know what had happened to its master. She mentally imaged Qorall's attack on the planet, so the Tla Beth ship could see all that she had seen.

Another blast of oxygen. This time, her fingers and legs went into intense cramp, but she relished it; the Tla Beth ship was saving her. But again, just one breath. Jen gathered this was some kind of bargaining: oxygen for information. But the silver worm began to retract out of her gullet. She guessed why. She had nothing to offer it. Its master was dead. She was nothing to it. But she realised she wasn't ready to die. Her arms still weren't working, so she clamped her teeth down on the worm just as it was pulling out of her. Her head lifted from the floor as it tried to extract itself. Jen knew this was her last chance. She focused, transmitting via her node: Kalaran; her time on his ship, fighting the dark worms, accessing the Hohash; anything she could think of. The worm paused, its head just inside her mouth, as if deciding. Then it shot back down her throat, and pumped her so full of oxygen that her gag reflex returned.

———

Pierre tried to keep up with Ukrull. He'd never realised how fast his reptilian colleague could run, covering ground easily with his zig-zagging gait. Pierre activated his suit rear-cam, to see behind him rather than turn around and risk tripping. It showed an image of what was chasing them, displaying it on the upper right section of his visor.

Beetle-like machines loped toward them, with eight legs and empty sockets where eyes might have been, and coiled protrusions on their skulls that could have been antennae. At least they had no wings, since there was no atmosphere, and no wheels either since the terrain was too broken up. Pierre had no doubt that the Machines could fabricate any form they needed. But the antennae were stretching in his direction. With alarm he saw more of the mechanized creatures to his left and right, closing in.

At last he was catching up with Ukrull. On second thought, Ukrull was braking, and Pierre saw why – a gaping fissure had opened up in front of them, too wide to leap across. A ship rose up from its depths, but it wasn't black like the other Machines; rather, it glowed blue. It lifted level with them just as the beetles arrived. A hatch opened, and a space-suited, helmetless figure stood in the doorway: Jen.

She waved to them to enter, though there was no need; Pierre and Ukrull bolted for the hatch. They dived in and the doorway disappeared as if it had never been there. As he got to his feet, Pierre found he couldn't focus on the interior, it was like being inside a liquid, pinks and blues and other coloured shapes forming and deforming, sometimes transparent, sometimes opaque. Secrecy. All he could resolve visually were Jen and Ukrull.

"This way," Jen said.

Pierre had a hundred questions, but an objection got there first. "Qorall has shielded the planet; we can't get off."

Jen turned. "It's good to see you both alive. Really."

Pierre slowed down a second: Jen looked like hell. He dared to ask. "Dimitri?"

Ukrull turned to look at Jen, too. Her eyes teared up, then she raised her chin to stop any from falling, and placed her right palm over her heart. Pierre understood. But it was hard to accept: Dimitri had been the closest human to a Level Five Pierre had known, smarter than most Genners. And Dimitri and Jen had been besotted with each other; that much had been clear. But before Pierre could speak, Ukrull emitted a low growl that grew into a roar; it fit how they all felt, a mixture of loss, anger and respect. But mostly anger.

Then Ukrull spoke, though it wasn't any language Pierre recognised. A Hohash arrived – not theirs, its frame metallic blue – it must have belonged to the Tla Beth guardian of this planet. It showed them an external view: ten or so of the beetles were clambering all over the Tla Beth ship, their antennae trying to syringe into the Tla Beth's exterior, but they couldn't penetrate the hull, and so instead they locked their legs around the external rings. Pierre wondered why the ship didn't rotate its rings to break free.

Jen, rather than Ukrull, answered his unspoken question. "It wants them. We're taking them with us."

The certainty in her voice led him to another question. "Are you in touch with the ship? Via your node?"

She nodded, then added, "Kalaran is out there, though apparently he can't break through this planet's shield. The good news is that Qorall can't either. We only know what's going on because this Hohash is communicating with one just outside the shield. Subspace movement is blocked, but not communication." Jen frowned. "According to the ship, the Machines aren't supposed to be able to do what they're doing."

Pierre suddenly felt optimistic. "Never mind, Jen. Kalaran is here! That's great news." Yet she didn't look happy, and neither did Ukrull. Pierre's optimism dipped. "Isn't it?"

Ukrull loped off through curtains of colour. Jen held out her hand. "Come on, Pierre, it's time to go."

They turned a corner and the colours dissolved, revealing a circular hatch leading to empty space – normal, not green – full of stars. Pierre didn't get it; had they left the planet and moved outside the shield? And if so where were the beetles? As he got closer he saw that there was a gossamer tube-like corridor leading from the hatch, twisting out into space, its walls like thin transparent plastic. He paused at the threshold.

"Jen, is this what I think it is? An inter-dimensional corridor? It shouldn't be possible."

She shrugged. "Level Nineteen, remember? Kalaran still has a few tricks up his sleeve. Just think of it as an escape chute, Pierre. You go first."

He didn't move. "We should stay and help Kalaran."

She shook her head. "You're not thinking. At best we'd be a distraction, mostly a nuisance, and at worst a liability. He wants us out. Now."

"Where's Ukrull?" Pierre stared into the infinite, empty corridor.

"Behind you," Ukrull grunted, and shoved Pierre in the back, knocking him over the threshold.

Immediately, with that single step, Pierre found himself flung far along the corridor, landing on hands and knees. The corridor's floor had a damp, spongy feel, his fingers making indentations; it felt terribly flimsy, as if it might tear and disgorge him into open space. He got up and looked behind, and could just make out Jen and Ukrull staring from the hatchway. Yet outside the corridor he'd moved a great distance; he estimated twenty thousand kilometres from the planet. He tried to step back toward Jen, but a single pace in any direction thrust him further down the corridor. Now he couldn't see either the hatch or Jen or Ukrull. But what he could see took his breath away, as this section of the corridor appeared to run close to the heat of battle.

Kalaran's ship jetted a stream of blazing violet fire at Qorall's asteroid-sized vessel. Most of it was deflected into the mouth of Qorall's black hole. Qorall's ship spewed forth jade-coloured forks of dark energy throughout the entire system. Pierre turned to see the Machine planet, in the path of those arcs of destructive power. The planet's dull shield came down long enough for a single ship – the one he'd been standing on a minute ago – to sprint out of the system towards a crimson mouth at the edge of the sector that swelled for a moment then swallowed the ship and vanished.

"Wormhole," Jen said, suddenly next to him. "Kalaran created it out of enemy ships and exotic matter. Hellera has opened the other end deeper inside the galaxy, at the Tla Beth homeworld.

"Why didn't we travel through it?"

She laughed mirthlessly. "Turned out Dimitri was right about that. Wormhole travel is possible in theory, but most matter gets pulped and cooked during transit. But the Xera are very tough. They adapted last time around – using some kind of Level Eighteen shielding – when they tried to escape this battle-field two million years ago."

Pierre saw the irony in what was happening. "Kalaran blocked them last time, didn't he?"

She nodded.

He turned back to the planet. It was being drawn into Qorall's black hole. But some of the Machines had escaped. Kalaran's plan all along.

Ukrull arrived. "Must go. Conduit sealed behind us. Won't last." Without waiting, Ukrull took another step and disappeared down the corridor.

"We have to go, Pierre," Jen said.

She held out her hand. He looked at it but didn't take it, not meeting her gaze. "I'll be right along, Jen."

She studied him a moment. "I don't think…" Her voice caught. She collected herself, and tried again. "I don't think Kalaran's going to make it, Pierre.

Qorall is too strong. I've lost one person I care about today, I'm about to lose another. Please don't make it three."

He had to force himself not to step back. Kalaran about to die? Impossible. Kalaran was way too smart. "I'll be there, Jen. I promise. You go."

She shrugged, took a breath and a step, and vanished into the distant swaying, cord-like corridor.

Pierre didn't believe Kalaran would, or even could, die. He was Level Nineteen, a sublime intelligence. For sure he had some trick up his sleeve, and Pierre wanted to see it; the scientist in him demanded it, and he still had a little time. He glanced back towards where the ship had been: the corridor undulated in space like a long rope cut loose. He swallowed, but stayed put.

Kalaran's crossbow-shaped vessel was closer to Qorall's now, the latter's asteroid-sized ship glowing red under Kalaran's relentless fire. The Machine planet whipped past both ships, arcs of green lightning skittering across its surface. It plunged towards the maw of the black hole, shattering into fragments before spiralling downwards. Its descent appeared to slow down, due to relativity, but Pierre knew the planet was already gone.

Pierre glanced back towards the corridor's original entrance, only to find it was rushing toward him, like the end of a deflating balloon. He stumbled backwards and found himself thrown way down the corridor, but the loose end was catching up fast. He got to his feet and was about to run when he saw in the distance the unthinkable: Kalaran's ship was engulfed in green shards of energy. *This can't be happening!* Turning to his right, open space was almost upon him, and he dived left just in time.

The scene was far away now, hard to make out. The whole sector was like a ball of green electricity. He heard Jen's voice as Ukrull's claws locked around him.

"Out of time."

Pierre was hauled off his feet, as the trio bounded towards the safe end of the corridor. He didn't struggle. The last glimpse he saw of the battle scene was a series of eye-searing flashes before it went dark. But in the afterglow Pierre witnessed the unmistakeable remains of Kalaran's shattered ship spinning into Qorall's black hole.

As the trio spilled into an empty white room – Pierre hardly cared where they were – Ukrull planted him on his feet. Pierre gripped Ukrull's claw and Jen's wrist.

"Kalaran's... dead." Pierre still couldn't believe it. Surely Qorall would win now; Hellera alone could not stand up against him. She would leave, and the galaxy would be lost. He felt dizzy, wanted to sit on the floor, to sink through it. Ukrull should have left him in the corridor.

In the silence punctuated only by Ukrull's raspish breathing, they stared at each other. Ukrull let his head roll back towards the ceiling, his fore-claws raised above his head like fists, as he began hammering the air, emitting the loudest roar Pierre had ever heard. Pierre glanced at Jen, then sat down, his back against the wall. He didn't have the energy to roar. Instead he stared into the floor, trying to make sense of it, to see the way out, but all he foresaw was their doom.

All his life he'd believed intelligence to be the only thing that mattered, and spending the last eighteen years travelling in a galaxy whose very basis was founded on the supremacy of intelligence had vindicated that perspective. But now the most intelligent being in the galaxy, perhaps the universe, had been felled. The universe had changed with Kalaran's passing, and Pierre wasn't sure he wanted to stay in this darker one.

Ukrull's roaring ceased, leaving a ringing in Pierre's ears. Jen joined him sitting on the floor, and took his hand and held onto it, while Ukrull paced, occasionally stomping or kicking at the walls.

Jen leant her head against his shoulder. "We're totally screwed, aren't we?"

PART TWO
BLAKE

Chapter 14
EXPERIMENT

Petra stared at the plazglass, wondering if it needed to be thicker. Blake – the golden version – was quieter now, finally. Kilaney had brought him back in a stasis capsule, a grim moment for the people of Esperia, seeing the one-time saviour of humanity sedated in a transparent casket surrounded by heavily-armed guards. Word spread quickly as to what had happened, that Blake had been contaminated – corrupted – and was now on Qorall's side. He'd been brought to Esperantia's hospital through the streets; most people had looked at him not so much with pity, but with fear. If Qorall could turn Blake…

That was yesterday. Since then a contingent of Ossyrian doctors and an Ngank surgeon had landed their egg-shaped ship right outside Esperantia's hospital. That was where Petra stood right now, staring at Blake, separated by a reinforced glass wall.

When they first woke him, he broke through his restraints – apparently by dislocating his shoulder – and managed to bite one of the Ossyrian doctors, infecting her. The others had evacuated and vaporised their comrade, even as her fur had begun to take on a golden sheen.

Sedation was no longer working. He just sat there, staring.

Kilaney entered through the Egg-ship's airlock. "Any change?"

She shook her head.

"The Ossyrians want to take him into orbit; less risk of contamination up there."

"No," Petra said. "He's my jurisdiction. He stays."

Kilaney took in a breath, as if about to give a speech, then apparently thought better of it. He walked up to the glass, fingertips of one hand resting against it. With speed that made Petra recoil and almost topple from her stool, Blake leapt forward and rammed the glass with his head. A dull boom filled the room. Kilaney didn't flinch. Where Kilaney's fingers met the glass, there was a golden smear on the other side. Blake returned to a standing position, his head apparently undamaged, and resumed his stare at Petra.

"He's no longer Blake, Petra. He's a rabid dog. Back home we shot rabid dogs."

"Not going to happen. We need a cure for this type of rabies, or else we'll all be infected sooner or later."

Kilaney turned his back on his erstwhile protégé and friend, blocking her view. "I'm no use here, Petra, not to him, not to you. I'm heading back out." He pursed his lips. "There are battles to be fought, and –"

"How long have we got till one of Qorall's Orbs arrives?"

He leant back against the glass. Petra winced as Blake became animated again, pounding the glass wall right behind Kilaney, his punches sounding like soft footsteps. Kilaney stayed where he was. She didn't know if he could feel it or not, but she reckoned he could.

"There's one traversing space at high transit speed, heading in our direction. It's already bypassed several sectors, which is unusual – Qorall doesn't normally leave any gaps in his advancing front."

"So, how long?"

"It isn't like the others. It's black, for one thing. We think it's been designed to get through the Shrell wires."

Petra snatched at a glimmer of hope. "The Shrell, could they –"

He shook his head in a way that told her they'd already tried and paid a heavy price.

She waited, lips pressed tight.

"A week at most," he said. "I'll be back before then."

Petra felt like slumping, but she didn't. The pounding ceased. Blake stood directly behind Kilaney so she couldn't see him at all. "No word from Kalaran?"

Kilaney shook his head. "Hellera is still in contact, though."

Petra stared at the floor. For some reason, nobody trusted Hellera as much as they trusted Kalaran, which wasn't much in the first place.

"Go," she said, wishing she, too were a soldier and could go with him. But as he moved past her she laid a hand on his arm, and he paused.

"None of us want to become like this." She nodded her head toward the glass. "If it comes to it, if Council decides, and gives the order… You understand me, don't you?"

"Understood, Madam President. But I doubt they will. Most likely Council will let individuals decide for themselves, and given human nature, that means if we're overcome we'll end up swelling Qorall's ranks."

"We will of course abide by what they say, though I already know my personal choice."

"As do I." Kilaney took a hard stare at Blake, then looked away.

She retracted her hand, and Kilaney stepped through the airlock. Petra returned to her vigil, watching Blake stare at her. She sensed his contempt – bordering on disgust – for the infidel he believed her to be, and wondered how she might reach him, all the time knowing there was no way she could. She'd already talked to him for hours, trying every counter-conditioning technique in the book, and a few Genner ones, too. It was no longer Blake, that much was clear, and yet she couldn't bring herself to accept it. Despite being a Genner and having no truck with amorphous concepts like souls, she wondered if, deep down, there was some vestige of the real Blake, wounded, aware of his state and screaming to get out. She almost hoped not, because for him this would be hell.

With that thought, she turned and headed to another compartment where the Ngank – a squid-like creature who never seemed to touch the floor – was communicating with the three remaining Ossyrians doctors.

"He's all yours," she said.

They barely paid her attention, so she spun around and left the vessel through the same airlock as Kilaney. Outside in the bright sunshine, on the dusty main street of Esperantia, she breathed in the dry air, picking up traces of lavender, one of the few Earth plants that flourished in Esperia's cool sunlight. She had work to do, a meeting with Vasquez and the militia to prepare, futile as she knew their defences would be. One week. Not enough time. She left and proceeded at a brisk pace to her office.

Brandt intercepted her. "Petra, we need to talk."

She knew what he wanted. "Not now," she said, and tried to out-pace him, pointless given his gargantuan size.

He blocked her path, though remaining at arm's reach. "Petra, you need to listen to me."

After two attempts to walk past him, she stopped, folding her arms. "Then how about 'Madam President', for starters?"

"That title doesn't mean anything to us Genners, and you know it." But he lowered his gaze.

"Then maybe you shouldn't have voted for me." But he looked hurt, in a way she thought only very large men could. "Well, go ahead, I'm listening." But her anger from the last two days boiled over. "On second thought, you listen, Brandt." She pointed back to the egg-ship. "I told Blake to go and do something and make it count. Have you seen him? Have you seen what they did to him? What they'll do to us in a week's time? Genners, Steaders, it won't make a damn of difference."

Brandt lowered his voice. "The Youngbloods are not going to wait."

Petra couldn't believe it. "They want to go and fight the Orb and die early, is that it? Then they'll be in the front line attacking us. Even Steaders aren't that stupid!"

Brandt shook his head. "They want to evacuate, Petra."

She thought she'd heard it wrong. "What?" The anger fled from her voice. "Where to?" It didn't make sense. The Youngbloods were warriors at heart; surely if anything they'd want to stay and fight. Petra realised she'd been spending so much time looking after the Steader population that she'd lost touch with her own people.

"Come to my office, Brandt, you'd better fill me in."

An hour later, Brandt had left, and she sat in her utilitarian alabaster office that was bereft of ornamentation, not even a pad lying on the antique oak table, the last of its kind. It had served four Presidents in eighteen years. She didn't see how there would be a fifth.

Vasquez sat on the other side of the table, frowning. "Evacuate? Where to?"

She told him the plan, and the reasoning, while gazing out the window, past the curve of the Dome to the cracked sky beyond. She ran through it quickly, summarising, because she didn't like it, despite its logic, due to a 'gut feel', something they'd all believed had been bred out of Genners. Brandt and the other Youngblood warriors had run the calcs. Qorall was coming for the Spiders, and even if Hellera could hold him off, humanity was likely to get torched in the process. Several Ossyrian vessels were going to pass by the system in a matter of days. They'd recently lost their homeworld and were going to fall back to a proto-world a hundred and fifty sectors away. They had room on their ships, a lot of room...

"What about Micah and the others?"

"If they succeed, we can send a message via the Hohash, and Shiva can rendezvous with us."

Vasquez stroked his stubble. "I don't know about this, Petra..."

She got up, then perched on her desk. "Tell me about it. But part of me wonders why I didn't think of it, or why no one else in Council has raised it."

"Kalaran and Hellera are two reasons. They're relying on us, though none of us truly understands why. And for the past eighteen years this ball of rock has been our home. We ran away before, Petra, the Steaders don't want to run again. And the Spiders are still here. And so is Blake. That's five reasons."

"Five reasons to stay here and die? Not a compelling business case, Colonel." Petra felt like the galaxy was closing in on her, the Shrell-wires a trap rather than a protective cage.

Vasquez stood tall, despite his years. "Call the Council. Put it to them."

She nodded, then something occurred to her. "The Spider's shield around Shimsha. You were trying to break through."

"No way we can, and we still don't know what it's for. Which is why I'm here, Petra. Three Spiders emerged an hour ago, I followed them here."

Petra was on her feet. "Where...? Blake?" She was out the door before Vasquez answered.

She walked fast to the ivory egg-ship, Vasquez a little way behind, as always maintaining his composure; she remembered Blake once joking with her that no one had actually seen Vasquez run, because when he did, it was too fast. As President, Petra knew she should also maintain a certain level of decorum, so she maintained a steady pace. Up ahead she saw a small group of people who had set up some chairs and a couple of tables in the forecourt nearest the Ngank surgeon's ship. Various religious groups were holding a vigil for Blake, some on their knees, palms clasped together in prayer. Petra doubted any of them knew Blake personally; this was symbolic, for everyone's survival. She'd never been religious, but right now she'd take any help she could get. Her heart pounded – what if the Spiders could cure him? To hell with decorum; she broke into a run.

A single Ossyrian sat at the hexagonal airlock entrance, its jet-black mane flowing out from underneath a platinum, sapphire and emerald headdress. Petra could read their shifting mercurial eyes a little, having learned from her godmother Chahat-Me. The Ossyrians and the Ngank surgeon had exhausted all options. She braced herself for what she might find inside.

The Ngank, two Ossyrians, and two Spiders crowded at the quarantine cell observation window. Vasquez had said there were three Spiders. She nudged politely in – the Ngank obliged by floating above one of the Spiders – and saw the third Spider through an inner airlock portal; it was about to enter. Blake sat motionless, staring at one of the Spiders next to her. The Spider began to stream light towards Blake, trying to reach him.

Vasquez arrived and took up a place directly behind her, and brought her up to date.

"The Ossyrians said it probably won't work, as the change has done something to his eyesight; he can't see colours anymore. Still, it's worth a try."

Petra ground her teeth together. That bastard Qorall thought of everything. Of course he did, she chided herself – he's Level Nineteen. And she'd heard that the Spiders weren't the only species communicating by colour. But she also considered that it ran deeper than that: in order to change the way people think, you have to change how they perceive. As if to prove her point,

Blake looked away from the Spider, momentarily caught her eye with a grim smile, then turned to face the airlock. A sense of panic gripped Petra.

"No!" she shouted. But there was a hiss. "I said –"

The Ossyrian to her left placed a paw on her arm, something Chahat-Me used to do when she'd wanted a younger Petra to be quiet. Out of respect for her deceased Ossyrian godmother, Petra shut up, despite guessing what would come next.

The hatch between Blake and the Spider opened. With a sinking feeling, she noticed a slightly darker pear-shaped patch on its left rear leg; it was one of Blake's friends, the one she'd seen most often with him. She folded her arms, as if holding herself. *Please, Blake...* She felt Vasquez' hand on her shoulder. Normally she'd have shrugged it off, but for once she didn't.

The Spider ambled into Blake's chamber. Its comms band rippled a soothing aquamarine. Blake was a statue. Around her, everyone else remained completely still.

Blake moved so fast, almost a blur, one moment sitting, the next a ball of fury attacking the Spider with fists and feet and elbows and teeth. The Spider made no response, not even defensive reflexes kicking in. One of its legs collapsed as Blake's foot shattered a knee-joint, and Blake's rigid golden fingers drove into the Spider's comms band like blades, again and again, until blue liquid spurted out. Petra's breathing was frantic, no one else seemed to be reacting like her, except that Vasquez held her shoulders firm. One of her knuckles went to her mouth and she bit hard as she watched Blake gouge and tear his best friend to pieces.

It lasted five minutes – she never once closed her eyes to it – before the Spider was on the ground, still twitching, but almost certainly dead. Blake's arms dripped blue gore. He stood, facing away from them, surveying his handiwork. Now Petra understood how Kilaney had felt earlier. She wanted to shoot this abomination, right here, right now. But she channelled her anger in another direction, as she turned around.

"Well, what was the point of that? We all knew what was going to happen, didn't we?"

The Ngank drifted down level with her face. It had two pink holes she assumed were eyes, and a spout on its face she hoped was a mouth. It surprised her by speaking English.

"Experiment successful."

For the second time that day, the anger inside Petra reached boiling point. "Are you out of your mind? He just tore his best friend to pieces. What kind of sick success is that?" She turned to the Ossyrians. "What is wrong with you all?"

Vasquez raised a hand. "Petra –"

"What? Since you seem to get it, Colonel, please explain it to me. In which galaxy does what I've just had to witness count as success?"

He pursed his lips, and took his time, presumably waiting for her to calm down, to listen. She didn't want to hear whatever he had to say, but his tactic worked, and she recovered a little. She spoke in a quieter voice, regaining some composure.

"Tell me, Colonel."

"What colour is the Spider, Petra?"

She stared at him as if he'd asked some ridiculously banal question, then spun around to the glass. It was black. Not gold. So far, every single being of any race that had been touched by one of Qorall's minions had been contaminated and turned in seconds, ending up gold like Blake, like the Orbs. Until now.

"How?" she asked.

The Ngank came close to her again. "Unknown. But breakthrough. Must prepare for autopsy." It drifted away, then came back. "Apologies for harm."

"I understand," she said, her voice quieter.

The Ossyrians and the Ngank disappeared into an adjacent room with the two remaining Spiders. Vasquez stood silently behind her. She stayed facing the glass. Blake still stared at the corpse, so she couldn't see his face. She turned to Vasquez. He held out a handkerchief. She stared at it and then remembered, and wiped the blood off her chin.

"Thank you, Colonel, I'm sorry for my behaviour just now. To be honest I don't feel fit to be President anymore. I'm too involved in all of this, I can't step back. Could you –"

"Nothing to apologise for. What we all just witnessed was… harrowing. You expressed what I felt. And no, we need a President who *is* involved, frankly, and your judgement and decisions have been sound so far." He smiled. "Besides, I'm not averse to some theatrics every now and again."

His smile infected her. "I can see why Blake had you as his right-hand man." Her smile faded. "Please call an Emergency Council meeting in an hour in the Dome, ask Brandt to address Council with his evacuation proposal."

"Will we see you at the Meeting?"

"I'll be there." She stopped him near the exit with a question. "Why doesn't Blake turn around?"

Vasquez shook his head. "He's gone, Petra, there's nothing left of him in there."

Vasquez quit the observation chamber. Alone, she returned to stare at the scene. Vasquez was right. If the autopsy was successful, they could terminate Blake – this zombie – and bury the man who had died inside it several days ago. Out of pure frustration, Petra walked up to the glass and punched it hard with her left hand, hurting her knuckles. She was about to walk away when Blake turned his head slightly, as if listening, then turned back again. She thought she noticed something. Yet it couldn't be; a trick of the light, perhaps, but she had to be certain. She called to the Ossyrians. One of them came in, its quicksilver eyes displaying more than a little irritation.

"Show me the view from that camera." She pointed to a camera located inside the cell, high up on the opposite wall.

The Ossyrian's eyes glittered dissatisfaction.

"Just do it!"

The Ossyrian moved to a console and activated a screen. Petra moved towards it. The Ossyrian was about to depart when it stopped, staring at the view of Blake's face. It called to the others, but before they arrived Petra barged in front of the display. She gripped the screen with both hands.

Blake's golden face was splattered with drying blue blood and pieces of gore, some of the Spider's fur matted to his chin. His expression was still as grim as it had been earlier, full of spite and hatred. But his cheeks showed unmistakeable streaks where tears had run, and his eyes were red.

As the Ngank arrived she seized two of its tentacles. "Blake's not lost," she cried. "He's still in there!"

The Spiders entered, and everyone moved out of their way so they could see the display. Petra's pulse quickened. She knew in that moment that whatever Council decided – even if it voted for evacuation – she wasn't going anywhere. She'd put Blake on this course of action, and was determined to get him back or else die trying.

She lifted her wristcom to her mouth, and was about to call Vasquez, when she changed her mind.

"Kilaney… Bill, I need you back here. Blake… he's still buried in there."

There was a pause.

"I'm on my way."

As the Ossyrians and the Ngank used robot arms to extract the Spider's corpse, the other two Spiders stood on either side of Petra, watching the operation. Without thinking about it, she rested a palm on each one, and patted them.

Chapter 15
PLAN F

Micah hadn't slept in two days straight. Vashta had given him something to keep him going, but it made him edgy and gave everything around him a slightly yellow tinge. She'd told him to take half an hour off the Bridge, so he sat in his quarters on the bed, his back against the wall, contemplating his next move now that Ramires and Ash had been taken. Clearly Plan F was called for, but he needed to be sure, and he needed to be focused. He wasn't, and he knew why.

He recalled an event some years earlier that led to him resign as President, an event he'd never told anyone about. He'd bumped into Sandy – an event in itself since she'd managed to avoid him for a long time – and they'd actually talked. She hadn't had much choice, as her son Gabriel, a mere boy then, had been seriously injured in a training bout, and Ramires had been away. Micah had gone to the hospital to see the boy, bringing one of the Ossyrian doctors with him, and Micah and Sandy ended up sharing an empty waiting room while the doctor performed emergency surgery.

After some pained pleasantries, they talked, over cups of tea. The talk had been mainly one-way, her talking, him listening. It had reminded him of a painting he'd seen somewhere in a virtual museum showing a saint tied to a tree, with many arrows sticking out of his body…

"I just don't think you're the right one to lead us if there's an attack," she said.

First arrow, a light one. He took a sip. "Of course not; there's Blake, Vasqu –"

"But you'd be commander-in-chief. You'd make the final call."

"I'm not sure I see –"

"You don't have the killer instinct, Micah. If Sister Esma attacked us again, and you had the chance to blow her to smithereens, would you?"

"Well, that would –"

"Thought not. You'd hesitate, she'd recover, and then come back better prepared next time, and we'd all pay the price for your decision."

Second arrow. He took another sip.

"And what about Louise?" She folded her arms.

Micah's breathing slowed. He felt he was turning to stone. He put down his cup. "What about her?"

"Well, if you'd screwed a hundred women, it wouldn't be so bad, but Louise – was she your first?" That arrow narrowly missed. His thirst deserted him. He shook his head.

"Let's be honest, Micah, you've probably had very few lovers, and Louise was one of them."

Another arrow. "Once," he said quietly. "We had sex once."

"So, here's my point. Look me in the eye and tell me you'll kill her."

He looked her in the eye. "I'll kill her."

She shook her head. "You're lying and you don't even know it. Do you know what your problem is Micah?"

He had a few ideas.

"You're too compassionate. You care too much about others, to the point that you're self-deprecating. That's okay if it only affects you, but when you're leader of the human race…"

He couldn't take any more arrows, and got up and left. That evening he resigned from the Presidency.

The next day Sandy came by his house, a first, but he refused to answer the door. She talked to him through it for two hours, saying it had all been displaced anger, that she'd been worried about Gabriel, that she hadn't meant him to resign. Micah didn't say a word, and eventually she left.

Antonia took over for two years as President before Kat came and told him it was burning her out, and persuaded him to take back his job.

He thought he'd be free of Sandy after that whole episode, but each time he heard about her his ears pricked up. She'd been well-respected amongst the outer communities, and especially with the Youngbloods, not only because she was married to Ramires whom they practically worshipped, but because she counselled them on a range of social problems, helped the fast-growing Genner kids deal with their Steader parents, relate to them. She'd worked unseen for a decade, creating a much-needed social glue that kept a fractious society from flying apart, though she never once appeared in or before Council, never took any credit.

He glanced at his watch. Five more minutes.

He knew why Sandy was angry with him, it wasn't just about Louise. There'd been Hannah, too.

Most people couldn't pinpoint the exact moment their lives took a course for the worse, but Micah could. On board a stolen Q'Roth vessel, roaming the Grid with Sandy, back when they'd been friends and on the cusp of becoming more, Sandy barely pregnant with Gabriel. Late at night they'd been talking, she'd come to see him, but he'd misread the signs, only realising it later. Unfortunately, the Alician Hannah called on him later that night while he was asleep, and crawled into bed with him; on top of him to be precise. Hardly awake, he'd thought she was Sandy. Then, fate being not merely cruel but vicious as it sometimes was, Sandy had arrived, and found them together. From that point on Sandy turned away from him, and towards Ramires, and Micah did nothing to stop it, confirming her later assessment of him.

Zack once told him that the whole point of life was to overcome your main flaw, which, funnily enough, could also be your strength. Micah hadn't thought too much about it until now, because of Plan F. Plan F would spill blood. He would have a lot of blood on his hands. Had Sandy been right about him? Was his compassion going to stay his hand when it came to the necessary, or if he was faced with Louise? Had he lied to Sandy and to himself on that day?

It was time, and he was out of time. He headed to the bridge, determined to be the man that the situation – and the whole of humanity – demanded him to be.

Micah sat in the command chair, Vashta at Tactical behind him. He replayed the scenario in his head again. Plan F – Ash's strategy. When he'd first heard it, Micah had winced, but it made sense, though he'd had a hard time hearing such an aggressive manoeuvre coming from someone as philosophical as Ash.

The Alician space station, a gleaming crystal city, lay ten kilometres dead ahead, hanging in space like a jewel, a marvel of engineering. Four Q'Roth battleships were docked there, while two Marauder Class vessels patrolled the perimeter. He checked the ship's chronometer.

"Fire," he said.

There was no recoil, no sound as the intelligent missile Shiva called a *Bleeder* shot like a flare towards its target, not seeming to be in a hurry. Micah counted down. *Ten, nine, eight...* A Q'Roth Marauder jumped into its path, pulse cannons blazing, lighting up space. The Bleeder punctured the ship's shields and hull. The Marauder's on-board lights flickered then went out, the vessel suddenly inert, adrift, all its energy haemorrhaging into a subspace rift left by the missile. The Bleeder emerged from the other side, homing in on its prize.

Five, four, three... It breached the space station's translucent shield, which flashed silver once, then vanished.

One.

There was no explosion. The only noticeable change was that lights began to fade and go out all over the space station. Two of the Q'Roth battleships had managed to detach before the Bleeder made contact, and tore towards Shiva's position, which hadn't deviated a centimetre.

Micah touched a panel. "Approaching Q'Roth ships, break off immediately or be destroyed."

The screens in front of Micah stuttered white and yellow as Shiva was bathed in plasma fire.

"Final warning," he said, not bothering to check Shiva's hull integrity.

The larger Q'Roth ship fired an anti-matter projectile; it was relatively small, but then if it had been even medium-sized, say twenty kilograms, the backwash from the energy release would have fried the Q'Roth ship. Micah tapped a remote cam and watched the illegal weapon scorch all the way around Shiva's elliptical shield, space dust erupting like fire-crackers around the hull before evanescing into gas, giving the impression Shiva had been dropped into boiling water flashing to steam.

"Take them out, Vashta."

It was like watching two trucks race headlong into a giant hammer swinging the other way. He'd heard about gravity weapons, but never imagined what they could do; this one had been Hellera's gift, an upgrade for Shiva.

The two battleships were first flattened, then turned inside out, as if a giant arm had reached down their throats, grabbed their tails, and pulled hard. Amidst the carnage, hundreds of Q'Roth warriors, most of them unsuited, flailed their limbs in cold space. Vashta targeted all of them with a dazzling shower of laser fire. In two seconds they were all dead.

Micah closed his eyes. "Was that necessary?"

Vashta spoke, the sound of her voice an unholy choir of out-of-tune fingernails scraping down an antique blackboard. "Better for them. Dying in space is agony."

He glanced back at the display. A single Marauder was intact. He touched the pad again. "Q'Roth vessel, the people aboard the station are still alive, but all power is gone, including life support. You may proceed to rescue –"

The ship jumped out of the system. Micah scratched his chin. The Marauder had gone for reinforcements, for sure. The whole point of Plan F, Ash had said, was brutality, creating shock in the enemy, to throw them off-balance, to make them realise you meant business. But Micah was at the helm, not Ash, not Ramires. He stared at the city, imagining hundreds of Alicians and Q'Roth beginning to chill, local gravity nullified, oxygen recycling ceased.

They'd all be dead in thirty minutes. His earlier self-debate about compassion versus the killer instinct arose in his mind. The station was incapacitated, he'd sent a message. There was a difference between spilling blood and creating a bloodbath.

"Switch it off, Shiva."

"Are we on a new plan, Micah?" Shiva's voice often had an aloof, slightly mocking tone.

"No. Switch off the Bleeder. Now."

A few lights flickered back on inside the station. Vashta arrived next to him, her voice grating louder than usual.

"Do you wish me to take over? You have reinstated a threat. If you feel unable to execute the plan –"

He tapped another panel while he looked Vashta in the eye. "Aramisk, blast the base of the tether."

Vashta's fast-moving quicksilver eyes stilled for a moment, then she returned to her station.

They waited ten minutes before seeing a wave like the curl of a whip travel up the tether. When it reached the orbital city, it snapped clean off, shunting the city out of orbit. The two Q'Roth ships powered up and undocked from the station.

"Your orders, Micah?" Shiva asked.

He imagined Vashta's eyes lasering into his back. And Sandy's.

Micah stared at the vessels, recalling the final battle for Earth, when he'd watched from a distance as the Q'Roth slaughtered billions.

"Ram the closest one."

Shiva's inertial dampers were so good that he felt nothing, simply watched the screen show wild movement as Shiva, a Scintarelli Scythe-ship, lived up to her name. Shiva tore away from the closest ship before looping back at terrifying speed. Micah barely had time to register the Q'Roth ship rushing towards him on the screen, then there was a flash of grey followed by open space again. The aft screen showed the two halves of the guillotined ship careening away from each other, internal explosions sputtering briefly before both halves grew dark. Micah doubted there would be survivors.

The last ship had moved off but had not yet jumped out of the system. Its commander hailed Micah.

"Enemy ship, identify yourself."

Micah and the others had discussed this at length. Technically humans and the Q'Roth were on the same side – Kalaran's – in the war against Qorall. But certain Q'Roth tribes had allied themselves with the Alicians. Micah didn't see any point in subterfuge.

"We are humans. This is a private matter between us and the Alicians. I suggest you stay out of it; you have seen what this ship can do. Return now to your Queen. Tell her that Kalaran favours us rather than the Alicians, and that she must choose her allegiances carefully. You can return for your colleagues tomorrow."

"Your name, human?"

"Micah."

The battleship jumped out of the system.

Micah relaxed a little, then took a breath. He'd spilled blood. But he knew it was one thing to do it from a ship, using superior firepower, and quite another to kill someone right in front of you. He had a nasty feeling that fate would test him, presenting him with the question Sandy had asked years ago. He felt certain he would face Louise.

"Take us down, Shiva. Prepare for ground assault."

Ash wondered why he was still alive. He couldn't feel his head, and could only see out of his right eye. What he saw was Louise. She hadn't spoken for ten minutes, just perched on a stool alternating between watching him and a screen to her right. He was strapped down to a semi-reclined operating chair; the restraints seemed unnecessary given that his muscles had been anaesthetised. He presumed they were there for another reason: Louise had operated on him, on his head. But he felt calm. He was more than prepared for death.

"I didn't recognise you at first, Rashid; or should I call you Ash? What's with the Mannekhi eyes, anyway?" She glanced at the screen. "No matter, the procedure is finished."

Curiosity got the better of him. "Call me Ash, please. What procedure?"

"I've split your brain, blocked the corpus callosum that joins your two hemispheres, so I can interrogate you. I perfected this approach a few years back; nice to have an opportunity to use it again."

That was why he could only see out of one eye. The right one. So, his conscious mind was active – the left hemisphere connected to the right eye. The analytic, linguistic half of his mind. The rational one. Which meant she was going to access the right hemisphere, the creative part, the truthful half that did not know how to lie.

"Actually, your two names make it easier to do this. I'll call you Ash, and the other one Rashid. Let's get started, shall we? What is your crew complement, Rashid?"

Ash heard his mouth list Shiva's crew. It was startling to hear his own voice as if spoken by another person. He tried to think of some way to stop this, to stop telling her everything.

"Good to know Micah's coming. Also, Kat owes me an apology. And another Ossyrian doctor might come in handy." She crossed her legs, leaning forward with her forearms atop her knees. "What is the plan, Rashid?"

Ash tried to stop talking, to hold his breath, to stop his mouth working, but to no avail. At least his right brain gave only the broad brush strokes, no details. But it was small comfort. During their travels together, Kalaran had once offered him a mental trigger, a way to think a series of thoughts that would initiate neural shutdown. Ash wished he'd accepted the offer.

"Ash, this Plan F, destroying Savange if you can't release the captives… it's a bluff, correct?"

"Why are you asking me?"

"Because your alter ego doesn't seem to be clear about it."

Ah, of course. Plan F was complex, and that wasn't the domain of the right hemisphere. "It is not a bluff."

She got off her stool and walked closer to him. "Bring the woman," she said.

Ash hoped it would not be her, but sure enough, Sonja was marched in by an Alician male.

"I believe you two know each other?" Louise went back to her seat, and crossed her legs again, looking relaxed.

Ash stared at Sonja, whom he'd not seen for a year of his time, eighteen of hers. But she hadn't aged appreciably, except that her short afro had touches of grey here and there. Her eyes were the same, but her expression was one of shock, presumably at seeing some contraption strapped to his head. Seeing Sonja rekindled emotions he'd convinced himself were long dead.

"Rashid," Louise said, "how do you feel about this woman?"

Ash heard his alter ego confess thoughts and feeling he'd denied for a long time. Yet despite the anger at Louise for this gross violation, Ash was surprised at the passion in his voice as he professed love for Sonja, and watched a tear trickle down her left cheek. Eventually his counterpart grew silent.

Louise stayed quiet.

Sonja's head bowed, then lifted, proud and honest as he remembered. "Is it true that you love me? Louise explained what she's done to you. I want to hear it from the other side, I need to know, Ash. Is it true?"

"We must not entertain Louise's games, Sonja. You know –"

Sonja stamped a foot. "Is it true? All these years while you were gone I've been wondering and waiting. Answer me, yes or no!"

She looked as if she might shatter. Eighteen years for her, one for him, unfair to the point of being tragic. Was it true?

"Yes," he said.

Louise got off her stool and moved behind Sonja, locking an elbow around her neck, her other hand on the back of her head.

"So, Ash. Is Plan F ultimately a bluff?"

Ash stared into Sonja's defiant eyes. He realised he no longer wanted to die, that he did have something to live for. Louise had outplayed him.

He closed his eyes. *I'm sorry Micah.*

"It's a bluff."

Shiva burst through the cloud layer, and raced down towards the purple savannah studded with green pines that led to Savange City. Micah found himself edging backwards into his chair as the tree-line rushed upwards.

"Er… Shiva?"

At the last millisecond, Shiva pulled up and cleaved a furrow between fir trees, bolting forwards at an altitude of twenty metres and a speed of five hundred kilometres an hour. The aft screen showed pine trees ablaze.

"Was that necessary?"

"I needed to verify certain subsystems were functioning optimally."

"Of course you did," Micah said, trying to breathe normally.

To the East, the orbital tether continued to fall from orbit, coiling giant loops that pummelled into the ground, flattening trees, sparking fires, and shattering boulders into plumes of dust. The city was to the South, so the natural spin of the planet meant the tether fell away from the inhabitants; Micah presumed they'd planned it that way, just in case.

"Kat," Micah said. "Are you in position?"

"Almost," she said, panting.

He looked at the timer. Ninety seconds. "You have –"

"I know!"

He leant back, tried to slow his heart rate, which his resident was inconveniently displaying in the corner of his right eye. "Vashta, you have all their life signs and locations?

A display next to Micah opened up: the terrain ahead, the city, and beneath, where all except Kat were. There was something wrong with Ash's signature: it was slightly out of phase, presenting a double image on the screen.

"Where's the Spider? I don't see it." This was the added complication to their mission – to recover or destroy the Spider at all costs; it must not fall into Qorall's hands.

"Unknown," Vashta shouted.

They flashed over a lake, and Shiva dipped lower, sending a fountain of water up into the sky behind them.

Micah cleared his throat. "We're not going for subtlety then, Shiva?"

"They are tracking us Micah. In fact they are firing at us."

"Let's see what they've got against a Level Fifteen Mind-ship."

The display blazed white, then red, then white again. Then the screen re-adjusted, filtering out the high energy plasma fire so he could see the tracer lines coming from two towers at the edge of the city. At first they reminded him of battleship towers, as if some giant vessel had been buried just below ground level. Each tower had an array of weapons turrets and cannons, almost all of which were firing simultaneously. The intensity of the energy bearing down on them was igniting everything between Shiva and the towers, creating a tunnel of fire. He wondered how they protected the city from the heat and backwash radiation, then he saw it; a shield, similar to the one around the orbital city.

"Take down their shield."

A mauve circle spat out ahead of them, unperturbed by enemy beams, and grew in size, then narrowed into a cone that sped off and disappeared. A second later, the shield fizzed and died, and the enemy beams cut off; an intelligent protection system, since there was no point having a defence grid that killed most of Savange's population.

Shiva slowed so fast that thunder roared around them, then she slewed lazily between the two towers. "Drop-zone," Shiva said.

"Okay, bore the hole." Micah turned to Vashta. "The Bridge is yours." He ran to the aft of the ship, knowing that Shiva was tilting to a vertical position, from whence she would core a deep shaft.

"Kat, tell me you're ready."

"Almost!"

Micah leapt aboard the sled as the aft door opened. Steam flushed in, then cleared, revealing a smoking hole, five metres in diameter. He engaged the sled engine and dropped out of Shiva, circling once, scanning the rim of the hole. "Kat, where the hell –"

She slammed into his back, and locked her arms around his waist, just as Shiva roared off to combat another weapons-tower.

"Go," she said.

He let the sled drop like a stone, no lights, his resident projecting an image of the polished cylinder around him, and the floor a kilometre below to the fiftieth level; where Sandy, Antonia and the other captives were, where Ash and Ramires were, and, he knew, where Louise would be waiting.

Ash watched Louise dart between displays and controls, like a wild bird suddenly trapped in a room, barking orders on her wristcom. She strode over to him.

"How do they know where we are, where you are? We're shielded." She looked away. "And even if they can track you, they couldn't know where the captives are, unless…"

Ash was sure of the next question, and glad she hadn't posed it to Rashid earlier. Hopefully now it was too late.

She stared at him. "Your eyes. They're not Mannekhi, are they? Tell me Rashid."

Ash heard his alter ego tell her they were a gift from Kalaran, and that they could link with a Hohash via subspace. There was no known shield in existence that could block subspace. Ash guessed what was coming next. It was okay, he told himself, he'd been blind before. The pain cut through his eyes like a jagged knife, even though he knew Louise had probably used a laser scalpel. Hot fluid splashed onto his cheeks and temples, then ran down his neck. Sonja screamed. It's alright, he heard Rashid say. This is how we met, remember? Sonja was sobbing. Ash hoped Louise wouldn't kill her.

He listened, a blind man's skill not easily forgotten. But Louise said nothing, furiously tapping displays. Then he heard the unmistakable sound of explosions, sonic grenades, and flashbombs further down the corridor, and the hissing of the gas canisters that would knock out all Alicians.

Plan F was right on schedule.

Micah and Kat had arrived.

Chapter 16
SIEGE

In the bowels of the Kalarash ship, Pierre stared into the bubbling pool that had just swallowed Ukrull and Jen. Pierre had always hated water, and had never learned to swim, a fact he'd managed to conceal during his astronaut training back on Earth. He hadn't told Jen or Ukrull either. But swimming through water should be easier than staying afloat. Besides, Kalaran was gone, and they needed to start working with Hellera. He checked his face-mask one more time, and plunged in.

The green-tinged fluid was warm, the visibility good. He saw Ukrull, so ungainly on land, tuck his fore-claws by his side, and use his long tail to swim easily, like a marine iguana back on Earth. Jen swam with a practical breast stroke and occasional dolphin kick, while he clawed his way through the fluid like a dog. He stayed at the rear.

The inside of Kalaran's ship, from what Jen had told him, had been as vast as Hellera's, filled with sweet air and small asteroids each with their own gravity field, with a mercury lake at the bottom. By contrast, Hellera's ship, though equally vast, was filled with liquid. Instead of the asteroids, there were purple or red bulbous masses that slowly changed shape from sphere to ovoid to long, flat tongues that occasionally broke and split, forming two new spheres. It was mesmerising, and he had to concentrate on keeping up with Jen rather than staying to watch and wonder what these masses were. He had no idea of the surrounding liquid's function or chemical composition.

Swimming upward through the water – he decided to think of it as water for now – was not easy, and it reminded him of their situation. He watched Jen; she had lost the most, first Dimitri, then Kalaran. Yet she swam onwards. He tried to mimic her actions, and after a while found a steady rhythm. He wondered why Hellera was making them do this, there must be an easier mode of transport. It occurred to him that a liquid made for good internal defence.

During the next twenty minutes Pierre saw shapes in the water, always just a little too far off to make out their details; human-sized, moving independently, swimming fast through the fluid. Several times Ukrull paused their ascent, waiting for something to pass overhead before continuing. Pierre's headset had no comms capability, so all questions would have to wait.

At last he saw the ship walls tapering to a neck above him. He tried to recall the external form of the Kalarash vessel: crossbow-shaped with a narrow shaft ascending to an arrowhead at the top. He guessed that was their destination. After another few minutes, he saw a ceiling. A hatch irised open and the three of them swam through it into darkness. It sealed beneath them, and then the water began flushing out through grooves beneath their feet, and the lights came on.

Jen was first to take off her mask. "Well, I needed a workout. It's made me hungry though. Glad there's a cockpit, I was beginning to wonder." She climbed a circular ramp up and out of the wet pit onto a dry upper deck. Pierre followed suit, Ukrull crawling out of the pit on all fours.

Ukrull illuminated consoles, and view-screens sprang to life. Pierre studied each one in turn. A holo arose showing a supernova. There were few in the galaxy, and Pierre had visited this one before, with Ukrull. "The Tla Beth homeworld," he said.

"Where?" asked Jen, suddenly at his side.

He pointed to the centre of the nebula-like explosion of green, scarlet, yellow and purple light, and almost immeasurable radiation. "Inside, masked in some kind of null-field. They live on an asteroid at its heart."

Jen walked closer to the screen. "How old is this supernova? They can last millennia, can't they?"

"This one far older," Ukrull grunted. He laid a fore-claw on Pierre's shoulder. "I go there now."

Pierre met Ukrull's yellow reptilian eyes. They didn't waver, or grow or shrink as they often did, and Pierre understood that they might not meet again. He gripped Ukrull's fore-claw as hard as he could. Ukrull grunted something in his native language, and all Pierre could do was nod and say "Good luck, my friend."

Ukrull crawled back into the pit, filled it with fluid, and disappeared through the hatch.

"One by one," Jen said.

"What?" Pierre asked, unsure he'd heard her correctly.

"Nothing." She busied herself with one of the consoles, fixing something to her temple. She seemed at home.

Pierre studied the holo of the supernova, Hellera's ship at its leading edge and, much further out, other ships, and something else.

"Nchkani, Level Sixteen, and dark worms," Jen said without looking up.

"Nchkani? But weren't they on our side?"

"Right tense, Pierre. They *were* our allies."

There were a lot of ships. But he'd understood that the higher the Level, the fewer in number, like the Kalarash, the Tla Beth, and even the Rangers.

Jen pored over her console, and answered his unspoken question. "One ship, one Nchkani."

The sensors in front of Pierre counted three hundred ships, and more were still arriving. Even at only one Nchkani per ship, this was possibly their entire race assembled in one place for one battle. And most of the Tla Beth were here, too. For both species it was about dominance. Nchkani and Tla Beth committing everything to the battle for second place after either Qorall or Hellera; only one of those second-tier species would walk away from here.

Pierre sat down. He was happier in the cockpit as Jen called it; the rest of Hellera's ship was too vast after years of travelling in the Ice Pick.

"Are there enough Nchkani to mount an attack?" Jen asked.

He stretched the ship's sensors far outwards to pick up inbounds, while he pondered. Hellera had presumably created this place just for them, based on Jen's travels with Kalaran. But Jen's question was the wrong one. She was thinking of a normal attack by hordes of worms and Nchkani vessels. Besides, what would you attack a supernova with? Hellera's ship was well inside the supernova remnant field that fluxed with intense, off-the-scale radiation, but only because her ship's super-dense alloys were from another galaxy; the Nchkani could not approach closer – yet.

"The question is what can they do with this many ships and worms," he said.

"Kalaran would have liked you; you talk like he does – did." She cleared her throat. "So, what do you figure is their game plan?"

Pierre had narrowed it down to three candidates. "First, they could try to feed energy into the supernova to destabilise it, causing it to emit a shock wave and collapse into a black hole or a neutron star, or even a Magnetar, a rather nasty neutron star variant; any of which could terminate the Tla Beth sanctuary."

"Wouldn't the Nchkani ships get caught in the shock wave?"

"Yes; it travels at ten per cent of the speed of light; pretty hard to outrun. Second option is that they use the dark worms as shields, and penetrate the supernova itself. I don't have enough information on the Nchkani vessels, but the worms are very large, and very tough. I'm pretty sure Qorall has tampered with their physiology."

"Sounds like that kid's vid-game, Meteorite Shower."

"I agree," he said. He'd mastered it when he was six, which lost him most of his school friends that year. He re-focused. "Hellera could certainly pick enough of them off to break such a manoeuvre. Third is a straightforward, old-style siege, keeping the Tla Beth and Hellera here while Qorall methodically tips the balance elsewhere."

Hellera's voice cut through, jarring him. It was the first time they had heard from her since arriving.

"It is the third. They are also hoping that to break the stalemate, the Tla Beth themselves will initiate the shockwave."

Hellera sounded so certain. "How can you be sure?" Pierre asked.

A holographic image of a Nchkani flashed up in front of him. Jen walked to Pierre's side. It wasn't a pretty sight; the octopus-like creature squirmed, its tentacles writhing, each one tethered.

Hellera spoke while they stared. "Qorall injected all Nchkani with a virus preventing me from downloading its memories, hence the use of old-fashioned but ultimately efficient methods."

The creature's central body mass shook violently, excreting steaming yellow pus from its pores. Its beak opened and closed sporadically. Pierre was glad there was no sound. A single metallic pole drove into what looked like its eye. Pierre swallowed. He was about to say something when Jen placed a hand on his arm, and shook her head. He understood. Hellera would see squeamishness on his part as weak. They were at war. Hellera snapped her finger and thumb and the Nchkani stilled, presumably dead. The hologram dissolved, much to Pierre's relief.

Jen filled the ensuing silence. "So it's a question of timing, right? The risks and advantages are shifting: more Nchkani ships and worms arriving here, Esperia vulnerable, Qorall doing who knows what, and the Tla Beth – what are they up to, by the way? I can't believe they are just sitting there."

"Your friend missed some variables, Pierre. Explain the battle math, I'm busy."

Hellera was gone again.

"She didn't mention Kalaran," Jen said.

Pierre was not surprised; he'd met Hellera once before. "We don't know anything about Kalarash emotional attachments, if they have any. Besides, I'm sure Ukrull has already briefed her."

"Still, Kalaran would have said something about her if the roles had been reversed."

Pierre gave her a look to convey that he, too, was busy, and Jen went back to her console. But she didn't stay quiet.

"Tell me how you are doing it."

Pierre sighed, then began articulating the mathematics. "I'm mentally constructing a four dimensional geometric plane that operationalizes real-time and predicted evolution of key dynamic variables – the ones already mentioned plus a few others – and looks for cusps or spikes in two opposing value utility factors; our favour and Qorall's. It will tell us the optimum time to… Oh."

"What?"

He turned to face her. "The optimum time for us passed thirty minutes ago."

Jen shrugged. "So when's the next one in our favour?"

"No, that's just it, there isn't one. From here on it's downhill. The odds get progressively worse for us, and Qorall's get better and better."

Jen got up, and headed toward the pit, picking up her mask.

He followed her and stood as the water rose over his feet and ankles. "Where are we going?"

"To get some answers. We're going to find a Hohash, and then talk to Ukrull on the Tla Beth homeworld. Something's going on there. A variable Hellera hasn't told us about, and isn't going to."

"Do you even know how to find one? And what makes you think any of them will talk to us?" The water reached his knees.

"I've been touched by Kalaran, Pierre. They sense it. I'm guessing even Hellera does, which is probably why she let me on board. She's not very sociable, is she?"

"What if her plan is too complex for us?" The water rose above his waist.

"You're a well-behaved Level Ten being, aren't you, Pierre, fitting nicely into the Kalarash's intelligence apartheid system called Grid Society." She splashed water in his face. "Wake up, Pierre. We have to stop playing their game, assuming what they are doing is best for us, or else we'll never be anything other than pawns. You're the bloody scientist, not me, you work it out."

He stared at her, then slid the mask over his face just in time.

She smiled at him, her mask sealed, and spoke through the intercom. "That's more like it. More like Dimitri." She touched a pad and the door opened, flushing them down into the ship's internal sea.

It took nearly an hour to reach the bottom. Pierre wondered if Hellera would intervene, but she didn't. They reached a surface layer between water and air. It rippled, mirror-like, and they passed through to the other side, then half-drifted, half-fell as gravity re-asserted itself and they stood on dry sand, looking around.

"This way," Jen said.

Pierre followed her gaze and spied something. As they approached, he recognised it as an ornate throne, which was odd, as whoever sat in it would survey nothing but desert. Hovering nearby was a Hohash mirror, in the shape of an elongated diamond. While Jen tried to access it with her node, Pierre wandered around the throne, careful not to touch it. On the way, he'd been considering the Grid hierarchy: its flaws and its benefits. Clearly the societal system worked, in that there were few wars; Pierre remembered Hellera's 'history lesson' showing how most space-faring civilisations sputtered into existence for tens of thousands of years before fizzling out. There had been no social fabric to bind different races together cohesively, leading to anarchy, wars, and species obliteration or obsolescence; until the Grid system. The intelligence Levels locked species into a role for a very long time, preserving the status quo of the hierarchy. It was sustainable, but it was also stagnant. Little evolution, few surprises. He wondered what Darwin would have thought about it all, or Fiyong Choh for that matter. The ultimate choice seemed to be between rigidity and chaos.

"I'm through," Jen announced.

Pierre walked over and stood behind her, and gazed at the Tla Beth homeworld, its tan surface against a violet and steel sky that raged like a brewing hurricane. In the foreground was Ukrull, with three Tla Beth and a robed female figure whose skin and long hair blazed white. Ukrull was gesticulating wildly, his tail thrashing. He didn't look happy. The woman was unmoved.

"Hellera?" Jen said. "I thought Kalarash couldn't leave their ships?"

"An instantiation of her." But his eyes were drawn to the background. It was some way off, but it was definitely a Kalarash ship, on the ground. He recognised the colouring, and assumed Jen did too.

"Jen, when you came back with Kalaran and brought the extra Kalarash ship –"

"Darkur's ship."

"Yes. Did you ever leave the cockpit?" But he already guessed the answer.

"She's there, isn't she, inside the supernova with Ukrull and the Tla Beth, and her ship. We're on Darkur's ship, on the front line between them and the Nchkani."

The woman in the image walked closer, staring at them through the Hohash connection. Her eyes were pure grey, the colour of slate. She opened her mouth, then the image vanished, the Hohash resuming its oil-film colouring. Pierre was relieved she was gone, but suspected the worst.

"What did she say, Jen?"

Jen stared at the mirror, her voice quiet. "We're alone on this ship, Pierre. It doesn't matter what we do. We're a decoy. We're…"

A sacrificial pawn. He placed a hand on Jen's shoulder, knowing this could tip her over the edge. But inside, he felt something boiling up into his chest. All his life, he'd been manipulated by others: first his father had genetically engineered him to be smarter and less emotional, then he'd been altered by the Ossyrians, and last time he'd met Hellera she had changed him yet again. But he was living proof of the fallibility of Grid Society's founding principle, that species stayed within their assigned Level. He was a Level Ten variant of a Level Three race. He was the scientist's infamous black swan.

"Come on," Pierre said. "We have to make our way back to the cockpit."

"What for?" Jen looked as if she was ready to crack.

Pierre held her by the shoulders. "We're going to make some chaos, Jen."

She stared at him a while, then a smile dawned across her face. "Finally, something in which I excel."

They swam back to the far end of the ship. Pierre felt lighter. Glancing downwards, he noticed the Hohash following. He'd often wondered about them; servants of the Kalarash, yes; but they also seemed to have an independent existence, perhaps even their own agenda. He didn't understand their role, and considered that they might simply watch from the sidelines as the war unfolded, recording everything no matter who won. But he reckoned they would act decisively at some point. Like him, they would stop being played, stop being pawns. He hoped he would be around to see it.

Chapter 17
SENTINELS

Ramires paced up and down like a caged animal in the glass-fronted cell, while Sandy and Antonia sat close together. An explosion rocked the ground, but he remained standing.

"How deep are we?" Sandy asked.

"A kilometre, more or less." He waved a hand dismissively. Not a problem for Shiva; she could sink a hole that deep in seconds. He resumed pacing, counting down the seconds based on the estimates Ash had made back on the ship.

The hiss of gas canisters venting made him pause. Sandy came to his side, put her arms around him. He should tell her. No secrets, ever; that had been their agreement. A single lie and it was all over. A secret was a lie by another name.

He turned, took her wrists. "They have fashioned another Gabriel, like the original one back on Earth." There, he'd said it. It sounded like an epitaph. His.

She tensed, her sandstone eyes transmuting from soft to hard in an instant. Still he held her wrists. A look of comprehension dawned across her face. It wasn't the prettiest face he'd seen in his lifetime, but it was the only one he cared to gaze upon.

"Clone?" She mouthed it rather than saying it aloud, in case the Alicians were still monitoring, though Ramires knew it didn't matter anymore. Micah's assault had begun, and Kat should arrive at any second, which was why he had to prepare her.

"He's on their side, so it isn't really Gabriel, just a shadow."

Her wrists slipped from his grip using the Bagwa move he'd shown her years ago, making him smile, and she put her hands on his waist. "Is he a Sentinel?"

Ramires' smile vanished. It was the only question that mattered. No secrets, no lies.

"Not yet," he said.

Sandy's breathing quickened, and she embraced him, just as Kat arrived. Antonia leapt up from the bench and dashed to the side of the glass closest to her.

Sandy didn't let him go, so he watched as Kat bent down and used something that looked like a pencil to scrape a door-sized arched groove in the glass. Kat stood back, but Antonia didn't wait, intuiting what the pencil did, and shouldered the impromptu glass doorway outwards, where it fell as if in slow motion and smacked onto the floor. In a second Kat and Antonia were locked in an embrace, too. Ramires unpeeled himself from Sandy.

"Seconds count," he said, another Sentinel phrase he'd taught Sandy. She let go, and nodded. She placed two fingertips to her lips, then to his. It almost made Ramires crack; Sandy knew, guessed what he foresaw. No secrets was a two-way street.

Sandy touched Antonia's shoulder. "You have to go now, deactivate the chemical weapon planted in our brains. Give me that device, Kat, I'll find and release the other captives."

Kat looked first at Sandy, then Ramires. "All the Alicians in the complex are down; nerve gas tailored to their physiology, based on the two we captured on Esperia."

Ramires nodded. "Go quickly. Remember that Louise is hybrid; it may not work on her." He watched Sandy depart, followed her spring-like gait, her hair bobbing up and down as she moved. She didn't turn around. He touched his fingertips to his lips, and then held them out in her direction. Then he lowered his arm, and stepped through the archway, and spoke to the person he sensed was just around the corner.

"They are gone, Clone."

"My name is Toran," he said as he emerged, carrying a staff, a sword and a knife in each hand. He tossed one set onto the floor in front of Ramires.

"The Alicians haven't been able to teach me anything useful for some time. Perhaps Louise could. But you can hone my Sentinel fighting skills."

Ramires surveyed his opponent. *Know your enemy.* The clone of Gabriel – this Toran, since he preferred that name to the one of a warrior he respected – had the eagerness of any avid student. But it was more than that; unlike Louise, also a clone but with her original identity and assuredness intact, Toran acted as if he'd been born yesterday, unsure of who or what he was. It was as if he craved anything to make him feel like true flesh and blood, to make him feel like a real person, not something engineered in a lab. Ramires guessed that whereas Louise had kept topping up her clone's memory frequently until she needed it, Toran had been grown years after the loss of the original Gabriel. Added to that, the Alicians had interfered with his values and morals, disrupting the original personality construct. It wasn't Gabriel. Yet the way Toran moved and held both himself and the sword, Ramires had no doubt that the martial arts memories were mature and coherent.

Ramires picked up the sword, hefted it in his hand, gauged its weight, and then picked up the knife, holding it so the blade pointed behind, its sharpest edge down.

"I will teach you how to die. You should never have been brought into this world. You are a shadow, nothing more. You have no soul."

Toran dropped the staff and held onto the sword and dagger, mirroring Ramires.

"We shall see. But you forget how much I know, how many memories I have, things Sister Esma downloaded from the real Gabriel before he died. That gesture you just performed with that woman, it is the final goodbye of the Sentinel. It is you who will die, Ramires, you know it already. But not before you teach me your fighting secrets."

Ramires reflected a moment. Toran didn't know who 'that woman' was, what she had meant to the original Gabriel. It didn't matter. Clearing his mind, he held both weapons, making them extensions of his arms, and circled to the right, pointing the sword's blade at Toran's eyes so its length could not be gauged.

"Knowledge is not the same as skill, Toran. But either way, today I'll teach you how to die."

Ramires attacked.

Micah held a small ball in his right hand, one of Shiva's more gruesome devices. A surprise for Louise. He walked along the corridor, stepping over inert bodies of Alician guards – unconscious rather than dead, despite Vashta's recommendation. He paused at each intersection, ready for an attack, but none came. His resident had been feeding him telemetry from Ash's vision, relayed via the Hohash, until Louise had used a laser scalpel to blind him. Micah heard voices up ahead, and sped up.

As he rounded a corner, he was confronted by the sight of Ash inside a large lab, strapped to a chair, his eyes slit, black streaks down his face. He looked like a nightmarish clown. Sonja talked softly beside him. Two Alicians lay prone on the floor.

Micah didn't enter. His resident detected a shimmer in the air in front of him, just inside the chamber, and enhanced the image: humaniform mostly, except for one arm; female; advanced stealth camouflage. Micah tossed the ball towards the image.

Louise cried out as a silver net wrapped itself around her. Her stealth field stuttered then failed, and she came into full view, in black one-piece coveralls. Micah didn't move. He watched Louise struggle to break free of the mesh, her Q'Roth claw snapping uselessly at the tightening fibres. Micah wrested the pistol from her grip as some of the fibres slid across her face, sealing her lips and forcing her eyelids closed. She staggered forward a pace then froze, locked down, barely able to breathe, an ungainly statue.

Micah's resident reminded him that if he didn't stop the process, it would begin to cut into her flesh, then her bones, then her organs. It would dice her. He watched its progress a few seconds longer, recalling all his encounters with Louise, flashbacks that usually ended with many people dead, people Micah had cared for, had sworn to protect, until the first thin traces of blood etched across her forehead and hands, then he sent the command for it to halt; at least until Kat confirmed that the device linking Louise's survival to the fate of the captives had been deactivated. Then they would decide, though he had no doubt how Kat would vote; it was his own vote that was in question. Sandy had been right about him. It was difficult to kill someone in cold blood, no matter what they'd done. Despite that, he vowed to do it when the time came. She was too dangerous to stay alive.

Micah had thought many times of all the things he would say to Louise when he next saw her, when he fulfilled his promise to kill her, but he said nothing. Instead he walked past her to Ash and Sonja.

"I'm sorry it came to this, Ash." He placed a hand on Sonja's shoulder. "We'll fix him, don't worry." He sliced through Ash's restraints with the same bloodied laser scalpel Louise had used earlier.

Sonja drew aside to look at Micah's handiwork on Louise. "Don't worry, Micah. I'll describe every aspect of that bitch's death to him in intricate detail."

Ash sat up. "Thank you, but I have witnessed more than enough death. Micah, we are not out of this yet. I have a bad feeling."

"Vashta will patch you up, Ash, and then we'll get you some new eyes, human ones this time."

Micah smiled, and for the first time in a long while felt a lightness, that humanity had turned a corner, had won an important victory, shown the Alicians they had met their match.

Shiva tapped into Micah's resident. *We have an incoming enemy ship, Micah; we must move fast.* Micah glanced back at Louise, blood welling in a line across her brow, a single drop threading its way over silver threads down her cheek. Enemy ship? Shiva sounded concerned. It couldn't be Alician, or even Q'Roth, they were no match for Shiva; in fact no ship for light years around posed a threat. For an instant he went into denial. He was tempted to allow the mesh to resume its work on Louise, but at that moment Shiva supplied more information: *a Level Sixteen Nchkani warship is nearing the planet. It is far more powerful than I, Micah, and we have used our only gravitic weapon. I will be destroyed on detection. I am also sorry to inform you that it has already destroyed the space station we cut loose; there were no survivors. We have five minutes, Micah. Where are the captives?*

Micah was still trying to process the sudden turn of events, when Kat and Antonia dashed in, nearly knocking Louise over.

Kat regained her breath first. "It's deactivated, Micah, the captives are coming. You can kill her, and we can all get the hell out of here."

He raised his wristcom to his mouth. "Aramisk, bring the Rapier as quick as you can."

Micah weighed things up. He guessed why the Nchkani had arrived: the Spider. They had come for it, to take it back to Qorall. But he still didn't know where it was, and the Nchkani clearly meant business and would turn the planet inside out to find it. He stared at Louise; she knew its location.

His eyes met with Antonia's, knowing she belonged to Kat again. "It's really good to see you," he said. "You look well."

Antonia nodded, her face taut, as if something else had happened, something he needed to know. But now wasn't the time. Aramisk's shouts echoed down the corridor.

"Sonja," he said, "Get everyone to safety, including Ash. You too," he said to Kat and Antonia.

Kat stood her ground. "She's going, I'm staying till we locate the Spider." She held up both hands. "No arguments from either of you, there's no time. I met Qorall once, remember? If he gets the Spider, dead or alive, the war is lost."

While Kat and Antonia embraced one last time, Micah turned away and spoke to Aramisk and Shiva.

"Captives en route. Shiva, once they're aboard, get them out of the system; that's an order. We'll take care of the Spider."

He turned back to see Antonia departing. Micah stepped out into the corridor to watch them go, and to catch sight of someone. But she wasn't there. He came back in and walked up to Kat.

"Where's Sandy?" he asked. "And where's Ramires?"

Sandy watched from a distance, barely breathing. Ramires fought like a dervish, but each time he appeared to be about to kill the clone, the Gabriel doppelganger managed to escape by a hair's breadth.

Earlier she'd run to each of the cells holding the captives, carving out doors as quickly as she could, all the time hearing the clangs of sword on sword in the background. At one point it had stopped, and she almost crumbled, fearing the worst. But then the sound of wood striking wood reverberated down the corridor. She'd released the last of the captives, told them which way to go, then double-backed to her cell. The two swords, daggers and staves lay on the ground; it was down to hands, feet, elbows and knees. She didn't care if Micah left without her, didn't care if Louise's device released a toxin inside her head. She just wanted Ramires to survive. But it wasn't looking good. No human, even a Sentinel, could keep up this pace. But an Alician could. No doubt Sister Esma had been unable to resist upgrading the clone with a few adjustments.

Sandy hung back only out of fear of distracting her husband at some critical moment. He'd fight better if he believed her to be safe. She'd been biting her lip for some time, realised it was bleeding, and forced herself to stop. She glanced toward the nearest sword. Back on Earth she'd been a competitive fencer. If Ramires lost she could attack the clone… It probably wouldn't make much difference, she wouldn't last more than a second, but… for so long now she had allied herself to Ramires. He'd once told her that Sentinels almost never took wives, because usually they also died fighting Alicians. She edged closer.

She'd watched Ramires train the Genner Youngbloods often enough to know which way it was going, and her breathing became heavy. The clone had one hand around Ramires' throat. They were both on the floor, Ramires' face away from her. The clone was choking him, pinning him down in a wrestling grip. Ramires' legs thrashed around but the clone was well-anchored behind him. Ramires' one semi-free hand tried to reach backwards to the clone's face, but it was no use.

Sandy darted forwards, sprinting for the closest sword. Ramires' legs were slowing down, his free hand clawing at air. She snatched up the sword and flung herself forwards, raising the blade high as Ramires had trained her years ago, and brought it downwards, aiming to decapitate the clone.

But the clone moved with incredible speed, simultaneously dodging the cut and tugging Ramires throat into harm's way.

The blade sliced through Ramires' neck and thwacked into the stone floor and lodged there, a sound like a bell ringing loud in the air, before fading into silence.

The sword's hilt slid from Sandy's fingers as she knelt next to her dead husband, his blood soaking her knees and shins.

The clone got up.

"He was already defeated. You hastened his departure by a few seconds, nothing more." He walked off a few paces.

Sandy stared, unbelieving. Dead words escaped her mouth. "Kill me. Now."

The clone walked towards her, then knelt next to Ramires' corpse.

"He was an extraordinary fighter, like nothing I've ever encountered." He prised the sword from the stone floor and flung it away. "There is a Tibetan prayer for the fall of warriors. We must honour him, but my memory is not perfect on such things."

Sandy placed three unsteady fingers on Ramires' bloody, cooling brow, closed her eyes and began the chant, tears streaming down her cheeks.

The clone joined in as best he could.

———

Micah tried to contact Shiva for the tenth time, with no luck. He had to believe they had made it. In the last few minutes a loud, pulsing hum could be heard everywhere. He had no idea what it meant, only that it couldn't be good. Kat was head down, jade light reflecting off her brow as she interrogated the Alician main computer, trying to locate the Spider.

"Do you know anything of these Nchkani, Kat?"

Kat shook her head, and pointed without looking. "She might."

Micah turned to the locked-down figure of Louise. He closed his eyes a second and gave his resident the command to release the wires around her head, so she could speak.

Louise gasped for a few breaths. She wasn't facing Micah, but spoke as if he was in front of her. "Nasty toys you have these days, Micah. Release me and I'll tell you –"

"Tell me in the next five seconds or I'll silence you forever. Don't think I won't do it, Louise."

"What's in it for me, Micah?"

"I know you, Louise. You still believe you can somehow turn this situation around, get free, re-capture the hostages and kill me into the bargain."

"When did you become a telepath?"

"Kill her now, Micah," Kat said.

Louise raised her voice. "Nchkani, Level Sixteen, changed to Qorall's side exactly a week ago. Their warships are impregnable except against Tla Beth Grazers, Level Seventeen Goliath Class ships, none of which have been seen since the Anxorian rebellion fifty thousand years ago. Nchkani warships are known colloquially as Shredders; they have kilometre long spines protruding from their hulls. One of their ships can take down an entire planet in a matter of minutes."

Micah moved in front of her, so he could see her eyes, and watch for lies. "Where is the Spider? Is it alive?"

She looked at him directly, though her head was bent slightly toward the floor. "Four kilometres deeper than we are now, a shielded chamber. It's dead."

Kat joined Micah. She put three fingers under Louise's chin, a Mannekhi gesture Micah had heard about, and lifted Louise's neck back against the wires at the base of her head, razor-slicing the flesh there, making Louise blink and take in a sharp breath. Micah didn't intervene.

"Did you kill the Spider as easily as you did Tarish and the rest of the Mannekhi crew who had served you so well?" Kat's fingers weren't particularly steady.

"We tried to study it, I guess it knew what we were doing, and it just shut down, though not before it killed one of my aides. I thought they were supposed to be pacifist? Anyway, when we arrived here, as we exited Transpace, we found it was already dead; I'm a little hazy on the details." Her voice softened. "I had planned to save you, Kat. You know that, don't you?"

Micah stored the intel that a Spider had killed, for later. It seemed unlikely, but if true it was a positive development; the Spiders could finally join the war effort. Micah saw Kat ease off the pressure, then remove her fingers from Louise's chin. He didn't know what exactly had happened between Kat and Louise during the two years Louise had kept her prisoner on board the Q'Roth Marauder. He guessed it was complicated; he didn't want to know more, and he didn't want to judge. But the clock was ticking. He changed tack.

"How do we get out of this, Louise?"

Louise spat a drop of blood onto the floor. "Tricky. I knew Kalaran would send someone, because of the Spider. So I contacted Qorall as soon as I could, said I would bring it to him. Evidently he has other plans."

"We can't give them the Spider, there must be –"

"You don't get it, do you?" Louise shouted. "If we don't give them the Spider immediately, they'll destroy this planet, and they'll make us pay first. They believe in crushing an enemy's spirit, their entire culture, before annihilation. They will destroy our defence infrastructure from orbit, then they will send a single soldier down to tear us apart, piece by piece, after they flood these tunnels with fire. They will leave nothing: no memory, no DNA, not a single artefact. They eradicate their enemies from history, Micah, consigning them to oblivion. We *have* to give them the Spider."

He could tell she was sincere. "Not going to happen, Louise. Qorall gets the Spider, the Kalarash plan fails, and we lose the galaxy."

"Your opinion. Change sides, Micah, you'll see it differently. I'm serious, you set me free, and I'll tell them humanity helped. They'll leave you alone."

Micah laughed in disbelief. "You'll say anything, won't you?"

"Think about it, Micah, it's all you're good at, but that's okay because in this universe it's all that matters. Hellera won't be able to stop Qorall alone, and then –"

"Kalaran –"

"IS DEAD!" Spittle dripped from Louise's lips. "You don't even have good intel, do you? He's gone, Micah, and Hellera is on the run. You want to save humanity? You'd better think really fast, because one of Qorall's Orbs is on its way to Esperia. Either way, your species is joining Qorall."

It was a reflex. He told the resident to silence her, and the wires gripped her lips, forcing them closed. Micah's hands shook. Kat took one of them.

"Micah. She's telling the truth." Kat's voice was fragile, like he'd never heard her before. "I just deciphered an info flash sent to Louise two days ago. She's still one of Qorall's spies, it seems, and… Kalaran was killed in a battle with Qorall, and… Hellera has left Esperia."

Micah felt he was losing his grip, as if everything was suddenly spinning out of control. He yanked a chair towards him, sat down and gripped Kat's hands. "How, Kat? We… we were so close. How can he be dead?"

Kat crouched in front of Micah, the strength in her voice returning. "Micah, whatever we decide, we have to act quickly. What do you want me to do?"

He recalled his one and only meeting with Kalaran, who had said they would not meet again. Micah had assumed that was because he would not make it back from Savange. But perhaps Kalaran knew of his own imminent demise. And if he did, then there was still a slim chance. Micah clung to it, because the alternative was something he couldn't face. At least Hellera was still around. But if Qorall got the Spider… Kalaran had told him to prevent this at all costs. Micah could only see one way out. Blake wouldn't do it, Vince would have in a second, Ramires… probably not. But he reminded himself he needed to do whatever it took to save humanity, to step up to the task. He made his decision.

He stood, and gave the command to his resident. The wires began loosening from Louise.

"Micah, what are you doing?" Kat backed off from Louise, aiming a weapon at her. Micah turned to Kat, his back to Louise, and mouthed a single word. *Wait.*

"It's okay, Kat. Louise, you guarantee our safety?"

Louise staggered out of the bonds as they fell to the floor, rubbing her neck.

"Agreed."

"However, I don't trust you, as I'm sure you understand. So, the only way out of this is if I tell the Nchkani the location of the Spider."

Louise bristled, her claw raising until a wave of Kat's pistol made her lower it again.

"They are expecting to talk to me."

"They are expecting to receive the Spider, and they will find they have a new ally standing alongside you, an already-trusted one."

Louise eyed him. "I don't trust you either, Micah. Why the change of heart?"

"All the things you said. Kalaran told me it needed two Kalarash to take down Qorall. Hellera will desert us. I don't want to return to Esperia and find nothing but Qorall's golden minions. I just freed the captives, but why bother if there's nowhere for them to go?"

The sound of an explosion echoed down the corridor.

"Not very patient, your Nchkani friends, are they?"

Louise looked tenser than Micah had ever seen her, breathing fast.

"I want your word, Micah; you'll hand over the Spider."

Micah kept his gaze level. "You have it."

"Say it. I need to hear you say it."

He felt he'd passed the point of no return, and hoped he was doing the right thing, or at least the wrong thing for a good enough reason.

"I give you my word, Louise. I'll hand over the Spider to the Nchkani."

Louise turned to Kat, and spoke a nine-digit code. "Enter it and you'll find the location."

Kat handed Micah the pistol, which he kept trained on Louise.

"Found it," she said.

Micah ramped up the power rating to maximum on the pistol. It hummed.

Louise glared. "What are you doing?"

"Kat," Micah said, "Is there a failsafe bomb in the same location? I'm betting there is, in case anyone tried to steal the corpse."

"Yep. A small anti-matter device. Won't leave anything."

"Micah," Louise said, taking a step forward, "Don't do this. I know the Nchkani, they'll destroy my people, all of them. And for what? You *must* hand over the Spider. The war's already lost!"

Micah didn't take his eyes off Louise. "I have to believe it isn't. I'm sorry, Louise. I'm breaking my word, which I don't do lightly, but I already promised Kalaran. Kat, detonate the device."

Louise's eyes went wide. She screamed "NO!" and leapt forward towards Kat. Micah fired. Louise used her claw to take most of the pulse round's energy, and was thrown backwards against the far lab wall, next to an open hatch. The floor shuddered, a dull boom like a deep gong resonating until it was silent. Louise was on the floor, but conscious. Three sharp cracks announced more explosions topside.

"It's done," Kat said. She turned to Louise. "Finish her, Micah."

Micah stared at Louise, raised the pistol, his finger on the trigger.

"Kill her!" Kat shouted.

He took a breath, imagined Earth's charred corpse, a Q'Roth transport carrying two thousand humans flown into a sun, Hannah's head rolled onto the floor in front of him, Vince killed back on Esperia, Chahat-Me vaporised during the struggle on the ship during the attack only six weeks ago. He squeezed the trigger, felt a tiny recoil.

Electric blue arcs skittered around Louise, leaving her undamaged. She didn't blink.

"Shit, her shield is working again," Kat said.

Micah fired several more times, with the same result. Kat picked up the laser scalpel.

Louise struggled to her feet, weakened from the pulse strikes. "I have to go now, try to save my people. But I'll be back, for both of you. And like the Nchkani, I'll cause as much pain as possible before I eradicate humanity once and for all. On that, you have *my* word."

Kat advanced with the scalpel, but Louise ducked through the hatch and sealed it behind her. More explosions and the sound of weapons fire echoed down from the surface.

"What now?" Kat said, slumping back against the ledge of a table.

Micah couldn't believe he'd let her escape again. The repercussions could only be bad. But the autopsy of his leadership decisions would have to wait.

"We're not safe here. The Nchkani will send down soldiers or drones for sure. I'd rather take our chances topside."

They made their way along the corridor until they found an exit leading to a drop shaft, a tiny pinprick of sunlight way above them. After his lie to Louise, possibly sentencing Savange's population to death, he felt as if the surface way above him was who he'd been just minutes earlier, and now he had fallen far from the morals that had guided his entire life. He felt worse for it, though he couldn't see what alternative he could have taken. He'd destroyed the Spider – primary mission achieved – and most of the hostages had gotten away. He began climbing the ladder, wanting not only to escape, but to return to who he was, even if only for the short time he had left.

Micah wondered if, by destroying the Spider, Kalaran's plan – whatever it was – was still salvageable by Hellera. Logically, the planet Savange, including him, Kat and Louise, would be destroyed by the Nchkani, but the escapees still had a fighting chance if they could make it back to Esperia. He hoped Ramires and Sandy had escaped and found Aramisk; he didn't want to think about losing anyone else. Yet he had a gnawing hunch that Louise would somehow survive, and do her utmost to make good on her promise to make him and mankind pay.

Chapter 18
PREPARATIONS

Defence was going to be a nightmare. Petra, dwarfed by Vasquez, Kilaney and Brandt, surveyed the holo of the terrain surrounding Esperantia and Shimsha. It stretched far beyond the Acarian mountain range, all the way to Lake Takamaka, two hundred kilometres distant, and included the tiny outlying settlements currently being evacuated. The residents there had not wanted to move, but the quartet leading the defence had all agreed they could not defend such a wide area. A few of the residents had refused, and so remained, or had fled to the caves. Petra already considered them lost. She nudged a control and the holo zoomed in to focus on a zone with a five-kilometre radius.

"General, walk us through the aerial defences again." They'd been through it three times already with nothing new emerging, but she was evaluating her chiefs of staff, looking for cracks that could splinter her leaders at crucial moments when the attack came.

Kilaney looked weary, a heaviness around his chest and shoulders, the way he leant on the table for support, eyes hooded; he was holding himself together with brute force of will. But this man had will by the bucket-load. Part of his fatigue was no doubt due to Blake's condition, unchanged since the experiment. It made it worse for Kilaney to know that the real Blake was trapped inside, screaming to get out. As for the general's genocidal choice back on the Zlarasi homeworld, she guessed that was a burden that would never leave him.

But he was a born commander, and knew how to channel every emotion into cold professional logic. She interrupted him.

"At what point will you give up on the aerial defence and join the ground battle?"

The others all looked at her. She was implying they would lose. If it came to a ground assault, the invading hordes would be unstoppable.

Kilaney smiled. "Back on Earth, Petra, I'd have recruited and groomed you to replace me. You're right, of course. There will come a decision point when I'll have to either order my men to run suicide attacks on the inbound vessels until we are no more, or enter the atmosphere and strafe as many as we can until we are shot down."

Petra stared at the image of Esperantia, her home her entire life.

"At what point will you land, General?"

Kilaney moved back a pace and sat down heavily in a cushioned chair. He gazed at the map of the town, and pointed, speaking in a low voice. "If I am not dead, and my ships are of no more use in space or above ground, and the invaders have breached the outer perimeter, and if you give me no further order, I will land and stand next to Blake, and I will make sure they do not take him alive."

Silence hung in the room after those tombstone words. This was what Petra had wanted. To know the absolute truth, where their devotions lay. "Good. That is what I was hoping you would say."

Kilaney looked up at her, studied her a moment, then got up again, and continued detailing his battle strategy with more vigour in his voice.

The rest ran smoothly. Vasquez would have men and automated defences in the mountains and outlying terrain, Brandt's Youngbloods would patrol the outer perimeter and the town itself. At Council, she had been outvoted on the idea of self-annihilation rather than being absorbed into Qorall's ranks. She had to admit that knowing Blake was somehow still alive on the inside had weakened her position. Maybe even if they were all converted, if Hellera, against the odds, defeated Qorall, they could be restored. But that felt like clutching at straws. She carried a vial of fast-acting poison in her pocket, as did

Kilaney and Vasquez, and a number of others. Freedom of choice for individuals, in case they were overwhelmed.

A single ship had almost left Esperia to flee the system. But few had signed up for it, and in the end it had been too late, the enemy already inbound, nearing the system. Any humans on a refugee ship would be picked up early, and become part of the invading force. All of them were in this together now. She'd expected recriminations, anger at her for not organising something earlier. But people understood. While Hellera had been in orbit, they'd seemed protected here. Her unannounced departure had changed the game, with little time to react. Petra berated herself for not seeing that one coming, but for now she had to focus. It helped that everyone seemed determined to fight, and she knew why.

When Earth had fallen, it had come as a surprise attack, most people not even grasping what was going on until it was too late. This time, if nothing else, they could prepare, and put up a fight, even if futile. And Genners like her, born on Esperia, also wanted to fight, carrying the scars of the previous generation in their hearts. They were angry, a new breed of humanity whose chance at life was about to be snatched away from them. But Genners channelled their emotions as Kilaney did. She knew they would all fight and die well.

They were done, and Kilaney and Vasquez left to go over the fine details, countless contingencies, and final preparations with their lieutenants. Brandt stayed behind. During the meeting he had stood upright, like the Genner warrior he was, second only to Gabriel. She knew Brandt had feelings for her, and like all Genners he was under-equipped to deal with or even express them. Now the others were gone, his posture was hunched over, accentuated by his size. He somehow looked like a giant child, who knew he couldn't have what he wanted. She reminded herself they were all still so young, she just eighteen, Brandt sixteen. For Genners, that meant the intellectual equivalent of a forty-year-old professor at his peak. Emotionally, though… that was a different story. Still, she did not want to lose her focus. Eventually he broke the silence.

"The Youngbloods are ready."

She nodded. Part of her wanted to dismiss him, before he could say more. But another part held her tongue. She thought about Gabriel, how long she'd loved him from afar, unable to tell him how she'd felt, not until the very end. So she understood this particular pain. Brandt seemed to read her mind.

"What did you say to him, Petra, at the end? Did he know?"

Now she wished she'd dismissed him. "Not fair, Brandt. Anyway, I said nothing, Micah spoke."

Brandt was very still, unlike his usual boisterous self. He looked her in the eye.

"What did he do when he realised how you felt about him?"

She looked away, remembering how Gabriel had held her on the disintegrating ship, embraced her, and kissed her while she wept like a little girl. Most nights she fell asleep thinking about those moments. "That's between us."

"Of course." Brandt got up, and headed for the door.

"Brandt, I need to know I can rely on you. Are we okay?"

He opened the door, and stood framed there, blocking most of the daylight, his back to her.

"Yes, Madam President."

She watched the door close with a soft click. Petra thought she'd feel relief, but instead, those words stung. *Dammit!* She got up to go after him. Midway to the door, the radio crackled into life.

"Petra, it's Bill. Xenic is here. You'd better come."

"I'm on my way." She rushed outside, her eyes sweeping the area for Brandt, but he was gone.

Petra didn't know Xenic well. He was a Mannekhi commander Kilaney had teamed up with during Sister Esma's attack on Esperia. He was tall, not an ounce of fat on his tanned body, with all-black eyes, a zero-nonsense manner. Xenic looked as if he'd come out of his mother's womb issuing orders.

"The enemy is inbound," he said, after a cursory nod of introduction. "No Orb this time, because of the Shrell wires, but fifty enemy ships are about to transit to this system. The black Orb was a decoy to give you a false sense of how much time you had; it has already attacked another system."

Petra didn't yet trust the Mannekhi; until a month ago they had all been working for Qorall.

"How did you get here without us detecting you?"

"Mannekhi can navigate through Shrell-fields. We also recently acquired Level Eight stealth-tech from an evacuating race."

"Evidently it works." It came out more aggressively than she'd intended.

Kilaney held up a hand. "Petra – Madam President – you need to hear him out."

Petra pulled up a chair and sat in it. "Please, Commander Xenic, you've come a long way. Tell me."

"The Mannekhi homeworlds – all twelve of them – were recently hit by Orbs in an unprecedented coordinated attack. It seems Qorall learned we had changed sides, and lost no time in absorbing us into his obedient ranks."

It was as she and Kilaney had feared. She stared into those black pits of eyes. "Then the fifty ships inbound are –"

"Mannekhi. Ten thousand soldiers, all gold."

"The Shrell field. It won't stop them, will it?"

Xenic shook his head.

Petra looked to both men. "I'm open to options, gentlemen."

Kilaney and Xenic exchanged a glance.

"There is one tactic that might help," Xenic said. "Mannekhi smugglers, when being chased by police vessels would use unorthodox tactics to nudge the ships giving chase into the wires, disabling them. I can show Kilaney how to do this. Together we can stop ten of their ships getting through."

"Leaving only eight thousand troops, any one of whom can turn us." Petra didn't bother to rinse the bitterness from her words.

"I can leave if you prefer," Xenic said.

She gazed up at him again. "I'm sorry, commander." She stood up. "Did any of your people escape the Orbs?"

"Some ships, here and there. Not many, and not nearly enough."

"Please don't take this the wrong way; I'm glad you came. But why *did* you come here? You could be trying to find surviving Mannekhi vessels, or joining other allies."

Xenic turned to Kilaney, and placed a hand on his shoulder. "In the last battle in this system, we learned that Mannekhi and humans have an ancestral link. You are as precious to us as our own kind, though I don't expect you to understand. Strategically you are important. Qorall's latest offensive is marshalling significant resources to take Esperia. There are battles going on in a hundred systems right now, but this is the one that matters."

Petra smiled. "We should feel flattered." Her smile faded. "But the truth is, we don't stand a chance, do we?"

Xenic laughed, causing Petra to frown.

"We have two sayings – had two sayings – back on Mannekhi Prime. The first is that the only certainty in battle is uncertainty."

Petra waited. "And the second?"

Xenic grew serious. "When you are convinced you will lose, the gods will desert you."

Petra nodded. "Understood. I will leave you two to make preparations. How long do we have?"

"They will be here tomorrow, by noon."

"Then I wish us all the luck your gods can spare."

Xenic tilted his head slightly. "Wait." He walked up to her and placed his fingers under her chin. Her mother Kat had told her of this gesture, and she knew she had to stay quiet and listen.

"Mannekhi eyes see more than human ones, and I read people. You have something eating away inside you. Make peace with your soul tonight."

She made to speak but he lifted his fingers, and shook his head.

"I am telling you, one commander to another. You need to be diamond clear tomorrow. My men, Kilaney's men, and everyone else need you to be one hundred per cent focused. Do you understand me? Whatever it is, fix it."

He removed his hand. Petra felt her cheeks flush, but Xenic had already turned away and called up a holo of the Shrell field, pointing out particular junctures to Kilaney, who glanced at her once or twice but said nothing. She left the Rapier, and marched back towards her office near the Dome. The light was beginning to fade.

Vasquez met her halfway, driving a skimmer.

"You'd better get aboard," he said.

Petra didn't conceal mounting frustration. "What now?"

Vasquez' face, with its cheekbones that normally looked as if they'd been chiselled out of marble, softened. "Would 'please' or 'Madam President' help?"

She climbed aboard, sitting behind him. He accelerated so fast she had to put her arms around him. He sped towards Hazzards Ridge, hit the incline and rocketed up the slope. Above the rushing wind, she heard two ships lifting off; Kilaney's and Xenic's. She had no idea what could be so urgent up here, but as they reached the crest, she saw. He slewed the skimmer to a halt, and she leapt off, unable to believe her eyes.

"The Spiders are leaving."

Vasquez passed her a viewer, but with her Genner eyesight she didn't need it. Small ellipsoids, like flattened pearls, were rising from Shimsha, piercing the shield and zipping straight up into the sky.

"Where the hell did they get those ships? They have barely any technology."

"Kalaran, most likely," Vasquez said.

It was dusk, and Petra lifted the viewer to her eyes. "They're not all leaving," she said, lowering the viewer. "Some are headed this way."

As she'd expected, Kilaney called in. "Petra, are you seeing this?"

"Unfortunately I am. Vasquez is with me. Most are airborne but a small group appears to be staying here. Make me happy, Bill. Tell me these ships are going to join you in defending Esperia."

"No such luck. They're heading clean out of the system, zig-zagging through the Shrell field like nothing Xenic has ever seen, accelerating all the way. They're gone, Petra."

And not coming back. She spoke to Vasquez, while watching the small procession of Spiders wind their way up the hill. "Ironic, isn't it? Qorall is coming here for the Spiders, and they'll be long gone by morning. Any chance the recoded Mannekhi will leave us be?"

But she guessed the answer.

Petra and Vasquez waited for the Spiders. There were fifteen of them. Four at the back steered two broad levi-panels stacked with short, stubby cylinders. She wondered what they were for, they looked oddly familiar. Then she remembered. They'd been at the top of the new towers surrounding the Spider city. She glanced back toward deserted Shimsha.

"The shield is down," she said.

Vasquez took another look. It was nearly dark. "I guess they don't need it anymore, they seem to be abandoning their home. Unless…"

But Petra had already set off down the hill to meet the Spiders. At last, some good news.

It took several hours to set up the shield emitters, get everyone inside Esperantia, and power up the shield. For the first time in weeks, Petra was cautiously optimistic. Vasquez was busy trying to find the Spiders somewhere to spend the night, what was left of it.

She wandered the streets a while. Xenic's rebuke played heavily on her mind. *Whatever it is, fix it*, he'd said. Most lights were still on. Few could sleep knowing what the morning would bring. She found herself in the Genner part of town, in the street where Brandt lived. She walked up and down it a few times, then approached his door. She lifted her hand, made a loose fist, then knocked gently, half hoping for no reply, or to hear another female voice inside mixed with Brandt's, laughing or worse. Instead she heard his heavy footsteps. He opened the door, saw her, and opened it wider, inviting her in. Petra looked down at her feet, poised at the threshold of the doorway in front of her. She took a breath, and stepped across it.

Chapter 19
RESURRECTION

He awoke, not knowing who he was, where he was, or how he had come there. He couldn't move or feel any part of his body. All he could do was see, and remember. He had killed someone.

"She deserved to die."

The woman's voice was cold, synthetic, like a discordant choir. But she was beautiful, tawny hair cascading over tanned shoulders, sitting in a high-backed metal chair like a throne. They were outside, on an emerald sea whose ripples faded as it stretched in all directions towards a blue horizon. The legs of the throne made dimples in the water, but it didn't sink. Her toes dipped into the emerald fluid but no drops clung to them; not water then. Two suns hung in the sky, the higher one blood red, the smaller one purple. But the light was white and grainy, like twilight, so they weren't suns. Nothing was as it should be. He turned his attention back towards her, and realised she was naked, her knees slightly apart. He looked away.

"Ah, I forgot."

She was suddenly clothed, a pale blue wrap barely disguising the contours of her body.

"Better?"

He knew the body before him intimately. His mate, his lover. But he could not remember her name. The persona was all wrong. This was not his mate, this was someone else. Something else.

"She died in battle. So did you. But your memories were salvaged. Most of them. Perhaps not those that mattered to you most. We are having this discussion to see how much you remember. If there is enough, I will reconstruct you. If not…" She shrugged.

His mind flooded with an urgent jumble of images and facts at the ready, his survival instinct strong. But then he stopped this information avalanche, as if pressing 'pause' on a vid. He knew he should be afraid of the implied threat, but he realised he cared less about his own survival than his dignity. He would not be intimidated. His mind emptied, then filled again, this time brimming with questions, one overriding all others. *Who am I?*

"Later. I respect your lack of fear. That alone may make you worth saving."

He knew he should feel anger at her complete power over him, but something about being disembodied was affecting him.

"Correct. You have no organs at present, no flesh, no hormonal systems. You are not visceral, so you are more detached." She cocked her head. "Your mind is clearer than it has ever been. Would you like to remain this way?"

He recoiled from the idea.

"I didn't think so."

He wondered if he was being 'stored' in some kind of computer.

She laughed. It was a grating noise, as if she was out of practice, or didn't know how it was really done. "Nothing so primitive. Here."

A gold-rimmed oval mirror approached across the wavelets, taking up position a few metres to the right of her throne. A Hohash. He'd been with one just before he'd died, before he'd killed and been killed. Who was his interrogator, then?

"Hellera."

The name meant nothing to him.

"I am the same species as Kalaran."

There was something off about the way she said 'Kalaran', an emotion he couldn't discern, but at least he recognised the name. One of the Kalarash, allegedly the most intelligent and powerful beings in the galaxy. They owned the Hohash. He remembered something else: Kalaran was at war with Qorall, the invader ravaging the galaxy, whose armies would soon reach Esperia, where the last human survivors lived.

"Kalaran asked me to resurrect you, but I haven't decided yet. If you are too incomplete, you will be of no help to anyone, a burden even to yourself."

He sensed a callousness about her, an indifference to killing. But his memories were degraded. He tried to recall the people he had grown up with, but it was like seeing a crowd from a distance; he couldn't make out their faces.

"How did your people arrive on Esperia?"

Her voice was sharper; the real test had begun. He recalled his lessons. It had started with the Alicians, a human tribe in the Himalayas who met visitors from another world – the Q'Roth – back in the eleventh century. They agreed to prepare humanity for culling over the next thousand years while the Q'Roth hibernated. Another group – the Sentinels, learned of this pact and tried to stop them, but failed. Then it all came to a head, Earth and Eden were lost, except for twelve thousand refugees who escaped to the planet Esperia, where they'd been protected by a quarantine while all human children – including himself, he remembered – underwent genetic advancement. He was a Genner.

"Factual memory usually fares best. Recent events now."

That was like trying to see through smoke. He had taken control of a ship, an Ossyrian pyramid vessel. The Alicians – they had come to Esperia to finish the job they had started, waiting for the quarantine barrier to come down. He'd tried to launch a pre-emptive strike. It had all gone badly wrong. Images reared up in his mind of dead Ossyrians and fellow Genners scattered across the battered ship's floor. He'd screwed up badly.

"Don't be too hard on yourself. If you had not acted Esperia would have been lost, Kalaran's secret along with it."

Secret? Ah yes, the human population wasn't alone on Esperia. The Spiders. Nobody really knew anything about them, except they mattered to Kalaran a great deal.

"Now, enough of your history. What do you know of ours?"

He stared, his mind blank. Almost nothing. Then he recalled a school lesson. Two billion years ago, the Kalarash had welcomed Qorall into their territory – the Jannahi galaxy – but Qorall had risen up against the Kalarash. A war had ensued, and as the Kalarash were about to win it, Qorall unleashed a terrible weapon, one that destroyed the galaxy itself. The Kalarash, all seven of them, fled to this galaxy, believing Qorall dead.

She let her head fall back, laughing again, doing a better job of it this time. Watching her, he recalled the name of the girl he had loved – Virginia. He wished he could somehow give his life to bring her back. The laughing ceased.

"No," she said, her voice cold steel. "Not possible."

He felt – organs or no organs – a deep well of sadness. He stared at the floor.

Her voice softened. "Kalaran's little lie."

That got his attention. The legend of the battle with Qorall was known by every race in the Grid. It was a lie?

She stood, then paced a little, tracing a small circle around the throne, hands clasped behind her back. "After all this time, perhaps someone should know the truth." She returned to her throne and sat down, once again facing him.

"We Kalarash number seven. We cannot procreate. We took Qorall in because he was Level Eighteen, the last of his kind, bordering on becoming Level Nineteen."

He understood. They had adopted him. But that meant…

"Qorall for us was… well, you would say 'a breath of fresh air'. We were on the verge of becoming obsolescent. He gave us new hope, our little project, and for the first time in aeons it bound us together again. And then he did something remarkable."

He waited, but he had a suspicion.

"Yes. He learned how to procreate, to make others of his kind." She looked away. "But he needed our help. In particular, he needed mine."

The skin on her face grew taut, and he understood. Hellera was female, whatever that meant in Level Nineteen terms.

She nodded, staring into the emerald depths at her feet. "Kalaran and the others didn't like the plan." She laughed, for the first time sounding right, but tinged with regret. "I considered it, but we were a democracy back then, and I was out-voted. They banished him, or tried to." She stared back at him again. "Qorall – there was a viciousness to his character we'd never perceived. His rage erupted in a war against us, the likes of which no being had ever imagined… and he was winning."

She stood. "Qorall didn't destroy the Jannahi galaxy. We did."

The Hohash moved closer to her, its silver mirror surface darkening to show an image. Seven ships shaped like elongated crossbows, each one a pair of rippling colours; sleek and beautiful, hurtled through space, leaving behind them a swirl of stars around a pure white central ball.

He heard a plaintive voice – Hellera's, he realised – from one of the ships. "We cannot do this!"

A choir of voices from the others: harsh, definitive. "We must."

In the image, Hellera did not reply.

Glancing briefly away from the Hohash, he saw the present-day Hellera facing away from him and the record of the past.

He turned back to the history lesson. The central core of what he guessed was the Jannahi galaxy began to shrink as the seven ships vanished into the inter-galactic void. As the white hot ball shrank it turned red, then grey, then black.

The view shifted so he was 'above' the galactic centre, which continued to shrink. He could almost feel the unimaginable power building. It seemed to disappear, and for a second he hoped… But then stars closest to the centre began to flash and wink out, and a radial wave swept outwards, extinguishing the galaxy from inside out. When it was done – he had the impression it had been speeded up for him – he witnessed the remains: ash, space dust, unrecognisable shreds of scorched tech and debris floating in space. Nothing left alive.

"So we thought," Hellera said, turning back to face him.

His mind freefell as the enormity of it sank in. Qorall's lust for revenge was in some ways a just cause. Qorall could have come all this way to exact revenge on Kalaran, and that would be more than understandable. But Level Nineteen beings were ultra-advanced, and it was just as likely Qorall had come here for another reason: Hellera. To breed. But if Hellera could fashion a human clone…

"It is not so simple with higher Levels, and almost impossible above Level Fourteen. But Qorall originated from a galaxy where understanding of organic science far exceeded our own, and he found a way. Still, he needs a specimen. He would kill me afterwards, of course; in fact he does not even need me alive to procreate, just a sufficient sample of my DNA. Unlike all the other Kalarash, except Darkur, I never fully merged with my ship. I am Qorall's best chance."

She folded her arms. "Then, he will hunt down the other five Kalarash, erasing their galaxies, too. Make no mistake, he will leave nothing of your precious Milky Way other than space dust, because higher Level species exist here in abundance, as in all galaxies the Kalarash have fostered. In the end Qorall will tolerate nothing above Level Six, because even if turned by him, they may one day rebel."

She circled the throne. Her hand briefly caressed the top of the Hohash.

"He will take his children to new galaxies where sentient life has not yet begun, or is in the fallow stage after the collapse of space-faring civilisations, and he and his progeny will expand his empire across the universe. With us gone, he will have time."

She sat again. "What we did may have been wrong, but we are Progenitors. We Kalarash breathe life into galaxies, cultivate civilisations and encourage species advancement to higher levels. Qorall will exterminate such species, and create followers who will be devoted to him and his children. He will build a homogenous universe, where he and his kind are so far beyond other species that they will be treated as Gods. They will be unassailable." She gazed toward the horizon. "Perhaps this is why even universes have a limited time-span."

He is what you made him.

Her eyes flared. "Careful!"

Why are you telling me all this?

She touched the throne and it vanished. "I have decided you are worth reconstruction. There is a task you must fulfil. I have embedded it in your subconscious. When you are in the right situation, it will override everything else and you will execute it. Although it may interfere with the plans of the humans, it is imperative that you carry out this mission, no matter who gets in your way. You will remember all we have discussed, except where it concerns this hidden task."

My name?

"It will be the first word you will hear upon awakening." She vanished.

The two suns turned grey, and the sea became absolutely flat calm. The Hohash faced him. He studied his reflection: he knew his body, but still could not recall his name.

As the sky around him turned to night, he tried to hang on to the memory that he harboured a hidden task. But he grew sleepy, knowing that when he awoke it would be gone.

Chapter 20
MASSACRE

Micah recalled the adage 'be careful what you wish for.' The Nchkani were attacking Savange, perhaps from their ship in orbit, perhaps via ground troops, he didn't yet know. The air above him in the drop shaft brimmed with sounds from outside: explosions, buildings collapsing, energy-beam fire, and Alician shouts, cries and screams. He and Kat reached the top and found themselves halfway up one of the seven hills surrounding Savange City. Micah scanned the area but there was no sign of the Rapier carrying Aramisk and the freed captives. For now he took that as a good sign.

"We'd best stay here, Micah, at least for now."

It was hard not to agree. Citizens of Savange were scurrying about the city, a large number heading to the West. At first he couldn't see why, then he noticed the black and white crab-like vehicle making its way down a main street. His resident zoomed in, so he could count the eight legs and see the turret at the top, spinning and unleashing fire in all directions. The Alicians tried to stop the crab with all manner of beam and projectile weapons, but it was shielded, and ploughed through manned Alician barricades like an armoured tank crushing sticks and ants. Occasionally, one of its legs lifted and fired at the base of one of Savange's many towers, sending a white hot wave up its length, leaving a charred structure in its wake with liquefied glass dripping down like rain. Micah glimpsed cremated corpses through some of the gouged windows.

Five craft Micah didn't recognise lifted off from the Western side of the city and headed to meet the Nchkani crab. They banked skilfully around the towers left standing then deluged the crab with high energy plasma beams. Undamaged, it let loose fireflies that tracked down the airborne craft, no matter their avoidance manoeuvres, and blasted them into glowing embers of ash as soon as they made contact. Micah noticed a single male spring up from a heap of corpses in the crab's wake and run towards it, holding a ball in both hands. Others attacked from the front, aiming to distract it, and were mercilessly cut down. The male reached the trailing legs and leapt up to the turret, banging down the ball on its cover.

The whole city was drenched in blinding white light, making Kat cry out and reel away, an elbow across her eyes. Micah's nannites instantly applied filters, protecting his retinas. A cylinder of light projected skywards. He reckoned it was some kind of channelled fusion device, as nearby buildings melted and crumbled, and people burst into flame. Six seconds later crackling thunder, accompanied by a blast of scorching heat, swept through the air for several seconds, before dissipating, leaving a ringing in Micah's ears.

The crab was motionless but intact, a heat haze shimmering all around it. The surrounding ground had sunk into a crater, and a new wave of Alicians ran towards the pit, some with wide hoses. They doused the crab with a glistening liquid.

Kat groped for his arm. "Micah, I can't see!"

He took her hand. "You're flash-blinded, it will pass in a few minutes." He recalled the aerial detonations over LA that left many flash-blind, unable to run from the shockwave that incinerated them. He recalled the last days of Earth, how quickly the Q'Roth overran the entire planet. Defensive nukes launched by desperate governments probably did more harm than good, but at least they tried.

"What's happening?"

He told Kat, relating the Alicians' actions. He presumed the liquid was some kind of crystalline polymer; they were trying to vitrify the crab in solid glass, probably liquid diamond. He almost hoped it would work, but he kept remembering how the Alicians contributed to Earth's demise, disabling its defences as the Q'Roth vessels appeared, even sending people to Eden for the first Q'Roth feed.

Turning to the West part of the city again, he saw children – precious few of them due to the Plight rendering most Alicians sterile – shepherded into rapid ground transports. His gaze caught on one particular figure, and again his resident zoomed in. It was Louise, overseeing the evacuation. He was surprised, he thought she'd be leading the defence, or even running to save her own skin. He unslung the rifle, and brought her into his sights. It was a difficult shot, but he could make it. But others kept running past in front of her, and several times she picked up children to put them into the transport herself. He waited, finger on the trigger.

"What's happening, Micah? Why have you gone quiet?"

"Louise," he said. "But I don't have a clean shot."

Through the targetter he saw Louise suddenly look to the East, just as he heard a massive explosion that spat fragments high into the sky. "Shit," he said, as his resident auto-tracked shrapnel headed his way. He dropped the rifle and pulled Kat towards him.

"Trust me," he said.

She clung to him, eyes scrunched closed. "Like I have a choice!"

A tumbling clump of jagged metal was falling towards them, but it was difficult to judge its size and final impact trajectory. In the last two seconds his resident worked it out and told him to dive left. He picked up Kat and threw them both sideways as the metal meteorite slammed into the earth, showering them with soil, and bouncing them off the ground. He landed on top of Kat in order to protect her, and rolled off, spitting out dirt and wiping it from his eyes.

"Thanks Micah, I think."

He sat up and looked to where the rifle should have been, but it was buried under a mass of twisted girders.

"I can see now," Kat said. "Where is she?"

Micah scanned the area where Louise had been, but there was no sign of her. He saw two dust trails heading to the West, but he couldn't see Louise.

"There!"

Micah followed Kat's pointing arm and saw Louise sprinting with a half-dozen Alicians to the base of one of the large defence towers cut in half by the Nchkani warship beams in the first seconds of the assault.

"What's she up to?" Kat asked.

A good question. Micah tracked east and saw that, as he'd expected, the crab had survived the fusion bomb and escaped its glass casket, and was on the move again. Fully half the city had been reduced to smoking ruins. No one was putting up a defence anymore. The crab killed anyone in its path.

"I hope you're not feeling sorry for them, Micah. It's rough justice, I know, just remember what they did to Earth. Seven billion dead; don't forget that for one second."

Micah wondered what the opposite of a conscience was. He wanted to ask all Earth's dead if they were enjoying watching this. He wasn't. If this was justice, it tasted bitter. But he knew he shouldn't be distracted by it, and he couldn't help them anyway. The Nchkani were clearly going to exterminate the Alicians. Micah decided he'd seen enough.

"We have to get moving, try and rendezvous with the others."

But Kat didn't budge, instead gazing to the West. "Micah, what was in those two transports?"

"Chil–" The breath went out of him. Two plumes of smoke and fire billowed from the vehicles. The Nchkani ship in orbit must have targeted them. His resident zoomed in for a second, before he asked it to zoom back out. There could be no survivors.

"Bloody hell! Now even I'm sorry, Micah."

He scanned the broken tower and found several figures half way up, staring out. Louise was one of them. She darted back inside.

He and Kat spent twenty minutes on the high ground, occasionally glancing down to the ongoing demolition of Savange, its surviving inhabitants pouring from its main gates and fanning out, presumably to offer too many targets to the orbital enemy. Yet they weren't in panic, instead moving methodically, helping each other. Micah respected them for that.

When he turned to see the crab, he stopped dead. Kat followed his gaze. Louise was standing in its path, holding some kind of bulky rifle. His resident identified it, and he told Kat. "Anxorian; Level Sixteen."

"I thought the Anxorians were extinct? Qorall must have given it to her."

Louise hefted it onto her shoulder, then fired a jet of mustard-coloured liquid at the advancing Crab. It stopped dead in its tracks. Nothing happened for ten seconds. Then its armour began to melt: the turret collapsed first, then the legs dissolved into muddy puddles. Soon the entire vehicle was reduced to mush dripping off the single Nchkani occupant, who floundered amongst the steaming residue. Louise raised an arm then dropped it. Out of the ruins men and women emerged with weapons ranging from pulse rifles to spears and knives. They fell upon the creature and butchered it. A long, ululating cry rang out across the city, echoed by all who heard it, until it reached the exterior, and those fleeing the city stopped and turned. Micah asked his resident to count the survivors. Savange had had a population of eight thousand. His resident counted two hundred and eighty-four.

Micah gazed upwards, waiting for the Nchkani response, which could well be planetary obliteration.

"Well, it's been nice knowing you, Micah," Kat said.

He braved a smile, then they waited for the killing blow to fall upon Savange. But it didn't come. Instead, a small, boxy craft descended, no noise whatsoever, until it hovered above the Nchkani carcass. Metal claws unfurled from its underside and scooped up the remains, forcing several Alicians to leap out of the way. Once collected, the ship rose into the clouds. Micah had the sense that everyone left alive was holding their breath, but the final strike still refused to come.

Aramisk contacted Micah via his wristcom. "Micah, there's been a development."

He almost laughed; a development. The city was decimated. "Where are you, Aramisk? Did you make it to Shiva?"

"Not yet."

Her voice sounded tense, but then, to Micah, she always sounded that way.

"We're hiding in a dormant volcano about a thousand klicks south of your position, but we've been watching everything via the remote cams Shiva sent out before the rescue. I'm in touch with Shiva, and she's intercepted a message from the Nchkani. They sent it broad spectrum, but I doubt the Alicians can translate it."

"What's the message?"

"The Nchkani want the weapon, the one the woman just used to kill a Nchkani soldier."

"It's just one rifle."

"You're missing the point. This is about technology. The Nchkani were Level Fifteen, the Anxorians were the Nchkani's patrons; quite good ones apparently. When the Anxorians were eradicated by the Tla Beth, there was almost nothing left of their culture, their science, or their weaponry, which rivalled the Tla Beth's own. With the rifle, the Nchkani could reverse engineer a whole arsenal, updating their capability at a pivotal moment in the war."

Micah didn't like where this was headed. "Why don't they just take it by force?"

"It has a self-destruct, a nasty one. The woman seems to know her way around it."

"And if the woman – Louise – gives it up?"

"They'll leave. They've already determined the Spider has been destroyed, and they've laid waste to the place and decimated the population. But they'll have to destroy the planet, Qorall would be angry with them otherwise; in his mind the Alicians screwed up by allowing the Spider to be destroyed. A planet-killer is already implanted underneath Savange's crust. However, they can set a delay on it."

"Otherwise?"

"Shiva might escape. The rest of us..."

Kat kicked a small rock, sent it tumbling down the shaft. "A bloody rifle. Unbefuckinglievable."

Micah reflected. The Alicians had paid a heavy price today. He looked upwards, trying to see any sign of the warship, but there was none.

"Aramisk, contact the Alicians. Tell them I'm coming down to sue for their surrender."

Kat folded her arms. "You're going to talk to that bitch again, aren't you?"

"Stay here, Kat, no point…"

But Kat had already moved in front of him and started scrambling down the escarpment towards what was left of the city.

Micah and Kat walked through the rubble, the only sound their footsteps and the creaking of metal still under heat stress, and every now and again a crash as yet another tortured building collapsed. He coughed once or twice, acrid fumes mixed with dust lacing the air. Alicians lined their path, creating a corridor that closed behind them. As they approached, he couldn't help notice that Louise looked like hell. But there was something else. In all the time he'd known her, she'd never cared for anyone else, except maybe Vince. Nothing fazed her emotionally. This time, however, she seemed devastated by what had happened, her manner less confident. But he'd learned not to trust anything about Louise.

She gave Micah a long hard stare. The rifle hung from her human hand. "Give me one good reason to believe all this."

Aramisk had relayed everything to Louise.

"How about two hundred and eighty reasons?"

"We'll die out soon enough. The children are dead. We can't have more."

"Alicians live for centuries. That's a long time to find a solution."

"There's nowhere for us to go. Besides, your fancy little ship will shoot us down as soon as the Nchkani are gone and we try to escape." She took a step forward. "That's what I'd do, Micah."

"We won't. I give you my…" He stopped himself.

"Exactly." She hefted the rifle.

Another voice cut in. "You have *my* word, Louise."

Micah turned around. It was Ash, being led by Sonja through the rubble. He stumbled, nearly fell over, but Sonja caught him, and he carried on walking.

"Ash," Micah began, "let me –"

"No, Micah. Let me." The Alicians moved aside as Sonja steered him in front of Louise, within reach of her claw.

"I'm listening," Louise said.

"I will come with you," Ash said. "Micah will not fire on your vessel with me aboard."

Kat reacted first. "Ash, excuse me, but have you lost your fucking mind? Sonja, talk some sense into him."

Sonja turned to Kat. "Where he goes, I go."

Ash continued. "We will head far from the front line, find a world, and a doctor who can perform the necessary genetic extraction. Sonja and I will give you some of our genetic material voluntarily."

Louise lowered the rifle, and stared at Ash a long while. Then, without another word, she deactivated the rifle and held it out to one of her aides, who took it. "Take it up to the hill, and leave it there."

Louise studied Ash and Sonja, then turned to another Alician, a female. "Call the southern post. Tell them to bring the ship once the Nchkani have left orbit. Take… escort these two to the boarding tower." She touched the Alician with her claw. "Treat them carefully. They are our future."

Kat muttered behind Micah. "This is a mistake."

Louise heard her. "Possibly. But death leaves one with so few options."

Micah noted that Louise was returning to form, becoming more dangerous again. But his prime concern was Ash. Micah pulled a hand out of his pocket and laid it on Ash's shoulder as he passed, depositing a comms micro-patch on his jacket.

"Are you absolutely sure about this? Do you want us to come and retrieve you?"

"Yes, I am sure, and no, Micah. It is time this rift was healed. The Alicians have paid for their crimes. I would ask you to take Sonja back, but she won't accept that, and the truth is, I need her."

Sonja spoke up. "As Zack would say, damned right on both counts."

Micah removed his hand. "Good luck, both of you. If you can send word –"

"No, it will be better to break contact. And I'm sorry Sandy didn't make it, Micah. She stayed behind, made sure all the other captives were freed. We think she went back for Ramires."

Micah had barely had time to think about it, but Ash was right, she must be dead, buried in the underground complex. He felt unsteady on his feet, but tried not to let it show.

As soon as they had gone, Micah and Louise faced each other again. She spoke first.

"We have preparations to make, I imagine you do, too." With that she headed back through the throng, the Alicians following her. Micah and Kat were left alone.

"I'm so sorry about Sandy and Ramires, Micah." She touched his arm, and lowered her voice. "I know how you felt about her."

"Do you?" His own voice sounded distant. He'd only just realised exactly how much she'd meant to him, now she was gone. All those years he'd never told her. Too late. It occurred to him to remain on Savange; after all, she was here, somewhere. Maybe she was still alive… But the tunnels had been flooded with fire during the Nchkani attack. Nobody could have survived, not even Ramires, and certainly not Sandy. He knew he wasn't thinking straight.

A screeching sound made him turn towards the hill where Louise had sent the rifle. A column of purple light shone down and then vanished. Micah presumed the Nchkani had taken the rifle.

Micah leant on Kat's shoulder a moment. She still had Antonia, and he had to get the other captives back to their loved ones too.

"Let's go find Aramisk and the others," he said.

Louise entered the tower. Toran stood with his staff, next to Sandy, who was cuffed, gagged and strapped to a chair. He spoke as Louise entered.

"I heard the deal with Micah on the Allcom. What do you want me to do?"

Louise regarded Sandy. "Carry on as planned. Take her with you. It will weaken Micah believing this one is dead, and unravel him when he finds out she is still alive. He still cares a great deal for her."

Sandy struggled in her restraints, but to no avail.

"Excuse me, but didn't Micah just save us?"

Louise lashed out with her claw. Toran blocked it with his staff, but it drove him back a pace.

"If he hadn't prevented me from handing over the Spider, all our people would still be alive. Use her as you like, to throw him off guard. Kill Micah and the girl-President, Petra, as well as Blake, too, if he still lives. Bring ten captives, then release the virus on Esperia."

"And what of this blind man, Ash?"

Louise's claw opened. "You are testing my patience, Toran. Thank yourself lucky I don't have a replacement to hand. Ash will be spared, his woman, too. Now go!"

Micah was glad to be back aboard Shiva. It was going to be pretty cramped, with sixty passengers – fifty-nine he reminded himself, with a pang. Shiva had run deep scans but found no trace of life in the caverns. Yet he kept seeing her face, expecting her to come sauntering around the corner with her buoyant smile, just like she used to back when they'd been friends. Somehow it didn't feel like she was dead. His head had accepted it, but his heart hadn't caught up yet.

Micah shook himself, and realised he'd not seen Antonia amongst the freed captives, nor Kat for a while; she'd disappeared somewhere.

He accessed Shiva via his resident. <Where are Kat and Antonia?>

<Medical bay. Antonia is undergoing surgery.>

Micah bolted from his chair and ran to the medical area, only to find the door sealed, with Kat outside.

"You can't go in, Micah, but she'll be fine."

"What happened?"

"As the captives were escaping the initial assault, the Rapier was hit by a plasma bolt. Antonia was next to a conduit that exploded outwards. She and three others were struck by fragments. Vashta is operating on them right now. They will all live. But she has to operate quickly, before we enter Transpace."

Micah leant against the door. "Where was she hit?"

Kat avoided his eyes, and took a moment before replying. "In the abdomen. She'll be fine."

Something about her reply made him wonder what she wasn't telling him. But he let it go. "I have to get back to the bridge. Please, when she wakes, give her my… best wishes."

Kat nodded, her face ashen.

"Don't worry, Kat, she's in good hands."

"Thanks. Now go, Micah. Get us away from here; get us home."

Micah glanced over to Ramires' empty tactical station. The last Sentinel, a legend, killed somewhere on the planet. They'd never been true friends, as there had always been underlying tension between them, but Ramires had been steadfast throughout. Micah felt it would have been a better result if Ramires had survived and he had perished. At least Ramires had helped bring the Alicians to their knees, eliminating the threat, perhaps for good. He didn't know if warriors who fought all their lives craved rest afterwards, but he whispered the words anyway: "rest in peace." Maybe Ramires and Sandy would be together again now; even if Micah didn't believe in an after-life, he didn't rule out the possibility. It would make sense out of such a senseless loss.

Aramisk stood in front of him. He gestured to Ramires' station. "Would you mind?"

"Thank you, I need something to do."

The central screen showed the planet from a safe distance, the Nchkani long gone, the sole Alician transport vessel also waiting to observe the destruction of their world. Micah guessed they needed closure.

Shiva informed Micah and Aramisk that it had begun, then added, "You might want to look away. This is a Hell-Class weapon. It is so named for a reason."

Micah took his command chair, stared at the screen, and braced himself mentally.

A red spot appeared on a major continent, and grew until it looked like a super-volcano. Magma spouted with such violence it shot into space. The volcanic mouth collapsed, leaving an even larger caldera, while red hot molten rock spewed upwards at a terrifying rate, as if the planet was vomiting its core. After several minutes the planet's surface began to crumple, dimples and gashes appearing on its spherical surface. The caldera imploded and the hole became an open wound, the planet's interior gushing relentlessly into space. After another minute the stream died down, and sputtered to a dribble. But it wasn't over. What was left was a shell of a planet, like a cracked and emptied egg. The edges caught fire, burning with a bright blue flame that ate up the shell until the last shred of the planet vanished into blackness.

It didn't seem right that Sandy and Ramires perished here, no trace of them left to take home. He vowed to make a grave for them as soon as he got back, and then head out into battle, wherever Hellera thought he and Shiva could be useful.

He noticed the Alician vessel preparing to leave, and wondered if any of them recalled departing a dead Earth almost two decades ago.

"Micah, it's Ash."

"Ash – are you alright? I wasn't sure the comms patch was working."

"It is, but I'll be out of range any second."

"Are you okay?"

"We are, so far. Micah, there's something you need to know, about Louise. She isn't here. She's not on the ship."

The Alician vessel jumped into Transpace. Micah asked Shiva to track them, but they were gone.

Chapter 21
BREACH

Kilaney stared at the star-filled screen, squinting to see the first indication of inbound Mannekhi ships. The dull beat of the TACAS, a device to detect opening Transpace conduits, pulsed steady as a heartbeat. Kilaney knew he had to wait. He got up from his command chair on the Q'Roth destroyer, and turned around to check his crew at their stations. They were all Youngblood volunteers: Siras at the helm, Janine at Tactical, Willem at Systems, and Annie on Comms. Siras was the eldest at seventeen, Janine barely fifteen. Kilaney had taken Vasquez aside when they'd been proposed as the skeleton crew.

"They're kids, for God's sake! You know as well as I do, none of us are likely to make it back."

"You've been away too long, Bill. They're Youngbloods. Do you remember when your blood was young, what it felt like?"

He hadn't answered. But watching them now, Kilaney had to admit they were all quick studies, having picked up the skills required to navigate and defend a mesa-class Q'Roth vessel in just a few days. Advanced spatial concepts that had taken him years to master were understood at the first telling by these Genned youngsters. He'd been unimpressed by Micah's decision to allow the Genning of all human children. Now, for the first time, he could see the point. The inbound Mannekhi turned by Qorall were Level Six; with a normal human crew he'd be overrun quickly, but with Genners aboard he had a fighting chance.

He returned to the command chair built for a Q'Roth general. The three metre recliner dwarfed him, made him seem like a child in an adult's chair. But he used to be Q'Roth, and though he no longer possessed the six limbs necessary to make full use of it, he knew his way around its controls. He tapped a pad.

"Xenic, any sign yet?" Kilaney glanced at a holo of the entire Esperian system covering twenty light minutes of travel. Xenic's Mannekhi Spiker was closer to Esperia, embedded well inside the Shrell field. Two ships against fifty didn't seem like good odds.

"We will know when they arrive. Never hasten an enemy's arrival; only see that he comes to you."

Kilaney wasn't a fan of military epithets, but they were preferable to Xenic telling him to relax. The TACAS pulse increased in pitch and frequency. Then it jumped again, a harmonic of the original steady tone. The Mannekhi were close.

Kilaney decided to air a question he'd harboured since Xenic's arrival. In battle, your life depended on your brother-in-arms, and he had to know he could rely on the Mannekhi commander.

"Xenic, I know they have been changed by Qorall, but they are – were – Mannekhi. Are you sure you can go through with this?"

There was a pause. "You would not understand. We Mannekhi have not been free for fifty thousand years, always managed with an iron claw by our patrons, any resistance met with brutal punishment. But in our hearts, our very DNA, that resistance, a simmering rage, is always there, deep down. This turning, what Qorall has done to my people… it is too much. I am freeing them."

Kilaney left it there. He spoke to Janine. "Prepare the Ricochet." That's what Kilaney had named it. Hellera had left it behind, cloaked in space until yesterday, when it had suddenly revealed itself, with a message for Kilaney. He'd seen one of these weapons in action before, when a Tla Beth had used it against Mannekhi Spikers. The trouble was, Qorall had seen it, too, and might have developed a counter-measure. Hellera's message had said it had to be combined with surprise. That meant hitting the enemy as they emerged from Transpace, when they would be vulnerable for a second or two. Kilaney had already primed it for Mannekhi ship signatures.

"Xenic, I want you well out of harm's way when I launch it."

"On that you have my complete agreement."

Kilaney stared at the star-field again, small pinpricks of light, serene, innocent, passive. The TACAS kicked up an octave, the pulses much faster, separating into three closely-matched tones. The TACAS was only approximate; it was difficult to predict exactly where and when ships would emerge from Transpace, but it already told him the Mannekhi attack plan.

"Xenic, they'll arrive in three waves."

Kilaney got up from his chair, and stood right next to the large screen. There was a flicker of space, as if a transparent film had momentarily shimmered. "There, Janine," he said. "Fire."

At first he couldn't see the Ricochet's trajectory, since the studded black sphere had no after-burn, but Willem was able to track it via its transponder, and Annie overlaid its course on the star-field. The TACAS pitch ramped up again, a shrill whine.

Annie shouted above the din. "Sir, do you want me to diminish the alarm?"

He shook his head. The Ricochet accelerated. Where were the Mannekhi ships? *Come on.* He only had one Ricochet, one shot. The sphere reached the designated area and slowed down, then stopped. Kilaney breathed a sigh of relief. *Smart boy!*

The bridge was filled with the TACAS alarm, when suddenly it shut off. As Kilaney had hoped, in the area where he had glimpsed the approaching bow wave of the Transpace conduit, ten ships, stretched cones of silver, sprang into view, popping back into normal space-time. He barely had time to make out any details before the Ricochet flared into action. A beam struck one ship, then bounced onto another then another. Within a second, a lattice of orange fire connected all ten ships. One by one they burst into crimson flame then snuffed out.

Thank you, Hellera.

Almost immediately the second wave arrived, this time twenty ships. The device fired at the first ship, but it alone was damaged. No ricochet effect.

The other nineteen fired purple beams at the sphere, which exploded silently; shreds of orange splattered across a vast area of space before they dissipated. The nineteen ships charged onwards, heading straight for Kilaney.

Xenic came online. "They're Dropships, Javelin Class, used for invasion. Once they land they cannot take off again."

The final wave of twenty ships burst into the sector.

"Back to the Shrell field," Kilaney said to Siras. The destroyer leapt forward in a single short-system jump.

"Janine, give me an outside view, one million klicks to starboard, enlarged focal area."

A holo showed a sideways view of the approaching fleet, and the Shrell field with Esperia at its core. The Dropships spread out, a hundred kilometres apart, spearing towards the field. He approached the holo, held out his hands, and flipped it around to get a frontal view. The Dropships were in concentric ring formation: the first ring comprised three ships, the next ring seven, the two outer rings twelve and seventeen respectively. But they were staggered, and they had shields. No beam could hit more than one ship, and no detonation from any of the weapons he had aboard had an effective blast radius larger than fifty kilometres against a shielded ship. The enemy had done their homework.

"Take us out of their path, Siras," he said.

"Sir?"

Kilaney hadn't had time to brief his crew on all the contingencies, and now wasn't the moment to start. "One thousand klicks should do it. Lateral, you choose the direction."

The helmsman complied, asking no further questions.

Kilaney tapped the ship-to-ship comms pad again. "Xenic, you'd better be ready, they're coming in hot."

"I am ready."

The Dropships seemed uninterested in deceleration, despite the fact that they could almost certainly see the Shrell wires that would razor through any ship, shielded or not.

"Siras, prepare to loop behind them and then chase them in."

"Sir, there's no way this destroyer can dodge the wires at their speed. They're smaller and far more manoeuvrable."

"I'm aware of that, son. Just follow my orders."

He watched as the first few Dropships neared the densely packed field that made him think of a ball of barbed wire. Halfway between the outside of the ball and Esperia was Xenic's ship. But the Dropships were designated Javelin Class for good reason. Travelling point first and at high speed, they were difficult targets, like trying to shoot at an arrow flying towards your face. Still, he would stick to the plan, because he had no better idea. If he'd stayed in their path, he'd have probably taken out three before the others blew him to kingdom come.

The first five ships flew straight into the field like needles.

"On my command."

He watched the holo, and waited until more than half the ships had entered.

"Now, Siras."

Although the destroyer was half a kilometre long, it could move very fast in open space, and its inertial dampers worked just fine. Kilaney collapsed the holo with his hands, and got back to his chair.

"Siras, take us in as fast as you can go. Janine, use the forward battery, don't stop firing till it's depleted. Willem, let me know if ship integrity is compromised. Annie, no in-comms except from Xenic, but stream our telemetry to Petra and Vasquez."

The destroyer plunged into the Shrell field. Siras made fine adjustments that Kilaney knew no ungenned pilot could manage at this velocity, even in a smaller ship. A wash of yellow spurted ahead of them as Janine ignited the main particle cannon, and it gushed forth the heat of a sun's core, seeking out the rear of the Dropships. Within thirty seconds Kilaney counted five hits. The others accelerated to get out of range, just as Xenic had said they would.

"Don't let them get away, Siras."

The destroyer accelerated, the forward view snapping to and fro even though Kilaney felt no movement. Then there was a grating noise and a jolt.

Willem shouted. "Sir, we just lost a piece of the aft superstructure."

"Keep going, keep firing."

More clanks, and two more hits. Make that three; no, four. The Dropships were shifting to try and escape, but Siras clung to them. And then Kilaney saw it – a funnel of wires dead ahead. The Dropships slipped through, but they were much thinner… The bastards had lured him into a trap. Dammit, these Mannekhi knew their way round a Shrell field. His destroyer raced towards the wires. He gripped the arms of the chair.

"Siras –"

"No good, Sir," Siras said. "Willem, now!"

A glistening cocoon ballooned around Kilaney and the chair, snuffing out all noise. Kilaney had forgotten about it, a device on Q'Roth ships to protect the commander, in case… He tried to stand up but the bubble didn't give him enough room. The destroyer braked hard but there was no saving her. The end of the funnel rocketed towards them. He turned to see Siras hunched over the controls, trying to minimise the impact – no, he was trying to save his commander. The other three also worked feverishly, despite knowing they were about to die.

The upper half of the bridge was shorn off, and Kilaney found himself hurtling through space in the bubble. It rolled, and he saw his ship carved into chunks, like meat through a grinder. He could no longer see the wires; this was an escape pod, nothing more. He tried to catch sight of his crew, but he was already too far away, and the ship fragments sputtered briefly with violet flame before going dark. He saluted his crew, intoning each of their names. As he continued to sail forwards at speed, he toggled the chair's inertial controls to stabilise the bubble and orient his view towards the planet, the remaining Dropships, and Xenic.

Now it's up to you, my friend.

Petra watched the holoscreen, Vasquez at her side, a skeleton crew with them in the cordoned-off room in the Dome, their hastily arranged Battle HQ. The waves of Mannekhi ships tore towards Xenic's lone Spiker. She zoomed in to see the front line of Javelins.

"Those three," Vasquez said, pointing.

She saw them. Three of the very front ships had altered course, converging towards Xenic. They were going to ram it – pierce it, slice it apart. "How do they keep managing to dodge the wires so easily?"

Vasquez rubbed the stubble on his chin. "The Mannekhi were born into this kind of briar patch. Nevertheless, it's impressive."

She wondered what Xenic was going to do. He hadn't told anyone. Nor had he fired a single weapon.

It was as if Vasquez read her mind. "Whatever he's going to do, it had better be fast." Vasquez walked closer to the holonet, then stepped inside, first through the planet, into the patch of scribbled wire filaments, until his face was right next to the image of Xenic's ship, needles sprinting towards his eyes. It unnerved Petra, though she knew it was just a holo. Still...

"Commander, please."

He turned around, looked her in the eye, and then walked back to her side.

"Ten seconds," one of the aides said.

They watched. *Come on, Xenic, whatever you're going to do, do it now.*

But the ship just sat there. Petra's hand went to her mouth as the three Javelins plunged into the Spiker, at first splintering it, then, as they passed right through the other side and continued on their way, the Spiker shattered.

Petra took a step backwards, but Vasquez took a pace forwards.

"Zoom in," he barked.

Petra stared, confused. All she saw was debris spilling in all directions, the second and third waves accelerating towards the debris field, and Esperia.

Vasquez grinned. "You sneaky son of a..."

Petra stepped forward. What? What was he seeing? She focused. The debris pattern. It was shifting. Then she noticed the spikes. They were all intact. She moved closer, in front of Vasquez, and like him, stepped inside the holonet, needles flying toward her face.

None of them touched her.

All the drifting spikes except one suddenly flared, each homing onto a Javelin, a needle against a needle, the combined speed destroying the spike but gouging the hull of each Javelin. Flowers of flame blossomed right in front of Petra's eyes.

A cheer arose from behind her, and Vasquez arrived at her side, his hand on her shoulder. With his other hand he pointed at the single remaining spike.

"No offence Ma'am, but I want to work for that man."

She let out a short laugh. "If we get through this, remind me to create some medals."

They both walked out of the net back to the central console.

"Zoom out," she said. "How many got through?" She tried to count the ones that had been on the periphery, too far for Xenic's spikes.

"Seven," came the reply.

Fifty down to seven. Bravo, even if it might not be enough.

She touched a console. "Commander Xenic, are you there?"

"Of course," came the reply.

She smiled. "That was truly exceptional, Commander." She cleared her throat. "What is your status?"

"I wish I had gotten more of them. My crew and I are in a single spike. We are trying to rendezvous with Kilaney. We may be late."

She thought about telling them both to stay up there, where it might be safer. But she didn't want to insult them.

She turned to Vasquez. "How long?"

"Twenty minutes till the Dropships land."

She nodded, then touched another button. "People of Esperia, know that Commanders Kilaney and Xenic have, against incredible odds, destroyed forty-three enemy ships out in space." She paused, waiting until she could hear cheering outside. "There are seven ships still inbound. The odds are still not even, but far better than before. Prepare yourselves for battle."

She clicked off comms, and turned to Vasquez. "Commander, I now hand tactical over to you."

"Yes, Madam President." He saluted her.

She made an effort to stand to attention, and saluted him back.

Vasquez spoke in a lower voice. "I need your access code, Petra."

She looked around at the seven aides, who were also standing to attention. "Are you sure?"

"We are all sure."

"Alright." She approached a panel, placed apart from the rest, and tapped in the code. Two small circles, a foot apart, lit up, pulsing yellow. Vasquez typed in his own code and their colour shifted to red. Now all it required was to touch both circles simultaneously, and the Battle HQ would be obliterated. They both stepped away from the panel.

Vasquez spoke to his men. "If they breach the Dome, they won't be adding us to their army."

Petra nodded. "I pray it doesn't come to that. Good luck, Colonel." She held out her hand, and he shook it. She walked to each to the seven other men and did the same, turned to go, then paused.

"Colonel, you've not asked where I'm going, what my plans are."

"You're going to stand with Blake and the Spiders."

She smiled as she walked to the exit. She'd left the right man in charge.

Chapter 22
STAR STORM

Pierre had never killed anyone. That hadn't been easy, having endured the Third World War on Earth, the fighting against the Q'Roth on Eden and Earth a decade later, and all those years gallivanting around a war-torn galaxy with Ukrull. The Ranger, being telepathic, knew Pierre's value structure, and had done the necessary whenever they'd been in a tight spot. But Pierre had kept it a secret from his human colleagues. Until now. Jen was fuming.

"What do you mean you won't take Tactical?"

She got out of her immerser chair where she'd been controlling Navigation, and walked right up to his face, then shoved him backwards, so that he fell into the seat controlling the ship's weapons. Jen was smaller than he was, but right now he'd prefer a Q'Roth warrior in front of him.

"It… against my morals, Jen. I've never in my life –"

"Look out the window and tell me what you see." She shoved his chin sideways so he faced the screen at the end of the compact cockpit set in the front of the *Duality*, the ship Kalaran had 'borrowed' from the Kalarash entity known as Darkur.

Pierre stared at the screen, and felt the blood drain from his face. Three hundred and thirty Nchkani warships, black and white ovoids with feather-like blades brimming with weapons. They circled the supernova concealing the Tla Beth homeworld, in opposing directions, like a coordinated ballet of electrons circling a nucleus. Beyond this inner ring of hostiles were swarms of the immense dark worms, their pattern more erratic, the very randomness more menacing, offering no escape. He couldn't see how even Hellera could fight her way out of this, and then the galaxy would fall into Qorall's hands.

"I see our doom, Jen."

"All the more reason to fight!"

"Jen, I'm sorry, I can't do it." He levered himself out of the chair and tried to push past her.

Jen slapped him hard across the face, the shock of it more than its force making him sit back in the chair. Red-faced, her lips quivering, she pinned him to the chair with a firm hand on his chest.

Her voice quavered. "You –" She closed her eyes a moment, sucked in a deep breath. "Listen to me, Pierre. Dimitri is gone, Kalaran, too. They died to save us. They didn't die so we could lie down and offer our throats to the wolves. You can't operate Nav. You're more intelligent than me, but you have no experience flying one of these."

He studied the interface in front of him, its array of symbols and displays. A touch here, a tap there, and lives would be snuffed out. Why was his life more important than theirs? He had no right…

"You still have a daughter, Pierre. Petra is on Esperia. They'll go there next." Jen pushed off from his chest, and turned away from him, folding her arms as if holding herself. She stood immobile, and the cockpit grew quiet.

Pierre tried to remember who he used to be, before being accelerated to Level Ten, to know what he might have decided then, before he'd set off around the galaxy ignoring Kat and the daughter he still barely knew. But not that long ago Hellera had put him on a downward course, restoring his humanity. He'd thought it had been done as a rebuke, but now he wasn't so sure. Feelings he'd almost forgotten had been returning. He didn't know if he could rely on them, but Jen was right, Kat and Petra were relying on him, and he owed it to Ukrull, Jen, and to Kalaran…

He took a deep breath, and placed a finger on the interface in front of him, making it come to life.

"Take your station, Jen. I'll do what I can."

They patrolled the circumference of the supernova once an hour, checking that the Nchkani had not approached from their own farther orbit. The Nchkani and the dark worms stayed out in the blackness of space, whereas Jen and Pierre skated along a perimeter of purple and blue ionised clouds of deadly radiation that concealed a dwarfed star at its heart. The star itself sheltered the Tla Beth homeworld – or asteroid – using unknown spatial manipulation techniques for shielding. Pierre guessed the Level Sixteen Nchkani would prize such know-how, wanting to steal the secret from the Level Seventeen Tla Beth before exterminating them. Perhaps that was why they hadn't yet attacked. No new ships had arrived in the past two hours, and he assumed their fleet had reached full strength.

He glanced across at Jen, her brow smooth, eyes closed but twitching as if in REM sleep, her mind immersed in the neural interface. Occasionally the corner of her lip lifted a fraction, coinciding with the ship threading through a loop in the cloud layer, or surfing a wave of radiation unleashed from the ongoing starburst reaction. She was clearly enjoying the challenge. Good, take what pleasure you can from all of this, Jen. He turned back to his instruments, unable to use a neural interface because of his nannites; the ship didn't trust them, though he wasn't sure why.

There was the usual outpouring of higher atomic weight molecules, the denser metals only given to the universe by supernovas. But there were odd concentrations. He found a particularly dense metal, far heavier than plutonium, streaming out and pooling in the neutral zone between them and the Nchkani, forming a molecular cloud. As the Duality completed the next circular tour, he identified six such streams and clouds, equidistant from each other.

Pierre hadn't heard from Hellera or Ukrull for some time. He wondered what they were up to. Ukrull's face suddenly appeared on the Hohash, making Pierre jump.

"Telepathic, remember?"

It was good to hear the reptile's growly voice. He recalled Ukrull once confiding that telepathy attenuated less over distance than other forms of communication, though he'd never disclosed its range. He'd also said that the longer a Ranger was in close proximity to another being, the stronger the bond became. That was why all Rangers ended up becoming nomadic, usually travelling alone. Pierre had asked Ukrull how he could tolerate his presence. He had laughed, saying that Pierre's thoughts were so dim, being only a measly Level Ten, that he could tune them out as random noise.

For the first time, Pierre began to wonder.

"So, Ukrull, are you going to tell me the plan?"

"No. If works, you see something always wanted, since small."

Ukrull never talked of Pierre's childhood, saying that the intellectual difference was so minimal, he could only discriminate between a human adult and a child in terms of physical size. Pierre had always appreciated Ukrull's sense of humour. A knot formed in Pierre's stomach, as he realised how much he would miss Ukrull, having spent nearly half of his 'tall' life with him.

He'd once asked Ukrull why he spoke such broken English, given his intelligence level. Ukrull had replied, "Less words, you listen harder. Redundancy comes from emotional weakness."

Pierre had pondered that a lot. He'd also tried Ukrull's form of speaking a number of times, but Ukrull had laughed off every single attempt. He thought of trying now, since this might be their last conversation, but he gave up on the idea.

"What do you want us to do, my friend?"

"Live."

Pierre smiled. "Is that all?"

"To live, must kill many worms and destroy one hundred Nchkani vessels."

"Oh."

Ukrull's yellow slit eyes narrowed. "Up to it?"

"If it's what I have to do in order to see what I have apparently always wanted to see, then yes." The knot in Pierre's stomach tightened. "What about you?"

Ukrull glanced at something Pierre couldn't see, then turned back to face Pierre. "Tell Manota…"

Pierre leaned forward. "The female Ranger? Tell her what?"

Ukrull flicked his forked tongue over his eyes. "Have to go now." The image vanished on the Hohash. Pierre's worried face reflected on its mirror surface. *Take care, Ukrull.*

"Pierre," Jen said, eyes open, her features soft. Had she been watching him?

"Pierre, they're coming. I'm bringing the Duality about."

He turned back to his console, and watched as a section of the outer layer of Nchkani ships moved aside, leaving a circular gap. Dark worms poured through, straight towards him.

"Do we retreat back into the nebula's clouds for cover?" He still couldn't see a way out of this, nor any practical offensive move they could make. It all felt futile.

"Pierre, look at me."

He tore his gaze from the screen.

"This is the *Duality*. It is a Kalarash ship. Today we fight for the Kalarash, the most powerful beings in the universe. We do not retreat. Ever. Is that clear?"

He nodded, reminding himself she'd been a captain of one of the refugee ships that escaped Earth. For the first time he could see why.

"I'm immersing now, I won't be able to talk to you until... after. And, Pierre, if you can't fire, I under–"

"I will fire."

She gave him a measured stare. "See you on the other side of whatever." She closed her eyes again and was immersed, in direct mental contact with the Duality's navigation and engine control systems.

Pierre shrank back into the chair as they burst forward towards the flood of leviathans. Wondering which weapon to fire first, he noticed a red disk light up in front of him. It said "Assist?" He almost laughed. Kalarash indeed. He pressed it.

It was like swimming up a waterfall. Each worm was three times the length and breadth of the Duality. The ship's weapons punctured the space around them, fans of light cascading from the ship as it twisted, its crossbow arms flailing superheated plasma beams like whips, lacerating the worms as they tried to engulf the ship. The aft of the Duality sprayed beams in its wake, aiming to finish off wounded worms. But there were so many. The screens could hardly see beyond the worms' huge hides. Pierre noted an indication of shield integrity. The worms were leaching energy, a few per cent a minute, not helped by the deluge of weapons fire, but if he stopped firing, the ship would be trapped, drained, and crushed. The bar already showed only fifty-five per cent of reserves left.

He selected an external view from a probe they'd released earlier, and saw that many of the worms had bypassed them and were heading straight into the heart of the supernova. The Nchkani were also edging closer. Jen must have noticed it too, because suddenly the Duality swung sideways away from the avalanche of worms, vectoring towards a group of Nchkani warships.

A panel indication lit up: gravitic net. He knew what it was, and recoiled at the idea. But he took a deep breath, and launched it. He watched it writhe its way toward the ships. That was when it all went wrong.

At around halfway point, the net slowed, stopped, and then headed back toward the Duality. *Merde!*

"Jen!" he shouted. At first he thought she hadn't heard him, but the Duality suddenly veered toward the flood of dark worms. With the gravity net on their tail, she aimed straight for a worm cluster. Pierre fired at them to get their attention, to bore a hole through them. It worked, just, and as they sped through the gap, the worms closed behind them. He switched to aft screens, and saw a group of worms caught in the net, squirming as they shrank together, crushed into oblivion.

"You told me Kalaran used a net on a group of Nchkani before he was killed, but at least one ship got away. They must have recorded data, taken it back to Qorall, and –"

"Hellera is using us to test their defences," Jen remarked, temporarily out from immersion, rubbing her eyes. "Makes sense, though she's off my Christmas card list."

Pierre stared at her. "How can you be so blasé at a time like this?"

"I hung around with Kalaran for a year. He had a very subtle form of humour I'm finally starting to appreciate. Back to work, Pierre. No more nets, please. Think of something else."

She was back 'in'. He recalled studying battle tactics during the American civil war. Often there would be two lines facing each other across a wasteland, neither side wanting to charge. Occasionally a lone rider would be sent out into no man's land to draw fire, and to try and goad the other side into attacking. Of course, in most cases the rider was shot dead before he got back.

Jen slung the ship around for another pass. The 'assist' button lit up again, but he didn't press it. They drew closer to the Nchkani ships. The assist disc changed colour from green to red. Still, he left it. He wanted to draw their fire, deciding that was what Hellera needed, and that it made strategic sense, even if he and Jen were the bait.

The four closest ships all fired at the same time, but it wasn't a plasma weapon. Instead, they sprayed the Duality with a gelatinous material, a mucous substance that tried to bind with the ship's hull. Jen instinctively pulled away, and Pierre fired at the matter streams. Single beam-fire didn't work, but he found he could use two intersecting beams to scissor through the mucous streams, choking off their momentum. Yet still enough of it reached the ship, and clung to it. Pierre called up the hull resilience display – those defence systems had gone into overdrive, but it was clear the organic material was eating its way through the hull, one molecular layer at the time. This had to be Qorall's artistry, it was way above the Nchkani level. Pierre knew Hellera would be seeing this, and they all knew now that this was no siege, the attack had begun in earnest.

Pierre perceived the genius in Darkur's design of his ship. As the sludge ate through the hull, the ship's internal fluid metamorphosed, creating more hull material. It couldn't stop the invasion, but it bought them time. Luckily, or through Jen's flying, none of the material had latched onto the cockpit area in the arrowhead at the front of the ship.

Jen raced the ship back to the supernova, twenty of the Nchkani ships in hot pursuit. Pierre now saw the sting in the Nchkani strategy. The worms that had already passed them earlier now moved to block their path, creating a wall.

The intention was clearly to corral the Duality and destroy it. The Nchkani no doubt preferred to capture and study such a ship, but then they would have to answer to Qorall. Pierre looked at the two screens, the pack of Nchkani ships behind, and a swarm of worms in front. No way out.

But he did notice something: one of the dense molecular clouds, full of heavy metals, was nearby. His display listed the metals, and as he'd suspected, Trancium was amongst them. He had no better idea. "Jen, take us into the cloud!"

Pierre.

He looked across to Jen, but she was still immersed in the neural interface. Besides, the voice saying his name had been inside his head, and had sounded… synthetic. He ignored it, whatever or whoever it was, now was not the time. He checked the hull again. The attacking agent was voracious. They didn't have much time, and they were beginning to lose power. Abruptly the engines closed down, and the Duality drifted into the cloud. Jen let out a gasp as she was dumped out of immersion; there was nothing more she could do. The Nchkani ships took up positions all around them, readying for the kill. Pierre watched them on the screens.

"This is it," Jen said.

He noticed movement in the cloud, black on black, hard to make out.

"Pierre, Jen." This time the voice was clear: Hellera. "Why do you think our ships are fashioned in the shape of a crossbow?"

Before he could think the answer, the screen blurred as the arrowhead containing them bolted out of the cloud, a long shaft of intact and uncontaminated hull behind them. They blazed out of the supernova region at terrific speed.

Pierre and Jen watched the main screen, where they could finally see the big picture, and Hellera's strategy. Something was happening to the six molecular clouds around the supernova. The Nchkani ships had been fleeing the one where the Duality had foundered, and were now adrift. The screen zoomed in. First, Pierre's heart sank as he saw the Duality: listless, blistered and corroded, as if attacked by leprosy. The ship was dying. But the Nchkani ships were clearly in trouble themselves. Black sores grew on their hulls, scabs stretching up their spines. Jen voiced what Pierre had already surmised.

"Machines. They were in the cloud, waiting."

"They're feeding on the Nchkani ships," Pierre added. "Hellera used the supernova to create nutrient pools the Machine race couldn't afford to ignore; they need heavy metals. The clouds were the bait, all along. Kalaran must have sent what was left of the Machines here."

"Funny, Kalaran and Hellera were working as a team all along," Jen said.

The Nchkani ships were in disarray, slowly succumbing to the Machines that would assimilate them and discard almost all the organic content as waste. Mucous streams fired at the Machines had little effect, because the Machine assailants were too small to target, until they mushroomed in size on contact with the Nchkani hulls. Pierre realised how like nannites the Machines acted, and felt a strange affinity with them – nannites had been an integral part of him most of his life, courtesy of his father's genetic engineering experiments on his own son.

Leaderless, the worms scattered. Hellera's ship emerged from the centre of the supernova, weapons blazing, carving through worm flesh. But Pierre sensed there was more to come. Hellera's ship fired six missiles, each one snaking towards a molecular cloud. Then everything happened at once: Hellera's ship tore out of the system; the supernova collapsed as if being sucked in, pulling the worms towards it. Nchkani ships struggled to break free of the gravitational force but they too slipped backwards. Pierre could barely imagine the energy being condensed, easily enough to create a black hole, or… He suddenly remembered what he'd always wanted to see. He jumped out of his seat.

"Jen, get us out of here!"

She didn't ask questions, but slipped back into the neural interface and executed emergency thrust. What Pierre witnessed in the aft screen was something he'd always wanted – and dreaded – to see, the birth of a white hole. At first he saw the six micro-stars Hellera had created from the Machine-infested clouds, the heavy metal explosions briefly burning hotter than normal stars; he guessed that was to exterminate the Machines rather than the Nchkani, as the former were tougher to kill. The six stars looked like the points of a diamond, with a white light growing hotter in its centre. Then the white hole expanded until it engulfed the micro-stars. It continued to grow all the way to the outer perimeter where the Nchkani had originally been. He doubted anything survived. With a shock, he realised an entire race, the Nchkani, had probably just been wiped out, maybe two if he included the Xera.

"She used the Machines, then destroyed them," he said.

Jen shrugged. "Kalarash are ruthless. They have to be that way to stay on top. Just remember Qorall is far worse. Be grateful Hellera's on our side."

He hoped Ukrull was aboard Hellera's vessel. The Tla Beth, too; he knew there weren't that many of them anymore, and their ships were small, though incredibly powerful. But their base had been destroyed; they would have to find a new home.

Pierre.

There it was again. Jen hadn't reacted. Only he heard it, inside his head. The Hohash came to life. As far as Pierre could tell, Ukrull was grinning.

"Well played," Ukrull growled.

Pierre shrugged. "Hellera's strategy was impeccable, not to mention her timing."

Ukrull's snout swung left and right, then he spoke in a quieter growl. "Twice, noise stopped. Hole in your thoughts. What happened?"

Pierre had forgotten Ukrull was monitoring his mind. So, twice, when someone had tried to contact him, Ukrull had not heard it. Somebody, or something, had blocked a Level Fifteen telepath.

"Don't know," Pierre said. There was no point lying to Ukrull.

"Later," Ukrull said, and broke the connection.

Pierre, we need to talk.

"Well," Jen said, "I have to say I'm pleased to be alive." She looked at him. "You did well, back there." She tilted her head. "What was Ukrull referring to?"

"Like I said, I don't know. Probably nothing."

Now, Pierre. We are running out of time.

Instead of being exhausted, Jen seemed to have been energised. "I'm going down to see what's left of our ship. Want to come and explore?" Her voice dipped. "Dimitri would."

"No, thank you, Jen. I'm going to rest here a while. Why don't you take the Hohash with you?"

She cast him a quizzical look, but decided it was a good idea. He watched her don a facemask and slip through the waterlock, the Hohash following her.

I'm alone, he thought. Can Ukrull hear me?

No. You know who we are, don't you?

He hadn't been sure until that moment.

Yes. The Machine race. The Xera.

We have a proposal for you.

Pierre listened, knowing that the longer he did so, the more concerned Ukrull would be. Eventually, the Ranger, despite the friendship between them, would be compelled to tell Hellera. Then Pierre knew he would find himself on the wrong side of the last remaining Kalarash in the galaxy.

Still, he listened.

Chapter 23
ANTIGEN

It rained on Esperia. Petra stared up through the transparent barrier erected by the Spiders, the protective dome made visible by rivulets chasing down its outer surface. It hardly ever rained on Esperia, but when it did, it was relentless. Several drops collected on her upper lip despite the peaked cap Vasquez had given her. She blew them off, and continued to search the sky. She wasn't alone. It seemed the whole town of Esperantia was gazing upwards, watching and waiting. But they often glanced in her direction. She recalled what Vasquez had said to her.

"You're the CIC, Petra, our Commander-in-Chief. This is a Military Op, the population is under imminent threat, and need to see their President out there. But you must stay out of the fray. If you enter it, then no one is in charge, and we're lost. I need to be here to manage the aerial situation and organise our ground troops, but you are the eyes and ears on the scene. Stay close to the battle, but don't be drawn into it. If things go bad, I'll be there before the end."

A raindrop entered her eye, making her blink. The barrier didn't stop all of the rain; she had no way of asking the Spiders how it worked, but guessed it had some basic intelligence. It made sense; such a shield could be used for an extended period – a siege – in which case it would be useful to allow rain to pass through while keeping out enemies and biological agents.

She glanced at the four Spiders standing behind her. They looked soggy, but otherwise unperturbed. In their midst was Blake, locked inside a grey metal body glove that came all the way up to his eyes. He could stand, but was otherwise immobilised. He was still golden; they had no idea if the medical procedure had truly worked, and until now had no way of testing it. Blake was potentially an antigen, a catalyst to trigger a reversal of the Orb virus that had already turned trillions of aliens into Qorall's minions. The Ngank surgeon had said that if it did work – and there were no guarantees it would – then it would activate on physical contact with a recoded individual, and would work faster than the original recoding, because the individual – like Blake – would be fighting it from the inside. But Blake was still golden, and was still infectious. She felt the device in her pocket that would release him from his bonds, noting that the nearest people – a trio of Youngbloods – were a good ten metres away, and returned to observing the sky.

Vasquez called on her wristcom. "Thirty seconds."

Loud cracks made her flinch: sonic booms, but she couldn't see the Mannekhi Javelin ships. Xenic called them Dropships; released from their Mother-ship just before entering Transpace. They'd fallen like needles navigating their way through the Shrell-field, and would barely slow as they entered the atmosphere, and would pound into the ground. More difficult to shoot down that way. The recoded Mannekhi inside would be in deep stasis, encased in inertia-dampening gel, but would emerge very shortly after landing, to invade the town.

More cracks stretched into scraping noises that grated in her ears, and then she heard shouts from behind. "There!" At first she couldn't see them, but then narrow glints of silver caught her eye. She counted: four, five… then all seven. The shield darkened, as if polarised, dampening light and sound. Yellow blotches erupted on its surface, accompanied by dull booms as the Javelins fired on the town. She heard children's' screams in the background, quickly hushed. The Spiders didn't move. The shield continued to darken, until Esperantia was plunged into night, fireworks billowing all around them. The ground shook, and Petra wondered how deep the shield penetrated Esperia's surface.

She could barely make out the Javelins amidst the bombardment. But then a bright object, like a comet, grew in size. She braced herself. One of them was going to try and break through the shield. The impact was like a sonic boom, and made her clamp her hands over her ears. The shield lightened, revealing the awful carnage of a ship flattened into an amorphous slime of blood and metal. A second later there was an earthquake as the six other ships slammed into the area outside the shield, knocking Petra off her feet. The shield became transparent again as rock and soil spurted high into the air, then rained back down. As Vasquez had predicted, the ships had landed in the valley just south of Esperantia, the closest one a few hundred metres from her position. The open landscape favoured a large ground force. She recalled that Blake had once told her that decisive battles in wars often came down to infantry. *Break the infantry, win the war.* But how could you defeat an invading force you could not afford to touch?

She got to her feet and noticed that the shield had stopped letting the rain through. Blake remained standing, his eyes looking toward where two of the ships had struck home.

Vasquez called her. "Now, Petra."

She used the translation flashlight device to ask the Spiders to open a hole in the shield for thirty seconds, long enough for four tactical groups to sprint outside and engage the enemy before they emerged from their ships. Two skimmers powered up behind her. She raised her hand until one of the Spiders flashed back in the affirmative, then she dropped it. The skimmers zipped past, one carrying three Youngbloods, the other a trio of Vasquez' militia, both teams loaded with heavy ordnance. The rush of wind from their wake blew her hat off. She let it go. Twenty seconds later another two skimmers dashed past – they had been stationed in the middle of town, just in case. She was relieved that Brandt wasn't among the Youngbloods, reminding herself that his size would have worked against him for this type of hit-and-run mission, as the skimmers were mainly designed to carry two people, not three.

The buzz of the engines powering the four teams towards the ships keened and then diminished. She turned back to the Spiders, and they raised the shield. Along with others, she approached the inner edge of the barrier. She stared through the rain coursing down its protective skin. Brandt arrived next to her, panting from having sprinted across town. She resisted the urge to embrace him, or even reach for his hand.

Craters smoked from where the two closest Dropships had landed, and through a viewer she saw the skimmers race towards them. *Go faster.* The Youngbloods arrived first, two of them crash-rolling off the skimmer, deadly packages clutched to their chests, while the driver slewed the skimmer to a halt. The first two ran to the crater and leapt over the edge. Seconds later they re-emerged and dashed back to the skimmer.

Nothing happened, and the Youngbloods waited.

She zoomed in on the second skimmer, crewed by Vasquez' militia, as it headed to the next crater. Before they arrived, Mannekhi burst out of the pit like angered ants from an anthill, armed and firing. The militia returned fire but were cut down.

She swung to the left and then to the right to see the third and fourth skimmer meet similar circumstances, in the latter case the skimmer was able to turn around in time. The Youngbloods still waited, despite a growing number of Mannekhi emerging from the other Dropships.

As she realised what they intended, she spoke to Brandt, trying to keep her voice steady.

"Tell them to come back."

"It was their choice, Petra."

She knew there was no point in further discussion, and put the viewer to her eyes again. The Youngbloods had booby-trapped the Dropship to explode as soon as its hatches opened. The Mannekhi inside knew that, but could afford to wait for reinforcements. She switched to the last remaining skimmer, racing back towards sanctuary. She judged the distance. They would make it. Then she noticed some kind of weapon emerging from one of the far craters, shaped like a cannon.

Vasquez came on line. "Petra, don't drop the shield. We don't know what that cannon does."

"They're your men, they can get back here in time." She could just make out their faces.

"They understood the risks. You put me in charge of tactical ops for a reason."

She watched them. The militia men might understand the risks and sacrifice with their heads, but they looked terrified. She turned to the Spiders, and used the flashcoder.

"Petra, what are you doing?" Brandt asked.

She didn't answer. She turned back to the last skimmer, raising her hand. But the skimmer changed course. She could see one of them touch an earpiece, and shout something to the other two. *Dammit, Vasquez!* The skimmer raced back towards the advancing horde, firing as they went. She saw one picked off, then another, rolling to a stop on the sandy ground. The driver, hunched behind his protective windshield, accelerated toward the advancing Mannekhi.

The front line of Mannekhi soldiers suddenly split, like a golden sea opening, leaving a passage in front of the skimmer. She didn't understand why until she caught sight of the cannon, which now had a direct line of fire at the skimmer. A long corridor of shimmering air lanced forth from the cannon, and enveloped both skimmer and the driver. The driver must have detonated the ordnance, because the corridor became a conduit of fire, stretching all the way to the shield. Flames bounced off a point just in front of where Petra stood, though there was no sensation of heat. The corridor vanished, leaving no trace of the skimmer or its driver.

Not a single Mannekhi had been killed.

"They were brave men, as brave as our Youngbloods," Brandt said.

She touched his hand, and zoomed in on the three remaining Youngbloods who had moved away from the crater into the horde's path. Each Genner warrior stood with arms outstretched, holding two daggers.

"What the hell are they doing?" she asked. "They'll be shot to pieces."

But they weren't.

"It's a Mannekhi fighting ritual," Brandt said.

"But they're Qorall's minions now."

"We'll see. We need to know."

The leading edge of Mannekhi slowed to a walking pace, then stopped in front of the three warriors. Three Mannekhi attacked them, and were quickly dispatched by the Youngbloods. Petra could feel the tension all around her, as everyone drew closer to the barrier for a better view. As another three Mannekhi fell to the floor, a hissing sound arose on her side of the barrier, in Hremsta, an encouragement Genners used in sparring matches to cheer their fellows on. Petra took a breath and made the same noise between tongue and teeth.

Three more Mannekhi died, but the blood of one of them spattered onto a Youngblood's face. He wiped it away, then buckled as if punched in the stomach, his face lined in pain. Petra zoomed in, and saw the first cracks of gold etch down his cheeks. She screamed a single word in Hremsta, cutting off the hissing, hoping her voice would carry on the breeze and be picked up by the Youngbloods' superior hearing. Brandt glanced at her with a look of surprise, then echoed her command in his far louder voice.

A fellow Youngblood moved to the infected warrior and slit his throat. A roar erupted from the Genners, chanting the same word Petra had used. Many of the Steaders tried to imitate the word, neither knowing nor caring what it meant. But the two remaining warriors were set upon by the Mannekhi until Petra could no longer see them. The chanting ceased, the crowd craning their necks to see. After a minute, the two Youngblood warriors emerged from the Mannekhi horde, their skin golden. They walked towards the lip of the crater, as the Mannekhi drew back. Petra grasped Brandt's hand, and squeezed hard. The turned warriors calmly disappeared into the crater. Five seconds later flame and dirt mushroomed from the crater up into the air.

Even before the dirt had come back to the ground, the Mannekhi from the last ship emerged. As one, the golden infantry advanced. Petra noticed armoured vehicles, several with serious-looking hardware and cannons of varying sizes.

She stood her ground. Everyone else did, too.

At last the invading army stood some ten metres from the shield. One golden man walked forward, only recognisable as Mannekhi by his eyes of pure black. He stopped at the other side of the barrier from Petra. At first she thought he was staring at her, that this was some other kind of pre-battle ritual. But it was always hard to know what a Mannekhi was looking at, and it dawned on her that he was studying Blake. The man returned to the front line, a mixture of male and female soldiers, all golden, and various vehicles and artillery.

"Now what?" Brandt asked.

"We see who blinks first."

Within the hour, Kilaney and Xenic had landed on the opposite side of town, but there was no way to let them in. Petra still faced the unmoving wall of Mannekhi, who were by now thoroughly drenched from the rain. It didn't bother them. Funny thing was, the rain seemed to be only on them, not on the shield directly in front of her.

Vasquez had informed her there were twelve hundred turned Mannekhi outside the barrier. Only a few needed to get through, and then the chain reaction of contamination would begin. She had to admit, this conversion ploy of Qorall's was brilliant, since in most wars even the winning side usually suffered devastating losses to its numbers, but this way, battles actually swelled Qorall's armies. Three ranks of heavily armed Genners and militia had taken up position in front of the horde, and the crowd of Esperian onlookers were ordered back to the town.

One of the Spiders nudged her hip, startling her. She tried to read its flickering comms band.

"What's it saying?" Brandt asked.

She stared at it. "I'm not sure." She whirled back to the cannons. They were silent. "Oh crap!" she said.

Brandt touched her shoulder, holding her in place. "Petra, speak to me. What did it say?"

She held his gaze while lifting her wristcom to her mouth. "Colonel, can you tell me the integrity of the shield? No? Can you detect if there is any energy signature from the cannons. Check *all* frequencies."

She sighed. "It said three minutes until barrier failure." She cursed herself. The Spiders assumed the humans knew; the cannons had probably been firing steadily since they'd taken up position.

Vasquez came online. "Sorry Petra, you're right. It's on a frequency we weren't monitoring and can't see or hear. Convergent beams from all six main cannons are focused on a spot right in front of you. You'd better move out of the way. I don't know if the whole barrier will come down, or if it will only create a small opening for the soldiers to come through."

She stared at the cannons, the Mannekhi soldiers standing in the rain, and the clear – and completely dry – barrier.

"The rain," she said. "That's why we can't see rain on the shield in front of us!" *Stupid! I should have seen that.*

She and Brandt moved back, but she noticed the Spiders remained where they were. A thought struck her. "Vasquez, tell me the moment the cannons stop firing." She switched channels. "Kilaney, Xenic, get ready to come through."

There was a sound like glass cracking, then fissures appeared in the shield. They spread outwards like ferns, then cracks opened up, stretching until a crude arch formed.

"They've stopped firing, Petra."

She whirled to the Spiders, gave them the command. "Kilaney, Xenic, you have five seconds." The Mannekhi soldiers began filing toward the arch. She signalled to the Spiders to raise the shield, just as militia took up position in front of her, armed with pulse rifles. Vasquez must have ordered them to open fire, because suddenly the noise of constant pulse fire deafened her. Backlash heat seared her face as Brandt dragged her backwards, away from the fray, though she watched, horrified as a mound of charred corpses built up in the arch. But more soldiers continued to pour through, despite appalling losses.

Eventually one made it through and flung himself towards the militia. They caught him in crossbeams, igniting him like a flaming torch, but that allowed two more to try the same tactic. The front rank of militia fell back, as the second rank opened fire.

"It's not working," she said. Brandt held her tight while she gripped the handle of her pulse pistol. The ten metre distance between the arch and the militia was strewn with burning bodies. There was a surge though the arch, and even though the militia caught the front wave, the ones behind continued the charge, carrying their dying comrades, and fell upon the front militia row. The second row paused a fraction of a second then opened fire on their fallen colleagues, trying to stem the flow.

Kilaney arrived, out of breath. He surveyed the scene. "Petra, what are the Spiders saying?"

She looked at him, not understanding, then followed his gaze to the Spiders, who had remained exactly where they had always been, Blake still in their midst. She read their comms bands, then reached into her left pocket, and clicked the release. The Spiders parted, and Blake stepped free of his restraints.

Petra found the scene surreal. The yells, screams, the buzzsaw of pulse rifles in freeflow mode, solid beams of yellow streaming outwards, devouring the soldiers, the searing heat, the stench of charred flesh, frenetic animalistic fighting on a carpet of corpses and boiling blood, and a single golden man walking right into the melee. The Mannekhi seemed to ignore him. Until he touched the shoulder of one of them, at the edge, and the man flinched, then staggered backwards, falling in amidst other men, the golden sheen on his face giving way to mottled patches of grey. Blake touched another, then another. The fighters at the front remained oblivious to Blake, but those at the back were not; they began to notice him. Three of them faced Blake, and crouched. Before Petra could react, Kilaney snatched her pulse pistol and drew his own, and sprinted forward, while Xenic yelled at the militia to restrain their fire in that direction.

Blake glanced at Kilaney for a split second and – she was sure of it – the corners of his mouth lifted a fraction. Blake began fighting, Kilaney protecting his back as golden Mannekhi soldiers swarmed around them. Those at the front line stopped advancing, and joined this new focus.

"Cease fire!" Xenic shouted, with such force and presence of command that the militia stopped, even though he wasn't their commanding officer.

Petra couldn't see. "Lift me up," she said to Brandt, and he hoisted her up onto his shoulders.

Kilaney and Blake were back-to-back as the Mannekhi soldiers tried to stab them both without being touched. Kilaney used his pistols sparingly; the object wasn't to kill them, but to convert enough to stem and then turn the tide. But each time Blake touched one and he began to turn, his comrades slaughtered him. She saw Blake shout something over his shoulder to Kilaney, the latter nodding, and then Blake dived forward, touching as many faces as he could reach, taking several knife thrusts in the process. Kilaney spun around and picked up Blake like a battering ram, his half-Q'Roth physiology keeping him upright long after any human or Genner could have survived, piledriving Blake through the soldiers until too many knives in his back and legs brought him down. And then Petra couldn't see; Blake and Kilaney were on the ground.

"Down," she said, then turned to Xenic and the militia. But Vasquez had arrived. A pulse cannon hanging from his shoulder.

"Ready, people," he said.

All the militia and Youngbloods stood in a single rank, weapons raised. Petra watched the crowd of Mannekhi soldiers. They shuffled this way and that, and then collapsed to the ground. No more Mannekhi pushed through the arch, and she saw the mottled grey affecting others outside the shield, spreading backwards through the Mannekhi ranks like wildfire. The antigen was working. She walked forward, shaking off Brandt's attempt to hold her back. By the time she reached the throng, most were on all fours, gasping, retching, all of them losing their golden sheen. She walked through them until she found the two men she'd been searching for.

Kilaney was dead, his eyes wide open but a grimace on his face she felt sure concealed a smile. Vasquez, Xenic and Brandt arrived, but she didn't look up. Instead she rolled Blake onto his back. His blood, still warm, soaked her tunic. Three knives were driven into his torso up to the hilt.

To her surprise, he was still alive, just. Blood oozed from his mouth, and his breath came in short sharp rasps. She knelt down next to him, no longer caring what happened to her. She tried to speak, but her throat choked up. But he looked at her, and the words came forth.

"You did it Blake," she said. "Like you always said, break the infantry, win the war. The tide will turn now."

He smiled, and made to speak, but blood poured from his lips. He looked up to the sky.

Petra bent forward and spoke softly into his ear. "Go to her, Blake. Go to Glenda." She kissed his forehead, and as she lifted away from him, saw that he was gone, and closed his eyelids with her fingertips.

The Spiders gathered around her and Blake. Petra bowed her head, as drops of rain coursed down her cheeks.

PART THREE
MICAH

Chapter 24
GOLIATHS

Pierre stood on the surface of the Machine asteroid as it hurtled through space. He was on an intercept course with one of Qorall's Orbs, standing inside a small bubble of tailored atmosphere shielding him from cold vacuum and hard radiation. The asteroid-sized Machine remnant – all that was left of the race after Hellera's deception – was solid metal, so there was nowhere else for him to go. The ground beneath him was flat and featureless. Since his childhood, he'd always looked to the stars; they had been his friends, the constellations a landscape sketching his hopes and dreams. But it was different seeing them this way, with the naked eye as opposed to via a screen or porthole back on Ukrull's Ice Pick, or through layers of atmosphere back on Earth. Now the stars looked starker, stabbing at him through silent space. Somehow they felt hostile, accusing, as if they knew what he was planning. He started walking on the grainy metal surface. There was nowhere to go, but he needed to move to help him think this through one last time, before there was no going back.

He started from when Jen had dropped him off, literally.

Jen had come back up from the lower part of the sliver that remained from Darkur's ship. As soon as she entered the cockpit, water dripping from her overalls and hair, he sealed the hatch, blocking the Hohash from entering. Frowning, she stared at him.

"Please don't tell me you want privacy, Pierre, because I'm really not –"

"The Machines, they've been in touch with me."

She froze, and glared at him through her wet, mouse-coloured fringe. Pierre had known her long enough to realise that she thought things through before she spoke – jumping several steps ahead. He wasn't disappointed.

"Your nannites? That's how they made a connection?"

He nodded.

She moved over to her chair, swung it around so she was facing him. She closed her eyes. "Dimitri – is he somehow..?"

He didn't answer. She opened her eyes again.

"Okay. So, some of them got away from Hellera's trap. What do they want?"

"Me," he said.

She cocked her head to one side. "How did the interview go?"

He decided to play it her way. "I got the job."

She folded her arms. "What's the pay like?"

"With their help I'm going to try and destroy the Orbs. All of them."

She studied him. "What do you want me to say to the three women in your life, Pierre? You remember them, right? Petra, Kat… Hellera?"

"I'll miss them." He cleared his throat. "Well, not Hellera, obviously."

She leant forward in her chair. "I don't think she's the forgiving type." She got up, tried to pace, gave it up as there was no room. "I'll need to give her a reason not to hunt you down, Pierre."

"Bishops."

Jen sat back in the chair. "Excuse me?"

"It's like chess. She knows chess. There are four enemy layers: rooks, bishops, pawns, and the king."

Jen folded her arms. "Let me see: the Nchkani are rooks, the Orbs are bishops, the turned races pawns, and Qorall, well, that's obvious. Hellera has just wiped out the rooks, and you think together with the Machines you can eliminate the Orbs. What about the pawns? And for that matter, who is Qorall's queen?"

He shrugged. "I'm not sure who the queen is." But a name arose in his mind: Louise. Could it be? She was a lowly pawn, and yet… no, he had insufficient information, and it was too unlikely. He got back on track. "As for the pawns…

not my jurisdiction any more. If the Machines go after the pawns – the organics as they think of them – they'll do more damage than Qorall."

Her smile faded. "What about *after*? What's your endgame, or for that matter, that of the Machines?"

That was the big question. If they survived the first Orb contact, the Machines would grow and attack others. But afterwards, they might decide to purge the galaxy of organic species again.

"Thought so," she said. "How much of a head start do you need? And on that subject, how are you going to get to work?"

He smiled. "An hour. And, out the airlock. They're outside. I've been working furiously to stop the ship's immune systems attacking them."

She raised both eyebrows. "Won't need a suit, then?"

He shook his head and stood up. Without warning, she got up and embraced him.

"I'll tell Petra and Kat that you did it for them, for all of us." She released him.

"It's not exactly true... But you understand my decision, don't you?"

She walked him to the airlock hatch. "Sure. Dimitri would have been tempted to join a hyper-advanced race. You scientists value intellect and exploration above everything else; it's your heroin."

She activated the hatch, which slid open without a sound. "But I'll lie to Kat and Petra, because they won't fully understand otherwise."

"I'm not sure –"

Her voice became firm. "Kalaran once told me that perception is the only reality that matters."

He acquiesced. Who was he to disagree with Kalaran?

She held out her hand, shook his. "Now, go and destroy all the bishops, and when you're done, take the Machines out of our galaxy, and never come back. Hard code it into them, Pierre, they must leave and never return."

He stared at her a moment. "You're a dark horse, Jen, far smarter than you let on. Only now can I begin to see why Dimitri loved you, and why Kalaran spent time with you."

"We all have our moments. Now, get out of here."

That had been an hour ago. He stopped walking, squatted down, and touched the hard surface. Did he trust the Machines? Of course not. That made no sense, they were logical creatures. Jen had used the right words – it needed to be hard-coded into them. But how? The Machines were in survival mode. Kalaran had awoken them, Hellera had used them and tried to eliminate them immediately afterwards. But the Machines would not feel anger, nor would they feel any remorse if they took over the galaxy by killing a few trillion organics, and not just those turned by Qorall. For the Machines, it was all about utility, propagation, and logical order rather than chaos. The idea of a new galaxy was an enticing prospect, and they had originally been designed by the Tla Beth to explore remote galaxies, but there was a lot of risk, and why should they leave this galaxy when they had what they needed here? The Orbs were a significant threat, but if they could be destroyed, then the Machines could sit and wait out the final battle between Qorall and Hellera and then make their move. Pure, cold logic.

The ground beneath his fingers rippled, and he glanced upwards, and saw it, a star that looked brighter than any other, with a golden light. He stood up, and opened his mind.

<Are you ready, Pierre?>

<Yes. You may begin.>

He tensed. This was the agreement. He wouldn't sign the contract with blood, but with his DNA, and his organic mind's force of will. That's what they needed to survive and defeat the Orb, which was nothing more than a super-virus that worked by re-writing organic software. Most organic species – following Kalaran's ankh template – had strong will, but their emotional and intellectual 'software' was beneath their conscious control, and so was vulnerable; their coding was weak, so re-coding via the Orbs was easy. In contrast, the Machine race's coding was very strong, ultra-disciplined, and had inbuilt intelligent monitoring and resistance. But the Machines lacked any organic sense of will; they had been designed by the Tla Beth to be servants, and so it was only a matter of time before the Orbs exploited such a basic flaw, a trap-door in their metal-clad coding.

That was where Pierre came in. He'd asked earlier why they hadn't used Dimitri to achieve the same effect, but at the time they had taken Dimitri purely for sustenance, a catalyst for their propagation, nothing more. Besides, they needed a tech interface, and Pierre had nannites. He'd also asked them why they hadn't considered this option before, during their brief reign of terror two million years earlier. They'd believed they could win by pure logic alone – they needed a miniscule amount of genetic material to propagate, but they abhorred organics with their clumsy and chaotic thought processes. However, the Orbs had presented a new challenge to the Machine race, requiring a new response. Logic dictated that a new strategy was needed. But to Pierre it was more than that; it was Darwinian evolution writ large, a new threat in a species' environment that would either kill it or make it stronger. And there was the risk: he was about to try to help a dangerous force become even more powerful. The lesser of two evils? He couldn't be sure. But he had made up his mind, he was committed.

He felt pressure on his feet, and glanced down. It had begun. Black metal vines crawled up his calves, his feet and ankles already encased. There was no turning back now. He took one last look at the Orb, at the stars he knew he would never see again this way, then closed his eyes, and held the vision of Kat and Petra in his mind, knowing he would never meet them again. The metal around his legs invaded his flesh, freezing pinpricks stabbing into him, making his upper body shake as his core temperature freefell. He opened his eyes, gasped and cried out. He could no longer feel his legs, only a wave of ice creeping up his chest. He lifted his arms in front of him, watched metal gloves wrap around his hands, and felt the ice-metal on his neck. Whichever way he analysed it, he was dying, there would be no more Pierre after this. He just had time to taste the names on his lips of the two women who had meant more to him than anyone else. He spoke their names into the echoless void.

"Petra, Kat, forgive me."

He could no longer see, the metal ice tightening like a tourniquet around his face, freezing tendrils drilling through his skull, skewering inwards. Pierre concentrated on one last thought, with all his being, with all his will, one single line of code.

Jen stood with Ukrull and an avatar of Hellera inside her ship, watching the event as if standing in space, as if they were right there.

The Orb dwarfed the Machine asteroid. As the two neared collision, the leading surface of the Orb bled outwards, reaching out to embrace the ball of solid metal. It slowly engulfed the Machine world, their entire race, until all that was left was a slightly larger Orb. Ukrull walked forward, to the other side of the scene, and growled at it, his tail thrashing behind him. Jen knew he wanted to help in some way, but they were all powerless in this particular struggle. The Orb paused, then continued on its way, steady against Ukrull's massive figure, stars whiplashing past in the background and foreground as it accelerated towards its next target. Jen felt her heart sink. But Hellera and Ukrull waited, saying nothing, so Jen stayed. She'd just decided to sit on the floor when a chair appeared. So, Hellera wasn't totally pissed off with her. It didn't look too comfortable, but Jen knew when not to be impolite, and sat down.

After what seemed like an hour, Ukrull snorted – she didn't know what that meant, but she sat up and paid attention. The apparent movement of the stars tearing past the Orb slowed, then braked to a dead halt. She saw a single ripple disturb the Orb's smooth surface. More followed, waves building; something was emerging. It was black.

She was out of her chair, standing next to Ukrull, staring. Cube-like black insects crawled out of an open sore on the Orb's surface. On closer inspection they were compact flat boxes with legs, reminding her of nannites, though their actual size must have been that of small ships. Her breath quickened. Waves grew on the Orb's surface, became tsunamis that smashed down on the giant nannites. But the Machines were unharmed, and more and more swarmed over the Orb from wounds splitting all over its surface. They scalpelled its flesh, skinned it alive, flinging swathes of gold-turned-brown matter into empty space. Jen squeezed her fists. *Kick its ass, Pierre.*

The core of the Orb could be seen, and it was metal. Gradually the Orb was completely shorn of its golden flesh, leaving the original black Machine asteroid shrouded in a cloud of detritus. Her only wish was that there could have been some blood as well. But she narrowed her eyes as she gauged the size of the Machine world.

"It's grown," she said, guessing that Ukrull and Hellera were well aware of it. The Machine asteroid morphed into the shape of a lozenge, then separated at its mid-point, creating two smaller asteroids. The process repeated itself. Four asteroids, and from her reckoning, each one was the same size as the original. Three of them flashed silver and disappeared into Transpace, no doubt in search of more Orbs. The last one hung there, not moving. A light gold spot appeared on its surface. It moved up, then down, etching a figure on the asteroid's surface. Not a figure, she realised; writing. As it continued, both Ukrull and Jen moved aside, so that Hellera could see – not that she needed to, given her faculties – but out of deference, because the first word had spelled out her name.

Jen reckoned Pierre was somehow still there, since it was too ironic an act to use the Orb's penchant for writing on its surface; a pure Machine intelligence would have found another way. It was a message for Hellera, but it also told Jen that Pierre had survived the process in some way. At last the message finished.

<Afterwards we will leave this galaxy and never return.>

The words glimmered a few moments in the cool starlight, then dissolved into black. The metallic asteroid vanished into Transpace. Jen caught one last glimpse of Hellera's avatar, poker-faced as ever, before that, too, vanished, leaving her alone with Ukrull.

"Pierre was pretty exceptional, wasn't he?"

Ukrull grunted.

"I didn't really get to know him," she said.

"Will tell you about him on way to Esperia."

Jen's heart quickened. She had mixed feelings; it was home to humanity, but she had nobody there who really cared for her.

"Wrong," Ukrull said.

"What?" She suddenly remembered Ukrull was telepathic.

"You will see."

Jen stood next to the screen of Ukrull's brand new ship, which he hadn't yet named. It had taken her nearly a day to get the full facts out of Ukrull, and now she couldn't sleep or even sit down. Hellera had sent a clone of Gabriel to Esperia. She knew it wasn't the real Gabriel, but part of it was him, his thoughts, his personality; whatever Kalaran had been able to download before Gabriel – the Genner Youngblood leader who was also her nephew – had blown up Sister Esma and himself into the bargain. And she was terrified of something happening to him; she'd lost too much these past few days.

Her skin itched on the inside. "Can't we go any faster?"

Ukrull laughed, as far as she could tell. "Like old times. Want? Will hurt."

"Has your telepathy stopped working?" Last time she'd missed Gabriel by a hair's breadth, only to find him dead. She wasn't going to let that happen again.

Ukrull's forked tongue flicked over his eyes, then he kicked a control with his claw. Jen found herself on all fours, a hammering inside her skull, gut-wrenching nausea in her belly, blotches before her eyes, and a roar in her ears like a rocket engine at full thrust. She ended up curled in a ball, forehead on the cold floor, hands over her ears, but she said nothing, and bit back the urge to scream. *Hang on, Gabriel, we're coming.* She swallowed with difficulty, then shouted a single word to Ukrull.

"Faster."

Chapter 25
GABRIEL

Sandy was thankful Toran hadn't harmed her, but that small vestige of gratitude didn't stop her wishing him dead. He'd killed her husband in front of her – that was the only way she could reconcile what had actually happened – and was set to take out the remaining human leaders. But there was nothing she could do. She'd been bound and gagged in her chair most of the six days it had taken his small ship to reach Esperia. She couldn't feel the back of her head; something was plugged in there, as evidenced by periodical drops of her blood dripping onto her neck, zig-zagging down several vertebrae before they congealed. At least he'd told her his Alician name, Toran; she couldn't bear to think of the clone as the original Gabriel, her one-time lover from those last fateful days on Earth.

But at last they had arrived back on Esperia, Toran's ship perched on the Acarian mountain range sheltering Esperantia. She tried to see as much as possible over his shoulder as he surveyed the chaotic town scene via the ship's viewer. It looked like a war zone, bodies scattered on the perimeter, some in small mounds. But the town buildings and streets were intact.

"They have prevailed," he said.

"We're not as stupid as you Alicians take us for."

He turned to her. "No, you are not." He returned to the scene, zooming in to see individual faces. She glimpsed Petra and Vasquez, and then flinched at seeing Blake's corpse being carried away by four Youngbloods, Brandt leading the way.

"I do not see Micah in the crowd," Toran said, "which means he has not yet returned. I need other targets."

"Go screw yourself," Sandy said.

He faced her again, framed by three frozen images on the screen. He touched a pad on the arm of his chair, and Sandy's vision became grainy. She heard a dispassionate voice, female. With a shock she realised it was hers.

"Petra, President; Vasquez, Commander of the Militia, Brandt, leader of the Youngbloods."

Her vision became normal again. She spat in his direction, but it failed to reach him.

Toran's voice was flat, devoid of emotion. "Normally I would have killed you for that, before your saliva reached the floor. But I want you alive when Micah arrives, to throw him off balance. I shall wait for him."

Sandy had turned away from Micah a long time ago, but knew he mattered to the war effort. She didn't want to see him executed. Toran had dispatched Ramires, so Micah wouldn't stand a chance. Besides, if he waited for Micah, Toran would have the element of surprise, whereas if she could get him to act early, Micah would arrive and maybe salvage the situation.

"He's not coming back," she lied. She felt a stab of pain behind her eyes. What had Toran done to her? She continued her lie, despite her vision almost shutting down, and a feeling like somebody drilling through her temples. She squeezed her hands behind her, sinking her fingernails into her palms to try and counter the pain in her head, and swallowed down an urge to retch. "Ramires told me, Micah is taking Shiva to join Hellera to battle Qorall. That ship is pretty advanced, remember?"

Toran studied her. She felt sweat run under her armpits, but the pain abated a little, and she could see again.

Toran turned back to the screen. He didn't seem that interested in Micah. Sandy understood; Toran was a warrior, not an assassin. He would rather fight hand-to-hand against a worthy adversary; his focus on Micah was purely on

Louise's orders. Sandy stayed quiet, letting him digest the lie. Silence could sometimes shore up a lie better than further words.

"Louise told me he loves you," Toran said, turning back to her. "That concept doesn't mean much to Alicians; it is mostly foolishness. We Alicians care for each other, respect each other, and of course make mating decisions according to preferences. Did you know Alicians mate for life with a single partner, and such relationships endure for hundreds of years? Would any human relationship last so long? There is no such thing as infidelity in Alician society." He turned back to his display. "You know so little about us."

Good, he was moving away from the Micah topic. She decided to push him, to goad him; something she reluctantly admitted she was good at.

"What I know is you've also wanted to destroy us for hundreds of years. Besides, you're a clone. How old are you, clone?"

He paused. "One year."

She tried to detect any emotion underneath that sad statement, but there was none. He was a cipher, little more than an automaton, filled with propaganda. But he clearly wanted to be more. That was his weakness. She attacked it.

"Then you know only what you've been programmed to know. You're a killing machine, that's all."

"I am Toran," he said. "And I know what I am. There are almost no clones in our society, even though we have the technology, and I of all… people, understand why."

"You have no soul, clone, you will never know love, or be loved, or even cared for." She hated that her husband had been killed by such a creature.

He fixed her with a gaze, and for an instant she thought she detected something real about him, a flicker of bitterness.

"Then I will have no guilt over what I am about to do."

Good. He was going to act, though she hated to think what he was going to do. At least Micah should arrive soon, taking Toran by surprise, or upsetting his plans.

He stood up, gathered several weapons together, including Ramires' nanosword.

"This human love keeps your species weak. Yet I am curious. Do you love Micah?"

She tried to turn her head away, but couldn't move, and her vision went grainy again, and she heard a single word escape her lips before her vision returned to normal. She needed to get him off that particular track.

"My turn to be curious," she said. "Why the lone assassin walking amongst them? Why don't you attack with this ship? You could do more damage."

"Three reasons. First, values: I am not an assassin, I am a warrior, as your mate was. I fight and die with honour. Whatever else you may believe, I have Sentinel values, albeit with a different allegiance. I look my enemy in the eye before killing him. Second, psychology: a ship attacking is one thing, but a lone man walking into the midst of human society and killing its leaders creates a deeper fear. Third, there is some kind of shield around the town. I need to dismantle it."

Sandy didn't like the sound of that. "Why?"

"If I survive I will take ten human captives – enough to facilitate successful Alician procreation, and then leave the planet, discharging a human-tailored toxin into the biosphere. Then I shall join the other Alicians."

"And Louise."

"No," he replied. "She has another mission." He turned away from her, studied the screen again.

The way he'd said it made it seem like a secret. "What mission?"

He didn't answer, and busied himself at the ship console.

She knew it must be important. "You said you had Sentinel values. I invoke Charok-Nor. You are going to kill me one way or the other, and you killed my mate, as you call him."

He paused at the controls, then told her. Sandy would have shaken her head if she could have. Louise was going to see the Q'Roth High Queen; the leader of all the other Queens spread across the galaxy; the ultimate ruler of all the Q'Roth tribes. Louise was going to offer the High Queen a deal to persuade her to work with Qorall, and she had the perfect bribe to clinch the deal. If the legions of Q'Roth turned against Hellera now… Sandy stored it for later.

"And if you perish?" she asked.

"In four hours, unless I send a signal, the toxin will be released automatically."

Sandy cursed under her breath. *Micah, wherever the hell you are, hurry up and arrive!*

"You Alicians truly are humanity's bastards. I wish the Nchkani had blown Savange to pieces with us still on it."

Toran's face remained neutral. "The feed in your head is wrapped around your upper spine. If you pull really hard, you may break loose, but you will be paraplegic and you will transect your vagus nerve, after which you will asphyxiate within two minutes."

He departed via the airlock.

Once he was gone, Sandy tried to let her head hang, but it wouldn't budge very far. Then she noticed he'd left the viewer running, and she scanned the sea of faces. She'd isolated herself the last fifteen years or so, and most of the people she saw were strangers. She'd never integrated. Now, for the first time in a long while, she felt a kinship towards them, and wanted to protect them, but there was nothing she could do. The only hope would be if Micah returned early. Reluctantly, she pondered the single word she'd spoken to Toran earlier, in response to his question about how she felt about Micah. It hadn't been the answer she'd expected. She'd thought she no longer cared for him. Evidently she did.

Petra was busy; she had to be to stay sane. Xenic and his small Mannekhi crew rounded up the restored Mannekhi soldiers, most of whom seemed bewildered and in shock. The Steaders and Genners had largely headed back into town, but she stayed near to the spot where Blake had died. The thought stopped her cold. She closed her eyes and took three deep breaths.

She heard Vasquez' sharp, clear voice.

"You should get some rest, Petra."

She opened her eyes. "The Spiders have left the shield up except for the breach. Why?"

Vasquez squinted in the direction of the invisible large hole, the sun dipping towards the Acarian Mountains.

"I assume you've asked them?"

"Of course. They chose not to answer." She glanced back towards the town; the Spiders had followed Blake's body an hour ago and not returned. Brandt had said that many people had walked next to them, trying to see the fallen heroes, the first time most had ever been close to a Spider.

She took in the hundreds of Mannekhi milling about in the near distance. "What will Xenic do? Where will we put all these Mannekhi? Their ships can't take off again."

Vasquez touched his earpiece. "Two ships have entered the Shrell field."

Petra's breath stalled; she couldn't weather another attack.

Vasquez paced while he listened, then he stopped and faced her. "Thank you," he said. "Keep me informed."

He walked to Petra and placed his hands on her shoulders, as if to steady her. "One is Shiva. Micah, Kat and Antonia are aboard."

Petra found that his steady hands were welcome, as she stifled a gasp of relief.

"The other ship?"

"Unknown, a small vessel already landed in the mountains. There's a third vessel on long range sensors coming in at a terrific speed, broadcasting a Ranger's code."

"Rush hour," she said. "The Spiders must know, somehow."

She saw Brandt walking towards them, but he was being followed a few paces behind by another man she didn't recognise, though he looked somehow familiar. Brandt waved to her, then stopped and spun around. Petra saw something in the other man's hand. Dread filled her, and she burst into a sprint towards them. But even as she approached, the two men had already become locked in a struggle. Brandt was much larger, but the other man moved like no one else she'd ever seen, barring Ramires. Vasquez followed her, bellowing orders, but most of the militia had already gone back to the town.

Brandt appeared to be winning, his tree-trunk arms wrestling with the man, but suddenly his head shot backwards and she heard a snap, and his body flopped onto the ground.

Vasquez, right behind her, tripped her, sending her sprawling to the ground, as he opened fire with a pulse rifle on freeflow, taking no chances. But the man stood unperturbed, the beam flowing around him like a river round a boulder; he had a personal shield, a defence she'd never seen. He stepped over Brandt's corpse and walked towards Vasquez as if taking a stroll. He pulled out a hand-held weapon and rapid-fired at six militia men approaching from the town. There were six staccato sounds as darts struck each man in the centre of the forehead. All six men crashed into the dust, eyes still open. Petra got to her feet, but Vasquez split away from her, the man following him. Petra dashed over to Brandt, keeping one eye on the killer and Vasquez. Brandt was dead, his neck snapped. Petra closed his eyes, and touched his lips with her fingertips.

"Old style," the man said to Vasquez.

"It never grows old," Vasquez replied. He unsheathed two commando knives, and carved the air before him in circular and spiral movements difficult to foresee. The man faced Vasquez, his hands and arms spread wide, inviting attack. Vasquez lunged but at the last second pulled back, avoiding a ferocious roundhouse punch. The intruder was incredibly fast, and spun like a dervish, savage kicks flicking outwards, forcing Vasquez to retreat even while he jabbed at the man's feet and legs, finding no flesh to cut. The outer edge of the man's foot whiplashed into Vasquez' right forearm then the left, sending both knives spinning from his hands. Vasquez recovered and his right fist smashed into the man's jaw, but the punch had little effect. Vasquez stilled, face-to-face with the attacker, then he looked down. Petra followed his gaze; the man's hand had punctured Vasquez' trunk just below the sternum, his fingers buried in Vasquez up to the knuckles. She got up as Vasquez collapsed to his knees, glanced at her once, and shouted a single word before he fell forwards:

"RUN!"

The man faced her, his right hand red with gore. Pulse shots ricocheted off the man's shield as Xenic's men raced towards them, but Petra knew they wouldn't make it in time.

"My name is Toran," he said. "I will make it quick."

Petra could have run, but she recognised this assassin's tactic, to instil fear in those around her, and so she stood her ground as he walked towards her. He pulled out a thin rod she recognised; so, he had killed Ramires. The electric blue nanoblade stretched from its sheath, as his arm curled in a backswing. She refused to blink, and stared him in the eyes, squeezing her lips tight so they wouldn't tremble. Her body tensed, but the blade stopped centimetres before her neck, a tanned fist locked around the assassin's wrist. Petra turned to see who had just saved her life, and then nearly stumbled as she saw the face of the new arrival. She whispered his name. "*Gabriel!*" She knew it couldn't really be him, but he looked so like the Youngblood warrior she had loved all her life, and whom she knew to be dead.

Toran whirled back into a defensive position, for the first time not looking serene, and faced Gabriel. Xenic and his men arrived, carrying heavy weaponry. Gabriel held up an open palm, and they lowered their weapons, instead forming a circle around the two men. Petra forced her way inside, and stood next to Xenic.

Gabriel looked different somehow, there was no fire in his eyes; they looked vacant, and he hadn't recognised her. She stared from Gabriel to Toran; the resemblance was clear as day, now she saw them together. There were no photos of the original Gabriel from Earth, but it must be two clones, father and son. And they didn't know. She made to move forward, to say something, but Xenic seized her arm and shook his head.

Toran launched into an attack with the nanosword, shrieking a fearsome warrior's kiai as he flashed the sword down, but the younger Gabriel blurred out of the way, the electric blue blade missing him by millimetres, while his fist shot like a piston into Toran's chest, sending him flying backwards. Petra knew no ordinary fist could hit that hard; the blow had sounded almost like metal on flesh. And no human or Alician could move *that* fast. The clone of Gabriel had been enhanced.

"Are you a Sentinel or an assassin?" Gabriel said. "It makes no difference to me, but to you it may matter how you die, who you choose to be when the killing blow comes."

Toran coughed on the floor, discarded the nanosword, and stood. He attacked with a flurry of blows almost too fast to see, Gabriel moving equally fast, evading and counter-striking each fist, foot and elbow, the impact sounds like a frenetic drumbeat, the last one a hammer fist down onto Toran's head, knocking him to the ground. Petra winced at the sound of his skull fracturing.

Toran got up, but could barely walk, as blood pumped from the top of his head, and ran down his face in streaks. Gabriel punched the man so hard in the chest even Xenic flinched as everyone heard Toran's chest-cage shatter, blood spraying from his mouth. He collapsed onto the ground, then managed to get to his knees and half stand up. She had no idea how he was even still alive. Gabriel walked over, locked his arms around the man and dragged him over to Petra.

"Finish him," he said.

Again she wanted to say something, but Xenic squeezed her arm.

"Do not speak, Petra. End this now."

She stared first at Gabriel, and then the broken man trapped in his arms. She wanted to tell Gabriel that this was his father, even if he was only a clone. Xenic released her and she stepped forward, her chest heaving. She looked Gabriel in the eye, but saw only a warrior's resolution. Toran looked up to her, his eyes drenched in blood, struggling to breathe. He closed his lips and nodded.

Petra knew the mechanics of it. She planted her right hand on the back of Toran's skull. He didn't struggle, but Gabriel held him tighter. Warm blood trickled over her forearm as she gripped Toran's chin with her other hand. She braced herself, but couldn't bring herself to do it.

"For Brandt," Gabriel said. "I remember him. He was my friend."

Without taking her eyes off Gabriel, she thought of her one-night lover lying in the dust, and snapped Toran's neck, feeling the inner crunch, and then let go at the same time Gabriel did, so that Toran crumpled to the floor. She lowered her blood-soaked hands and stared at them. She'd never killed before. She felt sick to her stomach.

A sonic boom followed by a ripping sound announced Shiva's return. She knew that later she'd be glad to see them all, that the mission to Savange had been a success, and that both her parents had safely returned, but right now she felt as if she'd lost so much, and she felt ashamed for taking another's life. She wanted to tell Gabriel that they had just killed a clone of his father, but to what end? She knelt down and touched Toran's head, and for the third time in the space of an hour closed dead eyes.

"Bury him with honour," she said. "Whatever else he was, he deserves a warrior's burial."

A group of militia ferried his body away, and she accepted a hand from Gabriel to get to her feet. She wiped her eyes, glancing over to Brandt's body, also being carried away by four Youngbloods.

"You look like Gabriel, but he was killed," she said.

"The Kalarash downloaded as much of me as they could before… I do not have good memories, though I remember Brandt. I am only sorry I did not make it here earlier. The one called Hellera sent me here in a capsule that whisked me to the surface, the Spiders dropped the shield for an instant to let me through."

She said nothing, just stared at him, trying to remind herself that those beautiful eyes were those of a clone, that the Gabriel she had loved was dead.

"You are Petra, aren't you?"

She nodded.

"You meant something to him, the original. But there was another, Virginia. Is she…?"

Petra shook her head. "Why are you here?"

He looked up at the sky, to the growing dot that was Shiva. "I have a message from Hellera, for the one called Micah."

Sandy heard voices. "In here," she shouted. "Come quickly." She'd seen Toran killed, but the four hours was nearly up, the toxin about to be released.

Micah entered along with the Ossyrian female doctor, Vashta. Micah came over to her straight away.

"No time, Micah, there's some kind of auto-release of a toxin about to happen, you need to stop it."

He and Vashta tried to read the console, but everything was encoded, except a digital countdown that registered five minutes and ten seconds remaining. He raised his wristcom to his lips.

"Shiva, tractor us up into space, as far from Esperia as possible."

Sandy heard a thunk as the hatch sealed, then felt her stomach freefall as they shot up into the sky.

"Free her," he said to Vashta, grimacing as he inspected the back of her head.

As they ascended, Micah seemed preoccupied, saying nothing until the blue of sky faded to black, and the stars became visible through the criss-cross pattern of Shrell filaments.

At last she was free, and could stand again, as long as she held onto something.

Micah moved closer. Without warning he hugged her. She stood stiffly, her arms refusing to embrace him, and he let her go.

"I'm sorry, Sandy I'm just relieved to find you alive. We all thought… But you must be grief-stricken over the loss of Ramires. He was… unequalled." He turned to the screen. "Did you see –?"

"Gabriel, yes. Is it really him?" She didn't dare to hope.

"I honestly don't know. Petra is trying to find out. She said he's a clone. I came straight to this vessel. To be honest I thought Louise might be here."

"Sorry to disappoint you, Micah." She mentally kicked herself. Why did she always do that?

He frowned. "What? No, I mean she escaped –"

"Stop, Micah. Please."

He looked crestfallen, and turned back to the screens. Vashta started patching up the back of her skull, and for the first time she felt pain rising like heat inside her head.

The countdown reached zero, and she heard a click from beneath the floor.

"Shiva," Micah said, "let us know when it's finished."

Sandy watched him from the back, wondering what to say; her head was a mess, filled with Ramires, and now Gabriel. She needed time. But she knew there wasn't any left. She cleared her throat.

"Micah, Toran told me something, something you need to know."

He turned his head a little, not enough to see her, just enough to show he was listening.

"About Louise." She hesitated, knowing what his reaction would be.

Vashta moved in front of her, quicksilver eyes dancing. She spoke in her grating choir voice. "There is a complication. What this Toran did to you. It is a Q'Roth interrogation technique, and works on the human left hemisphere, creating a short circuit to a particular part of the right brain and limbic system. Usually the subject dies eventually, but I have fixed you, mostly. You will live."

Micah turned around, looking concerned.

"Mostly?" she said.

"You must not lie, at least for the next week, as it may cause a neural cascade failure. If you do lie, either by telling a lie, or even by not speaking the truth and remaining silent, your vision will alter, you will notice it."

"Are you joking?" Her heart began to beat faster.

Vashta's quicksilver eyes stopped moving, just for a fraction of a second.

"It doesn't matter, as long as you live," Micah said.

But Sandy was terrified he'd ask her the same question Toran had asked. "Promise me you won't ask me anything, Micah."

His brow creased. "What? Why?"

"Just promise me."

He shook his head. "Fine," he said. He took his chair again, facing away from her. "You were saying something about Louise."

"Yes." She relaxed. This was safer ground. "Toran told me her plan."

"To join with the other Alicians –"

"No. To go to the Q'Roth High Queen."

He stopped moving. "Why?"

"To persuade her to switch sides."

Micah snorted. "What could she possibly offer the Queen to persuade her?"

"Nchkani technology."

Micah spun around. "But how?"

"When Louise surrendered the Anxorian rifle to the Nchkani, apparently there was a coded message to Qorall. The Q'Roth are only Level Six, but they're still the most formidable warriors in the galaxy. Imagine if they had Nchkani hardware…"

Micah paced, then suddenly slammed his fist into the hull.

"Micah, this is Shiva. The toxin release is over. I am going to decontaminate your vessel, then you can dock with me."

He slumped back into the chair, rubbed his hands down over his face. "I should have killed her."

"You know, I'm tired of hearing you say that, Micah."

But she watched him, saw how fatigued he was, how he was on the very edge. She wanted to say something to him, to let him know that she still cared for him, that she'd buried it all these years, but it was still there, deep down. Instead she said nothing, just watched him as her vision became increasingly grainy.

Chapter 26
MISSIONS

Micah counted the nine empty chairs at Council: Blake, Kilaney, Ramires, Dimitri, Vasquez, Brandt, Pierre, Ash and Sonja. He couldn't quite believe it; he could see their faces as clearly as if they were right in front of him. Wars displaced people, he knew that; some died, some went away for good. But three quarters of Council... It was one thing imagining the worst, and quite another staring it in the face.

Two emotional roller-coaster weeks had flown by, most people of Esperantia elated that they had survived the attack of the recoded Mannekhi, and plenty of happy reunions for the returned captives from Savange. Then one sorry funeral after another, uncertainty over what had happened to Pierre, and worry over how Ash and Sonja would cope surrounded by Alicians. Micah had left most people to their own grief, because he didn't want to trigger his own personal crisis over the loss of Blake, his mentor for so long.

As for the three women he cared about, Sandy had avoided him, Antonia had reunited with Kat, and Petra was befriending the new Gabriel, introducing him to the Youngbloods.

Jen had initially tried to get close to the new Gabriel, but there was no connection, everyone had seen that, he guessed because the original Youngblood had not known her, and this new version seemed less capable of emotional attachment. For the first time since he'd known Jen, he felt sorry for her, and also as if they finally had something in common: both back, yet both alone.

He'd spent most of his time with her and Xenic, another outsider, focusing on the war. That was what held him together.

Petra caught his eye, and he nodded. She called the meeting to order.

"Please take your seats; all except that one," she said, indicating Blake's chair in amongst the circle of twelve.

Micah counted. Jen, Xenic, Sandy, Gabriel, Kat, Antonia, Aramisk, Vashta, Petra and Micah. So, we are ten. He added Shiva, who was listening in via his resident. Eleven. And he felt that if there was anything *after*, then Blake would be watching, too. Then we are twelve, after all. He raised a hand, and Petra nodded. He took the central floor.

"I'd like to summarize our position and that of the galactic war." Jen and Xenic were sitting side by side. He acknowledged them. "If I miss anything out, please jump in."

He clicked finger and thumb and a holo sprang forth from a vid-projector, coalescing shimmering photons to form a white-centred spiral galaxy, more than half of it red, with small golden dots on the edge of Qorall's wave front signifying Orbs. A blue ring highlighted Esperia, almost at the red frontier.

"This is how it was two weeks ago." He clicked again, and heard gasps from some of the others. The red area had retreated, and the Orbs had entirely disappeared.

"We have this intel from the Hohash, and from occasional links with Hellera. The Machines have eliminated the Orb threat. As far as we can tell, all of them have been destroyed." He met Petra's eyes, and glanced at Kat. "We believe Pierre is to thank for this." Kat's face remained calm, though she took Petra's hand.

"As you know, almost immediately after…" His words stalled for a moment. "After Blake and Kilaney restored the Mannekhi, Vashta formulated both an aerosol and a Transpatial version of the antigen, and Ossyrian triage vessels and Shrell have been spreading it across worlds all along the front. As each race is freed from Qorall, they rejoin the war effort on Hellera's side, hence the reversion is proceeding exponentially."

"A double-whammy," Sandy said. She smiled, holding his gaze.

They were the first words he'd heard from her since rescuing her from Toran's ship. The first smile in his direction he'd seen in nearly two decades. He almost lost his thread.

"Actually, a triple. The Nchkani were defeated – that is, annihilated – at the battle that destroyed the Tla Beth homeworld. Other species who were wavering are now falling behind Hellera."

"So," Petra said, "are you saying we're winning this war?"

He turned back to the holo, and clicked his fingers again. A black gash appeared at the edge of the galaxy.

"Not yet. Jen?"

Jen stood and walked inside the holo. "Qorall is still here," she said, standing on tip-toes, just reaching the gash with her forefinger. "Hellera fears he has a doomsday weapon, one that could destroy this entire galaxy."

"He goes down, so do we?" Sandy asked.

"More like he goes, and we go down," Jen said. "He's remained at the edge of the galaxy for a reason."

"What about the Machines?" Sandy countered.

"Hellera feels if they approach, Qorall will cut and run. Her hope is that they leave the galaxy, along with whatever's left of Pierre." Jen re-took her seat.

Micah glanced at Kat, saw her lips tighten. But Petra remained stern. Her Genner emotional control no doubt came in handy, or perhaps her ability to see the larger picture.

"So," Sandy interjected, "Hellera and Qorall slug it out while we all wait either to cheer or weep?"

Micah shook his head. "No. Xenic will be leading his people and a growing armada to fight on Hellera's side, races all the way from Level Five to the Rangers, Level Fifteen, alongside the few remaining Tla Beth. The ultimate battle will be between Hellera and Qorall, but Qorall still has some species on his side."

"Those races will be defeated." Xenic was on his feet. "The Mannekhi, the Wagramanians, the Zlarasi and other restored races will make sure of that. Micah, I must leave. My new ship is calling. But first I need an answer."

"Ah yes," Micah said, and faced Petra. "A number of Mannekhi wish to come here, as protectors. They believe we are the descendants of a long lost Mannekhi tribe. They would be quite upset if anything happened to us."

Kat turned to her daughter and whispered something Micah couldn't catch.

Petra's eyes widened, then she cleared her throat. "How many are we talking about?"

Xenic answered. "We propose a mere ten thousand to begin with."

Antonia's mouth dropped open. "But we don't have the infrastructure, the food, the –"

Xenic raised his hand. "We will bring city crystals."

They all stared at him, uncomprehending. Micah's resident elaborated, and he filled them in. "They can fabricate – that is grow – cities in a matter of weeks, with everything from power cells to sewage treatment."

Antonia was about to speak again but Petra shook her head. She stared first at Micah, then back at Xenic. "Two thousand to begin with. That's one tenth of our population. We'll see how it goes from there."

"Acceptable," Xenic said, a smile stretching across his face; Micah had never seen him smile.

"They will be here tomorrow," Xenic said, then departed, the sound of his boots echoing after him.

Petra waited till he was gone. "Crystal cities, eh, Micah? Trying to do Antonia out of a job?"

Antonia smiled at him too, then looked away as if remembering something. Micah wondered what was going on. But that was for later. He cleared his throat. "Our part isn't over yet, I'm afraid. Sandy?"

She looked surprised, glared at him, then gathered herself. "Toran told me... Micah, why don't you tell it?"

Petra addressed her. "Sandy, why not address me? Or Gabriel?"

Sandy's eyes flicked to the reborn Youngblood, then back to Petra. "Louise is going to try and enlist the Q'Roth to fight for Qorall's side, with the promise of the spoils of war."

"But haven't they been fighting for the Kalarash all this time, on Hellera's side?"

Sandy stayed quiet.

Gabriel broke the silence. "Hellera downloaded a good deal of Grid politics into my brain; she said it would come in useful, and that there was room, given so many holes in my memory."

Micah noticed Sandy staring at him. So he'd heard, the two had said little to each other, although she had been the real Gabriel's mother. She watched him intently, no doubt searching for her son. But studying her, he realised it was the reverse – she wanted to convince herself this was *not* her son. And yet the way he looked at Sandy, he clearly had memories of her, fond ones.

Gabriel continued. "The Q'Roth were altered by the Tla Beth to become dogs of war. Their allegiance has never been one of choice, and in the past eighteen years they have lost billions of warriors in battles with Qorall, nearly ninety per cent of their population dead. No other species has willingly sacrificed so much in the war effort." He stared at the floor, as if viewing the memories there, or making sense of the stored information.

Petra was hanging on every word. "Please, Gabriel, continue."

He looked at her for a moment, then spoke. "In fact, the whole of Grid Society is rather feudal. It has not been a particularly happy society, even though it has endured ten million years."

Sandy cut in, her voice taut. "Is that Hellera speaking or you?"

Micah realised these two women had opposing feelings for this clone. He judged it best to stay out of it.

"Both, moth –" Gabriel stopped himself. "It is my assessment, but I believe both Kalaran and Hellera had already begun to see the flaw in what they fostered here."

Micah decided to end this. "Louise has to be stopped," he said. "Once and for all. The Q'Roth are still legion in number. And if, as Toran said, they gain some of the Nchkani technology and arsenal, who knows how much damage they could do. We have to go to the Q'Roth homeworld. Louise is probably there by now." He expected objections, shock, or something, but Petra took it in her stride.

EDEN'S ENDGAME

"When are you leaving, and who are you taking?"

Micah was caught off guard; he hadn't exactly planned it yet. "Tomorrow," he said.

"A small crew. Volunteers."

"Count me out," Jen said, rising from her seat. "I'm going to join Hellera. She's asked me to handle what's left of Darkur's ship." She shrugged. "I don't know why, I'm sure others would be better at it than me. But she's asked, and I owe it to Kalaran. Ukrull is in orbit. I don't do goodbyes."

With that, she faded from view and was gone.

Micah had never gotten used to whisking, though he wished Shiva had the capability to teleport.

Aramisk stood, silent until now. "Xenic has asked me to stay, to liaise with the incoming Mannekhi." She sat down again.

Micah noticed Antonia glare at Aramisk, while Kat studied the floor.

Gabriel stood, and was about to speak.

"You're staying here," Petra stated flatly.

Micah, along with all the others, stared at their President. Her face was stone. He realised he hadn't really talked to her since getting back.

"The Youngbloods need you here," she added. "They've lost so much, first you, I mean the other Gabriel, then Brandt…"

"I should go with Micah," Gabriel answered, utterly calm. "Who else here can fight a Q'Roth warrior, or even this Louise I have heard so much about. I believe Hellera fashioned me for this."

Micah was torn. Of all the people present, he needed Gabriel most. But Petra looked ready to crack.

She spoke slowly, with precision. "I… need… "

"I'll make sure he comes back, Petra," Sandy said.

Petra swallowed, puffed out her chest. "And how will you do that, Sandy?"

"I'm going along." Sandy looked at Micah, held his gaze. "Besides, somebody needs to make sure Micah pulls the trigger on Louise this time."

The Ossyrian, Vashta, also stood up and volunteered. Petra said nothing more, as Micah steered the meeting to a close. At last he and Petra were the only two in the room. She still sat in her Presidential chair. He approached.

"Micah, promise you'll bring him back."

"Of course," he said, knowing, as he knew she did too, that the likelihood was that all four of them were as good as dead.

"I mean it, Micah, if he doesn't come back I'll never forgive you."

"Petra –"

She got off her chair, and stood right in front of him, shouting. "You could have intervened, told him to stay here, he would have listened to you. I lost my Gabriel two months ago…" She turned away from him, and spoke in a quieter voice. "Don't come back without him. Promise me."

That was a promise he could keep. "I promise, Petra."

She walked away, leaving him alone in the chamber. He sat back in his chair, and again recalled the faces of former council members, and then added those of Zack and Vince, whose counsel he could really use right now, but there was only him and an empty room.

He realised that he and Vince had something in common, despite having totally opposing personalities: Vince had been decisive, a man of action, and ruthless to boot, cutting through all the emotional bullshit as Vince would have called it, to what mattered. Vince always got the job done, including killing Louise twice. Vince apparently had had a long affair with Louise, before the fall of Earth, and had slept once with Sandy on Esperia, the night before he'd been killed. Micah, by comparison, had had one disastrous fling with Louise, but had longed for Sandy for years, his realisation that she was the one he wanted gaining strength as time passed rather than weakening, despite her complete avoidance of him. He idly wondered why she'd never had more children with Ramires. Then he chastened himself; she was still in mourning, and one brief smile in his direction didn't mean anything. Besides, soon he would need to face down Louise again, finish the job this time, and almost certainly die on the Q'Roth homeworld. Vince would have told him to quit dreaming and get to it. Good advice. He got up and left the chamber.

Having made his preparations, Micah knew there was one last affair to be put in order. He wanted to know what was going on with Antonia. Feeling a tad idiotic, he picked some wild flowers he knew she liked, and marched over to her place as evening began to fall. Kat would be there too; all the better, he wanted to make it clear that 'it' was all behind them, his one night stand with Antonia before Kat had reappeared, and before Sandy had resurfaced. Approaching from the side of her small house, he heard raised voices. He slowed down, and though he knew it was wrong, stood by the exterior wall next to the open window so he could hear.

"You should have told him, Antonia. Part of me can't believe I'm saying this, but he deserves to know."

"He's about to go off to battle. It… It will undo him, Katrina."

Listening, his back against the wall, he mined the facts from the conversation. He slumped down until he was sitting on the ground, the flowers hanging limp from his loosened grasp. She'd been pregnant by him, until the battle on Savange. A son. Micah would have been a father. He'd given up the idea of having children a long time ago, but now, to have come so close and then have it ripped away from him… All sorts of images arose of how life could have been different, raising a son… Antonia was crying. He desperately wanted to comfort her, to share in her grief. But she'd chosen not to tell him, and she was back with Kat. He would get in the way, complicate matters. It would be best if he went off to the battle and never…

Quietly, he got up, taking the flowers with him, and stole into the night.

When he arrived at Silent Hill, the remnant of the moon that had been broken up during Sister Esma's attack on Esperia cast a pale light over the graveyard. Earlier he'd found two flat pieces of wood and nailed them together, the best he could do at short notice, and planted it in the ground near the fresh graves of Blake and Kilaney. He'd lasered onto the crosswise piece 'To the unknown soldier", so no one would know, and laid the flowers before it. He found he couldn't think straight until he gave the unborn soldier a name, even though he vowed never to tell another soul about it, not even Antonia. A traditional choice like his father's name was out of the question; they'd never got on, and he'd had no favourite uncles either. Blake and Zack sprang to mind as options, but that didn't seem right somehow. He recalled Zack saying that parents often wanted their kids to be better than them, to make up for faults the parents couldn't overcome. A single name came to mind, and resonated. It somehow fit, and it was about time. There had been a solider, an unsung hero who had helped save Earth and Esperia without a second's thought for his own survival, someone Micah wished he could emulate, though he knew he would always fall short. Antonia had barely known him, but Micah thought she'd be okay with the choice.

He remained on Silent Hill until the first rays of dawn, thinking of the life his unborn son could have had, then got up and faced the cross one last time before heading back to town.

"Rest in peace, Vince."

Micah stood at the ramp with Kat; the others had already boarded.

"Part of me is sorry you're not coming, Kat," he said, trying to sound upbeat.

Kat had seemed tense, and answered with some evident relief. "Me too, if I'm honest. But you saw how Petra is. And I can't leave Aramisk and Antonia alone together, they'd end up killing or loving each other, probably both." She tried to grin, gave up, grew serious.

"Come back, Micah. And do as Sandy says, kill Louise this time no matter what." She mock-punched him on the arm.

Micah nodded, though coming back wasn't on his agenda. She gripped his arm.

"What?" Micah asked.

She stared at him, hard. "Crap. You know, don't you?"

There was no lying to her; they'd been through too much together. "Tell her how sorry I am. That I wish…"

"I'll tell her, Micah. Truth is, I'm glad you know. But now I'm worried about your state of mind."

"Don't. It makes me all the more resolved to get the job done."

She searched his face. "Come back, Micah. Promise."

"Gotta go. Look after her."

She let go.

Micah took one last look towards the small crowd, waved once to Petra, and saw Antonia next to her. He held up his hand, braved a smile, then turned and walked up the ramp. As soon as the hatch sealed behind him, he leant heavily against the wall. Gathering himself, he walked slowly to the bridge, the purr of Shiva's drives beneath his feet. They'd already taken off. He quickened his pace.

When he arrived, Sandy took one look at him, then told him to sit down. Gabriel was in the pilot's chair, and the screen showed the blue fade to twilight, then to night, the Shrell wires looming close as Gabriel threaded through them at a dizzying pace.

Micah cleared his throat. "Is he flying manually?"

"Said he wanted to practice. Shiva's got override, just in case."

He nodded towards Gabriel, a few metres in front of them. "How are you and he…?"

Sandy had her arms folded. "He's not my Gabriel, Micah. Petra might convince herself." She lowered her voice. "He's a creature of Hellera, remember that, Micah. Kalaran might have promised Jen to restore Gabriel, but it was Hellera who actually delivered the goods." She spoke louder again. "Gabriel and I talked about it, actually – he's painfully honest – and he recalls my husband more than me…" Her voice caught.

He reached a comforting hand towards her but she drew away from it. "Sandy, I've not had a proper chance to say to you how sorry I am about Ramires."

She jutted out her chin. "The best man that ever was." Her eyes welled up.

"You'll get no argument from me on that point."

They said no more for a long time, as they watched Gabriel slalom his way out of the Shrell field encapsulating Esperia's system.

Micah stood. "Listen up, everyone. We need to talk strategy, we meet in the mess in five minutes."

"Aren't we going into Transpace? We won't be conscious until we arrive."

"Yes, and no," Micah replied. He touched a pad. "Vashta?"

The Ossyrian medic entered the bridge, followed by a Hohash and a lone Spider.

Scattered across the galaxy, all the remaining Hohash gathered. They temporarily phased out of normal space and morphed into subspace. Hellera's mind connected to each of them, as well as the Spiders. There was no speech, only a river of coherent thought. Hellera asked for an update, and each Hohash funnelled fused data cascades to her on the war, casualties, politics and alliances, army strengths and movements, weapons capabilities…

She took it all in. The tide of the war had turned; Qorall was losing, and losing fast. There would be one last major battle with his remaining armies, the decisive one between him and her. She presumed his original objective to capture and mate with her, or to use the DNA he would harvest from her dead and gutted ship for the same purpose, was off the table. She had pushed him into a corner. His game plan now would be either to win the war or destroy the galaxy. Then he'd hunt down and kill the other Kalarash one by one. Whilst her DNA was most favourable – because she was female – to create a line of descendants for Qorall, it wasn't beyond his ingenuity to adapt male Kalarash DNA for the same purpose; at least Kalaran had thought so.

The single unstable variable for the upcoming battle, the one that could tip the balance in Qorall's favour, was the potential Qorall-Q'Roth alliance. She had programmed Gabriel to deal with it, but knew it might already be too late due to Louise, a factor she'd underestimated. Another uncertain variable was the Machine race. They would leave the galaxy if Pierre stuck to his word, or rather, if his will still held enough sway with the Machines, now they had regained full strength. One Machine ship was still in contact with her, the one containing what was left of the mind of Pierre. Most of the other Machine ships were swarming at the outer edge of the galaxy. The deal stood, so far.

The main hazard was Qorall's doomsday weapon, the galaxy-breaker. The Hohash stationed in the galactic core had confirmed that Qorall has passed through the centre a year earlier, and left something there. No doubt a device for triggering a super white hole, one that would feed on the boundless energy there and trigger an explosive force with so much harmful radiation it would wipe out all life before spinning depleted stars and incinerated worlds into the inter-galactic void. If it ignited, she would have to abandon the galaxy, leaving most species behind; there would be insufficient time to build new ships capable of inter-galactic travel.

The Spiders were ready, their small ships cocooned within the depths of her own. She ordered the Hohash into position. Ukrull and Jen arrived, joining the fifty other Ranger scout-ships and the remaining Tla Beth vessels. Hellera commanded the armada forward, to Hell's End, where Qorall awaited.

Chapter 27
UPGRADE

Louise stayed perfectly still. One of the Q'Roth High Guard stood by her side with his mid-claw lightly closed around her throat. She avoided gulping; any sign of weakness might trigger a nervous twitch and end all her plans. The High Guard were taller than normal warrior Q'Roth, reaching four metres, and rarely left the Queen's side. Louise had learned that there were two types of Queen; those who journeyed out into the galaxy and set up hives, and the homeworld-based High Queen, supreme leader of all Q'Roth tribes. She was the one Louise had dared ask to see. But as soon as she had landed on the northern ice cap of the Q'Roth home planet, Korakkara, her ship had been impounded. Louise had been stripped and decontaminated, and made to stand naked for two hours with her neck on the line.

Losing Savange had been a cruel blow. She could blame Micah, but Qorall had been unnecessarily brutal, and Micah had actually saved the last Alicians from oblivion. The Queen had not sent reinforcements when Micah's ship had first attacked, nor had there been any offer of help with the Alician refugees. Louise knew how it went with the big players: no empathy, certainly no clemency; you stayed on their chessboard only as long as you were useful. After that, you were in the way, and not for long. Luckily she had sent a message prior to arrival, otherwise her ship would have been blown to pieces before it reached orbit.

She felt cold. One of her calf muscles began to tighten, as if it might cramp. She breathed deeper, willing her muscles to relax, so she could remain still – after all, the guard hadn't moved a millimetre, and Louise was sure she was being watched for any sign of weakness, at which she might be killed; they had the tech to extract the deal offered by Qorall from her dying mind, at least they thought they did.

At last she heard a rhythmic thumping sound, compounded by a dragging, scraping noise, like a horse dragging a sack of rocks along the floor. She'd never seen the High Queen; few had. She was brown, and there was a pungent smell like rotting fruit that caught in Louise's nostrils. But it was the Queen's girth that surprised Louise, the swollen ribbed belly that rippled with internal movement. Not eggs, that was for sure. Louise lifted her gaze instead to the Queen's head, an inverted triangle tapering to a sturdy neck. At the other end was a lizard tail with mace-like clumps at its end. They looked lethal, and although the Queen's movements seemed sluggish, Louise had no doubt this five-metre Q'Roth could react with lightning speed.

The Queen took up a standing position between two metal pillars, leaning on them with her upper claws. That was when Louise noticed something else, ultra-thin folds of skin tucked away below her armoured shoulder blades, stretching down behind her belly. So, the legend was true.

"State your proposal," the Queen said, each Q'Roth syllable razor-sharp.

The claw around Louise's throat loosened, allowing her to speak clearly.

"Level Sixteen Nchkani tech and weaponry in exchange for tactical support in the battle to be fought at Hell's End. After victory, the Q'Roth will be upgraded six Levels and become overlords in this galaxy."

The Queen's belly stirred, something writhing inside. Louise tried not to stare, and waited for the response to her proposal.

"Qorall's recode strategy is failing. The tide will turn. The Orbs have all been destroyed by the Machines." Her triangular head leaned forward, her six eyes flared. "He is losing."

Louise raised her voice. "Kalaran is dead. Hellera alone cannot defeat Qorall. The Tla Beth are few, the Rangers inconsequential. The recoding was a ruse, an experiment, nothing more. When Hellera is defeated, and you have Nchkani ships, Qorall will rule this galaxy the traditional way, a strong hierarchy, with the Q'Roth keeping everyone else in their place."

"Why us?"

"Despite considerable losses during the war, your Q'Roth warriors have time and time again proven their worth, often against Level Nine or even Level Ten species with far superior technology. Q'Roth resilience and tactical ingenuity are both legendary and feared."

The Queen didn't seem convinced. Louise remembered something else she had told Qorall about the Q'Roth. "You are also the species whose character is most like his own." She could go further, that the Q'Roth and Qorall were both defined by malice, and an unquenchable thirst for aggression, in Qorall's case forged through aeons of bitterness and a need for revenge, and for Q'Roth intentionally bred into them by the Tla Beth, and ultimately the Kalarash. What goes around, comes around.

"Tell me of the galaxy-destroyer."

"All I can tell you is that it exists, and it is located in the galactic core. A super white hole will ignite, and will burn its way through this galaxy, devouring all star systems."

"At the speed of light. We are very far from the core. It will not reach here for thousands of years. Why should we care now?"

Louise had asked the same question, though Qorall had inflicted severe pain in exchange for an answer. She'd barely grasped the math.

"Transpace carriers, subspace harmonics. Shockwaves, ripple effects. I already forwarded the simulation to your fleet Admiral in orbit. The galaxy will be gone in a year." And the Alicians along with it. Qorall had to be stopped, but if no one was up to it, he had to be helped in order to avoid his terrible endgame, equivalent to tossing the entire chessboard into the fire. There was a third way, of course, but she dared not even reflect on it in front of the Queen.

Something moved violently inside the Queen's belly, a savage kick. The Queen's head rolled back a moment as she emitted a hissing sound, then pitched forward again. There was a splitting noise emanating from the Queen's loins.

Louise tried not to watch as something dark and gelatinous began to emerge from between the Queen's lower legs. She was giving birth.

"Why you?"

The question took Louise aback, but she knew she had to answer immediately, even as a body slumped to the floor, twitching inside a transparent sack. She saw a mustard-coloured claw stretch the interior of the sheath and pierce it.

"I am but a messenger. I proved useful to Qorall before, and I am part-Q'Roth." Louise left out the fact that this switching of allegiances was her idea.

The Queen paid no attention to the hatchling. Louise wondered what it was. There was something different about it. Louise felt a shiver run down her spine. Hatchlings needed to feed almost immediately. The guardian's claw was still around her throat, and she had no weapons.

"The Nchkani fleet is destroyed," the Queen said, a nonchalance in her tone, as if the interview was boring, irrelevant, coming to a close, and the real purpose of Louise's presence about to be revealed. The hatchling, yellowish in colour, tried to get to its feet, and slipped in its own amniotic fluid. Its claws looked sharper than usual.

Louise watched the hatchling. It had a longer belly than a warrior, and was taller than normal, its mid-legs also longer, more spindly. With a gasp, Louise realised it was a Queen. No one – even Q'Roth she had worked with – knew where the Queens came from, the assumption being that they hatched from eggs like all other Q'Roth. The Queen who had given birth to this one must be special, and possibly very, very old. The new Queen stood awkwardly on its six legs, and faced Louise. It staggered a step towards her. The mother leaned forward, eager to watch her offspring take its first feed.

"The Nchkani had a secret process they called Resurrection," Louise said. "I can bring back the Nchkani ships, give you a fleet of them. Today. In your system." She glanced at the new-born. "Or not."

The claw tightened around her throat, almost choking her.

The Queen lurched forward from the pillars and landed right in front of Louise, pounding into the floor, making it shake. Her left mid-leg grabbed the hatchling at the neck, holding it in place. It acquiesced, and became docile.

"If you are lying, I will extract your mind before my new-born feeds on your carcass, and leave you in a torture loop for millennia. You will drown in your screams for eternity."

Louise had heard of this process, reserved for traitors and those who fled from battle; one reason the Q'Roth warriors were so disciplined and ready to die rather than suffer defeat.

The claw eased off a little so Louise could speak. "I never bluff. I carry the re-genesis material on my ship, but it needs my codes, cross-correlated with sixteen random memory fragments." You won't get all of them by post-mortem memory extraction, and you'll have nothing. "The sixth planet in this system will serve for re-genesis purposes."

The Queen lowered her head close to Louise's face, her six eye-slits waxing the colour of congealed blood. Then she lifted away again, shepherding the infant Queen to Louise's left. Louise heard the sound of feet. She tried to see, but could barely turn. Three chained, naked Alicians came into view, a male and two females. They had not been treated well. She recognised the male, Astara, the commander of the space station that had been tethered to Savange. These three must have been aboard the Q'Roth warship that escaped when Micah attacked the station. Astara's eyes locked onto hers.

"Ustraxia," she said. It was the name of a place from Alician history, a famous battlefield. Astara and the others stared a moment, then one by one nodded to Louise.

The Queen released her child who pounced on the trio. They did not defend themselves, nor resist, understanding Louise's command. The young Queen fed on them one after the other, its mouth clamping onto the top of Astara's skull first, sucking the life force out of him. The two women waited their turn. There were no screams. Louise watched till the last was taken. Her remaining human hand trembled, and Louise found she couldn't stop it, until the last was dead. The new-born Queen tilted its head back, and Alician blood sprayed from its mouth as it roared, its bellow echoing throughout the chamber. It departed.

The Queen returned her focus to Louise. "You have twelve hours. If you attempt to jump out of system, we will track you down, as well as your Alician refugees, and feed on you all."

"You will have your ships," Louise said. "I will go with your fleet to Hell's End."

The Queen raised herself and strode out of the chamber, her belly dragging on the floor as before. The guardian released Louise.

She walked to the three corpses and stood over them. She had never been religious – Alicians weren't, believing there was nothing afterwards – but she began to intone the Alician death ritual, then said it aloud, then louder, until it echoed around the chamber.

Aboard her vessel, she stared first at the harmless-looking doughnut-shaped object in the holding bay, the gift sent to her by Qorall himself, then at the holo of the dwarf planet below, originally an asteroid enlarged by the Q'Roth, who had used a process of accretion over decades, building a planet from a former asteroid belt; easier to mine that way. Six thousand Q'Roth, more or less, worked on this factory-planet rich in ores and complex alloys. The Queen hadn't warned them or given them time to evacuate, knowing that the resurrection process would require organic material. Louise had scanned the entire system prior to arrival, and this one had a 97% fit for the re-genesis requirements. She touched a control and the doughnut dropped from her ship down towards the planet.

The doughnut exploded at low orbit, sending a shimmering aurora around the planet. Rain the colour of rust fell all the way to ground level, nano-harvesters that broke down everything they touched, the Q'Roth included. She'd never seen Q'Roth warriors overwhelmed before, and wondered if they screamed in bewilderment as the bio-mechanised acids dissolved their flesh. Many raced to their ships but were unable to break through the aurora locking the planet down, their frantic calls for help unanswered. There was a time when Louise might have been impressed by the Queen's ruthlessness, her commitment to purpose, but not today.

She quit the bridge and headed to her quarters, and took a long shower to wash the three Alicians' blood from her feet. She sat naked on the floor, cold water drizzling over her, as she pondered her next move. She thought about the place she'd mentioned to Astara and the others: Ustraxia, the battlefield five hundred years earlier on Earth where Alessia herself had been overcome. It had been a ploy to make the Sentinels complacent, and fifty years later the Alicians had risen up and gained the upper hand, crushing all but a few of the Sentinels. Louise had invoked this name to persuade Astara and the two women that this was a worthy sacrifice, that their deaths would help Louise turn things around later.

For the first time ever, Louise considered that perhaps the Q'Roth were now their enemies, too. At the least, the Queen could no longer be trusted. The Alicians had outlived their usefulness to her; she could order her soldiers to cull all humans and Alicians left alive, and in so doing clean up her chessboard. Louise had fought alongside many Q'Roth warriors over the years, and found them to be honourable warriors; she respected them. But at the end of the day they did their Queen's bidding.

But did it matter to her? Unlike her mentor Sister Esma, Louise had never been that interested in Alician history, instead playing the renegade. But now she'd come back into the fold, and felt kinship with her fellow Alicians. With something of a shock, she realised she had found a cause other than her own survival. The image of the three Alicians being killed, their broken corpses on the floor, kept coming back to her. She couldn't remember the last time she'd felt this way… but then she could. Vince.

Louise had refused over the years to think about it, about him. They'd died together back on Esperia, courtesy of Micah. When her clone had awoken afterwards, she'd wept and raged in equal measure. She'd always seen Vince as her last chance at going back to any kind of normal existence. With him gone, she'd run around the galaxy for almost two decades, fuelled by cold anger. She closed her eyes, recalling times back on Earth – nothing remotely romantic, Vince hadn't been the type – but still, they'd looked out for each other, and that meant… She dared to think it, to let it surface: they'd cared about each other. She drew her thighs close to her chest, rested her brow on her knees, and recalled all their missions together, one by one, it made her smile.

She sat up, her head against the wall, the cold water numbing her back, and wondered what Vince would think of her choices over the years, all the bad things she'd done, knowing what his reply would have been. He'd have looked at her with those ice blue eyes, and said, "Louise, it only matters what you do next." She bit her lip, then whispered into the shower's drizzle. "I miss you." She started to shiver, and drew her arms around her shins.

Reluctantly, the other person who mattered in her life, if only as counterpoint, came into her mind. Micah. Since Vince's death she'd wanted nothing more than to watch the light fade from Micah's dying eyes. It was no longer important. For the first time they had a common enemy. She switched off the shower and towelled herself brusquely. Not having eaten for some time, she headed to the galley.

When she returned to the Bridge, the entire planet was coated in thick metallic mush that quivered as shapes swirled beneath the surface. Precisely two hours before the Queen's deadline, the first ship emerged, looking like a mechanical fish rising from a swamp. At first she couldn't see the trademark Nchkani spines, but as the ship climbed into orbit, slipping unhindered through the aurora, the black and white spines flexed outwards from its hull.

A Q'Roth Battlestar approached to intercept the Nchkani vessel. Louise let the vessel fire its full arsenal of weapons, none of which had any effect. She thought about instructing the commander to abandon ship, but knew it would do no good. Q'Roth tested everything through blood.

She instructed the Nchkani vessel to attack. A light-sphere riddled with electric blue arcs spat out from one of the spines and chased after the Battlestar, which tried to evade and fire at it, to no avail. The sphere engulfed the Q'Roth warship as the arcs dissected it into small chunks, as if the ship had been squeezed through a sieve. Individual Q'Roth warriors flailing in space were boiled alive inside the sphere. Eventually the sphere collapsed to a small ball, and returned to the Nchkani vessel, nourishing it.

The Nchkani had been brilliant. At Level Sixteen, they were few in number, but long ago had moved away from having dockyards to build ships, and had developed the re-genesis process, able to manufacture a fleet in a less than a day. And when they fought in battle and won, they recycled the enemy's energy and raw materials, rather than allowing their own resources to become depleted. From a war logistics point of view, it was pure genius.

And yet they were dead, gone, after who-knew-how many million years of existence.

The Queen contacted Louise. "How many more ships will we have, and when?"

"One hundred and eighty. By tomorrow. I will transmit command codes for all the others except this one, which I will command. They each need only one commander, no other crew are necessary. We should proceed straightaway to Hell's End. Qorall is waiting, and Hellera is on her way."

The Queen didn't acknowledge.

Louise watched the second ship emerge, then another. She wondered where Ash and the Alician refugees were by now, not missing the cruel irony of events, now that Alician society had suffered the same fate they had inflicted on humanity.

The fleet was ready to leave. A Q'Roth High Commander was in charge, Louise was to be at the rear. The Nchkani bridge was smaller than she expected, but then everything was done by neural interface. She was about to cut connection with her own ship when it informed her of an inbound vessel in Transpace. She had been given some of Qorall's tech to monitor Transpace, and had asked for notification of two signatures, the first the Alician flotilla led by Ash, the second, Shiva. It was the latter.

The Q'Roth/Nchkani fleet powered up.

Louise made up her mind, her adrenaline spiking as she did so. The third way. She'd received a visitor while in Transpace two days earlier: a Spider, and a Hohash. It was only then that she recalled clearly, for the first time, what had happened on her trip to Savange several weeks ago, how a Spider had interrupted her journey and stranded a Q'Roth ship in Quickspace, and in so doing, killed a number of her crew as well as Q'Roth. Qorall still didn't know the Spiders' capability, and she hadn't told him.

She presumed the Spider and Hohash had been sent to kill her. Instead they'd made an offer. She hadn't answered, and they'd left, and she'd woken up on arrival at Korakkara. She'd even wondered if she'd dreamt it, and had put it out of her mind while dealing with the Queen. Now, for the first time, she considered the offer, and Vince's favourite adage.

It only matters what you do next.

She transmitted an encoded message to her former ship, and ordered it into Transpace, where it would detonate and send an information spurt to Shiva. At Level Fifteen, Shiva would be able to intercept it, though no Q'Roth vessel could. A short message, captain's eyes only. She was convinced it would be Micah, despite the fact she had sent Toran to kill him.

Louise felt better than she had for days. She'd always believed in burning bridges behind her. As her vessel and all the others slipped into Transpace on the long journey to Hell's End, the message echoed in her mind. It had been simple, and above all it had been clear.

Kill the Queen.

Chapter 28
GHOST IN THE MACHINE

Pierre no longer knew where he was. His consciousness was distributed across eight hundred and forty-three sectors, wherever the Machines roved the galaxy, though nine-tenths had already assembled at the perimeter, awaiting the signal to depart. His thoughts were clear and pure. No more time spent self-guessing or worrying or considering the rights and wrongs of actions and decisions. No more self. Efficiency. Clarity. A larger perspective. But he could still speculate; that was one of his functions inside the Sublime Logic.

The Orbs were destroyed, and had nourished the Machines. Qorall's tentacles reaching across the galaxy had been slashed. Indigenous inhabitants everywhere were returning to normal, though many had become vengeful, and a motley armada of ships of all manner of alien species was making its way to outer spiral N117-E2, colloquially known as Hell's End, to do battle against Qorall.

The Machines had not interfered, simply eradicated the Orbs and aided in the distribution of the antigen, and so the local inhabitants did not fear the colossal black metal poly-structures sailing through their systems. Indeed, many alien infants had created toys mimicking the many forms of Machine city-ships traversing the galaxy.

It had not been like this the first time, Pierre knew. The Level Eighteen Machine race had been reviled, an object of terror and hatred, leading to a massive battle at N117-E2 two point zero three million years ago; which was how that region of space had gotten its name, where the last vestige of the once mighty Machines had been consigned to oblivion on the nameless tomb planet.

Things were different this time, and difference bred opportunity. The Machines were already spread too far and wide to be easily contained. Their closest rivals on the Intelligence scale, the Nchkani, had been obliterated. The Tla Beth were too few in number to resist, and only one Kalarash remained. The Machines could sit out the battle between Hellera and Qorall, then make their move and assert order. But there was a fluctuation in Pierre's thoughts, an asymmetry. He had promised Hellera and Ukrull that the Machines would leave the galaxy. And there had been individual aliens, certain personalities – he had difficulty recalling their names and faces – whom he had sworn to protect.

But that was before. It was more logical to stay. Order *was* protection. The Kalarash idea of a hierarchy based on intelligence was flawed. Resentment built up at lower levels and led to unrest and wars, or else stagnation. Organic species inevitably hated any overlords precisely because they saw that they could one day be in their place, so why should they serve them? But if Machines were the overlords, the psychology would be different. A vastly superior intelligence – a benign one that demanded nothing more than harmonious order and commerce, one that stayed in the background except to quell any unrest and to protect respectable citizen races from extra-galactic influences – would be god-like. The toys would in time become religious artefacts. With a Machine citadel on every inhabited world, ensuring justice and order; the galaxy would thrive.

Another discordant asymmetry arose. What if, no matter how benign, they saw us as oppressors? What if one day a race matched our own intelligence, and sought to replace us? Pierre tried to find the origin of this disharmony, but knew it could only have come from his own self. He felt schizoid: part of him had fully embraced the Machine intelligence's love of order and logic, its utter purity, but another part of him still clung to inchoate organic thinking patterns. It would be far easier all around if that smaller voice were silenced. *My point exactly*, the larger Pierre – the one distributed across half the galaxy – heard the smaller, less significant voice say.

Small Pierre continued. Why not play God more seriously? Eradicate all life in the galaxy and start again. Create life in the Machine image. A Machine galaxy. Though the larger Pierre knew this was being suggested more with irony than with sincerity, the thought had occurred. But the Machine race had always been designed to serve. It was written into their base code, their collective soul. It was who they were.

Code can be re-written, small Pierre said.

The distributed form of Pierre became aware of an external disruption. Contact with twenty Machine entities in sectors well inside the inner galactic rim had been lost. He had no idea why. The smaller Pierre seemed to know something.

I'll get back to you, small Pierre said.

Pierre found himself in human form again, with normal flesh, not even silver-tinged as it had been before. But he knew it was an illusion, first because the environment was a depthless blue, a floor with no walls or ceiling, and second due to the three others present: Kat, a Hohash, and a Spider.

"Hello, Pierre," Kat said. She looked worried. "How are you holding up?"

"Not too well, actually. Tell me, are you… real? I mean the real Kat here via node, or just another reflection of my mind?"

"Real. That is, I'm asleep back on Esperia, but the Hohash is by my bed. Anyway, it's me."

Surprising both himself and Kat, he rushed to her and embraced her, kissing her with a passion he'd rarely known during his physical life.

She gave him a crooked smile, her face flushed. "Wow, Pierre, being a Machine suits you. I feel a little embarrassed, knowing that back home I'm lying naked next to Antonia."

"I'm sorry, I shouldn't have done that."

Her smile lingered. "Ah, there you are, that's more like it. Don't apologise. In any case, I think we have business to do."

He glanced to the Hohash and then the Spider. "I gathered. First, how is Petra?"

"She's strong, that's what matters." She winced, squeezed her eyes closed, and put her fingertips to her temples. She opened her eyes. "Okay, the meeting has started. The Spiders want to know why you haven't left the galaxy."

Pierre nodded. "I'm losing that one, I'm afraid. The Machines are re-evaluating. They're in a strong position now."

"Interesting you say 'they', not 'we'."

"It's complicated. Part of me…" He didn't know how to explain it.

"It's alright. I know you're not coming back. I'm guessing you have no body anymore, and I can't exactly keep you hidden in a Hohash for an occasional secret midnight rendezvous."

He checked to see if she was mocking him, but although she was smiling, her eyes were sad, as if that was exactly what she'd like to happen.

He blurted it out. "They want to take over the galaxy, become our and every species' overlords."

"Of course they do, Pierre. That's why Kalaran got rid of them first time around, and why Hellera is terrified of them." She shook her head. "Funny, no matter how intelligent you are, you always remain naïve. Quite endearing."

She staggered forward a pace, as if someone had shoved her in the back, eyes squeezed shut, hands pressing her temples. She recovered. "Ouch. The Spider is getting impatient, and now I know why. Qorall has placed a device in the central core of the galaxy. Something about a super white hole, Transpace relays… Ah, this will be better. A Hohash scanned it so you can take a look."

Pierre watched the Hohash's mirror surface flash a set of detailed images in ever-increasing resolution, from macro to pico. The device was intricate, but with an elegance of design that was impressive, beyond the reach of his and the Machine's own intelligence level; Pierre felt a tinge of admiration. Its defences were impregnable; any aggressive or insidious attack would trigger the device; there would be no way to stop it. Though Pierre wasn't a physical being anymore, he felt like he needed to sit down.

"A doomsday device," he said. "We have to act now."

She frowned. "Why now? Surely Qorall will wait until the battle, and then decide whether or not to use it?"

Pierre paced up and down, thinking. "Not necessarily. We've been running data analyses on everything he has done since his arrival, gaining an insight into his psycho-pathology. But we didn't know about this device. Now I do, there's a ninety-eight per cent chance he will activate it now, but leave the relays open. That would start the white hole explosion, but without the Transpace relays the outpouring of radiation could only travel at lightspeed, and would take thousands of years to consume the galaxy."

Kat shook her head. "Seems crazy to me. What if he can't stop it? Thousands of years is the blink of an eye to Qorall."

Pierre recalled his earlier conversation with the larger Machine persona. "I'm afraid we might have been too successful. The whole galaxy is turning against him. The Orbs won't work again now that the antigen is everywhere."

"You think he'll cut and run?"

"He may yet try to capture Hellera during the battle, but if he is losing he will leave and burn the galaxy behind him. Even if he wins, he may quit this galaxy and start afresh somewhere else, incubating his young during the intergalactic voyage while all life here slowly roasts to death."

Kat looked crestfallen. She turned to the Hohash and the Spider, closed her eyes.

Pierre watched and waited. Kat became very still. When she opened her eyes again they were black; not like Mannekhi eyes; Kat's eyes were like holes in space. Pierre knew it wasn't Kat anymore. He glanced at the Spider. Then he noticed the Hohash showing a very odd vista with iridescent, multi-coloured contours. It looked like a different kind of space, and he wondered if he was looking at a different galaxy, the original home of the Spiders. In it were many Spider vessels, sleek rainbow-sheened ellipsoids.

"One who was called Pierre, six of your Machine vessels that were travelling in Transpace have been diverted into the central core. They will emerge near the device. They must surround it. Do it now."

Pierre was about to raise objections when he found that his mind was connected to those ships. The 'larger' Pierre, as he thought of him, wasn't present, or else six ships were not enough to allow larger Pierre's emergence. He morphed into the Machine ships' local intelligence and saw through their scanners. The device was shaped like a star, six pearl prongs glistening against a background of pure white. The heat and radiation were at the limit of the known scale; his Machines would not last long, the outer edges already deteriorating, metal vaporising in the heat, sloughing off layers at a tremendous rate. Transpace had been deactivated, no doubt the Spiders' doing. Under Pierre's control the six Machine cities began to flatten, growing thinner, until they were like sheets, lamina a few tens of metres thick, eroding fast. He guided them to connect and enshroud the device. That was when he noticed another object in the white haze, a single Hohash, dwarfed by the device and the shroud. It, too, was melting, cracks on its mirror face. He suddenly realised that this Hohash was keeping his consciousness there, and was also his lifeline back to where he had been moments before, outside the core. If the Hohash broke…

Via minimal remaining sensors he completed the shroud. Mentally joined to their sensors, he noticed from their internal chronometers that time slowed dramatically, or rather, everything was happening at a much faster rate. He knew why. They now had only pico-seconds in which to act, though he still did not see what they could do. As he'd predicted, the anti-tampering triggering system activated. In slow motion he saw the device begin to implode, like a balloon deflating.

"Switch off the Machine cities' intelligence now," the Spider said via Kat. "It will be more… humane."

He didn't question anymore, just complied, as if shooting a horse with a broken leg. He felt sadness, an emotion he'd almost forgotten.

The device had shrunk into a small pinprick of white. He knew what came next. It was as if the device had taken in a huge breath, and was about to explode outwards, endlessly, a silent scream that would engulf everything. The shroud was barely a metre thick.

But something happened. A slit in the brilliant white opened up, not quite dark, but a dim twilight that by comparison was almost night. The slit opened further, as if being peeled back, held apart by invisible hands against terrible pressure to close again. There was noise – though in space there shouldn't have been – the sound of a hurricane rising in pitch to a banshee. Pierre glimpsed ships, four of the Spider ellipsoids he'd seen earlier, stretching open the skein between two space-times. The shroud and the device were sucked through the grim portal, and a picosecond later it snapped closed.

The pure bright white returned, rippling at first, then becoming uniform again. The scorched Hohash, with only one small mirror fragment remaining, winked out of normal space. Pierre found himself back in the wall-less room.

"Where?" he said. "Where did you send the device? The intergalactic void? Another galaxy?"

"Another universe."

Pierre definitely needed a chair. One appeared, and without thinking, he sat down.

"How?"

"The Big Bang, as you call it, spawned multiple universes. There is one that is… darkness. It was stillborn, no stars, only gas clouds that failed to ignite, simmering at the low level of what you call the EM spectrum. The device can do no harm there, other than bring light."

"The four Spider ships, can they return?"

"A necessary sacrifice."

Pierre's mind was reeling. Who were these Spiders? Until now, he'd believed they were from another galaxy.

Kat was back, her eyes returned to normal. "Hello," she said. "That was a little weird. They had to take control, because the action was taking place too fast for my dumb little brain to keep up." A chair appeared for her, too, and she took it, and gazed at the Spider. "They're not from another galaxy. They're from another universe."

Pierre stared at her.

"One of the Kalarash found a way to cross over, Pierre. When he did, a Spider scout ship came through."

Pierre shook his head. "All this time, I've been exploring the galaxy when the most interesting species there could ever be was living next door on Esperia."

"There's more."

He looked into her eyes, and guessed it. "Kalaran. When he was in his ship in Esperia's underground oceans, he wasn't sleeping for those half million years, was he?"

She smiled, a non-crooked one. "I still love that you're smart."

"He crossed over, didn't he?"

She nodded. "Time runs differently there, so for him it was more like a year."

He remembered the brief vista the Hohash had shown him of Spider ships, in what must be their home universe. "Transpace is natural to them, isn't it?"

"Yep, that's how they can manipulate it. That's their last message to the Machines, by the way. If they don't leave, the Spiders will deactivate Transpatial travel in this galaxy. They can do it, something about interfering with the subspace harmonics that open up Transpatial conduits, via super-excitation of some exotic particles I've never heard of, probably because they're not from this universe… I couldn't follow it all. Sorry. They would need cooperation from the Shrell who inhabit subspace, but they already have it."

Pierre stared into the floor. "That would mean we – and anyone else – could only travel at sub-light speeds. Wormholes occasionally, but they're unstable, unfit for organics, and they chew up subspace."

"Exactly. It would kill trade and commerce, sending this galaxy back to an almost primeval state. But it would also negate the Machines' pan-galactic plans for a Sublime Order."

"This was Kalaran's idea, wasn't it?"

"Actually, it was theirs. And the Shrell's. They're pretty fed up with all of us invading their territory. Some of the Shrell are already defecting to the Spider universe."

Pierre stood up. "The Machines will leave. Tell them that, Kat. There would be no point in them staying. There are other plenty of other galaxies…"

"You were right, Pierre. They should re-write their base code. Find an empty galaxy, and fill it with Machines."

The Spider vanished.

"Meeting over?" Pierre asked. "I guess I should get back. They need me, I'm afraid."

"I know." Kat stood, looking a little sheepish. "But first… I asked for a little privacy."

"But the Hohash is still here."

She shrugged. "No Hohash, no us."

She walked towards him, put her arms around him, and kissed him.

Pierre felt other feelings rise up inside him that he thought he'd forgotten. Logic be damned, he thought, and kissed her back.

Kat opened her eyes and found herself back in bed next to Antonia, who was leaning on her elbow staring at her.

"Hello sleepy-toes. You've been dreaming."

"Oh," Kat said, blushing. "Sorry." She noticed the Hohash through the door in the next room.

"No need to apologise, especially as you were fondling me in quite an interesting way."

Kat's blush deepened. But she and Antonia hadn't had sex since they'd gotten back from Savange. Antonia had said she couldn't. Which meant they'd not made love for over two years, ever since Louise had taken Kat prisoner. Kat bit down on that thought, and made to get up out of bed.

Antonia caught Kat's shoulder. "Where do you think you're going?" Antonia slid on top of Kat, pinned her wrists to the pillow, almond eyes gleaming. "Promise you'll never leave me, Katrina."

"I promise," Kat said. "Anything else?"

Antonia released her wrists, and began kissing Kat's body.

Kat lay on the bed, listening to Antonia moving about in the bathroom next door. "Don't worry, I'll never leave you," she said quietly, more to herself, as the noise of a bath running masked her words. She got up and tiptoed to the Hohash in the living room. She leant her head towards it and connected via her node, searching. After a while, she smiled, and kissed its golden outer frame.

"Our little secret," she whispered, and headed to join Antonia.

Chapter 29

LAIR

Micah pondered the message from Louise, trying to see the deception. But he couldn't. Nor could Sandy, Gabriel or Vashta. "Kill the Queen," was all it said. Hard to read between the lines when there were only three words.

"Kill Louise first," Sandy offered.

"Shiva believes it was a parting message," Micah replied. "Transmitted just as she entered Transpace. Louise is probably long gone."

"Then go after her," Sandy replied. "Maybe Shiva can pick up her scent and we can change direction. She's enemy number one, Micah."

Micah wasn't so sure anymore. The last time he and Louise had met, he'd sensed a change in her. She'd seemed genuinely upset about what had happened to her people on Savange. *Her people.* She'd become loyal.

Gabriel joined in. "We came here to the Q'Roth system to find out what deal she has brokered with the Q'Roth High Queen. It might only concern Louise, or the Alicians, or Esperia, or the fate of the entire galaxy. All we know is what Toran told Sandy, but Louise may not have told him the whole story, or may have even lied to him. We need to know. Hellera needs to know. The final battle with Qorall is coming."

Sandy folded her arms. "I've watched this bitch lead men around her before, drawing them into her game. It never ends well – except for her."

Micah tried not to stare at Sandy. The past few days, awake in Transpace, he'd seen more of her than in years. Although he'd given up hope long ago, he swore he'd caught her looking at him once or twice. He dismissed it; he needed to focus. Sandy was right, Louise was treacherous. But Gabriel's line of argument was more immediate.

"We go in hot," Micah said. "Most likely they'll try to destroy us on the spot. Louise is half-Q'Roth, she may have gotten an audience. The only way we'll get one is by a show of strength."

Gabriel clutched the silver hilt of the nanosword in his hand. "I know I am a clone, that my memories – fragmented as they are – are not truly my own, but…"

"You want justice," Micah finished.

He nodded, addressing both of them. "It is odd. The Gabriel you know – your son, Sandy – wanted so much to avenge his father, slain on Earth. I can… see some of those thoughts. It is like reading a letter: I can see how he felt, but these are not my feelings. Nevertheless, I have a strong sense of duty."

Sandy walked up to Gabriel. Micah knew it was difficult for her: the clone looked just like her dead son, and his features resembled the original Gabriel, but it wasn't him. In the past few days Sandy had kept her distance from this Gabriel even more than from Micah.

"Then do your duty," she said, then added, "Gabriel."

He nodded, as a son to a mother. This time she didn't look or walk away.

The interaction reminded Micah that he himself had just narrowly missed becoming a father, and he felt a gnawing in his guts. Shiva contacted him via his resident.

<Are you alright, Micah? Your blood pressure just dropped, and several of your emotional centres spiked. Vashta noted it as well. We need you at peak performance.>

Micah turned his head to Vashta, who stood regally as usual, her mane of black fur framing quicksilver eyes that betrayed nothing. He gave her a small nod.

He turned back to Sandy and Gabriel. "Let's do this," he said. "Everyone take their stations."

Shiva emerged from Transpace to find herself surrounded by a dozen Q'Roth warships. They bathed her in fire without warning. As instructed, Shiva returned fire only to disarm the warships. Three Crucible Class vessels lashed out their anti-matter cables, trying to saw through Shiva's shields, but her artillery chopped off each strand at its base. More warships joined the fray, some jumping in from outside the system. Transpace conduits opened up like silver rips in space, disgorging ships around Micah and his crew.

Micah thought it was excessive, but then he recalled what Shiva had done to the Q'Roth warships guarding the orbital space station above Savange, cleaving them in two. *They think we've come to strike at their homeworld.*

"Stop firing," Micah said.

"Are you crazy?" Sandy asked.

"I want to talk to the Queen. I need to get her attention. How long will our shield hold, Shiva?"

"A while," Shiva answered.

"That was a little enigmatic," Sandy said. "I think Shiva's sulking, Micah. She's a warship, too, remember."

Micah said nothing, knowing that Shiva was Level Fifteen, augmented by Hellera herself. The shields were multi-layered, poly-phasic and regenerative, capable of shifting at the pico-second level, and harnessed a percentage of the inbound energy to reinforce themselves. It reminded him of the old aboriginal trick of cyclical breathing, which enabled ancient musicians to play wind instruments continuously, as if always breathing out. But it wouldn't last forever.

Gabriel left his station, stood next to Micah, and stared at the viewscreen, hundreds of ships now deluging them with beams, missiles, and anti-matter cables. Some of the frontline ships had to draw back or risk being fried in the radiation backlash.

"What are you searching for?" Micah asked him.

"I am not sure. I sense something out there, in the background, waiting."

"You sense something?"

"I am a creature of Hellera, Micah. Sandy is right on that point. You should not trust me. Sometimes…" He tore his vision away from the screen, and stared intently at Micah.

"Sometimes it is as if I can sense my mind hiding something from me. Other times it is as if someone is watching behind my eyes, seeing what I am seeing." He returned to searching the enemy fleet.

Micah rubbed the stubble on his chin. Then he got up, gestured for Gabriel to take his seat, and walked to the arch leading to the common room.

"Where the hell are you going?" Sandy asked.

"I need to think, and the battle is distracting me. I'm going to get an ultresso. I'll be back in a while. Want one?"

Sandy looked exasperated, but followed him.

He sipped the bitter, grainy coffee while he leaned against the wall, facing Sandy. There was a distant hiss, the only sound generated by the onslaught of Q'Roth enemy fire impacting Shiva's shield every second.

"How long are you going to keep this up?" Sandy asked.

"Until the Queen makes her next move, or Shiva tells me we need to fight back."

His resident was processing Sandy's body language and other parameters, analysing her. He switched it off. Micah sensed his own death approaching, and he needed some closure if he was to focus. He put his cup down, and spoke softly.

"Why, Sandy?"

Sandalwood eyes blazed beneath her fringe. "Why what?"

"For years you've refused to talk to me."

"Really? You want to do this now?"

He said nothing.

She clutched her cup near her lips without taking a sip, and spoke to the floor. "You had plenty of company, Micah, plenty of lovers over the years once you ran out of Alicians."

He placed his cup down on the table. "Louise and Hannah. Is it about them? My God that's ancient history, Sandy. Don't tell me you're still living there?"

She slammed down her cup and went to leave, but the door wouldn't open.

"Not my doing," Micah said.

"Shiva!" she shouted. But the door remained closed. She faced it, her back to Micah.

"You had plenty of lovers on Esperia, Micah."

"Two," he said, hearing the pathos in his own voice.

She uttered a single staccato laugh. "I heard it was eight."

"I didn't know you were listening."

She didn't reply for a time. "Antonia. You were always interested in her. You –" She cut herself off.

Micah felt blood rising to his head. Sandy must have known about Antonia's lost baby.

"What? Say it, Sandy. Or shall I say it for you?"

"Drop it Micah. Forget it." She banged her fist on the door.

He walked up close, right behind her. "At least you had a son. And you have a second chance. He's standing on the bridge right now."

"That… clone… is *not* my son." Her voice was quiet. "Please ask Shiva to open this door."

Before he had a chance, the door slid open. Sandy stepped into the corridor then paused, still facing away from him.

"I'm sorry about what happened to Antonia. And you, Micah. Really." She reached out a hand and grasped the doorframe, as if for support, her voice unsteady.

"I will tell you something I've never told anyone, Micah. All these years, Ramires and I wanted another child. He deserved it more than any man I know, and I wanted so much to give him his own son… But we couldn't. That is, he couldn't."

"But the Ossyrian doctors, surely –"

Micah saw her grip tighten. "They couldn't help, not this time."

Micah's mind reeled as he tried to imagine what that must have been like for them, for her.

"So, Micah, I have an inkling of what you must be feeling, to almost have something you might have wanted for a long time and then lose it." Her grip loosened. "But sometimes, even when your life turns to shit and everything seems lost, then out of the blue fate throws you a second chance. But if it's not the real thing… sometimes you just can't settle for it." She let go of the frame. "This Gabriel isn't my son. He's Hellera's. You'll see, Micah, before the end, of that I'm sure. So, please drop it."

All of Micah's angst had evaporated. She'd been through too much all those years, he'd had no idea. He wanted to comfort her, to hold her. But he had no right.

"It's dropped, Sandy. Thank you for telling me what you just did. It couldn't have been easy."

"It's never easy, Micah." She paused a moment, then left.

Shiva re-activated Micah's resident. <Micah, please come to the bridge, there is a development.>

He started walking. "Don't ever do that again, Shiva."

<Understood, Micah.>

Just before reaching the bridge he realised the continuous hiss of fire against Shiva had ceased. Gabriel vacated the command chair and Micah took it. The front barrage of Q'Roth warships parted, revealing a single black and white ship with long chequered spines.

Nchkani.

"Shiva, can you take it on?"

"Technically, no. The Nchkani vessel is more powerful. But Hellera sent me certain enhancements while we were on Esperia, Level Nineteen algorithms for new shield harmonics. Nevertheless, the odds are not in our favour."

Sandy moved next to Micah. "I thought their ships were all destroyed? I know Toran said Louise would offer them technology, but a ship?"

Her proximity distracted him.

"Shiva, is there only one?"

"That I can detect."

That was something. Also, it wasn't firing; a definite bonus, given that Shiva's shields had taken a battering in the past quarter of an hour. Shiva fed Micah's resident with a piece of Level Fifteen-only information from Hellera, concerning the ability of the Nchkani to replicate fleets in a matter of days, something about a resurrection protocol. Micah joined up the dots: Qorall's plan with Louise as messenger, the Q'Roth Queen as recipient, and Nchkani ships as payment. A fleet of Nchkani ships was an offer the High Queen was unlikely to refuse. He had to do something to make her wary of the deal.

"Vashta, transmit a message to the Q'Roth commanding that vessel. Tell him the following message is for the Queen: 'Louise lied: she is going to betray the Q'Roth.' Transmit as corroboration the message Louise sent us."

Sandy stood in front of Micah. "You've changed, Micah. That was… Ramires would have approved; Vince, too."

He gave a small nod to acknowledge the compliment, but knew full well it could be premature.

"That depends on what happens next." Micah noticed the Spider and Hohash enter the bridge, the Spider taking up position directly in front of the viewscreen.

The Nchkani vessel retreated slowly, and opened up a path through the Q'Roth fleet, towards Korakkara, the Q'Roth homeworld. Shiva followed through a seemingly endless tunnel of Q'Roth warships, until a planet emerged in front of them. Micah had seen an image of the Q'Roth homeworld once before, during humanity's Trial. But seeing it grow large on the viewscreen was something else. The world was dark, scarred by a dozen lava rivers, scarlet curves scratched across thousands of miles of black desert, terminating in magma seas; open wounds, as if pockets of flesh had been gouged from the planet's face. Extinct super-volcanoes rose tall enough to breach the upper atmosphere.

"How can even Q'Roth live there?" Sandy asked.

Gabriel answered, reciting something presumably lodged into his memory by Hellera.

"Their homeworld was once beautiful, purple oceans and forests of blue-woods that reached two kilometres in height, green snows in winter flushed away by rainbow rains leading to the amber period, when the forests produced a highly nutritious honey prized as a delicacy throughout Grid Society. This planet was once one of the galaxy's jewels. But it was attacked by the sole survivor of a Level Nine species the Q'Roth had helped to eradicate during one of the Grid Wars; one reason Q'Roth culls tend to be complete. The damage to the planet could not be repaired, nor could the degenerative terraforming process be reversed. The Tla Beth offered them a new homeworld, but the High Queen refused. The Q'Roth became nomadic, this planet a badge of honour. The core of the planet is now hollow, the High Queen living underground in catacombs with only a handful of guardians.

Micah studied Gabriel. At first the information seemed technical, but the last part was tactical. He would definitely have to keep an eye on him.

The Nchkani vessel hovered next to a gaping hole leading down inside the planet.

"Take us in, Shiva," Micah said.

Sandy put her hand on his shoulder. Whether it was for his or her benefit, he didn't care; he was glad for it.

As Micah suspected, the Nchkani vessel stayed behind, blocking the only way out.

They set down in a vast cavern bathed in green light, several tunnels leading away from it, one directly in front barred by the largest Q'Roth warrior Micah had ever seen.

"Vashta, Sandy, stay here, I have a feeling we might need a rescue and a quick getaway. Shiva, please work out how to destroy the Nchkani vessel."

He nodded to Gabriel, and they departed.

The air outside in the cavern was dank but breathable. They approached the guardian; Micah was sure its six eyes were a deeper red than those of a normal Q'Roth. The four-metre-tall warrior turned and led the way, Micah and Gabriel having to break into a trot to keep up. The tunnel twisted and turned, always descending, as they threaded their way through many intersections; Micah hoped his resident was keeping track of their pathway through the catacombs. As he'd expected, it grew hotter the deeper they went.

Finally, they emerged into a dome-like chamber, empty except for a square dais upon which stood two black pillars the height of a tall man. Four guardians stood in front of the dais, each carrying a three-metre barbed spear that shone like titanium.

There was a dragging, clomping sound, and Micah turned to see the High Queen enter, taller than the guardians. Her ribbed belly reached all the way to the ground and tapered off a couple of meters behind her in a coarse tail with three spikes. Her back was different to other Q'Roth he'd seen: two long bony rods hung straight down from either shoulder, corrugated translucent skin nestling in between. *Wings.* He hoped they were defunct, a throwback to a former Q'Roth age. She hauled herself onto the dais and leant on the two pillars using her mid-legs, leaving her forelegs free.

"The one you call Louise has given us Nchkani ships. You say she will betray us?"

She spoke in Q'Roth, Micah's resident translating; he hoped Gabriel understood. Glancing at the Youngblood clone, he noticed something odd about the way he was standing: completely relaxed, and his face… his expression was as if he wasn't really there.

"We are enemies of Louise," Micah said, "but the message we relayed to you comes directly from her, just as she left this system."

The Queen didn't seem surprised. "I will send word to have her killed as soon as the fleet reaches Hell's End."

The pieces fell into place for Micah. His tone didn't hide his disappointment. "You are changing sides, joining Qorall's ranks against Hellera."

"An offer of accelerated enhancement to Level Twelve, taking over from the soon-to-be-annihilated Rangers and intermediate species. And if Qorall loses, he will destroy the galaxy. It was not a hard decision."

Micah said the words, though he guessed they were to no avail. "You could have honoured your commitment, stayed loyal to Hellera."

"I fail to see why the Tla Beth allowed you humans to survive during your species' trial. You revel in Level Three thinking. I studied your world before we culled it; your lions and antelopes had a better grasp of the true order of the universe than you humans. You will not endure for much longer as a species."

Gabriel stood next to Micah, then spoke to the Queen in a strange voice; the intonations were all wrong, rising and falling randomly. It sounded so… inhuman. Micah had heard someone speak that way once before. *Hellera.*

"The Tla Beth re-engineered you, bred you for aggression, the perfect soldiers. They should have explained the rest: that you would never progress beyond your Level."

The Queen rose from her pillars to her full height, her upper legs flexing outwards. Ebony wings, like those of a bat, began to unfurl. "Enough! Qorall has given us Level Sixteen technology. No one can stop us now!"

The guardians began to close around Gabriel and Micah. Without warning, Gabriel placed a hand on Micah's chest and pushed, sending him flying across the room, until he landed and skidded across the floor. On his back he saw a second Queen, smaller and yellow in colour, high above Gabriel, hanging upside down from the ceiling. Winded from the push, Micah tried to warn Gabriel, but barely a croak emerged.

Gabriel continued to speak, unrushed, in Hellera's oscillating tones. "Technology does not equate with intelligence. These lowly humans, as you think of them, will dance on your unmarked graves."

The guardians attacked. Micah's vision could barely keep up with the blur that was Gabriel; frenetic movement interspersed with images of decisive slices from his nanosword, blue blood spraying in all directions as Gabriel decapitated each guardian in turn. But the smaller Queen hanging high above him dropped silently, her six claws stretched out, ready to thresh Gabriel to pieces, while the larger Queen watched.

Micah knew that although Hellera might be viewing events from inside Gabriel, she was still limited by his perceptual abilities. He yelled, but Gabriel stood his ground, and in the last instant threw the nanosword in Micah's direction.

The yellow Queen crashed onto Gabriel. Her lower claws nailed his torso to the ground while her mid and upper claws made short work of severing his arms and legs from his body.

The hilt of the de-activated nanosword rolled next to Micah. He picked it up as the yellow Queen's gash of a mouth yawned wide then clamped down on

Gabriel's skull. A gruesome sucking noise reverberated around the chamber. Micah began walking backwards toward the entrance, unable to take his eyes off the scene. The Queen released Gabriel's cracked open head and swiped his corpse aside in the pool of human and Q'Roth blood. Her head tilted back as she emitted a roar that sent chills down Micah's spine, then turned her head to look at him. But the larger Queen spoke.

"This one is mine."

Micah turned and sprinted for the exit, his resident snapping into action, showing him the way forward into the catacombs. He heard the slow beats of giant wings flapping in the windless chamber, but dared not turn around. Micah increased his speed to maximum, barely able to breathe in, desperate to reach the temporary sanctuary of the tunnel.

A strangled cry erupted behind him, and the beats changed, faster, and he realised the Queen was hovering in mid-air above him. Then she suddenly turned and flew back to the centre. Micah raced through the tunnel entrance and skidded to a halt. Forcing air into his lungs, he dared to pause to see what had happened. The yellow Queen – he had an intuition she was young – staggered left and right as if drunk, clawing at her head wildly before collapsing on the ground, legs twitching and flailing as her head bubbled and disintegrated, chunks of flesh sloughing off until she stopped moving. Micah understood. Hellera had used Gabriel as a weapon to take down the Queen, most probably using nannites. Sandy had been right all along. But Hellera hadn't factored in the appearance of a new Queen.

Micah knew what came next. With a sense of dread, he took a deep breath and bolted down the tunnel. He heard a long, gut-wrenching scream of anguish from the larger Queen, followed by the beats of powerful wings, and a heavy thud as she landed at the tunnel entrance. Micah then heard a sound he'd not heard in a long time; the jackhammer galloping of a Q'Roth running him down. Micah pumped his arms to run faster, navigating each turn as his resident showed his progress towards Shiva, and the Queen's position behind him, closing very fast. No chance. He needed a Plan B.

Micah's muscles strained to maintain his speed. The Queen was right behind him, and he imagined her raising her sharp upper claws for a slash that would stop him in his tracks without killing him. His resident flashed a sharp left turn. He didn't question it, darted to the side and ricocheted off the wall where, a moment later, a single Q'Roth claw slammed into it as the Queen skidded noisily behind him. Micah dashed through the passage. It was narrowing, but not enough.

He entered a bowl-like chamber, its walls sloping slowly upwards from the floor to a flat ceiling. A dead end. He tripped over something and ended up in a pile of bones and rotting hides. His panic peaked as he clambered over skeletons to the other side of the bowl.

He searched the walls frantically, but there was no other way out, only the entrance. He imagined the Queen chasing prey in here, watching them run up the walls in fear, only to slide back down to their doom. The Queen's steps were measured; she knew he was trapped. Micah willed himself to push down his fear and think. He wasn't Ramires, nor Gabriel. His only weapon was his brain. He focused. One entrance at the base of the bowl, the walls behind the entrance also sweeping up slowly to the ceiling. A blind spot.

At first he hoped she wouldn't be able to squeeze through the passage, even though the morgue around his feet testified otherwise. Her head appeared through the opening, and tilted towards the ground, then peered at him with all six eyes. One claw reached through the hole, then another, leveraging against the inside wall, readying to pull her body through. Micah knew it was now or never. He gripped the nanosword hilt, and ran around the rising edge of the bowl, obliquely at first, gathering speed. He ran up the sloping wall as he neared her, going high enough to be out of reach of her claws, then slid down the wall behind her, and activated the sword. He landed with his two feet either side of her neck, and rode her as he plunged the sword through the back of her head. She thrashed wildly, trying to reach backwards with her claws, but Micah held on, and dragged the sword to the left, and then to the right, until the top half of her head toppled to the ground.

He fell off the quivering body, and landed in the pile of bones now slippery and steaming with blood. He got to his feet and then chopped at her head again and again, recalling the billions killed by her command. Her body stilled, but it blocked his exit. Taking a deep breath, he used the sword like a machete, and hacked and chopped his way through her carcass so he could get back out into the tunnel. To keep going, he intoned a name with each slice, someone he knew and cared about who'd been butchered back on Earth twenty years ago. Tears ran down his face for all the people who'd been snuffed out. He continued to hack. It took him five minutes to get through. He didn't hurry.

As soon as he was through, his sword arm shaking, his breath ragged, he sagged to the floor, his back against the wall. He guessed there would be more Q'Roth warriors waiting for him outside, and that these were the last moments of his life.

While he waited, and his body calmed down, he recalled his father, the famous Grey Colonel, the WWIII hero who'd branded his fifteen-year-old son a coward all those years ago, during the first bombing of LA. Ever since, Micah had looked to role models like Blake and Vince, knowing he could never be like them. They'd had courage hardwired into them, Micah didn't. But for the first time in a long while, he thought of his dead father, wondering what he would think now.

Micah got up to go and meet his fate. There were four more Q'Roth Guardians outside, but they were all dead. The Spider stood over them, one of its legs twitching, the Hohash hovering behind. It flashed historical images from Shimsha, showing the Q'Roth invasion and culling of the Spider's ancestors a millennium earlier. Micah knew they had let the culling take place and offered no resistance, in order to protect their hidden egg fields on Esperia, as well as the whereabouts of Kalaran's ship; he'd been vulnerable at that time. The Tla Beth, who would have sanctioned the cull, must not have known about the Spiders' true nature, or that Kalaran was there, his ship hidden in the underground ocean. Strategy and sacrifice. Micah still didn't know the final role the Spiders – Kalaran's secret weapon – would play. But it was harrowing to watch an entire generation of them being slaughtered, their once-rainbow city bleached in the process. As if sensing his discomfort, the images shut off.

Micah glanced at the Q'Roth, trying to see how the Spider had killed them. The only clue was that their heads seemed to have caved in, as if their brains had been removed. He walked up to the Spider and placed a hand on top of its body, and stroked it. Then he gazed back towards the chamber where Gabriel had died. The clone had been less than a week old. Micah knew nothing of Sentinel protocol, but he bowed, then turned and led the Spider back towards Shiva.

At the bottom of Shiva's ramp, he noticed gossamer strands around the outside of the ship, almost like a web; the Spider had been busy. Both the Spider and the Hohash remained apart from the vessel; they weren't coming. The Hohash showed Micah an image, and tapped into his resident, depositing a sizeable chunk of information there, which made Micah stagger for a moment. At first Micah couldn't make out what he was being shown, but then he understood.

"I don't blame you," he said, then walked up the ramp and sealed it behind him.

When Micah entered the bridge, Sandy paled at the sight of him, and Vashta rushed to his side to check him over.

"Gabriel?" Sandy said.

"Dead. The Queen, too. We have to go. Now."

Vashta replied. "The Spider and the Hohash are still outside, and Shiva has not yet determined a way to destroy or evade the Nchkani ship."

"They're staying," Micah said. He took his position and activated the neural interface.

Shiva contacted Micah directly via his resident. <Micah, it would help if I knew your plan.>

Micah didn't reply, as the info-packet from the Hohash was still unfolding in the background of his mind. Shiva gave him manual control.

"Are you alright?" Sandy asked.

Micah lifted Shiva off the cavern and tilted her until she was vertical, facing downwards. He fired two missiles back up the shaft towards the Nchkani ship, and at the same time lasered into the rock below. The ground beneath crumbled and melted away, until a pit opened up. Micah drove Shiva straight down into it.

"The lava is on the outside," he said. "The planet is largely hollow."

He slalomed his way through a honeycomb of caverns, Sandy grabbing onto his shoulder despite the inertial dampers doing their job; there was no appreciable G-force – yet. A beeping commenced, signalling the Nchkani vessel chasing after them.

They passed several subterranean installations, one or two of which fired at them, but Micah had no intention of slowing down, and when his reactions were too slow or the turns too hard even for Shiva, he blasted through solid rock, carving a way through the planet.

The beeps grew closer in time, the Nchkani ship almost upon them, and then there was a succession of flashes, throwing everything into grey relief.

"Shiva, give it everything you've got, get us out of here on a direct vector, maximum speed." He concentrated on an image the Hohash had shown him, and transmitted it to Shiva via his resident.

This time there was a sudden thrust forward. Micah grabbed Sandy's wrist to prevent her flying backwards, and felt himself squeezed back into his chair. He heard a grating noise as Vashta extended metal claws to grip the floor. Micah's shoulder tore at him as he hung onto Sandy.

Rocks exploded in plasma fire up ahead of them, and they roared right into it, Shiva lasering an escape route through liquefying rock. It was like staring straight into the sun, and then suddenly there was the darkness of space in front of them; they had broken through the other side of the planet. The acceleration eased off. Shiva wasn't slowing down, but had reached her maximum in-sector velocity.

Sandy got up from the floor, and Micah rubbed his shoulder.

"What's going on, Micah?"

He touched a pad to bring up the aft view. The planet still occupied most of the screen, and the Nchkani ship chasing them was visible, but slipping backwards. Planetary rivers and seas of boiling magma were fading, and then were gone.

"Talk to me, Micah!"

But Micah didn't feel like talking. Instead his chest felt heavy, as if he was being sucked back towards the planet. For sure the Spider and Hohash were already dead.

Vashta drew alongside Sandy. "A black hole is forming," she said. "Inside the planet."

Blotches of red mushroomed on Korakkara's surface, then vanished, as if the planet was being shot from within, its blood immediately sucked back inside itself. Micah knew what came next. The Nchkani vessel tried to open a Transpace conduit, a bad idea, one the Hohash had made clear not to attempt until well away from the planet. The Nchkani ship shimmered for a second, then plunged like a silver nugget deep inside the planet.

Sandy whacked Micah's shoulder. "You did this! You're destroying their home planet, like they did to us. We should be better than them!"

"Not my doing, Sandy. The Spiders are exacting revenge."

The planet had grown smaller and without warning shattered, briefly exploding before imploding into a smooth black disk – a black hole. Shiva's engines strained with a grinding noise that increased to a shrill whine. In reality it was the Spider's web that would save them: the Hohash had conveyed the idea that it would help act as anti-gravity against a black hole, since the strands were from a different universe, exotic matter that didn't behave according to the local laws of physics.

Micah was still gaining knowledge from the Hohash transmission; it felt odd, as if he was remembering facts he had forgotten, but in reality had never known. The Spiders were from a different type of space, a different universe, one where violent gravitic storms were commonplace. Over countless aeons they, and several other indigenous species, had adapted to be able to counter gravity. He realised that Kalaran's interest in the Spiders hadn't necessarily been altruistic; he had probably wanted to learn from them, to understand how they could manipulate gravity and space so effectively.

He judged that the black hole was far enough away now, but still he watched, knowing what came next.

The fleet of Q'Roth ships that had engaged him earlier were dragged towards it. Many of them also tried to jump into Transpace, only to be pulled in faster. In the end, it made no difference. Micah knew that the other two planets and asteroids in the system, and eventually the sun, would suffer the same fate.

"Genocide," Sandy said.

Micah recalled something the Queen had said, and adapted it. "Lions like the Q'Roth will never stop hunting antelope," he said. "This was the Spiders' plan all along, and Hellera's too, I believe. We're barely a pawn in this war, and Hellera has just taken out a Queen and a whole host of her pieces."

He checked the distance. According to the equation the Hohash had shown him, it was safe. He signalled Shiva to prepare to enter Transpace for Hell's End.

After a while, Sandy spoke again. "The clone… Gabriel… How did he die?" She seemed closed in on herself.

Micah stood up, and dug something out of his pocket. "On his feet, fighting." He handed her the nanosword hilt, offering it holding both palms upturned, one of the very few Sentinel gestures he knew.

Sandy stared at it, then placed her hands on its smooth surface. Her fingers closed slowly around the hilt, remaining in contact with his palms. Micah closed his own hands gently around hers, and she looked into his eyes, just as her face and every surface around her turned quicksilver as they slid into Transpace.

Hell's End, Micah thought. This is where it all ends, one way or another.

He was ready.

Chapter 30
HELL'S END

Hellera surveyed the warscape. Qorall's asteroid ship hovered just off the event horizon of his customised black hole, a few million miles from a rip in the galactic barrier's fabric. Surrounding him in space tinged a ghostly green were three fleets, the first two cannon-fodder, Level Seven and Eight species she no longer cared about. Some had very large, Mega-Class ships, ten times the size of her own Crossbow, but after Level Fourteen one learned that bigger ships only meant easier targets. The third fleet was more of a challenge: Nchkani vessels, a hundred and eighty of them. They were manned by Q'Roth, but that didn't make them any less dangerous, and Qorall's greenspace neutralised Hellera's gravity-based weapons.

On her side were a dozen fleets, the ones that mattered being the twenty-seven remaining Tla Beth Gyroscope ships, forty-seven Rangers in assorted small but well-armed scout ships, and fifty Ossyrian Diamond ships. The latter had drawn her attention, not because of their fire-power – they were no match for the Nchkani – but because the Ossyrians had obviously retrograded, escaping their pacifist yoke, and had quickly fabricated war ships that had terrorised the galaxy many aeons earlier. Each Diamond ship was fashioned from the joining of the bases of two hospital pyramid ships. Hellera reflected that directive evolution was painstaking, requiring careful steps over hundreds of millennia, whereas species regression, by comparison, was as easy as falling off a cliff.

She waited for one more ship to join her armada. She switched her sensors to show the Spider ships and Hohash in the underlying subspace, contingents of Shrell accompanying them. Qorall could probably see them too, and must be wondering about their capability. At least he appeared to have no soldiers in subspace.

Hyper-assessments had yielded uncertain results: the emergent predictions of who would win remained unstable. Reluctantly she downgraded into a more basic analytic framework. Kalaran had trusted these humans, and had confided in her that there was something about the crude and undisciplined nature of their thinking processes that had tactical value, so she uploaded one of the templates Kalaran had extracted, Blake's, and fed it with data using a ridiculously small bandwidth.

The black hole: that was the problem. Neither she nor Kalaran had been able to fathom what it was exactly, as it was certainly not a normal singularity. Each galaxy she had visited – quite a few during her lifetime – tended towards a maximum number of black holes, reaching an equilibrium. They were nodes, intersections between universes, but not necessarily portals. Only twice had the Kalarash broken through to another universe, the first time it had been a one-way trip and their colleague was never heard from again, and the second was one where the laws of physics were different, the habitat of the Spiders. Their universe was smaller and ran faster – it would end long before this one – hence the Spiders had also been keen to explore other universes than their own time-limited space. They had travelled to fifty other universes, but few contained the conditions for sentient life; some had already fizzled out, others would stretch endlessly without organic species, bland space deserts spattered with dark stars in an endless ocean of space marred by vicious gravitational fluctuations.

In strategy terms, she held more firepower than Qorall. She should win. But since Qorall had defeated Kalaran, she had doubts. Qorall had been a game-changer since starting this current war: penetrating the Galactic Barrier, using organic weapons, the Orbs… Perhaps he had not yet run out of surprises.

Shiva arrived. Hellera contacted the ship mind and downloaded all its data. All had gone according to plan, except the second Queen, but Micah had handled that one. She was about to dissolve Blake's template, but elected to keep it running in the background.

She signalled all her fleets to prepare to engage. On a whim, one that was possibly a hangover from Blake's template, something to do with honour in war and some ancient surprise strike against a place known as Pearl Harbour, she sent a message to Qorall. It was a question, a warning, and a challenge. It was also a single word:

<Ready?>

She wasn't expecting a reply, but she got one.

<Ultimate stakes>

Hellera stared hard at his black hole, his fleets of ships, and his greenspace. She realised she was missing something. He must know by now that his super white hole device at the galactic core had been neutralised. Yet Qorall had never bluffed before. He had, as Blake would have said, something else up his sleeve. She had no idea what it was.

Micah stared through the clouds of ships, unable to fathom any pattern or formation. "Vashta, what do you see?"

The Ossyrian's mercurial eyes danced for a few moments before pronouncing.

"Intersecting helixes on our side, recursive phalanxes on theirs. An old argument in space battle strategy."

Sandy interjected. "Did that mean anything to you, Micah?"

He laughed. "I wish it did, Sandy. Shiva, what's our role in all this?"

Shiva spoke bridge-wide. "Hellera wants us to hang back."

"But you're Level Fifteen." Micah said. "We could inflict a lot of damage."

There was a pause, and Micah knew it was for his benefit, for him to reflect, as Shiva thought far quicker. "She said to wait, Micah. There is an unknown variable at play, she wants us in reserve."

Having seen Gabriel killed, and having just hacked his way through a Q'Roth Queen, he wasn't in a patient mood. And since Hellera's ruse with Gabriel, he wasn't sure he trusted her anymore.

"How about we leapfrog behind enemy lines? A short Transpatial jump? I know in-system jumps are very tricky, but you could do it, couldn't you?"

"Qorall's greenspace prevents any jumps; no conduits will open here."

Shiva switched to private comms, for Micah's ears only, via his resident.

<Micah, Hellera has sent a subspace message to all her commanders. Because information is crucial in battles, and Qorall must not be able to anticipate our moves or our capability until we are deployed, and also because she cannot predict his moves, she will only release tactical instructions as events unfold. However, she expects instant response on your part, and no unnecessary comms.>

Micah shook his head. Great. Management by surprise. But he couldn't fault her logic, and knew she could take in all the real-time data from the ongoing battle, even anticipate up to a point, and make immediate and optimised tactical decisions. Still, he would have liked a task.

Shiva spoke bridge-wide again. "Micah, Hellera said to keep an eye on this ship."

Micah stared at the screen as Shiva highlighted one of the Nchkani vessels. It was the lead ship in the last arrowhead formation of Nchkani vessels.

"Louise," Micah guessed. "I still don't get what her game plan is."

"Kill her, Micah," Sandy said. "Then extract it from her brain afterwards. That's what the Alicians would do."

She walked in front of Micah, obscuring his view.

"Whatever she does, Micah, it will be for her benefit and ultimately our loss, she has to go down. You told me what she did to Hannah, remember? Not forgetting the two thousand on Ash's ship that she plunged into a sun." She leant forward. "And not forgetting Vince, either."

Micah held her gaze a moment then looked aside. He hadn't forgotten any of it, and her mentioning Vince's name rattled him. He zoomed out, and studied Qorall's massive fleet. Of all the people he'd like to be here with them now, it would be Vince, even more so than Blake, because Vince had been a ruthless tactician, and because it had taken Vince to bring down Louise last time. He envisioned all the carnage Louise had wreaked over the past twenty years, and what else she might do if she survived this war. Yet he recalled a conversation a lifetime ago, back in his Optron lab before the fall of Earth, before he'd known she was Alician, when he'd seen a glimpse of another Louise. Sandy must have read his face, seen a crack of doubt, because she moved right in front of him, close to his face.

"You know why I chose Ramires instead of you? One of several reasons, actually."

It was as if someone had thrown a bucket of cold water over him; Micah's senses snapped to attention.

Sandy held the nanosword in her hand, weighing it. Her voice unsteady at first, then solid as rock.

"You're an analyst. Analysts always leave their options open, playing the uncertainties, the angles, retreating into nuances. Ramires was a man of action, Micah. He swore a blood debt. Warriors make a decision and stick to it, ignoring the shifting sands around them. I'm telling you this because soon we'll be in the heat of battle, and there may be a crucial moment when you can either act decisively, or reflect and analyse, and the window of opportunity will be lost."

Her voice softened a little. "Maybe it's an inferior way of thinking, maybe it locks us into Level Three, I don't know, but you have a choice to make today. There's a Sentinel saying that how you die defines you. In any case, now you know how I feel. And we, too, are in your hands, Micah."

Micah wanted to respond that all this was probably futile, that Qorall would destroy them, and that Louise's ship might be blown apart by another vessel, but such arguments would only confirm everything she'd just said. All verbal options sounded hollow, so he said nothing. He thought of that split-second when Gabriel had looked to him just before he was killed by the Queen. Micah's mind cleared, the analyses, the hypotheses and counter-hypotheses, all of it stopped.

Sandy spoke more quietly. "You slew a Queen back there, didn't you? On your own."

He nodded.

"Then whatever else happens, I'm proud of you for that."

Vashta intervened. "All ships are powering weapons and maximising shields."

Sandy returned to her comms console. Micah touched a few pads to bring up multiple displays. Shiva contacted him via his resident. <A gift from Hellera.>

Another view superimposed itself onto the screens, via his resident, so that only he saw it. Around thirty Hohash were arranged in a sphere around a white funnel, which he realised from normal view was Qorall's black hole. Next to each Hohash was a stubby cigar-like rainbow ship – the Spiders. Shrell swooped around them in undulating arcs. He'd never seen them before; they reminded him of manta rays, the edges of their wings waxing silver.

Only three hours ago, the Spider and the Hohash back on the Q'Roth homeworld had opened up a black hole. It occurred to him that it must have needed both of them to do it, perhaps the Spider affecting space and the Hohash amplifying or stabilising it somehow. But here were thirty! All he knew about the Shrell was that they could lay down tripwires in space, as they had done around Esperia. But he recalled someone saying that most of the time Shrell *repaired* sub-space, after it had been damaged by too much Transpatial travel. Like him, they were all waiting to be brought into play by Hellera.

He focused on the foreground, in particular the Ossyrian Diamond ships, and addressed Vashta.

"I didn't know Ossyrians still had weapons tech. It's been aeons since you last waged war."

Vashta took a few moments to reply. "After Level Seven there is never species memory loss. That is why when certain species rebel, they are completely eradicated."

"You were lucky, then."

Again, there was a pause. "It did not feel lucky, Micah."

Micah was about to apologise, when Sandy interrupted.

"Xenic has just arrived with the remains of the Mannekhi fleet. He'd like a word."

Micah nodded, relieved to see a fleet of black and purple Spikers enter the system.

"Xenic, glad you could join us, but there's some pretty heavy firepower out there."

"Do you see the black ships with two prongs at one end?"

Micah did, they reminded him of scorpions.

"Those are Tazani, our overlords for fifty thousand years. As Kilaney would have said, it's payback time."

Micah felt he should point out the obvious. "They are Level Seven, Xenic."

"We brought along some new friends."

Micah peered at the viewscreen and at first saw nothing, then massive Transpace conduits opened, revealing snake-like ships in the lead that rippled aquamarine. Shiva informed him they were Zlarasi Serpent-ships. He knew what Kilaney had done to them, destroying their home planet in order to salvage Blake, and was about to ask Sandy to contact their Commander when the Zlarasi commander opened a channel.

"Do not worry, human, we know who the enemy is. And Kilaney's actions have proven effective."

Micah was relieved, and wondered whether humanity would have been so forgiving had the roles been reversed.

Wagramanian Hammer-ships arrived, behind the Zlarasi Serpent-ships, and Micah recalled that the Wagramanians – the first to be recoded – had recently been restored. When he saw what they were towing, however, he stood and walked up to the viewscreen.

"Worms? You brought dark worms here?"

Xenic's sharp laugh cut across the bridge. "The Zlarasi tamed the ones Hellera didn't kill; that's why there's not been much activity."

"What do you propose to do with them?"

"Use them as shields, Micah. And if we get close enough, as mass-drivers. You'll see."

He doubted they would perturb the Nchkani vessels, and Qorall could use his black hole to swallow any amount of matter spewed in his direction. Then he remembered something; the worms, whose natural habitat was the intergalactic void, could excrete anti-matter. That might make a difference.

"Have you told Hellera?"

"She's the one that made it happen, Micah, she's been calling in favours across the galaxy. Kalarash aren't above a little politics now and again."

Of course. Micah kept forgetting that humanity was just a pawn, and there were more skilled players.

"Don't get killed, Xenic. I've buried too many friends recently."

Xenic replied in Mannekhi and broke the connection. Micah glanced back to Sandy for a translation. After a second she looked up from her console, a small smile on her face.

"He's been reading up on Earth culture. 'Only the good die young.'" Her voice caught on the last word, and she locked her face onto her displays again.

Micah focused on the arrays of ships again, imagining a gigantic chessboard: Hellera and Qorall at opposite ends, their armies lined up ready for the battle, waiting for one or other side to make the first move. He had a feeling it wouldn't be particularly subtle.

A klaxon sounded aboard Shiva as Qorall dispatched three waves of Tazani battle-cruisers and attendant fighter ships towards Hellera's position. The Wagramanians launched the worms – presumably anaesthetized – towards the first wave. Three Hammer-ships and a Serpent-ship skulked behind each dark worm, hidden in the giant folds of the creatures. Micah zoomed in on one, and saw a pulsing green cable protruding from the worm's neck; the Zlarasi were controlling them directly.

Mannekhi Spikers accelerated towards the attacking front, over-taking the worms, their purple spines spitting fire at the Tazani. In return, each of the Tazani ships' two prongs forged a beam between them that launched lozenges of energy at the Spikers, ignoring the worms. Space lit up like a firework factory exploding, but without sound. Shiva filtered out the glare. Micah saw the Mannekhi suffering heavy losses, many of the Spikers blown apart by the energy impact, spilling Mannekhi into space. None of the Mannekhi ships retreated, and nausea gripped Micah's stomach. But as the worms reached the centre of the battlefield, the Wagramanian Hammer-ships engaged, living up to their name as they spun like tomahawks towards the less manoeuvrable Tazani battle-cruisers, weathered the defensive energy lozenges, and smashed headlong into and through the cruisers. Once a Tazani cruiser was damaged, Spikers descended on it like vultures, to finish the job.

Bronze ships that looked like giant squid entered the fray, and Shiva tagged them as Level Eight, Hushtarans. They began capturing the Wagramanian Hammers with long tentacles of antimatter, burning their way through the Hammers' fuselage. Hellera deployed the Ossyrian Diamond ships. Micah didn't actually know what weapons the Ossyrians possessed, only that they had once been feared across the galaxy.

The crystal diamonds approached the squids and split into two pyramids, then began cutting each Hushtaran vessel, slicing through its hull, twisting and turning, the two halves of the diamond working together, gouging and dismembering the ship. Soon the Hushtaran fleet was listless in space. Micah zoomed in to one that was in pieces, but detected no bodies. Shiva informed him that Hushtaran pilots merged organically with their ships; they were one and the same.

Micah knew that this battle, though terrible, was all a preamble to the real one, and at the moment a ploy by Hellera to get the Nchkani vessels to enjoin battle. But it wasn't working. Instead, Qorall fired his famed spatial lightning bolts, criss-crossing the space with green plasma arcs of awesome power. Any Spikers, Diamonds and Hammers that didn't make it quickly enough to the leeward side of the worms were vaporised, as were the remaining Tazani and Hushtaran ships, evidently collateral damage as far as Qorall was concerned. Micah prayed that Xenic was still alive.

Sandy must have been thinking along the same lines. "Xenic's ship is still intact, Micah."

He nodded a thank you, then turned to Vashta. "Sorry for the Ossyrian casualties, Vashta."

"You have no idea, Micah, how proud we are to be here, fighting, after so many millennia of enforced pacifism. We are complete again."

Micah stared at her awhile, and realised that whatever happened here today, whoever won, ten million years of ordered Grid Society was going to be torn down. He wondered if Hellera knew, and then decided that of course she knew, she was Level Nineteen.

The Rangers' assortment of small scout ships swept in like fireflies, dodging the green lightning bolts with faster-than-eye movements, and for the first time Micah appreciated how physically robust the reptilian Rangers must be to survive such manoeuvres. Still the Nchkani hung back. Instead, hundreds of copper-coloured vessels shaped like corkscrews appeared out of nowhere, reminding Micah of old-style solenoids.

For the first time ever, he felt a jab from Shiva via his resident, and guessed it was her equivalent of a flinch. He interrogated, and Shiva replied: <unknown – this ship unseen before now.>

Micah paced the length of the screen, thinking. Unknown and some kind of stealth tech. It only made sense if Qorall had concealed them all this time, during nearly twenty years of war. The discipline behind his strategy was breath-taking.

"Are we out-manoeuvred, Micah?" Sandy asked.

He mentally flicked to the subspace view. The Spiders, Hohash and Shrell remained in position.

"Not yet," he replied.

The corkscrews took up a network formation, a lattice barring the way through to Qorall. Inside each corkscrew, orange beams formed, ready to fire. Micah saw what was coming. But Hellera's fleets remained in place. Why didn't Hellera do something? The beams grew brighter, building up power. Still, no command to attack or retreat. It suddenly dawned on him that Hellera might be willing to let numerous ships be destroyed in order to let Qorall think he was winning; a feint, but at huge cost in lives. He had to do something, he wasn't about to watch Xenic and countless others fried. Maybe he could prompt Hellera…

He dashed to Sandy's station. "Give me fleet-wide comms!"

"But Hellera –"

"Doesn't care about collateral damage, Sandy. Do it now."

She tapped feverishly. "Channel open, though Qorall will hear it too."

As he'd hoped. "All vessels, those corkscrew ships are about to deluge the battlefield with fire."

There was a sharp burst of comms that sounded like a chainsaw snagging on metal.

"What was that?" he asked.

Shiva answered. "Hellera ordered her fleets to fall back, except the Zlarasi and the Rangers."

He heard an ice-cold female voice. "Do not do that again, Micah."

But myriad ships retreated from the worms; not the Zlarasi, and he knew why. If they disconnected, the worms would be Qorall's again.

He walked to the centre of the bridge as the corkscrews continued their advance. The light of a sun ignited inside each one, then flamed out either end like a giant double bladed nanospear. The solenoids began to rotate and twist, synchronised, a pattern designed to flail every millimetre of space.

He looked towards the fleets of ships allied to Hellera, many still in the kill-zone.

"They're going to die," he whispered, but then something happened he hadn't anticipated. A new ship arrived out of nowhere. It looked like a stocky arrow, and he recognised from its rippling coloured shaft that it had to be a remnant of a Kalarash Crossbow ship: *Jen*. She launched toward the front in a looping manoeuvre, and swept up a hundred assorted ships inside her leeward shield, even as the light blades slammed into her, scorching her hull. Micah sat back in the command chair and gripped its arms, waiting for the ship's shield to falter, but it held, and she escorted the ships to safety. He breathed out, and had an urge to punch the air.

"Sandy, contact –"

"I'm okay, Micah," Jen said on intercom. "I managed to save some of our allies, but my ship is crippled. I'm out of the game."

"Take them out of the system, and get to safety, Jen."

"With all respect, Micah, get real, I'm staying till the end, but I'll send the allies out of the sector." She broke contact.

Sandy caught Micah's eye. "She hasn't changed."

He laughed. "I don't care, she saved them." He turned back to the screen. "Shiva, would we –"

"No, Micah, we would not survive. We must wait until Hellera plays us."

The entire space between the two sides was engulfed in energy, like a sprawling sun. Grey saccadic anti-matter flashes told him the worms were being systematically destroyed, no doubt taking most of the Zlarasi ships with them. Then the super-sun flamed out. Through blotchy eyes Micah counted half the Ranger ships still on course. There was no sign of the worms or any other ship except the Nchkani on Qorall's side. Finally, the Level Sixteen black-and-white, feather-bladed ovoids began to edge forward, spreading out like predators: the Nchkani ships piloted by Q'Roth warriors, and in one case, Louise.

The Rangers closed ranks, briefly presenting a single target, before they burst apart, each one attacking a single Nchkani ship. At that exact same instant, the Tla Beth ships speared forward, heading straight for Qorall's asteroid ship. It caught the Nchkani ships off-guard, but quickly half of them raced to intercept the Gyroscope ships. Micah realised the odds were two-to-one in Qorall's favour.

For the first time, Micah truly faced the likelihood that Hellera was going to be defeated. He stood back from it all, imagining again the battlefield as a giant chessboard, Hellera and Shiva held back on one side, Qorall on the other, the middle of the board awash with ships and carnage. He realised Hellera could still cut and run, but decided there and then that whatever happened, Shiva was not going to desert her allies.

Micah didn't know how long it lasted, maybe three minutes, maybe five, but he watched fifty duels play out, trying to guess what weapons were being used and what counter-measures were employed in response, while space shimmered and rocked, spilling sprays of raw energy into space, sometimes ending in a Nchkani vessel exploding, but more often a Ranger vessel turned incandescent before vanishing from sight, or a Tla Beth vessel shattered into a cloud of fragments that flared scarlet before fading to dust.

He checked with his resident, and with Shiva, and then pronounced what was staring them in the face. "We're losing this."

Sandy spoke quietly. "Are you thinking of –"

"We're not leaving," he said, "until we either win this or are destroyed."

"That's more like it," she said.

"We'll give Hellera a little more time." But not much; soon it would be too late to have any effect. His left hand hovered near the thruster control panel.

Then one of the Nchkani ships began attacking its own kind, neutralising fifteen of them in a single coordinated fire-burst. The targeted ships had been well-chosen, too, saving Rangers about to be defeated, and breaking both the Nchkani attack and defence lines, freeing up Rangers and Tla Beth ships, who rallied to their colleagues' defence. The tide of the battle turned. Micah could scarcely believe it. It must have been her. Louise had made a decisive move. Five of the Nchkani broke off from fighting the Rangers and circled Louise's ship, determined to destroy her vessel, spraying it in blue fire. Micah found his hands hovering above the engine controls.

Sandy shouted from her console. "Don't, Micah. Let them kill her."

His outstretched fingers curled into fists, then he folded his arms.

The battle became a rout. Several Tla Beth slashed their way through the remaining Nchkani ships, until all of them were laid to waste or – like Louise's – inert and drifting in greenspace. There were no more intermediaries.

The Tla Beth and Rangers re-grouped, then sped directly towards Qorall's asteroid.

Micah felt what happened next, as Shiva and all other ships were savagely tugged toward the black hole. At this distance, Shiva and the others could resist, but he knew the Rangers and Tla Beth would find it harder given that they were already accelerating towards it. Qorall's asteroid ship, inactive until now, began to glow green. The black hole was no longer pure black, like an unfathomable iris. Instead, its surface had texture, like a black-and-green sea of deep ocean swells. An enormous wave started from its circumference and swept toward the centre of the hole, until it collided with itself. A second later, Micah was knocked out of his chair as the entire ship lurched forward in space.

"What just happened?" He glanced over to Sandy, who was getting back to her feet; Vashta too.

"Ripples in space-time," Shiva said, "of immense power, not normally seen except…"

Micah's mind leapt ahead as his resident showed him the energy levels. Qorall was tapping into the most primal energetic event ever.

"A Big Bang. Shiva, the black hole, it's a doorway to another universe, isn't it, one that's being born, or dying?"

"This is known as a never-event, Micah," Shiva said, "because it must never be allowed to happen. It is of ultimate risk. No beings, neither Qorall nor Kalarash, can control such forces. He must be stopped."

Micah did a full sensor sweep. At least twenty ships in greenspace had been crushed, flattened into wafer-thin disks. The Ranger ships and even the Tla Beth Gyroscopes had been blown back and scattered like flotsam as if struck by a tsunami.

Hellera's Crossbow sprang towards Qorall's asteroid-ship. Micah was out of his seat. At last!

His resident activated, and he saw that the Spider ships and Hohash lying in subspace around Qorall's black hole were moving. Then they disappeared, and the subspace image vanished. He couldn't believe it. Had they deserted Hellera? Where had they gone?

Another wave began on the circumference, and just afterwards, the rainbow-hued cigar-shaped Spider ships appeared there, dotted around the lip of the black hole.

He heard Hellera's ice-cold voice again.

<I am leading the attack now. Evacuate all ships below Level Fifteen.>

He'd been hoping for such an instruction, it was down to the heavy-hitters now.

"Shiva, tell all the ships around us to get out of here. Transpace should work if they are heading out of the sector." But he wondered why she'd called him, not a higher-ranking commander. Then he understood. Shiva was Level Fifteen, Micah and his crew were staying.

He watched the wave sweep inwards, growing in size. He wasn't sure, but it looked bigger than the first one. On another screen he saw ships flare briefly and wink out of the sector. But the Tla Beth and Rangers were still inside Qorall's greenspace; they could not escape. Hellera's Crossbow reached the leading edge of the attack when the second gravitational tsunami struck. Micah thought he'd been hit by a hover car. Sandy had managed to anchor herself down, and Vashta had clamped her claws onto her console.

The sensor displays flashed erratically, some of the pictures distorted.

"Shiva?"

"I have sustained... damage... Micah. I can no longer control flight, I have handed over full manual control to you. We do... not have long. Lost... contact with Hellera."

Micah got back to his seat. Hellera's ship was stationary, firing a continuous red and white beam at Qorall's asteroid. The few Tla Beth and Ranger ships that weren't dead in space had joined her, belching forth a torrent of fire that looked like a waterfall in space, drowning Qorall's vessel. But the next wave had already started. It was colossal this time, taking longer to build.

"Sandy, Vashta –"

"Whatever you're going to do, Micah, just do it," Sandy said. "We're with you."

He hit full thrust, and Shiva sprinted towards the titanic struggle between Hellera and Qorall. The wave was still building, grey froth boiling at its top, and then it started to move.

But something else was happening. Blue dots appeared around the black hole, well inside the event horizon, and began to expand, all in the same rotational direction, until a ring of sapphire surrounded the hole. Micah made an educated guess as to what was happening. The Spiders were opening up a rift into another space, the Hohash acting as amplifiers, the Shrell most probably stabilising the rift or preventing it widening too much. He'd heard of Quickspace, an anomaly that had occurred a few times every million years, and led to a few unlucky ships disappearing out of Transpace, never to be seen again. That had to be Hellera's game plan: not to destroy Qorall – he reckoned she couldn't – but to send him elsewhere.

As Micah sped towards the asteroid, he kept one eye on the wave. It was nearing the centre, but now thin blue lines stretched forward from the edge of the hole, spiralling inwards. The wave foamed, then lost cohesion as the black and green sea suddenly caved in, and a sapphire vortex opened up, spanning the entire width of where the black hole had been. Rainbow-sheened arcs reached upwards towards Qorall's asteroid ship and looped over it, criss-crossing each other in a grid. Not a grid, Micah thought: a web.

Qorall fought back, streams of energy whipping against Hellera's Crossbow and the Tla Beth ships, two of which exploded in bright flashes and were gone. Milky tendrils grew from the asteroid and reached away from the vortex, hooking onto Hellera's ship. Neither her firepower not the Tla Beth or Rangers had any effect on the tendrils. Slowly, Qorall's asteroid ship reeled Hellera towards him.

Micah brought Shiva's still-active weapons to full readiness, particularly the forward shear system – effectively a giant nanoblade – and accelerated to maximum speed. Shiva was a scythe-ship, after all; time for her to live up to her name. Klaxons sounded, warning of imminent collision.

"Sandy, sorry it has to end this way," he shouted.

"I'm not," she replied.

Shiva dove down beneath Hellera's ship and headed straight for the tendrils. Micah reaped tendril after tendril while Vashta fired at Qorall, and tried to neutralize his weapons fire on them. Micah kept one eye on the main battle display; Qorall's asteroid was still resisting the tug of the vortex and the Spider net. Micah ploughed on through the last line of tendrils even as Shiva was rocked back and forth by enemy fire.

"It's Hellera," Sandy shouted.

<Micah, prepare to be whisked to my ship as soon as you have cut the last tendril.>

He stared at the battle display again, and made up his mind. He turned to Sandy and shouted his reply to Hellera.

"Take these two now, Qorall needs a little distraction."

Sandy's eyes flared, and she was about to voice complaint but then she and Vashta vanished. He activated tactical at his console, and slewed Shiva around, banking briefly before aiming her straight at the asteroid.

"See you in hell, Qorall," he said, and hit full thrust.

The screen blanked as Qorall switched his main beams onto Shiva, and all Micah saw was brilliant white. He heard a metallic scream like a battle cry, as his resident told him the front hull sections had almost boiled away. He squinted as the asteroid's surface raced towards him, and then Shiva broke clean through its outer crust. Kat had once told him Qorall's asteroid was hollow, and now he saw it with his own eyes. Instinctively he pulled Shiva up from its dive straight towards what looked like a boiling lava sea. Sure enough, above him was a gaping hole, showing blackness criss-crossed with deep blue lines. The inner surface of the protective shell surrounding Qorall's ship was grey rock, with patches of orange where Hellera and the remainder of the fleet were still firing at it.

He skimmed Shiva just above the surface of the lava sea, and headed towards a land region of steaming boulders. Random fire tornadoes coiled upwards from the sea, and it took all Micah's concentration to dodge them. The tactical display warned that something was following him, and gaining, though he couldn't see anything. He accelerated again. Then he saw what he'd been looking for, in the distance. It fit Kat's description of Qorall: a colossal skeletal structure, like femur bones joined together into the rough shape of a cube, each strut or bone partly covered by flesh, but no evident head or torso. It clumped along slowly, and as he sped towards it, a slit formed on the closest upper bone, and a mouth opened. Micah fired at it with everything he had.

A tactical alarm whined, and Micah knew that whatever was chasing him was about to make contact, but he held his course.

Shiva came back on-line. <Thank you, Micah.>

He didn't understand but without warning his command chair shot upwards and backwards out of the ship. He felt searing heat as Shiva simultaneously struck Qorall and was blown to smithereens by his defences.

The chair he was in careened to the side, and rocketed towards a narrow gulley between two oversized boulders. He bumped, bounced, and skidded to a landing, ending up thrown out of the chair, rolling onto the rocky floor before coming to a halt. He tried to get up, as every surface was red hot, but his left arm refused to work, and he saw a bone protruding through bloody flesh on his forearm. Just as he was wondering why it didn't hurt, searing pain burst through with a vengeance. He staggered through scalding steam that rose from cracks in the rocks and smelled strongly of sulphur, making his eyes water, and managed to make it to the remains of the chair, whose fabric had already started to smoulder. He touched his face and found blood there from a gash in his forehead. He could just see Qorall moving off in another direction, one of his upper bones fractured where Shiva had struck home. No doubt Qorall was more concerned with Hellera and the vortex. Micah would not even register on the nuisance scale now that Shiva was gone, and would soon be dead in any case. He clutched his left elbow, trying to find a position that minimised the pain.

A sound like thunder made Micah look up to the ceiling. Large metallic flakes, a light blue colour, stuck to the asteroid's shell, triggering cracks and fissures in Qorall's primary defence. The first flake broke through, and fell until it plunged into the lava sea, fizzing and steaming before disappearing below the surface. Another broke through, then another. Energy beams flooded through the resultant holes in Qorall's protective shell, one of them vaporising a boulder not far from Micah's position. Micah could barely see, but a turquoise metal fragment sailed downwards and crashed into the landscape not far from him. Before it settled, Micah saw part of a symbol on one side: an ivory ankh. *Kalaran's ship.*

A roar exploded all around him, the heat intensifying, and Micah covered his face with his right hand as his skin began to blister. Something nudged him, almost knocked him off the chair, a section of which had just ignited. He turned and saw a Spider, and behind it one of the Spider ships, the hatch open. Micah ran, the soles of his feet burning with each step, and threw himself into its dark interior, trying to protect his left arm as much as possible. The hatch sealed behind him, and with a shock he realised the Spider was still outside; there was only room for one. The last thing he saw was the Spider climbing a boulder, its fur aflame, possibly to get a better vantage point of the battle as it died. Then Micah decided it was probably helping Hellera target Qorall.

The small ship lifted off the ground and oriented itself towards one of the holes in the roof and shot upwards. Micah hurt all over, but as he panted, his flesh stinging, hands and forearms covered in blisters, and his scalp singed, the ship spun around so he could watch Qorall's crumbling asteroid descend into the sapphire vortex, dragged down by the Spiders' net. Fragments from Kalaran's ship – they must have been there all along, waiting just beneath the event horizon of the black hole where even Qorall couldn't see them – continued to attack Qorall's asteroid-ship. Micah caught one last glimpse of Qorall himself descending into the lava sea. A few seconds later the entire landscape, and what was left of the roof, boiled off into space in a series of startling flashes that hurt his retinas, leaving behind nothing but a black pearl, which Micah reckoned to be the core of Qorall's ship. It looked impregnable.

Hellera stopped firing.

The remnants from Kalaran's ship had been vaporised, but the Spiders' blue net was still intact. The black pearl sank into the vortex, foundering in Quickspace. It was like watching a setting sun, one Micah hoped would never, ever rise again. At last it was gone, and the vortex snapped closed, leaving behind a dozen Spider ships and Hohash. The greenspace had vanished. Stars re-appeared, and his ship turned and headed towards Hellera's burned and battered Crossbow.

He sat with Sandy and Vashta. Sandy had tried to give him a hug when she first saw he was alive, inflicting great physical pain, and had then berated him for having her whisked off the ship. Vashta had silenced her by simply saying, "Thank you." Vashta had injected him with something, so he felt no pain whatsoever, and said she would patch him up later. She'd also explained how Qorall, in a last fit of rage, had tried to send trigger signals to a hundred and fifty homeworlds throughout the galaxy, all booby-trapped with planet-breakers. The Hohash had intercepted and neutralised all the carrier waves, saving trillions of lives.

The avatar of Hellera appeared. He had to admit she'd played everything flawlessly.

But she hadn't been alone, at least not at first. "Kalaran?" he asked.

Her ice cold voice answered, for the first time tinged with sadness. "This was his plan all along. We knew we could not destroy Qorall's ship. But we could send it to another universe, a very short-lived one."

Micah pondered: Qorall had planned his conquest for millions of years, but then so too had Kalaran, with the aid of the Spiders, all the time waiting till the last moment. Micah found he had to pose the question…

"Is Kalaran really gone?"

Hellera stared into the distance. "Yes. And perhaps, no. He imbued the Spider race with traces of his consciousness. He believed they could fast-track their development, surpassing even us and reaching Level Twenty within a million years. When they reach Level Nineteen, the embers of his consciousness may coalesce, and his mind will live again."

"He'll come back for you."

Hellera stared at Micah with all-grey eyes. "You humans truly embody pathos: it is your defining characteristic. Though I begin to see why Kalaran tolerated you."

Micah countered: "You took a risk when you whisked Sandy and Vashta onto your ship. Any such transport drains significant energy from your ship. I'm surprised you did it. It wasn't tactically sound."

"You humans infected Kalaran's mind with compassion. I told him so. But at the end, I knew what he would have done. It seems I am not immune either. I left Blake's template running, and it said 'We don't leave people behind.' Besides, your suicide run towards Qorall distracted him – made him blink – at a crucial moment. Kalarash always reward merit."

"Then, I have something else to ask. The Nchkani ships, are they all –"

"The Rangers have destroyed all the surviving ships, except the one that rebelled."

Sandy folded her arms.

Micah pressed. "The one called Louise, she –"

"I made a deal with her, Micah. Her rebellion was part of the plan."

"She has committed atrocities –"

"I am aware. But the deal stands. Kalarash do not break their word, either. You will not harm her. You may ask something else, but not this. I will send you a Hohash. You have a week to decide. After that I am leaving this galaxy. Louise and all her Alicians are coming with me. I will find them a new home, in a distant part of the universe."

It sounded final, and non-negotiable, but Micah wouldn't let it go.

"I'd like a word with her first."

Micah found himself standing on an endless sandy beach under a stark sun, with nothing present but a Hohash, and Louise.

"Before you get any ideas, we're not really here," she said. "If we were, you'd be dead by now."

He studied her. She looked weary, older. "Why did you change sides?"

"Don't get your moral hopes up, Micah. It was survival, plain and simple. After Qorall's tactics on Savange, I realised that even if we helped him win, afterwards we'd be squashed or abandoned, and if he lost…"

"If you ever come back –"

She laughed. "You share humanity's biggest flaw, Micah: you think you're more important than you actually are. I have no intention of ever returning, and Hellera is sending us far away across the universe. Given relativistic travel, even if we did return one day, it would be thousands of years in your future, possibly millions."

He hadn't thought of that, but it was true. "Be kind to Ash and Sonja," he said.

"I plan to."

Micah realised she was sincere. He recalled her trying to save Alician children during the bombardment of Savange. "Something has changed in you, Louise."

She shrugged. "Not that much. For example, I'll live another five hundred years, maybe longer, and I'm happy to know that I'll still be young when you're dying of old age."

Micah countered. "And I'm happy to know that if you or any other Alicians ever come back we'll be far more advanced than you by the time you arrive."

"Unlikely." She paused. "You've changed, too, Micah. It suits you."

There was nothing more to say. Their eyes met once, and then he was back with Sandy and Vashta.

"She won't bother us again," he said.

After an hour, a door slid open and a bruised but grinning Ukrull arrived, a Hohash at his side. There was another Ranger with him, Micah reckoned a female.

"I take you home," he growled. "This is Manota," he added. "She's coming too."

As they boarded his cramped ship, Sandy, who had said nothing since Hellera's last words and Micah's encounter with Louise, finally spoke to him.

"Do you know what you will ask of Hellera?"

Micah nodded.

She sat next to him, laid her head on his shoulder, and fell asleep.

Micah stayed awake as long as he could, but exhaustion crashed over him, and he slipped into a dream of what he was going to ask for.

Chapter 31
DIASPORA

Micah and Petra watched the Youngblood sparring match, as they sat in the top row of one of the four wooden pavilions erected in front of the Monofaith church, each stand packed with onlookers for the tournament. The sun beat down on everyone present, the cracked sky finally dismantled by the Shrell. This was the last stage of the tournament, the other trials including a simulated space battle, won convincingly by a single individual. Micah hadn't been surprised. This last stage, though, was about martial abilities, in honour of Ramires.

The four white stands encircled a crude arena of sand, where a row of young men – some Youngbloods, some Mannekhi – waited in line to try and beat the new champion. Xenic was loudly berating two of his warriors who'd just been defeated; Micah thought Xenic looked perfectly at home.

Petra's eyes lingered on the undefeated recent arrival. "He's even less like Gabriel than the one before," she said.

"Best Hellera could do," Micah answered. "She was reluctant to even try it a second time, something about breaking a Kalarash rule, though she wouldn't explain why."

"It's alright, I'll take it – I mean him." She then lowered her voice so much that Micah wasn't sure he was meant to hear. "If he'll take me."

He touched her hand. "I've seen the way he looks at you, Petra."

She turned to him, eyes narrowed. "You didn't ask Hellera to… to make him…?"

"What? No, of course not. I'm not even sure she could…"

Petra stared at him a long moment, then returned her gaze to the match. Micah hoped she couldn't see the relief on his face. Hellera had not been impressed by the suggestion, but had agreed to 'tip the scales a fraction'. In Micah's mind Petra had suffered too much already; losing a third Gabriel would wreck her.

Another Youngblood hit the deck, cheers rising, with many people on their feet cheering at the prowess of the clone. Hellera had said he was Level Six. Micah hadn't told Petra that either, but she'd figure it out soon enough. It was necessary for mankind's evolution, although it would take at least a thousand years for the rest of humanity to catch up. If there was one thing he'd learned from the Kalarash, it was the value of thinking long term.

As the energetic applause died down following a young Mannekhi's defeat in the latest bout, Petra regained her Presidential tone. "So, she granted you three wishes in the end. How exactly did you manage that?"

Micah laughed. "Ukrull helped, actually, as did Vashta, given what I asked first."

"How is that going, by the way?"

"The few Rangers who agreed to stay are fast-tracking the Ossyrians' augmentation to Level Nine. It will take a few centuries, but they've already started to take up their new role as galactic peace-keepers. They're going to try and undo what the Tla Beth did to the Q'Roth tribes, too, those who survived."

Petra gave him a look. "Heavily armed doctors; you have a strong sense of irony, Uncle."

She hadn't called him that in a while. He squeezed her hand. Gazing across to the pavilion opposite, he spotted Kat and Antonia sitting close together, talking, ignoring the match, ensconced in each other's company as if sitting alone in a park.

"Will the other higher races accept it?" Petra asked.

"The Grid hierarchy is finished. Races will advance at their natural speed, no longer held back, locked into intelligence Levels, and the Ossyrians are going to help that process. In any case, most species are busy licking their wounds and re-building; several are heading off with Hellera, certainly the Tla Beth, what's left of them."

"With Louise and the Alicians."

Micah stared at the latest bout, five Youngbloods circling the new Gabriel.

"And Ash and Sonja," he said. He forced himself to be more upbeat. "Hellera will deposit them in a distant galaxy to fend for themselves. Then she'll go exploring, maybe force a reunion of the remaining Kalarash."

"With Jen."

He nodded. He'd really thought Jen would stay, but she'd said she wanted to remain with the Kalarash, that Dimitri would have wanted her to explore the universe. And the latest Gabriel didn't really know her. Micah never thought he'd miss Jen. "Hellera accepted in an instant; after all, Jen had been with Kalaran for quite a while."

"Won't she miss human contact?"

Micah arched his eyebrows.

"Okay, silly question. Maybe she'll push Louise into that mercury lake at the bottom of Hellera's ship."

Micah grinned.

Petra grew serious. "So, Micah, she gave you a new version of Gabriel, and has left the Ossyrians in charge. How long before your third wish?"

Micah drew in a long breath. "There's no fast-tracking that one, I'm afraid. We won't see it, Petra, nor your grand-kids."

Another cheer erupted from the crowd, who began chanting Gabriel's name. He thought he detected Petra blush. She cleared her throat.

"Let's not get ahead of ourselves, Uncle. Anyway, that reminds me. What's the deal with you and Sandy?"

"There is no deal," he said.

She nudged his elbow. "Ask her."

He gave Petra a look. "And what *do* I ask, exactly? She's avoided me since we got back."

Petra laughed. "Still hopeless in that domain, I see."

He shrugged. "I aim for consistency." But his eyes searched the crowd, and he found Sandy, down on the arena floor. She handed a thin rod to Gabriel, and gave him a kiss on the cheek. Sandy then turned and glanced surreptitiously in Micah's direction; he thought he detected a smile.

Micah stood up. "I think I'll go and congratulate him, too."

"Sure," Petra said. "What happened to consistency, though?"

Micah didn't reply, and took the steps down to the arena two at a time.

EPILOGUE

Anca and Jolan stared down through the skyship's portal to the planet's surface below. The terraformers had finally returned to orbit a few weeks earlier, after two centuries of painstaking work. Now it was up to the planet.

A break in the cloud layer allowed them to see. "There," Anca said, feeling a stab of excitement as she pointed to a slash of lush green in the ruddy landscape, a small herd of brown quadrupeds grazing on a hillside. "It's taking."

"I admit I had my doubts," Jolan said.

"It means we are only days away." She resisted taking Jolan's hand. Their relationship had not yet been announced, and now was not the time. "We've dreamed this dream for so long."

He nodded. "Your great-great-grandfather would have been proud."

She glanced at her lover, the leader of the Youngbloods, his all-blue eyes signalling his mixed human-Mannekhi heritage. But this was an official trip, and they had not been able to sleep with each other for a week. She mind-de-activated the cams for a moment, took his hand and kissed it, keeping eye contact. Then she let go, and re-activated the cams. She was President, after all.

Jolan asked the question publicly, the one they had debated privately in her bed chamber before the journey.

"How many will move here?"

"Not all, not at first." Even she would miss Esperia, though she longed to set foot on the virgin planet below.

"Do we name it Earth, as it was before?"

She shook her head. "No. The time-seal on the file opened this morning." This part had not been choreographed; nobody had known what Micah had decided two centuries ago, the name for his famed third wish. Anca knew the revelation had to be authentic, and so had not told Jolan. Everyone on the ship, back home, and in the Colonies was watching.

Jolan was clearly surprised, perhaps a little hurt, but if so he masked it well, and played his role. "What name did he propose?"

She was about to speak when the gravity of it all swept over her, and Anca found she had to suppress her emotions more than usual. She paused, not for dramatic effect, but rather she wondered if Micah had been right to give it this name. But it had been his legacy. And he had added in the file something she didn't quite understand, which she would have to check with the historian later: *third time lucky.*

She allowed the cams access to her emotional state, so those watching could feel what she felt, if they so wished; it was part of her duty, and might persuade more to come here. She waved a hand, and the cams captured the view through the portal, down through thinning clouds, to the sparkling blue waters underneath. So odd to see ocean rollers above ground, glittering in the sunlight, unlike Esperia's grey underground seas. Remote sense-cams nearer the surface relayed the sight, sound and smell of waves crashing onto the shore, followed by the hiss of surf retracting over pebbles, mixed with the salty tang of seawater. Somewhere out of view a bird called in a high-pitched shriek.

To hell with decorum. Anca reached out her hand, and after a moment's hesitation, Jolan clasped his fingers in hers, and she knew it was the right name for the planet, and spoke it aloud for all to hear.

"Eden."

GLOSSARY

Eden's Aliens, Artefacts and Ships

Achillia – personal guard of the Alician Supreme Leader.

Alicians – neo-human race genetically altered by the Q'Roth to increase intelligence, resilience and longevity. Alicians are named after *Alessia*, their founder, who brokered a deal with the Q'Roth in 1053 AD to prepare humanity for culling, and to eradicate Earth-based nuclear and nano-based weaponry, in exchange for genetic advancement and patronage. Alicians are Level Five, and are led by Sister Esma. Louise is an Alician renegade imbued with too much Q'Roth DNA.

Anxorians – Level Sixteen race, originally patrons of the Nchkani, who were annihilated in a rebellion fifty thousand years ago by the Tla Beth and the Q'Roth, for reasons that remain unclear. The best hypothesis relates to their military prowess, which possibly began to threaten the Tla Beth. The Nchkani took their place.

Dark Worms – leviathan-like creatures that live in the space between galaxies, feeding off both dark and normal energy sources. They are very difficult to kill. Normally they are kept outside by the Galactic Barrier, which was breached by Qorall's forces.

Esperantia – the principal human town on Esperia, population circa 20,000.

Esperia – formerly Ourshiwann – the Spider planet serving as mankind's home after the fall of Earth and Eden, with only two major cities: human-occupied Esperantia, and Spider-occupied Shimsha.

Finchikta – Level Nine bird-like creatures who administrate judicial affairs for the Tla Beth, e.g. during the trial of humanity in 2063.

Genners – following the trial of humanity, prosecuted by the Alicians and the Q'Roth, mankind was quarantined on Esperia for its own protection and all children genetically upgraded to Level Four (with Level Five potential) by the Ossyrians. 'Genners' surpass their parents intellectually by the age of twelve.

Grid – ring-shaped ultra-rapid transport hub that runs around the inner rim of the galaxy, for ease of commerce. **Grid Society**: established by the Kalarash ten million years ago, based on a scale of levels of intelligence running from one to nineteen, with Kalarash at the top. Mankind initially graded Level Three.

Hohash – intelligent artefacts resembling upright oval mirrors, designed by the Kalarash, known as omnipaths due to their powerful perception, communication and recording abilities. Their true function is unknown.

Hushtarans – Level Eight race with squid-like ships that use anti-matter cables similar to Q'Roth Crucible ships.

Jannahi Galaxy – original home galaxy of the Kalarash; destroyed during the first war with Qorall.

Kalarash – Level Nineteen beings originally believed to have left our galaxy. Only seven remain in the universe. Little is known about them. They are called Progenitors by many Grid species, as the Kalarash fostered civilisation in the galaxy, based on a strictly hierarchical intelligence-ranking system. The Kalarash never leave their Crossbow ships.

Korakkara – volcanic Q'Roth homeworld, partly destroyed by an enemy race, largely uninhabited except for the High Queen and her personal guard.

Mannekhi – Level Six human-looking alien race except for their all-black eyes. They sided with Qorall in the ongoing galactic war, due to millennia of oppression by the Tazani under Grid rule. Mannekhi use Spiker ships for war, as well as Javelin Class Dropships for incursions.

Nchkani – Level Sixteen warrior race infamous for their brutality in war and insurrections, especially with their ships known as Shredders, and tank-like Crabs for ground assault.

Nganks – full name Ngankfushtora – squid-like Level Twelve cosmetic surgeons whose services are usually reserved for higher-level species. Their hospital ships are known colloquially as Lozenges, and smaller triage vessels are known as Egg ships, both due to their shape.

Node – an implant developed in 2050, shortly before WWIII, that allowed direct interaction with the web and all social media. Banned due to psychotic and fatal accidents. Kat and Jen each have one. They allow direct communication with the Hohash.

Orb – deep space vessel with gravity-based and organic viral weaponry, mode of propulsion unknown; new weapon unleashed by Qorall.

Ossyrians – dog-like Level Eight medical race, charged as humanity's custodians after the trial, their eighteen-year long stay on Esperia led by *Chahat-Me*. Their hospital ships are known as Pyramid ships. Such ships visited Egypt five thousand years ago. Rapier ships are used for short in-system transit.

Ourshiwann – Spider name for the planet Esperia.

Qorall [kwo-rahl] – ancient enemy of the Kalarash, and invader of our galaxy. His ship is embedded inside an artificial asteroid the sits just above the event horizon of a black hole. His weapons include 'greenspace', which changes the nature of local space, preventing Transpace conduits from opening, and using the black hole to trigger gravitic shock waves.

Q'Roth [kyu-roth] – Level Six nomadic warrior race who culled Earth as part of the maturation process for its hatchlings, in a deal with the Alicians. Currently engaged as soldiers trying to stop the progress of Qorall's forces across the galaxy. The Q'Roth are the formal Patrons of the Alicians. Q'Roth have a number of warships from the Mega Class Battlestar and Crucible warships, to Mesa Class Destroyers, inter-stellar Marauders and Hunters, down to the short-haul Raptor.

Quickspace – very rare spatial phenomenon (the spatial equivalent of quicksand) where the fabric of space breaks down due to external factors. Ships and beings caught in Quickspace founder and slip into other spatial realms, usually destroyed by spatial riptides, and are never seen again.

Rangers – Level Fifteen taciturn reptilian creatures working for the Tla Beth. The Ranger Shatrall crash-landed in Tibet in the early part of the twelfth century and realized the Q'Roth had targeted humanity for culling. He was unsure the Level Three assessment of humanity was correct, and so unofficially warned a local warrior tribe who became the Alicians' principal adversary, the Sentinels.

Resident – an internal alien-designed symbiote implanted in Micah's head prior to the Trial of humanity, which acts as a semi-intelligent Level Five translator, with various additional survival-based functions.

Savange – new home planet of the Alicians, ruled by *Sister Esma*.

Scintarelli – legendary Level Twelve shipbuilders, whose shipyards dwell in gas giants. Their star-ship designs include the interstellar Starpiercer, the Scythe warship, and the one-man Dart.

Sclarese [skla-ray-zee] Nova Stormers – Level Nine semi-intelligent stealth missiles based on energy amplification technology, aimed at turning stars nova. Built by the Sclarese.

Sentinels – blood enemies of the Alicians, involved in a silent war over a period of nine centuries. Last remaining Sentinel alive is *Ramires*. Sentinels were famous for their nanoswords, able to slice through a Q'Roth warrior's armoured flesh.

Shimsha – home of the Spiders on Esperia.

Shiva – a Level Twelve Scintarelli Scythe-ship (a Cutlass Class warship) upgraded by Hellera to Level Fifteen. Shiva is a mind-ship, completely autonomous with its own personality.

Shrell – Level Nine matriarchal ray-like creatures who live in deep space, guardians and 'gardeners' of the space-environment, invisible to most other species as they dwell in Transpace. As well as protecting and fixing spatial tears, they can also poison space. They work for the *Tla Beth*.

Spiders – Level Four race harvested by the Q'Roth one thousand years prior to the culling on Earth. Homeworld called Ourshiwann, renamed Esperia. Visually-oriented race, otherwise deaf and mute. They live in Shimsha, near Esperantia, humanity's last city.

Steaders – the 'non-genned' human population on Esperia, so-called because of the preponderance of farms and homesteads surrounding Esperantia.

Tazani – Level Seven patrons of the Mannekhi. Their battle-cruisers fire energy packets capable of destroying Mannekhi Spikers.

Tla Beth – Level Seventeen energy creatures, rulers of the Grid in the absence of the Kalarash. Their homeworld is located inside a supernova. Their small but powerful ships are called Gyroscopes. Their famed Mega Class battleships were called Grazers, believed to be defunct.

Transpace – a form of hyperspace allowing instantaneous travel across light years without relativistic effects. Transpace, however, does not use wormholes, which do not allow organic transport and can cause rips in subspace.

Transpar – Blake's pilot Zack was transformed by the Tla Beth into a glass-like transparent living witness, unable to lie, and devoid (mostly) of his original personality, as part of the judicial procedure during the trial of mankind.

Wagramanians – Level Seven forest-dwelling tripeds famed for art, but also employed by the Tla Beth as shock troops during times of inter-stellar war, in their famed Hammer ships.

Whisking – short-range teleportation; requires vast amounts of energy, and only Level Fifteen ships and above can do it. Most ships, even at Level Fifteen and above, do not have the capability, and it is used in emergencies only, except by the Kalarash.

Xera – Level Eighteen Machine race developed by the Tla Beth, who had to be put down due to their war two million years earlier against 'organics'. Their City ships were feared by an entire galaxy until they were neutralised in the battle at the edge of the galaxy in a place later named Hell's End.

Zlarasi – Level Six aqua-farmers living in the oceans on Alagara. They use three ships: Conch ships (mass drivers), Diamond warships (anti-matter core and weaponry), and Serpent ships.

Printed in Great Britain
by Amazon